Winter, a former FBI profiler who u
serial criminals. The Jefferson Winter Thriller
Broken Dolls, *Watch Me*, which was shortlisted for
Specsavers Crime Thriller Book Club Best Read, and
e-book novellas, *Presumed Guilty* and *Hush Little Baby*, set during Winter's FBI days.

When he's not writing, James spends his time training horses and riders. An accomplished guitarist, he relaxes by writing and recording music. James lives in Hertfordshire with his wife and two children.

For more information please
visit www.james-carol.com

Praise for *Watch Me:*

'You'll finish this book and be straight online to find out when the next one's coming.' Mark Billingham

'I loved him. I thought he was a really interesting and different character . . .' Kate Mosse

'James Carol is a non-American who has mastered the idiom of the US thriller . . . Carol is no [Lee] Child clone, and carves out his own menacing canvas with real panache.' Barry Forshaw, *Independent*

Prey

A Jefferson Winter Thriller

JAMES CAROL

FABER & FABER

First published in 2015
by Faber & Faber Ltd
Bloomsbury House
74–77 Great Russell Street
London WC1B 3DA

Typeset by Faber & Faber Ltd.
Printed and bound by CPI Group (UK) Ltd, Croydon CR0 4YY

A CIP record for this book
is available from the British Library

ISBN 978-0-571-32231-2

FSC
www.fsc.org
MIX
Paper from
responsible sources

For Niamh,
You light up each and every one of my days.
Love you, sweetheart.

I

Jefferson Winter noticed the blonde the second he stepped into the diner. She was hidden behind the pages of a newspaper at the back table, a coffee mug in front of her. Three nights running he'd been coming here and this was the first customer he had seen. The newspaper dropped and she met his gaze. There was nothing in the look. No curiosity, no smile, no invitation. The newspaper went back up as quickly as it had come down, and the moment passed.

He pulled the door closed behind him and walked over to the counter, glad to get out of the cold. Early October in New York and the days were mostly pleasant, but the nights were starting to bite. The place was tiny, just eight tables and one guy taking the orders and doing the cooking. It was long and narrow, the tables lined up against one wall, the counter and grill along the other, a walkway in-between. The air smelled unhealthily good and was layered with grease so thick you could feel it on your skin. It was a smell that got better with every step. 'Love Me Tender' was playing quietly on a stereo perched on a high shelf, the old Elvis song working in counterpoint to the rumble of the dying heater.

Winter could see the woman's reflection in the mirror behind the counter. The newspaper was in the way so all he saw was a pair of black leather gloves and the top of her head. Her gloves were tight enough to make out the outline of her fingers, and the fact that she wasn't wearing any chunky rings. It didn't look as though there was a wedding band, but it was impossible to say for sure. The harsh lighting created the illusion that her platinum-blonde hair was actually white.

There was no evidence to suggest that she had company. The other three chairs were pushed hard up against the table and there was only one mug. So what was she doing here? She could be waiting for someone but, given that it was two in the morning, he wasn't convinced. If it had been the middle of the day then the question would be redundant since it wouldn't be that big a deal. A woman on her own enjoying a lunchtime coffee wouldn't raise any eyebrows, however, anyone sitting on their own in a diner in the middle of the night would. So what was her story? Winter could see a number of possibilities. Maybe she'd been out clubbing, or maybe she was a shift worker. Or maybe, like him, she suffered from occasional bouts of insomnia.

'Same as usual?'

He turned from the mirror. The cook was standing there wiping his hands on his dirty apron. His accent was impenetrable, the words barely comprehensible. The dark hair and complexion placed him somewhere to the south of the Mediterranean. He was in his fifties, skinny and tall, and he walked with a slight stoop, like he was apologising for those extra inches.

'Same as usual,' Winter replied.

'Everything?'

'Everything.'

The grunted response meant they were done talking. The cook poured a coffee and Winter added two sugars then looked for somewhere to sit. He was tempted by the tables at the rear where it was warmer, but habit won out and he went for the table next to the window. He preferred window seats because he liked watching the world go by. Not that there would be much to see. This time of day, even New York slowed down.

Winter shook off his jacket, draped it over the back of a chair and got himself comfortable. He'd had the jacket for years. Suede on the outside, sheepskin on the inside, and as comfortable as a well-worn pair of sneakers. He dug out his Zippo, clicked the lid open and flicked up a flame. For a moment he just sat there watching the fire dance, then he clicked the lid shut. *Click, flick, click.* The smoking ban was a pain in the ass.

The cook was busy at the grill, singing along to Elvis in a tuneless monotone. Judging by the way he was shaping and twisting the words, he'd learnt the lyrics phonetically. Winter tuned him out and unwrapped his cutlery. He laid the fork and knife neatly on the table and stared out of the window, losing himself in the neon-streaked darkness.

For a while he just sat there, staring at nothing. He'd been in New York for the past eight days helping the city's police department hunt down Ryan McCarthy, a serial killer who'd targeted young businessmen. As much as he liked the city, now that McCarthy was in custody there was no reason to stay. His next stop was Paris, where he had another killer to hunt. That's the way it had been since he left the FBI. Finish one case, move on to the next. The truth of the matter was that things hadn't been much different when he was with the FBI. Unfortunately, he existed in a world where there would never be a shortage of monsters.

He sipped his coffee, the details of the Paris case turning through his head. He already had some rough ideas, but nothing he was ready to share. The files the police had sent through were lacking in detail, and prompted more questions than answers. This was nothing new. Written reports tended to lack detail because the people writing them were so overworked.

The squeak of a chair moving against the floor tiles pulled him away from Paris and back to the diner. He looked up from his coffee and saw the blonde reflected in the window. She was walking along the narrow aisle between the tables and the counter. She moved gracefully, feet padding, body rolling.

The first thing that struck him was how thin she was. Her facial bones were pressing tight against the skin and her leather jacket was sitting as though it was a couple of sizes too big. She would never be classed as pretty, but nor was she unattractive. She sat right in the middle of those two extremes. With a little make-up she could be made to shine. He estimated that she was in her mid-twenties, and more or less the same height as him, five-nine, give or take an inch. She was wearing a pair of scruffy Levi's jeans and her baggy leather jacket was zipped up to the chin. Her Converse sneakers were old and battered.

He was wondering again what she was doing here. The way she was dressed didn't provide much in the way of clues. They were clothes that could be worn to work, or worn to a bar. If she was an insomniac she'd probably got up and put on the first thing she could find. That's what he'd done. He studied her reflection more closely and decided that she hadn't been out drinking. She was walking straight and steady, and seemed to be in full control of her body. Nor was there any food on her table. The reason you came to a place like this after a night out was to get a plateful of carb-heavy food to soak up the alcohol.

Not that it really mattered why she was here. He was leaving for Paris, and she was about to disappear into the night. That's how this one played out. Life could be broken down into a series of encounters, some significant, most not. For the tiniest slice of time his orbit had coincided with hers. In a world of seven billion people, the likelihood of their orbits ever colliding again was zilch.

Three strides from the door she changed direction and stopped at his table.

'May I?'

She nodded towards the empty seat on the opposite side of the table. It took Winter almost a whole second to process the fact that the question was aimed at him.

'Be my guest.'

She smiled and sat. The smile was playful and bright. Up close, her eyes looked too green to be natural. Interesting. She dressed casually but then disguised her eyes with contact lenses. Her platinum-blonde hair had clearly come from a bottle, and was too long to be classed as short. It looked like she'd styled it herself with kitchen scissors. She stared across the table at his dead-rock-star T-shirt and the scruffy hooded top, stared at his white hair. Then she laid the folded newspaper on the table and placed a gloved hand on top of it. Winter glanced at the newspaper then met her gaze.

'It's good to meet you, Jefferson.'

Of all the things she could have said, this was the last thing he'd expected. He looked at her more closely. He'd never seen her before. That much he was certain of. 'Who are you? More to the point, how do you know who I am?'

'I'd rather not say.'

'Okay, since you know who I am, how about you tell me your name?'

For a moment the woman said nothing. She was staring across the table again. Studying him. Checking him out. Winter waited for her to speak first.

'You know, I expected you to be taller. More impressive. But isn't that always the way? You build someone up in your mind, then, when you finally meet them, it's always a disappointment.'

Winter said nothing and the woman laughed.

'I've read the psychology books, too, Jefferson. Keep quiet and your opponent will be compelled to fill the silence. That's what's going on here, right? You're playing mind games with me. You're trying to suss me out.'

Winter smiled. 'What do you expect? Since you know who I am, I'm assuming that you also know what I do for living.'

'So what have you got so far? And don't play innocent and pretend you've got nothing because you've been checking me out since the second you stepped through the door.'

'I could ask you the same thing.'

The woman tutted and slowly shook her head. 'I asked first. And I want the truth. I'm a big girl. Believe me, there's very little you could say that would hurt me.'

The last statement was intentionally loaded. Was there a story, or was she just trying to make herself out to be more interesting than she actually was? Winter gave it a couple of seconds in case she had anything else to add. She smiled across the table and nodded for him to go on. Her eyes were wide. He could see the edges of the coloured lenses.

'You're a game player,' he said. 'That much is clear from this conversation. It's all move and countermove. You're also narcissistic. As far as you're concerned you're sitting there slap bang at the centre of the universe. Also, you want me to believe that you're this great big mystery that's just waiting to be solved.'

'Have you looked in the mirror lately? You could be describing yourself.'

'You don't know anything about me.'

'That's where you're wrong. I know exactly who you are. What's more, I know *what* you are.'

'And what am I?'

'You're a work in progress.'

Winter laughed. 'And what the hell is that supposed to mean?'

The woman didn't answer. She tapped the newspaper with her fingertips, then lifted her head so she was looking over his shoulder. Her gaze was aimed at the street, but she wasn't really seeing anything out there. Winter waited for her to speak again. He was more than comfortable with long silences. He was also comfortable dealing with crazy people. Right now, he was just trying to work out what brand of crazy she was.

'Have you ever wondered what it's like to kill someone?' she asked.

'No.'

'Liar. You're the man who gets inside the heads of serial

killers. You can't do that without imagining what it's like to kill.'

'Okay I'll concede that much, but you're talking about actually killing a person. What I do is light years away from that.'

'Liar.'

'Believe what you like.'

A movement by the counter caught Winter's eye. He looked up and saw the cook coming through the flap with a plate in his hand. The woman glanced over her shoulder, following his gaze. She looked back at Winter and waited for him to meet her eye.

'We could kill him,' she whispered. 'That would be fun, don't you think?'

Winter said nothing.

'Anyone is capable of murder if they're pushed hard enough.'

'You're wrong. Murder is a choice. You don't have to pull the trigger, you *choose* to.'

She shrugged. 'We'll have to agree to differ on that one, Jefferson.'

The cook stopped at the table and put the plate down. Winter said a distracted 'thank you' then turned back to the woman. Before he could say anything she pulled a food knife out of her pocket and stood up. She grabbed hold of the cook, then spun him into her body and cupped the back of his head in her left hand. Her eyes were sparkling and she was biting her bottom lip. She took a sharp intake of breath then plunged the knife into the cook's eye, all the way to the hilt. Surprise flashed momentarily in his good eye, his face went

8

slack and he dropped to the floor. The sound of his body hitting the tiles got Winter moving. He went to stand but the woman put her hand up, stopping him in his tracks.

'Whatever you've got planned, it won't work. Right now, I can think of ten different ways to kill you.'

Winter looked up at her, every muscle in his body tensed. Elvis had moved on to singing 'Suspicious Minds'. The emphysemic heater was banging as loudly as his heart. She leaned forward and he caught the scent of her shampoo, the scent of her soap. She was close enough to reach out and grab hold of. But then what? He'd come bottom in every self-defence class he'd ever taken at Quantico. Mind games he could manage, but when things got physical he was clueless. She moved closer, her lips brushing the edge of his ear.

'If you follow me I will kill you. But don't worry, I'll be seeing you again real soon.'

She stepped back and smiled, and Winter stayed very still. He was working hard to keep his face passive, his breathing easy. She was looking for a reaction, but there was no way she was getting one. Her smile turned into a laugh and she turned to leave. A second later the dull bell above the door clanged and she was gone.

2

The woman checked for traffic then crossed the road, squeezing between the cars parked on both sides of the narrow street. She was moving quickly, almost jogging. Winter tracked her progress along the sidewalk, willing her to turn her head so he could see her face one more time. It didn't happen. Another five strides took her all the way to the corner. He counted every single step. At the very last second, she looked back. A quick over-the-shoulder glance, then she disappeared from sight.

Winter settled back into his seat and lit a cigarette. He inhaled deeply and let out a long smoky sigh. The cook was lying in an awkward sprawl on the tiled floor a couple of yards away. There was no point checking for a pulse. He was wearing a wedding ring, so presumably he had a wife. What about kids? Someone out there was going to miss and mourn him, that was for sure. It was yet another example of someone being in the wrong place at the wrong time.

He knew that he wasn't to blame for the cook's death, but there was a world of difference between knowing something and believing it. On one level he understood that you couldn't be held responsible for the actions of others. He hadn't stabbed the cook. That one had been all down to the woman. She'd made the decision to take that course of action, and had followed through.

For the most part Winter bought into these justifications, but the bottom line here was that the cook had been murdered to get his attention. There was no other reason for what had just happened. It was pure theatre. You didn't put on a show like this without an audience. But why do that? And what the hell else was she planning on doing to get his attention? Paris was going to have to wait. Until she was caught it would be impossible to even start to find a way to be okay with what had just happened.

The intro to 'Heartbreak Hotel' started playing, and that was enough to get him moving again. Elvis's voice was annoying enough at the best of times, but right now it was one distraction too many. He got up, stepped over the body of the cook, and went behind the counter to turn off the CD player. He picked up a bowl to use as an ashtray, then walked to the rear of the diner and slid into the chair where the woman had been sitting.

The only evidence she'd ever been here was the coffee mug on the table, and a wisp of her scent that was there and gone so fast he was left wondering if he'd imagined it. He ran a finger down the side of the mug. No heat. She'd been here long enough for her coffee to cool, but the coffee hadn't been touched, and she'd been wearing gloves, so no DNA and no prints.

He settled back in the seat and tried to imagine the world from her perspective. It was a good choice of seat. The door on the left no doubt led to the back alley. If you needed to get away fast, it was always best to keep your options open. The seat also gave a good view of the other tables and the front door. Wherever he'd chosen to sit, she would have been able to watch him easily.

So what now? One thing was for sure, he couldn't do this on his own. He needed access to the police's databases, he needed information. Also, he was probably going to need a car.

This last one was the simplest to achieve. All he had to do was call Avis or Hertz and request the fastest car they had in their fleet, then go pick it up. The first two needs would be tougher, but not impossible to satisfy. One of the last things Carla Mendoza had said when he signed off on the McCarthy case was that she owed him one. The way she'd delivered this gave the impression that she was filling a hole in the conversation. That said, she was a homicide detective. Once she'd heard what had happened here, how could she not want to get involved?

Winter crushed the cigarette into the bowl and took out his cellphone. He found Mendoza's cell number and hit dial. The call went straight through to voicemail, which was understandable. It had taken eight long days to hunt down Ryan McCarthy and she no doubt wanted to catch up on her sleep.

He tapped his cell phone against his chin, wondering what to do next. If he'd had her home number he would have called that. Unfortunately, she'd never given it to him. He knew she lived in Brooklyn, but he didn't know where exactly, otherwise he'd just jump in a cab and drive out there. He went through everything in his head one more time, looking to see if there was any way he could do this on his own. There wasn't. He needed Mendoza. Or, to be more accurate, he needed the resources she had access to. He tried her cell one more time, but it went straight to voicemail again. He hung up, cutting the message off in mid-flow, then punched in 911.

'911, what's your emergency?'

The voice was male. Geographically, the accent originated from somewhere in the Midwest.

'I need you to get a message to Sergeant Carla Mendoza. She works out of the NYPD's headquarters at One Police Plaza. Tell her she needs to call Jefferson Winter immediately. I need you to stress that this is urgent.'

'Sir, this is 911. We don't pass on messages.'

'With all due respect, that's exactly what you do. You take information from your callers then pass that information on to the appropriate party, whether that's the cops, the medics or the fire department. This time I need you to relay a message to the cops.'

'Sir, I must warn you that it's a criminal offence to make hoax calls to 911.'

'That's good to hear. Okay, when you get hold of Sergeant Mendoza, she's probably going to give you some sob story about how it's the middle of the night and she doesn't want to be disturbed. There will probably be some shouting, and I'd be surprised if there's not a fair bit of cursing. Tell her that there's been a murder and my prints are all over the murder scene. By the way, I'm at a diner called O'Neal's over on the Lower East Side.'

Winter hung up, pushed the cellphone into his jeans pocket, and walked across to the counter to get a clean knife. He carried it back over to his table, stepping carefully over the body of the cook to avoid the blood. Then he sat down and started to eat.

The woman had left her newspaper behind. It was lying neatly folded on the table. Winter flicked it open and laid it down flat. The *Hartwood Gazette* was printed in a curly script at the top of the page, and the bold headline beneath read: COUPLE SLAIN IN BRUTAL MURDER. The byline belonged to someone called Granville Clarke. He took a closer look and saw how the pages had begun to darken and yellow with age. According to the header, the newspaper dated back to January six years ago.

To the right of the article was a picture of the dead couple. They were young, wholesome and smiling, their eyes filled with dreams of a bright future. This was a portrait rather than a snapshot and, although the smiles were suppressed and the pose staged, you could tell they'd been happy together. The caption named them as Lester and Melanie Reed.

According to the article, Lester and Melanie had been in their early twenties when they were murdered, and they'd lived in Hartwood their whole short lives. There was mention of the Monroe County Sheriff's Department, which placed Hartwood in upstate New York. Lester had worked at the family store, while Melanie taught in the town's elementary school. They'd only been married for a year. It was a life that had been halted before it had really gotten started.

There was more padding than substance to the story, and Winter had the impression that it must have been written in a hurry. Most likely the murders had coincided with the newspaper's deadline. If that was the case then everything would have been in chaos and there wouldn't have been time to dig deeper.

The newspaper had been left behind on purpose. If it had been the latest issue of *The New York Times*, then, yes, he could accept that it was an accident. But it wasn't. This was an old newspaper. It wasn't one that she'd just happened to have lying around. It had been left for a reason. Then there was the way that she'd kept tapping it while they were talking. She'd wanted him to notice it.

He quickly flicked through the rest of the pages. The only story of any note was the one about the murders. The other stories were the sort of thing you'd expect to find in a small-town newspaper. Births, marriages, deaths, local interest pieces. Which meant that she'd wanted him to see the story about the murders. But why do that? The only reason Winter could see was that she'd been involved in the murders. Given what she'd done to the cook it was a distinct possibility.

He took out his cell and did a quick Google search. The *Hartwood Gazette* didn't have a website, but the *Rochester Democrat & Chronicle* did. Rochester was where the sheriff's department was based, so it was the logical next place to go looking. Unfortunately, the online archive didn't go back far enough to be of any help.

Winter was still eating when a police cruiser came roaring into the street. The siren was howling and the light bar painted the night red and blue. Two cops burst from the car, their guns already drawn. Neither one was Mendoza, which didn't surprise him. The Seventh Precinct's station house was only a couple of blocks away, so chances were that's where they'd come from. Mendoza had to get here from Brooklyn so it would still be a while before she showed up.

The bell gave a dull clang and the door banged open. The guy who'd been driving entered first, covered by his partner. He looked at the body of the cook, looked at Winter.

'On the ground! Hands behind your back!'

Winter shook his head. 'Not going to happen.'

The cop gave him the look. It was an expression he was used to. Part disbelief, part perplexed, and part *what the hell?* This guy was smaller than his partner, but obviously older and more experienced. Mid-forties, black hair, blue eyes, and permanent frown lines etched into his forehead. According to the badge on his jacket his name was Pritchard. The name badge on the partner's jacket read Collins. Winter cut off a piece of egg and popped it into his mouth. Pritchard raised his gun and aimed.

'I said down on the floor.'

'Or what? You're going to shoot me?' He shook his head again. 'I don't think so. The other thing I'm sure of is that you're not about to come over here and drag me out of this chair. This is a crime scene and if you end up contaminating it, you'll be in all sorts of trouble. I can't contaminate it because I'm part of the scene, so, if you don't mind, I'd like to finish my breakfast. Chances are I'm not going to be eating again any time soon, so I might as well eat now.'

He scraped some hash browns on to his fork and ate them. Pritchard was giving him the look again. He was staring, his mouth slightly open. He stood frozen for a moment longer, the gun still pointed at Winter's chest, then he lowered it and conferred with Collins.

While they talked, Winter quickly finished his breakfast, washed it down with the last of his coffee, then wiped his mouth and hands on the serviette. He folded the serviette into a neat square, placed it on to the table, then rocked back in his seat. It was the pointlessness of the murder that got to him the most. It just wasn't right. The cook should have been flipping burgers and singing along to Elvis for years to come, but instead, he was going to get measured for a box and consigned to the flames.

He stared at the two cops until they stopped talking and gave him their full attention. Without a word, he stood up and stepped over the cook's body. Then he turned around, put his hands behind his back and waited for the handcuffs to be snapped on.

3

The handcuffs clicked tight and Pritchard recited the Miranda warning. Winter tuned him out. By his reckoning it would take about half an hour to track Mendoza down and get her here. Five minutes had passed since he called 911. Only twenty-five minutes to go. All he had to do was keep his head down and work the system.

Pritchard got to the end of his spiel and asked if he understood his rights. Winter said that he did, and Collins took this as his cue. He grabbed hold of Winter's arm then marched him outside and bundled him into the back of the police cruiser. The car smelled like someone had vomited in it recently. The leather seats been wiped clean but a trace of the smell still lingered. The back of the car was separated from the front by a partition. The thick Perspex window made it easy for the cops up front to keep an eye on him, and the crisscrossed grille next to it had been put there so they could tell him to shut up if he caused trouble. The door handles and window winders had been removed.

A second police cruiser turned into the street, lights flashing, and skidded to a halt nose to nose with the car Winter was in. The Perspex distorted the view through the windshield but he could see enough to work out what was going on. He watched Pritchard and Collins walk over and shake hands with the two uniformed officers. Words were exchanged and there was some arm waving, a few laughs. Pritchard was clearly filling the new guys in on what had gone down in the diner.

The conversation wound up and Pritchard climbed into the driver's seat and started the engine. He waited for Collins to shut the passenger door and get settled in, then hit the gas and reversed quickly back along the narrow street. Fifty yards later, he swung the wheel hard to the left and backed into an alleyway, throwing Winter across the rear seat. By the time he'd got himself upright they were facing the correct way and accelerating.

'Can you believe what an asshole this guy is?'

Pritchard's question wasn't answered straightaway. Instead, Collins glanced over his shoulder and waited for Winter to meet his eye. 'Yeah, what a douchebag.'

The name calling didn't bother him. It was something he'd had plenty of experience with as a kid. After his father's arrest, his mother had gone into flight mode in a futile attempt to escape the shame. Between the ages of eleven and seventeen they'd lived in fifteen cities in ten different states. All those new schools equated to a whole lot of name calling.

Pritchard and Collins moved on to talking about the Giants' season and a couple of minutes later the car pulled into a parking space outside the Seventh Precinct's red-brick station house. Despite the hour, the lights were burning bright. The rear door of the police cruiser swung open and Winter shuffled out. For a moment he just stood there breathing in the night air, the noise of the city filtering through the dark. By his reckoning, in twenty-two minutes he'd be a free man again.

'Get moving!'

Pritchard gave him a shove and he started walking towards the entrance. It took twenty minutes to process him. Mugshots, fingerprints, paperwork. He kept one eye on the clock, and started dragging his heels as they approached the twenty-two minute mark. Still no Mendoza. At twenty-eight minutes he was led to a chair in an interview room. The door banged shut and he was left alone. Ending up in an interview room had not been a part of the plan.

Mendoza should have been here by now. Her name would have been flagged up by the 911 operative, and he'd been sure to give enough details to track her down, so where the hell was she? It wasn't rocket science. A single telephone call to One Police Plaza would have confirmed that she existed. Personnel would have her home number on file, and someone would have rung it. Even if she was ignoring her cell, it would be hard to ignore a ringing landline. Unless, of course she'd taken it off the hook.

Winter had factored this possibility into his original calculations. If that had happened then a squad car would have been despatched, and someone would have knocked on the door until she answered. This time of the night, the Brooklyn Bridge would be clear of traffic. The roads would be clear, too. It should only take twenty minutes to get here from Brooklyn, maybe not even that.

He told himself to relax. She'd be here soon. It crossed his mind that she might be staying at a boyfriend's house. Or a girlfriend's. He wasn't convinced though. All the time they'd been working together he'd seen absolutely no evidence that she was in a relationship with anyone of either sex.

No quick furtive cellphone calls, no secret texting. She didn't wear rings, so if she was married then she wasn't advertising the fact. She was good at compartmentalising, that much was clear. Even so, Winter reckoned he would have picked up something. And even if he had missed it, her colleagues wouldn't have. She worked in an office full of detectives. Someone would have noticed something. An environment like that, secrets were practically non-existent. If that was the case, then someone would know where to find her.

He sat down and did his best to get comfortable. His hands were still cuffed behind his back, his arms starting to go numb. He stretched in the chair and tried to shake some life back into them, then took a quick look around. The room was like a hundred other interview rooms he'd been in. Cheap scuffed linoleum tiles on the floor, cheap grey paint on the walls. The table was bolted to the floor and there were four chairs, two to a side facing each other. The accused and their lawyer would get the side facing the large one-way mirror, while the interviewers got to sit with their back to it.

There would be someone in the room behind the mirror. Probably more than one person. Winter had been on the other side of the interview table often enough to know how that one worked. Right now, they'd be studying him closely and thinking about the best strategies to employ to get the most out of the interview. They'd be getting their game plan together, and all the time they'd be looking for weaknesses that they could exploit.

He had a strong urge to get up and walk over to the mirror. It was something he'd seen countless times. Without exception, any suspect who wasn't chained to the table or the floor would get up and go over to the mirror and stare into it. Most would tap the glass. Even though they'd seen enough cop shows to know the score, it was as though they needed to satisfy themselves that there was a room on the other side. That they were being watched.

As the minutes ticked by a trickle of anxiety wormed through his stomach. What if he'd overplayed his hand and the police couldn't get hold of Mendoza? If that happened then he might be in trouble. The interview wouldn't go on for ever. At some point it would end and he'd be transported down to the cells, and right now that prospect worried him more than anything else. He'd been in enough prisons to know a five-nine guy, weighing in at 140 pounds with no self-defence skills whatsoever was going to have a rough time.

Right now, he wasn't just the number-one suspect, he was the *only* suspect. And that was the problem. Why would the police go looking for the real killer if they already had someone in custody? It all came back to taking the path of least resistance. People rarely went out of their way to create more work for themselves. And if you'd pulled the night shift, then that was definitely going to be the case.

Winter took a deep breath and tried not to think about it. There was nothing he could do to affect the outcome, so there was no point worrying. All he could do was wait and see what happened next. With or without Mendoza, the truth would eventually come out. He shuffled around in his seat to get comfortable, shook his arms again to get the blood flowing. Then he shut his eyes and counted off the seconds.

4

The door swung open and a black guy entered. Everything about him was average. Medium height, medium build, and one of those faces you wouldn't look at twice. The lack of a uniform marked him out as a detective. His suit was off-the-rack and didn't fit particularly well. It was navy blue and crumpled. His tie was red and sitting slightly crooked. There was a sheet of paper and a pen in his left hand, a thin folder and a small digital recorder in his right.

The detective took the seat opposite him, placed the folder and the recorder on the table, pressed the record button, then went through the preliminaries. Date, time, the fact that Winter was here on suspicion of murder. He gave his name as Darryl Hitchin, his rank as sergeant.

Hitchin pushed the sheet of paper across the table, and Winter leant forward so he could read through it. Slowly. It was a standard Miranda waiver form. He'd seen plenty of these, so many that he could have recited what was written there by heart. Even so, he read through it like it was the most important document he'd ever seen. He rattled the handcuffs against the chair back, drawing Hitchin's attention to them

'If you want me to sign this, you're going to have to take these off.'

'Sure, but they're going straight back on afterwards.'

'Seriously? Do I look dangerous?'

'Looks can be deceptive.'

The detective was acting cool but Winter wasn't fooled. Inside he must have been celebrating. He had a murder suspect who was willing to be questioned without a lawyer being present. That didn't happen every day. Winter had contemplated asking for one so he could send them out to find Mendoza. The problem was that it was the middle of the night. If the lawyer was delayed then he might be moved down to the cells. Issues of personal safety aside, that would create another delay. The deeper into the system he went, the longer it was going to take to get out. Every minute spent dealing with this bullshit was a minute wasted. It was a hassle he could do without. Time that would be better spent doing something constructive, like finding out more about the Reed murders.

Hitchin came around the table and unlocked the handcuffs. It was good to have them off, albeit briefly. The steel had been pressing uncomfortably against his bones and had left indentations in his skin. Winter rubbed his wrists then picked up the pen and signed the form. Instead of putting his arms behind his back, he held them out to the front. Hitchin just stared at him without saying a word.

'Come on,' said Winter, 'I came in quietly enough. If you don't believe me, ask your buddies. So far I've been a model prisoner. No trouble whatsoever.'

Hitchin looked at him. He started at the white hair and worked his way down past the hooded top to his worn jeans and sneakers. Then he fastened the handcuffs, went around to the other side of the table and sat back down.

24

Winter waited for him to get settled. 'What was the cook's name?'

'Excuse me.'

'The dead cook, what was he called?'

'Why do you want to know?'

'Because he shouldn't be dead. He just happened to be in the wrong place at the wrong time.'

Hitchin raised a questioning eyebrow.

'Don't get too excited. That's not an admission of anything. Not even close.' He hesitated. 'Okay, I know how these things are supposed to work: you ask the questions, I answer them. On the basis of that I can understand why you might be reluctant to give me a name.'

Hitchin was watching him from the other side of the table, eyes narrow, not saying a word.

'Okay, let me make this real simple. If you answer my question, then I'll be more than happy to answer all of yours. Whatever you want to know, just ask. You want to talk for the rest of the day, that's absolutely fine with me. However, if you don't answer my question, then I'm afraid I'm just going to sit here and exercise my Fifth Amendment right to remain silent. You won't get zip.' He paused and smiled, waited until Hitchin met his eye. 'So what do you say? It's just one little question. Where's the harm?'

The detective just sat there for a moment, then flipped open his file and thumbed through the pages. There weren't many. This investigation had just got started.

'His name was Omar Harrak. He originated from Morocco and had been living here in the US for almost a decade. He was married with a couple of kids, a boy and a girl.

Immigration knows all about him. He got his green card a little over four years ago. No police record, not even a traffic violation.'

Winter closed his eyes and repeated the name under his breath a couple of times. In his mind's eye he saw the moment when Omar was stabbed. He opened his eyes and looked over the table at Hitchin. 'Thank you.'

'Quid pro quo. What were you doing in that diner in the middle of the night?'

Winter didn't answer. Instead, he stood up and walked over to the one-way mirror, aware that Hitchin's eyes were following every step. The fact that the detective wasn't shouting at him to get his ass back in the chair pretty much confirmed his suspicions. He studied his reflection for a second, saw the hint of a grin tugging at the corners of his mouth, then he banged hard on the glass.

'Come on out Mendoza! I know you're in there!' He banged again, the dull boom of his fist hitting glass echoing around the room. 'I'll give you to the count of ten then I'm coming in there to get you. One, two, three.'

'Sit down!' Hitchin was on his feet, moving fast.

'Four, five, six.'

A heavy hand landed on his shoulder and he was dragged back to the table. Hitchin dumped him roughly into a chair then sat down and glared across the table.

'I asked you a question. What were you doing in that diner?'

Winter flashed him a tight smile then turned to look at the door. 'Seven, eight, nine, ten,' he whispered.

5

The interview-room door opened again, and this time it was Mendoza. Her long curly black hair was tied back in its usual ponytail and her olive skin still retained a memory of the long-gone summer. She looked even more pissed off than usual, which no doubt had everything to do with being dragged out of bed in the middle of the night to deal with Winter.

Mendoza walked slowly across the small room. It was almost three-thirty in the morning yet she was immaculately turned out. No creases in her jacket or pants, no creases in her blouse. Her black patent-leather shoes were shining. The left side of her jacket had been let out to accommodate her shoulder holster. The first time they met, he had her pegged as the girl who'd done the popular girls' homework in order to fit in at high school. He'd been wrong about that. Carla Mendoza couldn't care less what other people thought about her.

Mendoza stopped beside Hitchin and laid a hand on his shoulder. 'I can handle this from here, Sergeant.' Her accent was pure Brooklyn, all hard syllables and menace. Even though she was a non-smoker, she sounded as though she got through a couple of packs of cigarettes a day.

Hitchin stood up and snorted. 'Yeah? Good luck with that.'

Mendoza slid into the seat the detective had just vacated and waited for him to leave. 'Why were you in the diner?'

'I was getting breakfast.'

'At two in the morning?'

'My body clock's all over the place at the moment. The middle of the night and it feels like the middle of the day. It's one of the downsides of spending a large part of your life stuck in airplane cabins.'

'Why O'Neal's? It's kind of off the beaten track.'

'I found it by accident a couple of nights ago. I woke up hungry in the middle of the night, so I headed out to find something to eat. I didn't have any real plan where I was going, I just let my feet find their own way. Because the food was so good, I came back again the next night, and the next.'

'If the food was as good as you say, then why did you kill the cook?'

'Omar,' Winter corrected her. 'His name was Omar.'

Mendoza nodded once. 'Okay, why did you kill Omar?'

'I didn't kill him.'

'If you didn't do it then who did?'

Winter hesitated. This was the hard part. Omar had been stabbed right in front of him and he was still having trouble believing it was real. 'How about I tell you what happened and we can work from there?' he suggested.

Mendoza settled back in her seat. 'You've got thirty seconds to convince me.'

Winter took a moment to order his thoughts, then closed his eyes and told her everything. He started at the moment he walked into the diner and went through to the point where the woman disappeared into the night. As he spoke he could see the whole thing unfolding on the back of his eyelids, every single detail. He could smell the grease. He could feel the hot air blasting out of the heater. He could hear Elvis. He finished talking and opened his eyes. It took a lot longer than thirty seconds, but Mendoza let him finish. It was clear that she didn't like what she was hearing. She was frowning across the table, her head going slowly from side to side.

'And you expect me to believe all that?'

Winter said nothing.

'You're supposed to be on a flight to Rome.'

'My flight doesn't leave until six. And it was Paris, not Rome.'

'And you're missing the point. You know, I distinctly remember our last conversation. When I told you that it would be good if we didn't see each other for a very long time, I meant every word.'

'We're not quite remembering this the same way. See, what I remember is the bit where you told me that you were eternally grateful for all the help I gave you in hunting down Ryan McCarthy. What was is it you said? Anything you could do, just holler?'

'I did not say that I'd be "eternally grateful". And I would *never* use the word "holler".'

'I know how this looks, and it's not good. But I also know that you know that I didn't kill Omar.'

Mendoza shook her head. 'What I know is that you think like a serial killer. Now, that turned out to be helpful when it came to catching Ryan McCarthy, but it's creepy.' She paused a second. 'Okay, how about this? Maybe something inside your head just finally snapped and that's why you stabbed him.'

Winter laughed. 'Seriously?'

Mendoza didn't reply.

'I did not murder Omar. If I had, I would have done it very differently. For a start I wouldn't have just been sitting there when the cops turned up. And I'd have an alibi. You can count on that. The other thing you could count on is that it would be one hundred per cent airtight.'

'And what am I supposed to think when you go and say something like that?' Mendoza leant forward. 'Now, I'm sure you could probably tell me a dozen different ways how you could have killed that cook and gotten away with it. And the reason for that is you've thought long and hard about this. Because that's what you do. You spend your days imagining what it's like to be a killer. But what if it's no longer enough just to imagine? What if you decided that it was time to get some first-hand experience? What if you finally decided to cross the line?'

'His name was Omar,' Winter said quietly. 'And why are we wasting valuable time here? We should be out there hunting this woman down. That's why I dragged you out of bed in the middle of the night. She's a killer, which means our job is to catch her.'

'No, no, no,' Mendoza interrupted. 'There is no "we" here. This is your mess, Winter.'

'I did not kill Omar.'

'Fine. Prove it.'

He lifted his hands up and rattled the cuffs. 'That's a little difficult while I'm sat here with these damn things on my wrists.'

Mendoza settled a little deeper into her seat and folded her arms. Winter dropped his hands and laid them palm down on the table.

'Okay,' he continued, 'the good news is that we don't need to go looking for this woman because she's going to find us. The last thing she said was that she'd be seeing me again real soon. So, in the meantime, we go through everything we can find on the Hartwood murders. We'll need to contact the cops up there to see what they've got to say. She's pointed us in that direction with the newspaper, so I say we see where that leads us. And we'll need to work Omar's murder as well. I'd be surprised if there's any direct connection to the woman, but his family deserves answers.'

'There are so many things wrong with what you've just said, I don't know where to start.' Mendoza reached for her ponytail and wrapped the strands tightly around her fingers, the tips whitening as the blood circulation was cut off. She tugged hard on the hair band to straighten it then held her left hand up in the air, the fingers curled into a fist. 'Okay, one.' She slowly straightened the index finger. 'All of this is based on the assumption that your mystery woman actually exists. Right now, all we've got is your word for that. Two.' The middle finger slowly unfurled. 'Like I said, there is no "we". Whatever the hell is going on here, it has nothing to do with me.'

'Come on, Mendoza, I can't do this chained up in here, and I can't do this on my own. I need you. And you've got to admit that we make a great team.' He smiled his widest smile. 'Plus, she does exist.'

'Winter, I'm booked on the noon flight to Vegas, and I fully intend to be on it. Not because I want to take a vacation, but because it's an order and, unlike you, I follow orders. You want to know the truth? The thought of taking a vacation makes me feel nauseous. Even though it's only a week, in my opinion that's still a week too long.'

'Okay, here's an idea: since you've been ordered to take a vacation, why not take it in Hartwood? I've heard it's beautiful up there at this time of year. You could do some walking, read a book.' He paused and his face lit up with a grin. 'If you get really bored you could help me investigate a six-year-old murder.'

Mendoza actually laughed at this. She tried to keep it in, but it was out there before she could get a hold of it. 'Jesus, you don't quit do you?'

'Admit it, this one's got you curious. So, what do you say?' When she didn't reply he grinned at her again. 'You're tempted, I can tell.' He held his hand up, thumb and forefinger a quarter of an inch apart. 'A teeny-tiny-weeny bit tempted.'

'You're wrong. Way off the mark.'

Winter leant back in his seat, saying nothing. Mendoza was keeping her mouth shut too. For almost a whole minute they sat staring across the table at each other. It was Winter who eventually broke the silence.

'Look, if we do nothing then this woman is going to kill again. You know that, and I know that.'

'Assuming she exists.'

'Do you really think I had anything to do with Omar's death?'

'Honestly?' Mendoza shrugged and shook her head. 'Right now, Winter, I don't know what to think.'

6

Mendoza walked out of the interview room, leaving Winter alone. The door closed quietly behind her and for the second time that night he was forced into a situation where all he could do was watch. It was like being back in the diner again, watching through the window as the blonde walked away.

He glanced down at the handcuffs, glanced up at his reflection in the one-way glass. Things were not going how he had imagined, and that concerned him. The way he'd seen this playing out, Mendoza had come charging to his rescue. In his fantasy she'd been pissed and cranky like always, but at least she'd got him out of these damn handcuffs and they'd got straight down to the business of looking into the Reed murders.

Except that hadn't happened.

Mendoza hadn't told him where she was going, or why. She hadn't said anything. She'd just got up from the table and left the room. And why shouldn't she? Winter had been on the other side of the table enough times to know how this game was played. Right now, she was watching from behind the mirror, planning her next move. And while she did that all he could do was sit here getting more pissed off and frustrated with every passing second.

It wasn't a complete surprise that she was acting like this. One of the first things he'd learned about Mendoza was that she didn't take things at face value. For the most part this was a good thing, but not always. What was happening here proved that.

Mendoza was still pretty much a mystery to him. He'd done some digging, but hadn't come up with much. Everything he'd discovered so far was connected to her work. He hadn't found out anything personal. Again, this highlighted how good she was at compartmentalising. She'd been careful to keep her work and personal lives separate.

One thing that everyone seemed to agree on was that she was a good cop. Winter had first-hand experience of how thorough she was. The work she'd done on the McCarthy case had been exemplary. She'd joined the NYPD after she left college and Winter expected that she'd stay until she retired. He'd met a lot of cops over the years. Some did the job for the money and some did it because it was what they were born to do. Mendoza was born to do this. No question about it.

He replayed Omar's murder in his head. He was looking for something he might have missed, something that might help him to get out of here, but whichever way he approached it he came up empty-handed.

The interview room was feeling much smaller than when he first got here, the walls beginning to close in. He wanted to stand up and pace. He wanted to go and study the mirror. He wanted to bang on it with his fist again. He wanted to do all the things that he'd observed time and again from the other side of the glass. Even though he was innocent, he was beginning to wonder. That was the effect this room was having on him, which was as it should be. This was a place designed to encourage guilt. It might say 'interview room' on the door, but make no mistake this was a cell, albeit one without a bed or a toilet. In fact it was worse than a cell. It was more like limbo. If things went south he was heading to hell. If they played out how they should then he would soon be a free man again. The uncertainty was like torture.

His father had been in prison for two decades before he was executed. Winter had occasionally wondered how he'd kept going for all those years. If their roles had been reversed, he doubted he would have survived. He might have managed a couple of years, but at some point he would have taken matters into his own hands. A life without freedom was no life at all.

The door finally opened and Mendoza came back in carrying a laptop. He expected her to sit in the same seat as earlier. She didn't. Instead, she put the computer down on the table and came around to his side. He gave her a quizzical look, but she wasn't giving anything away.

'Show me your hands.'

He answered with another look, and when she didn't respond he lifted his hands up. She produced a key and unlocked the cuffs. Winter rubbed his wrists and watched her walk back around to the chair on the other side of the table. He waited until she was seated then gave her a smile. 'Thanks. You have no idea how good it is to have those things off. So what happened to change your mind?'

Mendoza answered him by opening the laptop and hitting a couple of keys. She turned the computer around so that he could see the screen. The video that was playing had the low definition of a cheap CCTV camera. The picture wasn't great, but it was good enough.

According to the time stamp, the film had been shot at eighteen minutes after one this morning. The screen was taken up with a distorted blurry wide-angle shot of a store that was on the same street as the diner. A couple walked past, arms wrapped around each other. They were laughing and clearly having a good time. Nothing for almost a minute then a woman appeared. She was walking fast, her eyes fixed on the sidewalk ahead. Nothing for another thirty seconds then the blonde walked into the shot. Because of the angle, Winter could only see part of her face, but he recognised her from the way her shoulders rolled as she walked.

'That's her,' he said.

'That's what we figured.'

Mendoza leant over the top of the laptop and hit another couple of keys. A new video started playing. The time on the screen had jumped forward to three minutes to two, but everything else was almost identical to the first film clip. Same street, same store, same angle. One second passed, two, three. A man walked in front of the store.

'And that's me.'

Mendoza hit another couple of keys and a third film clip started playing. The clock in the corner of the screen had jumped forward to twenty-one after two. The woman walked past the store again, this time in the opposite direction. Mendoza hit pause, freezing her in mid-stride.

'On the basis of this Lieutenant Jones thinks we should give you the benefit of the doubt.' Her voice was flat and life-less, her face tense.

'And you clearly disagree with his decision. So, what? You'd rather I was a murderer? Then again that wouldn't reflect well on you, would it? It would mean you missed that one the whole way through the Ryan McCarthy case.' He smiled. 'You're not going to Vegas, are you?'

Mendoza glared at him. 'The good news is my forced leave has been cancelled. The bad news is that until we have this woman in custody, I've been ordered to assist you in apprehending her.'

'That's good to hear.'

'No it's not. There's nothing good about this situation whatsoever.'

'You get to go to Hartwood.'

'I'd rather go to the dentist.'

'And just so we're clear here, that's a joke, right? You don't really want to go to the dentist. I mean, nobody in their right mind wants to go to the dentist.'

Mendoza shot him a dirty look. 'Okay, you need to tell me what happened again, from beginning to end. And I want the full story. Everything. Don't leave anything out. Got it? Not a single goddamn thing.'

7

Winter went through the whole thing again, only this time Mendoza broke up his narrative with questions. Poking, prodding, clarifying. As far as he could tell she didn't get anything new. Omar's murder was seared into his memory and he'd covered everything in full the first time around.

'You seem pretty convinced that this woman murdered the Reeds,' she said when he'd finished.

'I am. What she did to Omar proves that she's capable of killing. And why leave that newspaper behind? She was pointing us in the direction of the Reed murders for a reason. It's the only reason I can see.'

'Makes sense to me. Okay, so let me make sure I've got this straight. This woman was here when you arrived, she came over to your table, spoke to you, stabbed the cook, then left. And the attack was completely unprovoked.'

Winter nodded. 'She accused me of not taking her seriously, but, yeah, I'd say that the attack was unprovoked.'

'And you've never seen her before?'

Winter shook his head. 'Nope.'

'And she used your first name?'

A nod.

Mendoza frowned. 'So she was waiting specifically for you. Which means she's been tailing you and you didn't notice. Which means you're losing your touch.'

'This has nothing to do with me losing my touch and everything to do with her being the real deal.'

'*The real deal?*'

'We're agreed that most criminals are idiots, right? After all, that's how they get caught. Every now and again, though, you come across one who's smart, one who plans everything down to the last detail. These are the ones who love what they do, and want to keep on doing it. That's what we're dealing with here.'

Mendoza laughed and shook her head. 'Of course you're going to say that. I mean, what's the alternative? That you were outsmarted by an idiot?'

Winter ignored the dig and shut his eyes. She was trying to push his buttons and that really wasn't helping. He went through everything in his head again, trying to see how it all fitted together. The camera added a new dimension. He opened his eyes.

'Go back and check the camera footage. You'll see that she followed me to the diner on Monday night, and Tuesday. She would have visited a third time as well, possibly during the day, to scope the place out. Because I'd been there two nights running she assumed that I'd go there again tonight and timed it so she arrived before I got there. We're looking for someone who's around five-nine, but if she's wearing heels she'll appear taller. Chances are she won't have blonde hair during her earlier visits, and I doubt she'll be dressed in jeans and leather. The hair was fake. Eye colour, too.'

Mendoza considered all this for a second. 'I'll get someone to look into it.'

'I wouldn't bother. It's a waste of time.'

'But it was your idea.'

Winter shrugged. 'And now that I've had time to think it through properly I'm telling you it's a waste of time. All you'll do is prove that she's methodical, and that's something I'm prepared to take at face value. It's a tangent we could do without. We need to focus on the road ahead, not the one that's disappearing in the rear-view mirror. She's given us Hartwood and the Reeds, and she's done that for a reason. I want to know what that reason is.'

They fell silent and Winter glanced over at his reflection in the one-way mirror. In his mind's eye he saw the woman cross the street and disappear around the corner. He heard a ghostly echo of Elvis singing 'Suspicious Minds'.

'Where do you stand on the nature versus nurture debate?' he asked.

'I think both arguments are valid. Some people are born bad, some are made bad.'

'I'd agree with that. And in my opinion this one was born bad.'

'How can you be so sure?'

Because I looked into her eyes and saw myself reflected back. The thought flitted through his head but didn't reach his lips. Instead, he said, 'Do this as much as I have and you get a feel for what flavour of crazy you're dealing with. This woman's a psychopath. Omar's murder was all about control and manipulation. She's toying with me. Basically, she's saying that she owns the board.'

'Okay, I can buy that. So, the next question has got to be why. Why is she's doing this? From what you've told me, we're clearly dealing with an organised offender, right?'

Winter nodded. Broadly speaking, serial killers fell into

two categories, organised and disorganised. Dr Harold Shipman was one of the most prolific murderers in recorded history, and a perfect example of an organised killer. He was intelligent, ruthless and manipulative. He'd been active in the UK for more than two decades, and during that time it was estimated that he killed more than two hundred and fifty of his patients. Disorganised killers were a lot more chaotic in their approach. As a result they tended to have smaller body counts and were usually caught more quickly.

'So why target you?' Mendoza asked again.

Winter shook his head. 'I've no idea.'

'Okay, assuming that she was following you, surely you would have noticed. You would have seen something, in your peripheral vision perhaps, or picked up that something wasn't quite right. Even if she was using a disguise, you're too switched on for that not to have happened.'

He met her gaze. 'Was that a compliment?'

'No, I'm just stating a fact.'

'The reason I didn't notice was because I had no reason to.'

'Explain.'

He took a deep breath. 'Okay, I found the diner by accident a couple of nights ago. Because the food was good I came back again last night. Ditto for tonight. Three nights in a row establishes a pattern. Now, counter-surveillance 101 dictates that you mix up your schedule. If you're going somewhere on a daily basis, you never go the same way two days running. And you never eat at the same diner two days in a row, never mind three days.'

Winter and Mendoza locked eyes for longer this time. She nodded for him to go on.

'But the Ryan McCarthy case wasn't the sort of case where I was going to be targeted, and I'm not in the habit of employing counter-surveillance techniques just in case. That road leads to paranoia and lunacy. If needs be, I'll up my level of vigilance, but there has to be a credible threat. Ryan was a shy boy. He had his fun in the dark and the shadows. There's no way he'd be brave enough to go after the people hunting him.'

Mendoza studied him. 'It's okay to admit that you screwed up, you know.'

Before Winter could respond, there was a knock on the door and Hitchin came in. He was flushed and breathing fast, and he was carrying a small notepad. If anything, his suit looked even more crumpled than it had done earlier. His face was just as forgettable, though.

'You wanted to know as soon as I heard back from the Monroe County Sheriff's Office.'

'What have you got?' Mendoza asked.

'Okay, I can confirm that Lester and Melanie Reed were the victims of a double homicide that took place six years ago in Hartwood, a small town upstate, twenty miles from Rochester. I can also confirm that as far as the sheriff's department is concerned, the case is closed. The murders were carried out by a local kid.'

'So they're not looking for anyone?'

Hitchin shook his head.

'And you're sure about this?'

Hitchin laughed. 'As sure as I can be given that it's the middle of the night and I'm talking with someone who lives out there in the middle of nowhere.'

Mendoza turned to Winter. 'Bang goes your theory that your mystery woman killed the Reeds.'

Winter frowned. 'So why draw our attention to the murders? What's that all about?'

'No idea. Maybe she's just screwing with you.' Mendoza turned back to Hitchin. 'Have you got a name for this kid?'

The detective flipped his pad open. 'Yeah. Nelson Price.'

'What can you tell me about him?'

'Absolutely nothing other than he was twenty-one when the murders took place. That's another downside with it being the middle of the night. I'm talking to people who are accessing computer records rather than people who were actually involved in the investigation.'

'Any idea where Nelson's being held?'

Another shake of the head. 'Sorry, I wasn't able to get that information.'

'Who was the lead investigator?'

Hitchin consulted his notepad again. 'The person I spoke with said it was most likely someone called Jeremiah Lowe. He was the Monroe County Sheriff's Department's number one go-to guy in homicide at the time. Unfortunately it doesn't really help since he's dead. There is some good news, though. Hartwood's Police Department was first on the scene, and the same chief of police is still there. Some guy by the name of Birch. I tried their number, but got diverted to the answering machine. No real surprise there. Hartwood's tiny. They probably operate on office hours.'

'Anything else?'

Another shake of the head. 'That's it for now.'

'I need you to get someone to take another look at the

camera footage. We think that Winter was under surveillance.' She smiled across the table at Winter. 'Roughly what time were you there on Monday and Tuesday night?'

'Around two.'

'On both nights?'

'On both nights.'

She turned back to Hitchin. 'She might be in disguise, so bear that in mind. Also, get someone to check the daytime footage for Tuesday and Wednesday as well.'

'Will do. Anything else?'

'No, that's all for now.'

Hitchin left, closing the door gently behind him.

'You're wasting your time,' said Winter.

'Okay, here's how this works: you butt out and let me do my thing, and I'll do my best to butt out and let you do yours. Understand?'

He answered with a smile.

'I'm serious.'

Winter waited for her to continue, but she was done for now. He gave it another couple of seconds to be sure, then closed his eyes and pictured himself back in the diner again. He replayed the conversation with the woman, looking for something he might have missed and coming up with nothing. He could hear the tone of her voice, the pitch, the slight whispering tail-off at the end of her sentences. He could see those bright green eyes studying him from the other side of the table. What he couldn't see was what the hell she was playing at. He opened his eyes and saw Mendoza watching him across the table.

'What's going on here, Winter?'

'I was just asking myself much the same thing.'

'And?'

'And I'm pretty sure that we're not going to get answers sitting around here. I vote we head on up to Hartwood. If we leave now we'll miss the morning rush.'

Mendoza was staring at him like he'd just suggested two weeks in Vegas.

'It's only upstate New York,' he added. 'It's not like you need shots and a passport. If we leave now, I reckon we'd get there by ten, maybe half-nine if we really push it.'

'Jesus, you're serious about this. You heard Hitchin. Nelson Price did it. Hauling our asses up there will not change that fact. Believe me, I've got better things to do with my time than this. Read my lips: I am not going to Hartwood.'

'Is this the point where I have to remind you that Lieutenant Jones has ordered you to assist me?' Winter smiled. 'You want to know what would help me out here? What would help me out is for you to get your hands on a really fast car.'

8

Mendoza kept her foot down all the way and they made the distance in just over five hours. She'd called in a favour with a buddy in narcotics and got hold of a BMW M3 that had been confiscated in a drug bust. The car had been pimped accordingly. Darkened windows, leather upholstery, metallic white paintwork, and a sound system that turned the car into a nightclub. They'd been pulled over twice. The first time as they'd skirted past Binghamton, and then fifteen miles south of Syracuse. On both occasions Mendoza had shown her badge and they'd been back on the road again a couple of minutes later.

For the last ten miles the roads had been getting narrower and more rural, the trees taller. Despite the tight turns, Mendoza was still driving fast, and that was fine with Winter. The quicker they got there, the better. He would have preferred to be behind the wheel but at least she wasn't hanging around. The further they got from New York, the more relaxed he was feeling. The interview room was a distant memory, and there was a sense that things were finally moving in the right direction.

They passed a signpost that read HARTWOOD: THE SMALL TOWN WITH THE BIG HEART. Up ahead, was an old wooden kissing bridge that had been painted a rustic brown. It was in pristine condition. A photo opportunity, if ever there was one.

Mendoza glanced over from the driver's seat. 'If this turns out to be one of those *Twilight Zone* towns and I end up murdered in my sleep, I'm coming back to haunt you. Are you hearing me?'

Winter laughed. 'And it would be nothing less than I deserve.'

'I'm serious.'

'I don't doubt that for a second.'

They crossed the bridge at fifteen miles an hour, wood clattering all around them and the sound of that big engine bouncing back off the roof. The BMW rumbled out the other side and was swallowed up by the trees again.

'So why did you become a cop?'

'Where did that come from?'

'It's just a question.'

'I don't do personal.'

'Nor do I.' Winter left the statement hanging there and waited for Mendoza to look over. 'The reason I joined the FBI's Behavioral Analysis Unit was because I was trying to make sense of what my father did. The reason I left was because I'm still trying to make sense of that. Okay, your turn.'

Mendoza didn't say anything for a bit. She kept stealing glances at him from the driver's seat.

'My dad was a cop,' she said eventually. 'So was my grandfather. I guess you could say that it's the family business.'

'Is your dad still a cop?'

Mendoza shook her head. 'He retired ten years ago. Him and my mom moved up to New Hampshire.'

'What about your mom? Was she a cop?'

'No, she was a cop's wife. She was the one who wanted to

47

move. After thirty years she just wanted to get as far away from New York as possible.'

'I'm guessing she wasn't exactly thrilled when you decided to follow in your dad's footsteps.'

'No she wasn't, but she wasn't surprised either. Okay, no more questions.'

A couple of minutes later they reached the town. As they cruised slowly up Main Street, Winter experienced a sense of temporal dislocation, like they'd travelled back in time to the turn of the last century. There wasn't a single chain store in sight. No McDonalds, no Walmart, no Starbucks. A red-and-white striped candy pole turned lazily outside the barber's shop. The drugstore had a sign saying APOTHECARY, and the largest building belonged to the general store. The garage sold gas, and repaired cars, and was one of those businesses that had probably been passed down from father to son for generations. Winter started humming *The Twilight Zone* theme and Mendoza ignored him.

Hartwood's police department was located in a small one-storey concrete office building halfway along Main. Mendoza parked in an empty slot and killed the engine. The dirt-streaked Ford Crown Victoria next to them was more than ten years old and probably had two hundred thousand miles on the clock.

'You think that's the only car that the Hartwood PD own?' Winter asked as he opened the door.

Mendoza ignored him again.

Winter got out and attempted to stretch away the miles, his fingertips pointing to the heavens. He shrugged his muscles loose, then put on his sheepskin jacket and zipped it all the way up to his chin to keep out the chill. The trees lining the sidewalk were alive with every shade of brown, red and orange, and the sun was burning low in the sky. It was going to be one of those beautiful fall days where you could almost trick yourself into forgetting that December was just around the corner.

Mendoza straightened her suit and headed for the entrance, Winter tagging along a couple of steps behind. The door opened on to a single room with a long counter separating the business and the public side. Access from one to the other was gained through a yard-long bar-style flap.

There were two desks and no sign of any ancillary offices, which indicated that the Hartwood Police Department was strictly a two-man affair. Tucked away in one corner was a small six-foot-by-six-foot holding cell. Metal bars, and a metal bedframe that had been bolted to the floor and walls. No toilet, which was probably a blessing. A large map of Monroe County was fixed to one wall, and there was a door in another wall that presumably led out back.

The guy behind the counter was in his mid-twenties. There was something in his expression that gave the impression that he wasn't particularly bright. Maybe it was the vague look in his eyes, or maybe it was the way he was staring like he'd never seen real-life city folk before. Or maybe he'd just never seen a thirty-something man with white hair. Whatever the reason, it was clear this wasn't the guy in charge.

Mendoza pushed her sunglasses on to the top of her head and walked over to the counter. She flashed her badge. The cop stared some more, then slowly lifted his head until he met her gaze.

'Chief Birch isn't here yet.'

He was soft spoken and timid, and if Mendoza had said 'boo' he would probably have died on the spot. His uniform was clean on and neatly pressed, the seams dead straight, and Winter wondered if his mom still did his laundry. The name tag read Peterson.

'Maybe you can help us since you are here,' Mendoza suggested. 'We need some information about the Reed murders.'

Peterson just stared at her like she was speaking in a foreign language. It took almost three whole seconds for him to process what she was saying. *One Mississippi, two Mississippi, three Mississippi.*

'Chief Birch should be here soon.'

'Yes, but you're here now.'

His eyes narrowed. 'I don't know anything about the Reed murders.'

'The number of murders that happen in Hartwood, I can see how this one slipped your mind.'

Another three whole seconds passed before Peterson responded. 'Chief Birch should be here soon.'

'Define soon.'

Peterson gave her a blank look.

Mendoza sighed. 'My guess is that things don't get too exciting around here, right? But every now and again you'll get an emergency. So your boss leaves a number you can contact him on in case of an emergency.'

'But it's not an emergency.'

'Just call your boss, okay?'

'I can't do that. He doesn't like to be disturbed when he's having breakfast.'

Winter had heard enough. He flipped the counter up and made a beeline for the desk on the left. This was obviously Peterson's as the computer was on.

'Hey,' Peterson called out, 'you're not allowed back here.'

Winter ignored him and sat down. He opened the top drawer and went through it, and struck gold straightaway. He lifted out the contact list and scanned it quickly. Birch's cellphone and home numbers were right up at the top. Mendoza had followed him through and was standing at his shoulder, her cell already out. Winter handed her the list and she punched Birch's number into the phone.

'You need to get back on the other side of the counter,' said Peterson, but he was talking to himself.

'Chief Birch?' said Mendoza. There was a short pause while she listened to the reply. 'My name is Sergeant Mendoza and I'm with the NYPD. I'm currently running an investigation that's led me to your beautiful corner of the world, and I'd really appreciate it if you could give me a couple of minutes of your time.'

She paused again, listening. 'That's correct we're at the station house. Officer Peterson is making us feel right at home.'

Birch said something that made Mendoza laugh. There were a couple of 'Uh-huhs' in response to whatever he said next, then she hung up.

'He'll be here in ten.'

9

Chief Birch's ten minutes was closer to fifteen. He came waddling into the station house wearing a wide politician's smile. His waistline was at least fifty inches. This was a man who would definitely get pissed if he missed a meal, so Peterson's reluctance to disturb him at breakfast suddenly made sense.

He wasn't just wide, he was tall, too, at least six-three. Early fifties, black tidy hair, red cheeks, three chins, and a heart attack waiting in the wings. He squeezed through the gap in the counter and the effort wiped the fake smile from his face. He didn't offer to shake hands, and he didn't look happy to be there. A quick glance at Mendoza, then a longer one for Winter. He stared at the hair, stared at the Jim Morrison T-shirt, stared at the worn Levis and the scuffed Converse sneakers.

'Who the hell are you?'

'Jefferson Winter. I'm working with Sergeant Mendoza on this case.'

The eyes turned suspicious. 'You're not a cop.'

'No, sir, I'm not. I was with the FBI's Behavioral Analysis Unit for more than a decade, though. Nowadays I work freelance.'

'Behavioral Analysis, eh? That's where you try to get inside the heads of killers, right? I've seen the documentaries on TV.

All a load of BS, if you ask me. It's right up there with getting psychics to solve crimes.'

Winter was tempted to tell Birch about how his overeating was the result of low self-esteem, and how that in turn was rooted in his miserable childhood. But he held back. That fat kid was still there, every time Birch looked in the mirror. No matter how tempting it was, poking him with sticks was not going to help, not if they wanted to get him on side.

Birch stared a second longer, then turned to Peterson. 'Get me a coffee. And I want real sugar, not those crappy sweeteners my wife told you to use. I can taste the difference, you know.'

'Yes, sir.'

Peterson disappeared out to the back rooms, and Birch waddled over to the chair Mendoza was in and stood next to it until she moved. He sat down heavily, coughed a couple of times, then sniffed. 'So, what can I do for you folks?'

'We need information on the Reed murders,' said Mendoza.

Birch stared at them one at a time, brow creased, puzzlement on his face. 'Now, why on all that's holy would you want to know about a murder that happened out here years ago?'

'I'm afraid I can't go into specifics because the investigation's ongoing.'

'Fine, don't tell me. But I've got to say, I can't see how what happened to the Reeds could have any bearing on anything that you might be working on. That was local business. The Reeds had no connection with New York. They were born and bred here. They can't be involved in whatever it is you've got going on. I'm telling you now, if you're looking for some sort of connection, you're looking in the wrong place.'

'Maybe so, but since we've driven all the way up here, the least you can do is humour us by answering a few questions.'

Birch laughed. 'Sure, why not?' He stopped talking and looked at Mendoza like he was waiting for her to start firing off questions. When she didn't say anything, he added, 'I was involved in that investigation from start to finish. Those jokers from the sheriff's department tried to push me out, but that was never going to happen. This is my town. I was the first cop on the scene when the call came in about the Reeds. In all my years I've never seen anything like it, and I pray to God I never see anything like it again.'

10

'How about you walk us through what happened?'

Winter matched the pitch and cadence of his speech to Birch's. Mirroring might be an old trick, but it was also an effective one. Show people a reflection of themselves and it helped to relax them. The more relaxed they were, the looser their lips got. If they were going to get anything useful from Birch, he needed to follow Mendoza's lead and tread warily. One push in the wrong direction and the chief would clam up.

Birch dragged a hand down over his mouth and squeezed a sigh between his fingers. 'Six years ago, but it seems like yesterday. We don't get many murders around these parts. Mostly when a murder does happen we're dealing with an argument that's got out of hand, and thank the Lord, those don't happen too often. What happened to the Reeds, though, that was something else entirely. You know what I remember most was the blood. Sweet Jesus, there was more blood than you could ever imagine.'

Winter nodded. He'd seen enough crime scenes to know that eight pints of blood could go a long way. And Birch was talking about a double homicide, which meant sixteen pints. Two gallons of blood could make one hell of a mess, and had obviously left one hell of a lasting impression. Before he could say anything else Peterson came back in. Birch took the coffee mug from Peterson without a word of thanks, sipped some, then put it down on the desk. CHIEF was written in big gold letters on the side.

'Where did you find the bodies?' Mendoza asked.

'In the living room. Both of them had been stabbed. There was blood sprayed all over the walls. It was all over the floors.'

Winter nodded at Mendoza then moved closer to Birch. He wanted to try a cognitive interview. Reliving the event in this way, the quality of the information was so much better. People remembered things they would never have remembered otherwise, and what they came up with was sometimes the difference between solving a case or not. He needed to go carefully though. If Birch worked out what he was up to he'd probably show them the door. A cognitive interview would definitely be classed as 'BS'.

'Where were you when the call came in that the Reeds had been found?' he asked.

Birch rubbed a meaty hand over his mouth. 'You know, I can't recall where I was. You're talking six years ago here. That's a whole chunk of time.'

'Okay, what time of day was it? Morning? Afternoon?'

'It was definitely morning. I remember that much because the bodies were found by Dave Henderson. He was delivering the post. The door was open when he got there, which it never was. The Reeds both worked. He called their names and when he got no answer he went inside. That's when he found them.'

Before Birch could get started on the blood again, Winter said, 'We'd like to talk to Henderson.'

'In that case it's a shame you're not a psychic as well as a mind reader. He died last year. A heart attack.'

And right there you had one of the big problems that came with investigating cold cases, thought Winter. 'Okay, if it was morning, you were probably here at the station.'

Birch rubbed his mouth again, his fingertips stroking his chins. He nodded. 'Henderson called and he was in a hell of a state, as you can imagine. He was in such a state it took me a while to work out who I was talking to, and I'd known him since we were kids. Anyhow, I calmed him down and he tells me this story about how he'd found the bodies. He wasn't making much sense and I thought he might have been drinking. It wouldn't have been the first time he'd been drunk at that time of day.'

'So what happened next?'

'Well, once I'd established he was sober, I told him to stay where he was then rushed straight over.'

'What was the weather like?'

'Excuse me?'

'Was it raining?' asked Winter.

Birch opened his mouth to say something then snapped it shut again. He ran a hand over his face. 'Now you mention it, yes it was raining. Later that day we were hit with one of the worst snowstorms I can remember. The rain was the start of it. How did you know that?'

It was an educated guess. This part of the world, in the middle of winter, rain was more likely than sun. Winter wasn't about to admit that out loud, though. 'So you pull up as close to the Reeds' house as you can get because you don't want to get any wetter than you need to, and you hurry up to the house because you don't want to get cold. Where's Henderson?'

'He's sat on the porch staring into space. My first thought was that he *was* drunk, then I realised he was in shock. He'd thrown up into a flower bed. He got up and said he'd show me where the bodies were and I told him to stay put. The house wasn't that big. I didn't think I was going to have much trouble finding them. And I was right. All I had to do was follow my nose.'

'What was the first thing that struck you when you stepped into the living room?'

'The bodies and the blood.'

The answer was pretty much what Winter expected. Six years added up to more than two thousand days. During that time Birch would have recounted this story out loud and in his head on numerous occasions, and on each retelling he would have focused increasingly on the gore and the devastation until those details eclipsed everything else. People didn't want the basic details, they wanted to know about the horror.

'And what was the second thing you noticed?'

'How neat the table was. It was all set out like they were about to have a dinner party. Place mats, wine glasses, knives and forks. There was even a candelabra. Damn weird was what it was. I remember thinking at the time that it was all a bit much.'

'And this was a weekday night. Do you know if the Reeds were celebrating anything? A birthday? An anniversary?'

'Not without looking at the files.'

'And you found Nelson Price's prints in the house?'

'They were all over the house.'

'What about the knocker or the doorbell?'

Birch looked flustered. His face was turning redder by the

58

second. 'How the hell am I supposed to remember something like that? This happened years ago. Why do you want to know anyway?'

'Because I'm trying to work out if Nelson broke in, or if the Reeds let him in.'

'I guess there might be something in the files.'

'We'd like to see those files, please,' Mendoza said.

'I'll get Peterson to dig them out for you.'

Birch whistled to Peterson, then gestured to the door that led out to the back rooms. Peterson hurried off, the door banging shut behind him.

'Can you remember where the bodies were?' Winter asked.

'Melanie's was by the fireplace and Lester's was next to the dining table.'

'Okay, let's stay with the dining table. I want you to close your eyes and tell me again how it was laid out.'

'Excuse me.'

'I just want you to close your eyes and tell me what you see.'

'I heard you. I take it this is one of those weirdo ideas they teach you in the FBI. Tell you what, let's do this the old-fashioned way. I'll have a little think about things and tell you what I remember. Does that work for you?'

Winter shrugged. 'Sure.'

'Okay, for starters the dining table was set for four.' Birch delivered this piece of information like he was laying down a winning hand.

'You seem pretty sure about that.'

'I am. A hundred per cent certain. There were four places set. One on each side.'

And you didn't think to mention this earlier, he thought but didn't say. 'Were Lester and Melanie expecting guests?'

'No, it was just Lester and Melanie. Nelson set the table out after he killed them. It's the only explanation that fits. That was my theory, by the way.'

'Why do you think he did that?'

Birch laughed. 'Because the kid was as crazy as a shithouse rat.'

'What else can you remember?'

'The tablecloth was white and the place mats were red. They'd used their best cutlery and their best flatware. Same goes for the china and the drinking glasses. Everything was the best they owned. It was like they were expecting a visit from the president.'

'Tell me about the candelabra.'

'It was solid silver with red candles.'

'Did it belong to the Reeds or did Nelson bring it along with him?'

'And why would he do something like that?'

'Because he's as crazy as a shithouse rat,' Winter suggested.

Birch just stared.

'Okay,' Winter went on. 'We know that the murders were carried out by Nelson Price, but before he was caught were there any other suspects?'

Birch shook his head. 'Nope. No suspects.'

'There must have been someone. Lester or Melanie must have made at least one enemy over the years.'

'The reason we didn't have any suspects was because we didn't need any suspects. Nelson Price was seen at the Reeds' house and his prints were all over the murder weapon. It doesn't get much more open and shut than that.'

'But before it become clear that Price did it, was there anyone else you were looking at? Anyone at all.'

Birch eyed Winter suspiciously. 'I'm getting the feeling
that something's going on here and I'm only privy to part of
it. Do you know how much that pisses me off?'

Mendoza fielded this one. 'My colleague was approached
by someone we believe might be connected with the murders.'

'Connected how?'

'He thinks they might be the killer.'

'And that's what brought you all this way?'

Mendoza nodded. 'Yes, sir.'

Birch's laughter filled the room. 'Well, I'm sorry to say but
it looks as if you've had a wasted journey.'

'Where is Nelson Price being held?' Winter asked. 'We
need to talk to him.'

Birch laughed again. 'Not going to happen. He's dead.'

For a moment Winter just stood there thinking. It would
be useful to talk to Dave Henderson or Nelson Price or
Jeremiah Lowe, the original lead investigator in the Reed
murders, but they were all dead. That could be viewed as
overly convenient, except this was a six-year-old murder and a
lot could happen in that time.

'What happened to him?'

'He hung himself in the family's barn.'

'And I'm taking it that this happened before he could
confess.'

'Nelson Price did it. No two ways about it.'

Winter nodded to himself. 'So he hung himself before you
got a confession.'

Birch looked from Winter to Mendoza then back again. The sudden change in his body language made it obvious that they were done talking. 'I've got a busy morning ahead of me, so I'm afraid our time is up.'

Winter fired a sunny smile at Birch. 'Before you get too deep into your busy morning, you said we could see the file.'

Time stopped. No one moved.

'Peterson,' Birch called out, eyes still locked on Winter's. 'Where the hell's that file?'

There was some banging and scrabbling from the back of the station house, then Peterson reappeared. His cheeks were flushed, his hair was a mess and his uniform was wrinkled and sprinkled with dust.

'I can't find it,' he said.

'What do you mean you can't find it? Have you tried under R for Reed and P for Price?'

'I've looked everywhere, sir. It's not here.'

'It has to be there,' Birch hissed.

Winter searched Peterson's desk for a sheet of paper and a pen. He scribbled down his cellphone number then got up and laid it neatly on Chief Birch's desk. 'If the file turns up, please give me a call.' He headed for the door, paused with his hand on the handle. 'One last thing: I'm going to need directions to the Reeds' house and a couple of flashlights.'

11

'I guess this means we can head back to New York,' said Mendoza when they got outside. 'It's an open and shut case. Nelson Price did it. Your mystery woman's off the hook.'

Winter stretched and shook his head. 'What about Omar? She definitely killed him.'

'Right now Omar's in a freezer in New York waiting for a post-mortem. He was murdered in the city, he worked there, he no doubt lived there, too. Are you seeing a pattern here, Winter?'

'And I'm sure Hitchin and his buddies are doing a fantastic job working the murder at that end. However, she wanted us to come here for a reason, and I want to know what that reason is. As far as I'm concerned, we're currently in the best place to do that. Why else would she have pointed us in the direction of the Reed murders?'

'That's one interpretation.'

'There's another?'

'Yeah, maybe Nelson isn't the only one who's as crazy as a shithouse rat.'

Winter ignored this and lit a cigarette. He pushed the pack back into his jacket pocket, zipped up, then took a long drag and stared to the east. The sun was still sitting low against the sharp blue sky. A flock of birds swooped and squawked in the distance, tiny dots of black moving in random patterns.

'The dining table at the Reed house is an anomaly. Why set four places if only two people are eating? I'd like to see the crime scene photographs.'

'Maybe the Monroe Sheriff's Department have some they can email over?' Mendoza suggested.

'Good idea. And say it's urgent. That way we might actually get them this side of Christmas.'

Mendoza took out her cell and made the call. It took a couple of minutes of bouncing around the switchboard before she managed to speak to someone who could help. She hung up with the promise that they'd do what they could.

'Why Vegas?' Winter asked her.

'Why not?'

'Because it doesn't strike me as a first choice vacation destination for you. People go to Vegas because they want to have fun and, no offence, so far you haven't shown much inclination towards fun.'

'Who says I was going on my own?'

'I say. The times don't add up. While Ryan McCarthy is getting settled into his cell, Lieutenant Jones is ordering you to get on the first plane out of the city. This whole situation defines the concept of last minute, so it's unlikely that your partner would have been able to get time off, not at such short notice. Assuming, of course, that you have a partner. And before you say anything: yes, they would have a job. No way would you be bankrolling a boy toy, not on what the NYPD pay.'

Mendoza just stared, and Winter laughed and held his hands up in mock surrender. 'I'm just saying.' He took another drag, his face turning serious. 'So, why don't you like me?'

The question caught Mendoza off guard. Her eyes darted to the left and the start of a blush painted her cheeks. She went to say something, then stopped and took a deep breath. She met his gaze again. 'Who says I don't like you?'

Winter said nothing.

'Okay, it's not that I don't like you. It's just that when you do that thing where you commune with your inner psychopath, it kind of freaks me out.'

'"Communing with my inner psychopath"? That's the first time I've heard it called that.' He paused. 'You've got to admit, though, it gets results.'

'And that's why I tolerate you. So what now?'

'Now we go to Lester and Melanie's house. I bet you lunch that no one lives there. Not after what happened. Not in a town this small.' Winter held his hand out but Mendoza made no move to shake it. He gave her a puzzled look. 'It's real simple. If I'm right then you buy lunch. If I'm wrong I'll buy. We seal the deal with a handshake.'

'I don't gamble.'

'Seriously? So why were you going to Vegas?'

'Because I like the shows.'

Without another word, Mendoza turned and walked over to the car. Winter watched her go for a second, then shook his head and followed.

12

Chief Birch's directions took them to a small house out on the edge of Hartwood. Like Winter thought, nobody had lived there since the murders. A rust-streaked mailbox stood lopsided at the head of the weed-infested driveway, the front yard was overgrown with waist-high grass, and the doors and windows were boarded up. There was blistered, peeling paint on the clapboard and the wooden porch furniture had started to collapse in on itself.

Winter stood on the sidewalk and scanned the street. There were eight other houses, all of them different but essentially the same. It was the sort of neighbourhood you came to if you were starting a family, or you were retired and wanted to downsize. The yards reflected this. Regimented flower beds and tidy lawns for the older folks, basketball hoops and toys for the younger ones. He could guess what the neighbours thought about the Reed's house. Having an abandoned murder house in your street did nothing for property prices.

Winter and Mendoza walked up the driveway side by side and stopped at the bottom of the porch steps. The wood was mouldy and had started to rot, making him wonder how sturdy they were. Mendoza was clearly thinking the same thing because she waited for him to reach the top before joining him. While she checked the boards nailed over the door and windows at the front of the house, he checked the back.

The wood was sound, the space between the boards tight. Getting inside wasn't going to be as straightforward as he'd hoped. He walked back around to the front of the house.

'We're going to need tools,' said Mendoza.

'Someone around here must have some we can borrow.'

'That's what I'm thinking.'

There was no answer at the first house they tried, but the widow living at the second was happy to help out after Mendoza showed her badge. The dead husband must have been a DIY nut because the garage was filled with tools. All of them were arranged neatly, and all were coated with a layer of dust. They left with a pry bar, a hammer, and a bag of nails for putting the boards back on later.

Getting the boards off posed no problem whatsoever. It was a five-minute job, if that. The door was locked but that wasn't much of a problem either. Lock picking was one of the more useful skills Winter had been taught in the FBI. He put his lock picks back into his jacket pocket and opened the door with a flourish. Mendoza turned on her flashlight, then pushed past him and went inside.

'You're welcome,' he called after her.

Winter took a minute to examine the door, running scenarios through his head. The lock was a Yale, straightforward to pick if you knew what you were doing. But Nelson Price was just a kid at the time of the murders, and how many kids had the patience or motivation to learn something like that? The most likely explanation was that he'd knocked on the door and either Melanie or Lester had answered. Maybe they'd looked through the spyhole and recognised Nelson, maybe they hadn't. Whichever way it had played out, the door had been opened. Chances were the security chain hadn't been attached. Most people tended not to bother with them.

Winter turned on his flashlight and walked into the hall. Shadows shrank and grew in the narrow beam, dust motes danced in the air. He sniffed the air. All he could smell was stale air and rotting wood. No one had been here for years, that much was clear. The house had the feel of a tomb. It was as though the door had been locked after the murders and hadn't been opened again until today. Even the local kids had given it a wide berth. There was no evidence that they had been here. No empty liquor bottles, no cigarette butts, no used condoms. If they'd broken in the place would have been trashed. Graffiti on the walls and devastation everywhere.

Mendoza was a couple of yards ahead of him, the beam of her flashlight bouncing in all directions. 'This place gives me the creeps. It's like a goddamn haunted house.'

'I didn't have you down as being superstitious.'

'I'm not. I've just watched too many horror movies. Doesn't it give you the creeps?'

'Not really.'

The corridor running parallel to the stairs had two doors leading off it. The first one they tried opened on to the living room. He aimed the flashlight at the fireplace, saw the faded bloodstains on the floor and the arterial spray patterns on the nearby walls. There was a smaller stain on the floor near the dining table. The markings were consistent with where Birch said that Lester and Melanie had died. Mendoza crouched down by the fireplace and examined the stained wood, the beam of her flashlight playing back and forth.

'Judging by these, I'd say that Lester got off easier than Melanie.'

'That's how I'm reading it.'

'Poor kids.'

Winter went over to the dining table and laid his left hand on the wood. Birch had been right about this, too. It was roughly five feet by three feet, big enough for four. You could get six on it, but it would be a squeeze. He closed his eyes, saw the table set for four, but he couldn't picture the scene as clearly as he'd like. He opened his eyes and headed back out into the hall.

'Where are you going?' Mendoza called after him.

'To find a tablecloth.'

'Ask a stupid question.'

The next door along led to the kitchen. It looked tidy enough, albeit with the layer of dust and the deserted feel that came from abandonment. Winter wondered who'd tidied up after the crime scene investigators had left. Lester's parents? Melanie's? He went through the drawers and cupboards and found most of what he was looking for on his first pass. Flatware, plates, wine glasses, candles. No candelabra but he did find some candlestick holders, There were cloth napkins and place mats in one of the bottom drawers. The mats were black instead of red, but they'd do. The only thing he didn't find was a tablecloth. He heard Mendoza walk into the kitchen, saw the beam of her flashlight bouncing over the collection he'd put together on one of the work surfaces.

'Take these back through to the living room,' he told her

as he headed back out to the hall. 'I'm going upstairs to look for a bed sheet.'

'This time I'm not even going to ask,' she shouted after him.

Winter went back along the hall and took the stairs two at a time. There were three doors leading off the landing, all closed. The first door led to a small bathroom. There was just about space for a toilet, sink and bathtub. He heard Mendoza's footsteps on the stairs, heard her walk along the landing. She stopped at his shoulder and looked past him.

'No bed sheets in here.'

'Nope.'

He closed the door and tried the next one. This room was painted a pale yellow colour and there was a crib pushed into one corner. White furniture, sky blue drapes and soft toys. There were brightly coloured dancing jungle animals on the walls. Elephants, tigers, giraffes and monkeys. On closer inspection, it was clear that the mural was hand painted. Mendoza let out a long heartfelt sigh.

'Birch didn't say anything about the Reed's having a baby.'

'That's because they didn't have one.' Winter walked over to the cradle and plucked out two teddy bears. One was pink, the other blue. He held them up for Mendoza to see. 'They were trying for one.'

Mendoza was looking around the room. She was somehow managing to look both angry and sad. 'This job really sucks at times.'

'No arguments there.'

'You know, I deal with this shit day in, day out, and I think I've got immune, then I walk in on something like this. Lester and Melanie were just kids really. They had their whole lives ahead of them and that was stolen away from them. It's not fair.'

'No, it's not.'

Winter went over to the closet. There were some crib sheets on the top shelf but they were too small for what he had in mind. He went back out on to the landing. The last door led to the main bedroom. All the bedding had been stripped away, leaving a bare mattress. No doubt this had been done during the original investigation. He found a double sheet in the closet and went back downstairs to the living room.

Mendoza helped him put the sheet on the table, then they set it together, working efficiently around one another. Winter lit the candles and placed them in the middle of the table. Then they turned off their flashlights and sat down, Winter at the head, Mendoza at the foot. He looked around, shook his head. 'This isn't right.'

He got up and moved counterclockwise to the next place. It was just Lester and Melanie who were eating, so they would have sat opposite each other on this part of the table. Sitting at the ends would have been too formal. He looked around again, shook his head. 'Still not right.'

'What's not right? If you can be more specific, then maybe I can help.'

Winter ignored her and took out his cell. He looked up the number for the Hartwood PD and connected the call. Peterson answered and put him straight through to Birch.

'What do you want now?'

'You said that the Reed's table was set like they were

71

expecting a visit from the president. They'd used their best plates and cutlery. They'd even used a tablecloth. Are you sure about that?'

'Positive. Why do you want to know?'

'Was there any blood on the tablecloth?'

'I should imagine so.'

'You imagine or you know?'

'It was six years ago.'

'Any luck with that file?'

'Not yet.'

Winter hung up and tapped his phone gently against the tablecloth.

'What are you thinking?'

'I'm thinking that the murders happened on a weekday night, and both Melanie and Lester worked. Eating would have been approached from a functional point of view, not a celebratory one. It was more likely they would have eaten off the bare wood. Cutlery dumped down in the middle of the table, no candles, no tablecloth. As much as it pains me to admit this, Birch was right. Nelson must have set the table.'

'What? He brutally murders two people then lays the table? Sorry, I don't see it.'

'I've seen weirder things than this, Mendoza.'

'Okay, so why would he do it?'

'Because it was part of his fantasy. As for what that fantasy was, until we've got more information all I can offer is my best guess.'

'Is that your way of saying you don't know?'

'No, it's my way of saying that we need to be careful with making too many assumptions.'

72

'So what do you know?'

'I know that if we don't catch this woman she will kill again.'

They fell into a short silence. It was Mendoza who broke it. 'Do you have any idea how defensive you can be? It's okay to admit you don't know something.'

'I'm not defensive.'

Mendoza stared at him.

'I'm not.'

'You know, I still can't work out if you're a good guy or a bad guy. So which one is it?'

'I help you catch Ryan McCarthy and you've really got to ask?'

'That's a deflection.'

'What are you really asking here?'

'Your father was a serial killer, and you catch serial killers because you think like one. On the basis of that, it seems to me that maybe you're more alike than you'd care to admit. Nature rather than nurture, right? So, what I'd like to know is where you draw the line.'

She met his gaze across the table, looked him straight in the eye. Winter could see the candle flame reflected in her pupils.

'I've never killed anyone in cold blood.'

'But you have killed. Cold-blooded or hot-blooded, that's just a detail. The bottom line is that you are a killer.'

'There's a world of difference Mendoza, and you know it. You're a cop after all.'

'Okay, here's something else to think about. Maybe the difference between you and your father is that you've managed to find a way to kill and get away with it. If the kills are righteous then that makes everything okay, right?'

'That's bullshit.'

'Probably, but since you're not giving me anything else to work with, what am I supposed to think?'

Winter didn't say anything straightaway. The silence between them stretched longer, growing more uncomfortable with each passing second. 'It's complicated,' he said finally.

'And that's yet another deflection.'

13

'So what now?' asked Mendoza when they got back to the car.

'Now, it's lunchtime.'

'It's just after eleven.'

'I know, but my body clock's telling me it's lunchtime. I'm starving and my blood sugar's about to crash. I vote we head back to Main Street. I'm sure I remember seeing a diner there.'

Mendoza pulled away from the kerb and a short while later they were cruising along Main. There was only one diner, which made the decision about where to eat an easy one. They parked as close as they could and got out.

The diner had dirty windows and ancient paintwork. On the basis of that alone, it was the sort of place Winter would normally avoid. He didn't want to be a Petri dish for whatever bugs were growing in the kitchen. If the outside looked this shabby it didn't give much hope for the interior. He opened the door and got another surprise. The outside might have looked rundown, but inside it was a different matter. The tiled floor shone bright enough to see your reflection, and each of the tables had a small vase of freshly cut flowers on top of it. There wasn't a speck of dust anywhere.

Mendoza moved her sunglasses up on to the top of her head and pushed past him. Winter followed her inside. There were a dozen people sitting at the tables, five pairs and a couple of singletons, all of them staring. He felt like he'd walked into the saloon scene from every John Ford Western he'd ever watched.

'Take a seat and I'll be with you in a second.'

Winter tracked the voice to the waitress behind the counter. She was well into her fifties, with a square face that was all hard angles and suspicion. The stone in her engagement ring was larger than he would have expected from someone working in a diner. It was probably an heirloom. She smiled, but there was no warmth there.

The window seat was already taken, so he made his way to an empty table at the rear, Mendoza following him this time. The eyes of the other customers watched his progress and he did his best to ignore them. He removed his jacket, unzipped his hoodie and sat down with his back to the wall. Mendoza sat opposite him with her back to the other customers. One by one everybody went back to their coffees and breakfasts. The last person to turn away was the old guy who'd claimed the window seat.

The waitress came over and poured two coffees. Winter added two sugars to his, paused a moment, then spooned in a third. It would be too sweet, but he figured he was going to need all the extra energy he could get today. Sleep deprivation was a bitch.

'What can I get you?'

'I'd like an egg-white omelette and as much coffee as you can spare,' said Mendoza.

'And I'll have a cheeseburger and fries, and a large piece of cherry pie, please,' Winter added. 'The same goes for me with regards the coffee.'

'Cheeseburger, an omelette and a piece of pie coming right up.'

The waitress wrote their order down on her pad then headed back to the counter.

'So what do we know?' Mendoza took a sip of coffee, then started counting off on her fingers. 'One, our mystery woman wants you to prove that she didn't commit a crime that she says she's accused of committing, even though the cops say different.' She held up a second finger. 'Two, the Reeds' case file is missing.'

'Maybe it's been stolen.'

'That's one way of looking at it. Another explanation is that the file was out back but Birch didn't want us to see it, so he got Peterson to pretend it wasn't there.'

'Not buying. If anything had passed between them, it would have needed to have been pretty direct for Peterson to get it. Peterson does not do subtle, nor does he do anything without Birch's say so. He probably puts his hand up if he needs to use the bathroom.'

'Yeah, you're right.'

Mendoza's cell phone beeped in her pocket. She checked for new emails, her eyes widening in surprise.

'What is it?' Winter asked.

'See for yourself.'

She handed him the phone, and his eyes widened too. Wonders never cease, he thought. The Monroe Sheriff's Department had come through on the crime scene photographs. Winter recognised the Reeds' living room straightaway. There were differences. To start with the bodies were in situ. Secondly, the way that the table had been laid was even more elaborate than he'd imagined. Birch had been right about the three-pronged candelabra, and there was flatware for a three-course meal. Starter, main, dessert. Winter swiped through the crime scene photographs, looking for a close-up of the table. He found one and used his fingertip to navigate the photograph, zooming in so he could examine every inch of it. He handed the phone back.

'This clinches it. Nelson definitely set the table.'

Mendoza was studying the photograph, her finger moving back and forth. 'This is why you asked Birch about the blood-stains, right? If the tablecloth had been there when the murders took place it would have been covered in blood. No way would a bright white tablecloth have escaped without a mark. So Nelson kills the Reeds then cleans himself up and lays the table. Why the hell would he do something like that?'

'I don't know.' Each word was formed carefully, like he was talking in a foreign language.

'See, that wasn't so difficult. Okay, so what now?'

Winter looked over and saw the waitress coming towards them with their food. 'Now we eat.'

The plates went down, thanks were said, and Winter took a large bite out of his burger. He finished it before Mendoza had got halfway through her omelette, then started on his cherry pie. Three forkfuls in he became aware that she was watching him. He looked across at her.

'What? Have I got crumbs around my mouth?'

'No, I was just wondering if you were brought up by wolves.'

Winter laughed. 'Remind me again how you ended up be-ing a cop. You hate doughnuts, hate burgers, and who in their right mind orders an egg-white omelette? What's the point in that?'

Mendoza answered by carefully cutting away a small bite-sized section of omelette and popping it into her mouth.

Winter finished his pie then arranged all his cutlery so it was lined up straight in the exact centre of his plate. He wiped his hands on his serviette, then folded it into quarters and placed it neatly beside the plate.

'We need to find out where they carry out autopsies around here. See what the coroner has to say.'

'How about this? Maybe he's going to tell us that this is a six-year-old murder that's already been solved and we should just hustle back to New York and work Omar's murder from there.'

'With all due respect, you going on and on about New York really isn't helping here. Do I need to remind you what Lieutenant Jones said?'

Without another word Mendoza stood up and headed towards the restrooms, her annoyance punctuated by every short, sharp footstep. Winter watched her go. Her back was too straight, and her arms were swinging awkwardly by her sides. He pulled out his cell and found the police department's number. Birch answered on the seventh ring with a terse 'Police'. No 'hello', no 'how can I help', just that one word. The guy really was an asshole.

'Earlier you mentioned that the sheriff's department tried to push you out of the investigation, so I'm figuring that the autopsies were held over in Rochester?'

'I'm assuming this is Winter.'

'We'll make a detective of you yet, Chief.'

Winter heard a sigh. There was a slight pause then Birch said, 'Yes, they were.'

'I'd like to speak to the medical examiner who carried them out. I don't suppose you remember who that was?'

'Sorry, I can't help you there. It was six years ago.'

Winter heard the lie in his voice, the thin veil of glee. Birch was trying to bait him. 'No problem. Thanks for your time.'

Winter hung up before Birch had a chance to respond, then called the county ME's office. The woman who answered was a damn sight more helpful, but the hold music was painful. Bach's *Air on the G String* on an endless loop. Forty-two seconds on hold and he wanted to scream. The music stopped, and the woman came back on the line.

'Are you still there, sir?'

'Yeah, I'm still here.'

'The autopsies were carried out by Dr Rosalea Griffin, the Chief Medical Investigator. Dr Griffin has been out all morning, but we are expecting her back soon. If you'd like to talk to her she'll be here between two and three, and then she's out at meetings for the rest of the day.'

Winter looked up and saw Mendoza coming out of the restroom.

'Would Dr Griffin be able to spare five minutes if I dropped by at two?'

'That shouldn't be a problem. Just remind me, what did you say your name was, Detective?'

'Mendoza.'

Winter spelled out the name, said a quick thanks and goodbye, then hung up. Mendoza pulled out her chair and sat back down. She studied his face, glanced at his cell.

'Who were you talking to?'

'Birch. I was asking him about the missing file.'

'No news, I'm guessing.'

'Nope.' He gave it a second then added, 'I've been thinking that maybe we're going at this all wrong. We're being too reactive. We need to take a step back and try and get some perspective. How about we wipe the slate clean and start again? Let's pretend that the Reeds have just been murdered. There are no theories, no hypotheses, and no mystery woman waving a newspaper around. We go right back to first principles. We'll need to start by looking at the victims and build things up from there.'

Mendoza took a long sip of her coffee. 'We're talking about a murder that happened six years ago. Do you have any idea how much I hate cold cases? They're a pain in the ass to investigate.' She sighed long and hard, air whistling between her teeth. 'So where do we start? The coroner?'

'Let's forget about the coroner for the moment. The person we really need to speak to right now is Granville Clarke.'

Mendoza frowned. 'And who the hell's Granville Clarke?'

'He's the guy who wrote the newspaper article about the murders. A small town like this, it's the journalists who really know what's going on. If they don't know, then it isn't worth knowing.'

The waitress came back over and topped up their coffees. This time Winter went for his usual two sugars. Mendoza finished her omelette and they headed to the counter. Winter settled the bill and gave the waitress a tip that was almost as much as the whole meal.

'That was excellent pie, by the way.'

The waitress smiled at the compliment. 'Glad you enjoyed it, hon.'

'I wonder if you could help us out. We're looking for the *Gazette*'s office.'

'It's on Main, a couple of hundred yards up from the police department. Not that it'll do you much good. The paper shut down last year.'

The way things were going, this was no great surprise. Dead ends and dead witnesses, that seemed to be the way things were rolling today. 'We really need to see Granville Clarke. I don't suppose you know where I can find him?'

'Now that one I can help with.' She nodded to the old guy at the window seat. 'That's Granville sitting right over there.'

14

'Do you mind if we sit down?'

'Fine by me since it's a free country,' replied Clarke, 'But if you're wanting to talk, you're going to be talking to air. I'm just leaving.'

He studied them from behind his wire-framed spectacles for a moment, then stood up and shook himself into his coat. He was a tall, skinny man with cheekbones that were so prominent they were almost cutting through his skin.

'Put my breakfast on my tab, please,' he called over to the waitress.

'And when exactly are you planning on settling your tab?' she shouted back.

'The end of the month.'

'That's what you said last month, Granville, and the month before that.'

'See you tomorrow, Violet.'

Clarke flipped a loose wave over his shoulder then pushed through the diner door and headed outside. Mendoza and Winter followed and found him standing in the middle of the sidewalk staring up at the sky. Winter followed his gaze but couldn't see anything except a whole lot of blue. Even the birds and clouds from earlier had gone.

Mendoza was staring, too. 'What am I missing?'

Clarke looked at Mendoza, then Winter. In this light his

milky blue eyes looked gentle and friendly and disarming, and Winter was sure they were all those things, but that was only a part of it. The old guy might have been in his eighth decade but he was as sharp as they came.

'Chip away the hard edges and Violet's got a heart of gold,' he said. 'I wish she'd clean those damn windows, though. You can't see a thing out of them.'

'What's that all about?' asked Winter. 'The windows, I mean. The rest of the place is spotless.'

'That one's down to Zak. He owns the place. Not that you'd know. He spends his whole time in the kitchen and never comes out. Zak hates tourists.' Clarke chuckled softly to himself. 'Actually you could probably widen that particular net to encapsulate every man, woman and child on the planet. But tourists he hates with a passion. The dirty windows and crappy paintwork, that's to deter them from coming in. The town committee can't stand it, but there's nothing they can do.'

'Why? The way I see it, a small town like this, you'd want all the business you can get.'

Clarke smiled at Winter. 'Get right to the heart of the matter, why don't you? You know, my father taught me that if you want the story, you need to know the right questions to ask. It's the only piece of advice he gave me that was worth a damn, but it was a gem.'

'So why does he hate tourists?' Winter asked again.

'Because his wife ran off with one. At least that's the way he sees it. Ask anyone around here and they'll tell you that Zak got what was coming to him. The only real surprise was that she stayed with him so long.' Clarke's face suddenly turned serious. 'Now talking about the right questions to ask. Who the hell are you, and what do you want?'

Mendoza showed her badge. 'I'm Detective Carla Mendoza, NYPD.'

'That's one question cleared up.' Clarke smiled at Winter. 'And what about you young man? You'd like me to believe you're a big-time New York City cop, which is why you're stood there keeping so quiet. But, if you were a cop, you'd have been as quick on the draw with your badge as your friend was.'

Winter smiled and nodded. *Busted*. 'My name's Jefferson Winter. I used to be with the FBI's Behavioral Analysis Unit. These days I work freelance.'

'Freelance eh?' He turned back to Mendoza. 'I guess that answers the who, so how abouts you tell me what you want?'

'We're looking into the murders of Lester and Melanie Reed.'

Clarke laughed. 'With all due respect, that ship has well and truly sailed.'

'We believe that their deaths might be connected with a murder that happened in New York in the early hours of this morning.'

Clarke stood nodding to himself on the sidewalk, processing this. 'Okay, you've got me curious. How about we head over to my office so we can talk about this some more?'

'Violet said the *Gazette* had shut down.'

'It has, but that doesn't mean I don't still have an office.'

Without another word, Clarke crossed the street and headed off down the road towards the *Gazette*'s building. Winter and Mendoza looked at each other, then followed him. Clarke had his keys out before he reached the door. He unlocked it and gave it a shove where the top edge had stuck to the frame.

Stepping into the reception area was like taking another step back in time. The place looked as though it hadn't been decorated in a while. Like the station house, the room was divided in two by a long counter that ran the entire length of it. On the business side there were filing cabinets, a desk, a coat stand, and a dated computer. Relics from a bygone age. The wall calendar was set to July of last year.

The place had been abandoned in a hurry, like the *Mary Celeste*. A coffee mug and paperwork lay on the desk, and the chair had been pushed back like the occupant had gone to use the restroom and would be back soon. The light covers were filthy, there was a layer of dust everywhere, and the windows were as dirty as the diner's.

Clarke caught him looking and smiled sadly. 'This is the sad truth of our existence. In the end everything is just dust and memories.'

'And that's way too profound for this time of the day.' Mendoza turned to Winter. 'Remind me why we're here again.'

Winter pressed a finger to his lips and Mendoza rolled her eyes.

'You know,' said Clarke, 'it's hard to believe that this place was once filled with noise and bustle. I came to work here as a cub reporter in the fifties, when I was fifteen. Back then, my grandfather was the editor, my father was news editor and I made more coffees than I care to remember. It was my grandfather who started the paper in 1897. It would break his heart to see this. It sure breaks mine.'

Without another word, Clarke walked off towards the door at the far end of the counter. Winter started to follow him but only got a couple of steps before Mendoza grabbed his shoulder and pulled him to a stop.

'Fascinating as this trip down Memory Lane is, I've got to wonder what the hell we're doing here.' She was talking in a fast harsh whisper that emphasised the Brooklyn in her accent.

'If you want, you can go wait outside.'

'Seriously?'

'Seriously. We need background on the Reeds, and Clarke can give us that, so I'm staying.'

He turned and headed for the door that Clarke had just disappeared through. Mendoza gave it a couple of seconds before following. He could sense her irritation in every breath and heavy footstep. The door led to a steep narrow staircase. Clarke was almost at the top and Winter hurried to catch up. There was a small landing at the top with three doors leading off. Clarke took a key from his pocket and unlocked the first door on the left.

Unlike the reception area, the office was clean and tidy. It was a room filled with significance. The oak desk was old, maybe even dating all the way back to Clarke's grandfather. There was a green leather blotter, and, in pride of place on top of it, an Olivetti typewriter. The telephone had a rotary dial and the answering machine used a cassette. Both looked ancient. There was no computer or any other high-tech gadgetry, nothing to indicate that this was the new millennium.

The chessboard on the small round occasional table was frozen mid-game, and both the in- and out-trays on the desk were empty. These two details said more than anything else. They told a tale of how the world had moved on, of how this was a place where time had stopped. Winter studied the chessboard for a second. Checkmate in five for white.

On top of the filing cabinet was a peace lily with a single white flower. The greens and whites were so vibrant they looked artificial against the faded backdrop of the rest of the office. Clarke walked over and carefully wiped the leaves. Mendoza was shuffling impatiently, watching but trying not to. He finished polishing the leaves, then sat down behind the desk and clicked back into the room again. He waved to the seats on the other side. Winter and Mendoza took that as their cue to sit.

'You're dying, aren't you?'

Clarke stared at Winter with those milky blue eyes. There was so much in the old guy's gaze, more than he'd ever seen in a single look. Hope, despair, happiness, sadness, a whole lifetime. And plenty of curiosity, too. Despite everything, there was no hiding that one.

'How did you know?'

'Outside the diner when you looked up at the sky, it was like you were looking at it for the last time.'

Clarke didn't say anything for a moment. 'You know, you always imagine that finding out you're going to die would be one of the worst things that could ever happen. It's not. If you allow it, it's actually one of the most liberating. All the day-to-day bullshit becomes irrelevant, and what you once thought of as mundane suddenly turns into a miracle. Who cares if the bills get paid? I sure as hell don't.' He looked over at the peace lily. 'I cried when that flower appeared. Actually broke down and wept. Partly because I realised it would be the last time I ever saw it bloom, but mostly because it was the most incredible, awe-inspiring thing I'd ever witnessed.'

'How long have you got?'

'A week, a month. The doctors told me a while back that I wouldn't live to see the summer, never mind the fall, so who knows. It's cancer, in case you're wondering.'

Winter motioned to the wedding band on the old guy's left hand. 'Your wife died last July, didn't she? When that happened you decided it was time to shut the paper down.'

Clarke looked down at his ring, then back at Winter. 'It was an aneurism, so at least she went quick, which I guess was a blessing. The last edition of the *Gazette* came out the week I buried her. For the last couple of years it was just the two of us working here. When she died, I didn't see the point in carrying on.'

He fell silent, a distant look clouding his face. For almost a full minute the only sound was the sound of breathing, and the occasional squeak as Mendoza shifted impatiently in her seat.

'To every thing there is a season, and a time to every purpose under the heaven,' Clarke said eventually.

'Ecclesiastes Three.'

'You know your Bible?'

Winter nodded. He'd read it from cover to cover. That didn't necessarily make him a believer, though. The things he'd seen made that impossible.

'We've all got our ghosts, Mr Winter. This is where I keep mine. Where do you keep yours?'

For a split second Winter was back in the execution

chamber at San Quentin Prison. His father was lying strapped to a prison gurney, smiling and staring at him. Winter had stared back, determined to win this last round, this final battle of wills. And then his father had mouthed three carefully formed words, three words that changed everything, and nothing. They changed everything because of the possibility, however slim, that there might be some truth in there. And they changed nothing because this was something that he had already considered on countless occasions when the hours before dawn seemed the longest.

A three-word curse.

We're the same.

15

'So what can I tell you about Melanie and Lester?' Clarke asked.

'Well, you can start with what they were like,' Winter replied.

'That's what you might want. But all your friend wants to know is why Nelson Price murdered them.'

'You've got a point,' Mendoza put in. 'So why do you think he murdered them?'

Clarke chuckled gently to himself. 'The only person who could answer that is Nelson Price, and he killed himself. There were plenty of mysteries surrounding the murders, but, for me, the big one was always why. It was an apparently motiveless attack. As far as anyone could tell the Reeds were random victims.'

'How about you give us everything you've got?' said Winter. 'And I mean everything. I don't care how irrelevant it seems, I don't care if it's gossip or hearsay, I want to know.'

Everything turned out to be a lot more than he was expecting. Clarke might have been old but there was nothing wrong with his memory. Half an hour later he was still talking.

Both Lester and Melanie had grown up in Hartwood. Melanie was the only daughter of the town's pastor, and Lester's parents had run the general store. They'd known each other since kindergarten and nobody was surprised when they became high school sweethearts. They were engaged at eighteen, married at twenty, and dead at twenty-one. Lester was the elder of two, and he was set to take over the family store. Melanie taught in the town's elementary school and she was one of the more popular teachers. According to Clarke, both Lester and Melanie loved living in Hartwood. They'd been born here and had no intentions of moving anywhere else.

Melanie had made no secret of the fact that she wanted kids. She was fourteen weeks pregnant when she died, a detail that came out at the autopsy. Because it was still early days, she'd kept it quiet. Nobody knew about the pregnancy except her and Lester. The reason they'd kept the news to themselves was because Melanie had previously suffered a couple of miscarriages.

It came as no great surprise that Clarke knew all this. Winter had first-hand experience of the way that murder stripped away any illusion of privacy. When someone was murdered, it wasn't just their death that went under the microscope, their whole life entered the public domain. It was the final atrocity. Not content with stealing the future, murderers also corrupted their victims' pasts. Nothing was sacrosanct.

Clarke had made the Reeds out to be the perfect couple, but Winter wasn't buying that. Nobody was perfect. The whole might be greater than the sum of its parts, but it was still going to be flawed. The truth was that the Reeds prob-ably existed some way to the south of perfect. From what Clarke was saying, they'd been decent people, and Winter could buy into that. However, they would have had their ups and downs just like everyone else, because that's how life worked.

'And what can you tell us about Nelson Price?' Mendoza asked when Clarke had finished.

He smiled. 'Not as much as you'd like. The Prices lived out on the edge of town and kept themselves to themselves. They moved here when Nelson was still small. Soon after, his mother committed suicide. She hung herself in their barn. Nelson and his sister, Amelia, found the body. Nelson was about ten or eleven when this happened. Amelia was a bit older.'

Winter felt his heart suddenly speed up. An image of the blonde pushing the knife into Omar's eye flashed into his brain. 'Tell me more about Amelia. Is she still here in Hartwood?'

'Yes she is. She still lives at the Price place out on the edge of town.'

'She'd be in her mid-twenties?'

'Closer to thirty, I'd say. Nelson was twenty-one when he committed the murders. Amelia was a year or two older.'

'What else can you tell me about her?'

'She's the shyest, saddest creature I've ever seen. I see her around town every now and again, head down, hiding behind her hair, but I've never spoken to her. Few people have. Come to think of it, it's got to be a couple of years since I last saw her.' He paused for a second, then nodded to himself. 'Yeah, it's got to be that long at least. Last I heard she was working as a nurse over in Rochester.'

'What colour are her hair and eyes?'

'Her eyes? I couldn't tell you. But her father definitely had

93

blue eyes. I can still see them now. Even when he smiled they looked cold. As for her hair?' Clarke went quiet and studied the peace lily for a second. 'Light brown, or maybe a mousy brown colour.'

'Are you thinking that she's your mystery woman?' Mendoza asked.

It was possible, thought Winter. Amelia was the right age, and anyone could disguise their hair colour. He closed his eyes and pictured her sitting at his diner table. Her platinum-blonde hair had looked almost white underneath the artificial lights. Maybe she'd been wearing a wig, or maybe it was dyed. As for her eyes. Maybe they were blue like her father's and she'd disguised them with green contact lenses. He thought it through some more and saw something that didn't add up.

'Well?' Mendoza prompted.

Winter opened his eyes. 'It could be her. The sticking point is their personalities. Amelia Price is shy, the woman who killed Omar was anything but. Could someone fake their character for all those years?' He shook his head. 'I don't think so.'

'Any idea why the mother killed herself?' Mendoza asked Clarke.

'Sorry. She didn't leave a note.'

'But that doesn't mean you don't know why she killed herself,' Winter put in. 'What about rumours? Something like this happens in a place as small as Hartwood and everyone's going to have a theory.'

Clarke didn't answer straightaway. He tapped his fingers on his desk and glanced over at the peace lily. 'The mother's name was Linda Price. If ever there was a woman who was constantly walking on eggshells, it was her. Like Amelia, she wouldn't meet your eye. Occasionally she had bruises.'

'Her husband?'

A nod. 'I never liked Eugene Price from the get-go. Never trusted him. He was pleasant enough, but he was too smooth. It was almost as though he was trying a bit too hard to be liked.'

'So, Eugene had been beating his wife and when things got unbearable she killed herself.'

'That's my take. Ask a dozen people around these parts what happened and you'll get a dozen different stories, but most of them will be a variation on that particular theme.'

'Okay,' said Mendoza. 'Let me take a shot at what happened next. Eugene brings up the kids on his own, only now instead of Linda turning up with bruises, it's the kids.'

Clarke shook his head. 'That's not what happened. After Linda killed herself, everyone was keeping an eye out for those kids. If Eugene had been beating them then they would have been taken away.'

'But?'

'Hindsight is a marvellous and truly frustrating thing. There weren't any bruises, but there was something going on. Everyone knew that but there wasn't a damn thing that could be done about it. Child Services were called in to investigate, but the kids were allowed to stay with their father so they presumably didn't find anything. Who knows, if they'd looked a little harder then maybe Lester and Melanie Reed would still be alive.'

'So Eugene raises the kids and then one day Nelson snaps

and kills the Reeds. Is there any way that the police might have made a mistake about Nelson being the killer?' Mendoza glanced over at Winter as she asked this.

'No. His fingerprints were all over the murder weapon, and there were witnesses who put him at the crime scene. Add in the fact that he was so guilt-ridden that he hung himself afterwards, and there's no doubt in my mind. He definitely did it.'

'The same barn as his mother?'

'The same beam.'

'What about Eugene? What happened to him?'

'Nelson killed him.'

'Before or after he murdered the Reeds?'

Clarke gave Mendoza a quizzical look, and she added, 'I'm just trying to get an idea of the timeline here.'

'It's impossible to say for sure. Eugene's body was never found so there wasn't an autopsy. Also, Nelson died before he could be questioned. And before you start jumping to conclusions, Eugene is dead.'

'How can you be so sure?'

'Because he left without packing a case, or taking his passport. His car was parked in the garage. Does that sound like someone who's done a disappearing act?'

'Actually it does,' said Winter. 'If I was going to disappear that's how I'd do it. I wouldn't want to take anything with me that connected me to my previous life. I'd be looking for a fresh start.'

Clarke studied him for a moment. 'Okay, I can see that, but I'd still bet everything I've got that Eugene Price is dead.'

16

Winter folded the page of notepaper into perfect quarters then tucked it into the inside pocket of his sheepskin jacket for safekeeping. Clarke had passed the note to him as they were leaving. Underneath his contact numbers were directions to the Prices' house. The sun was burning a pale yellow that was almost white. Everything suggested a pleasant summer's day, but it was all an illusion. The trees lining the street were turning, and leaves the colour of fire lay scattered over the sidewalk. The breeze was cold against his skin. He lit a cigarette and squinted through the smoke.

'Wishing you were in Vegas?'

Mendoza said nothing. She put her sunglasses on, then reached behind and straightened her ponytail. Her back was to the sun, and her face was in shadow.

'What are you thinking?' he asked her.

'How many triple homicides do you think Birch has worked?'

'Triple? Since there's no body for Eugene Price, you might want to rethink that one.'

'Okay, how many double homicides?'

'If I was being generous I'd say one, maybe two.'

'Well you're more generous than I am. So we're agreed that Chief Birch was out of his depth?'

'Well and truly.'

Mendoza frowned. 'There's no way Eugene Price's murder was investigated properly. Not a hope in hell. Everybody would have been too focused on the Reeds. They were the primary victims. Eugene Price was just an afterthought.'

Winter finished his cigarette and crushed it out on the sidewalk. He picked up the butt and dropped it in a nearby trash can. 'So what have we got? Nelson goes off the reservation and murders the Reeds. Either before that or after, he also murdered his father and hid the body so well that even now, six years on, nobody's found it. That's the official version of events, and people were prepared to believe it because it's the easy explanation. So, the first question's got to be: alive or dead?'

'If Eugene Price is alive then he's done a really good job of disappearing.'

'And if he's dead, then Nelson was busy.'

Mendoza nodded.

'Here's a question for you,' said Winter. 'Is Nelson Price guilty or innocent of the Reed murders?'

'So far everything points towards him being guilty. I can see the cops screwing up with Eugene Price, but not the Reeds. They had fingerprints and eyewitnesses. It sounds air-tight to me.'

'Which once again leads us back to the woman who murdered Omar. Why did she follow me? And why the hell did she point me in the direction of the Reed murders? It makes no sense. What does she stand to gain? I've never seen her before. I don't have a clue who she is.'

'And you're sure about that?'

Winter closed his eyes and imagined himself back into the

diner again. He saw the blonde sitting at the back table, saw her in the mirror behind the counter, saw her sitting opposite him. He opened his eyes. 'I've never seen her before. I'm absolutely certain.'

'Could she be connected to a case you've worked?' Mendoza suggested. 'A girlfriend or wife of someone you've put in prison, perhaps? I'm guessing you've made plenty of enemies over the years.'

'Sure, but someone I can connect to this?' Winter shook his head.

Mendoza's cell phone rang. She pulled it out, checked the display, frowned. Her finger was hovering over the answer button. 'It's Lieutenant Jones.'

'Ask him to get someone to look at Amelia Price. And make sure they call the local hospitals to find out which one she works at.'

'I can't just start giving my boss orders.'

'Why not?'

'Because he's my boss.'

'So?'

Mendoza looked as though she was going to argue some more, but she didn't. Instead, she sighed and answered the call. Winter sat down on the kerb, the sun warm on his face, his mind spinning in overdrive. He closed his eyes and replayed Omar's murder from the points of view of the main characters. His perspective first, then the cook's, then the blonde's. No matter what direction he came at this from, it still made no sense. He'd walked in, ordered breakfast, sat down. The woman had come over, they'd exchanged a few words, then she'd stabbed Omar and left.

If she had wanted to get his attention, then she'd succeeded. But why would she want to do that? That was the question he kept returning to. Why? She'd gone to a lot of trouble, and you didn't do that without a good reason.

Mendoza said a terse 'Bye' and he opened his eyes.

'Is Lieutenant Jones going to get someone to look into Amelia Price's background?' he asked her.

'No. He's passed the buck on this one. The murder happened on the Seventh Precinct's turf, therefore it's their problem. We're to liaise with Darryl Hitchin.' Her cell sounded a text alert. 'And that'll be his direct number.'

The call to Hitchin lasted longer than the call with Jones. Long enough for Mendoza to tell him that they'd just got started here, and for Hitchin to tell her that they weren't getting anywhere in New York. She killed the call and dropped the cell phone into a pocket.

'He's going to get someone to look into Amelia Price.' Mendoza stood there for a second, biting her lip. 'Okay, we need to talk to the coroner's office.'

'All arranged. We're meeting up with the ME who carried out the Reeds' autopsies at two.' Winter ignored the quizzical look that Mendoza was giving him and added, 'Which means we've got plenty of time to keep looking at Melanie and Lester. Clarke said that Lester's family owned the general store. I vote we start there.'

17

The general store was back along Main, a couple of doors down from the diner. The paintwork was peeling but, unlike the diner, the windows had been cleaned. Mendoza followed Winter inside, the bell above their heads jangling brightly.

The woman at the till was in her early twenties and clearly related to Lester Reed. The only photograph Winter had seen was the one on the front page of the *Hartwood Gazette*, but there was no doubt in his mind. They had the same wide eyes, the same blonde hair. The younger sister was his best guess. There was no jewellery whatsoever, no necklace, no bracelet, no rings, not even a watch. No make-up, either. She was wearing a baggy denim shirt and faded jeans.

Mendoza flashed her badge and the woman smiled nervously. One of her front teeth was slightly crooked, but rather than detract from her beauty it enhanced it. A perfect imperfection. A glance for Mendoza, a slightly longer one for Winter.

'How can I help?'

'You're Lester Reed's sister?' Winter asked her.

A nod.

'What's your name?'

'Hailey.' She frowned. 'If you don't mind me asking, what's this all about?'

'Where are your parents? We'd like to talk to them.'

'They're on vacation. I'm looking after the store while they're out of town. Can I help?'

Mendoza moved in front of Winter. 'We'd like to know more about Lester.'

'Lester? Why?'

'His name has come up in connection with an investigation we're working.'

'I'm sorry there must be some mistake. Lester's dead. His wife too. They were murdered.' She struggled with that last sentence, the words trailing into a staccato whisper. Even now, six years on, the pain was still there.

'We're aware of that.'

'How could he be involved? I don't understand. How did his name come up in the first place?'

'The investigation is ongoing, so I can't answer that.'

'Do we have to do this now?'

'It would really help us out.'

'I spoke to the police at the time and told them everything I knew. I don't see how I can help.'

'All we need is five minutes.'

'Look I'm really busy. I've got loads to do.'

The way she said this made it sound like the end of the conversation. Winter glanced around but couldn't see anything so urgent that it couldn't wait five minutes. Her reluctance had nothing to do with a packed schedule and everything to do with her revisiting a whole load of painful memories that she'd spent the last six years trying to escape from.

'Hailey,' he said softly. She turned her head to face him. 'Do you mind if I call you Hailey?'

She nodded reluctantly.

'A man was murdered this morning. He had a wife and two children. Right now, they're going through the exact same emotional process that you went through six years ago. Do you remember that? The shock, the denial, the anger? Somewhere later down the line they'll want answers. They'll want to know how this happened. You must remember that, too. That almost obsessive need to find out what happened?' He paused a moment to let her process this. 'Our job is to try and find those answers, but to do that we need your help. Now, I know this is painful for you, but all we're asking for is a couple of minutes of your time.'

Hailey was looking down at the counter like the scratches scored into the surface were the most interesting things she'd ever seen. Winter could see the tears threatening to break loose. She looked up and gave a small, almost imperceptible nod.

'Thank you,' he said. 'So how would you describe your brother?'

'Funny, clever. He was kind, too.'

The line felt rehearsed. It was an automated response informed by the need to protect Lester's memory rather than anything truthful, or useful. 'I'm sure he was all those things, but I'm betting that he annoyed the hell out of you as a kid? After all, that's what big brothers do.'

Hailey went to say something, then stopped. She glanced over Winter's shoulder towards the shadows and cobwebs in the corner of the store. Her face was filled with sadness, eyes still heavy with tears.

'What are you thinking?' he asked gently.

'I guess he could be a pain at times.'

She paused in a way that made it obvious she had more to say. Winter kept his mouth shut and waited.

'Whenever he got into trouble he always managed to make it look like it was my fault,' she said eventually. 'And my parents adored him, so they always sided with him. I lost count of the number of times I got blamed for things he did.'

'Give me an example.'

She went quiet again for a second. 'Okay, when he was thirteen, he started stealing from the store. Candy bars, cans of soda, that sort of thing. He was taking them into school and selling them to his buddies. My father realised that this stuff was missing, and Lester managed to convince him that I was responsible. It didn't matter what I said, he wouldn't listen. I got grounded for a month.'

'How did that make you feel?'

'Angry, but there was nothing I could do. This wasn't the first time something like this had happened, and it wouldn't be the last. That's just the way things were. Lester would do something wrong, and I got the blame.'

'I'm guessing your plan was to get out of Hartwood at the first opportunity.'

Hailey let loose with a tiny humourless half-laugh. 'Yeah, that was the plan.'

Winter leant against the counter, closing the distance between them. 'Where were you headed?'

'Chicago. I was trying to get into college there. My boyfriend at the time was a bit older, and that's where he'd gone.'

'And then Lester was murdered.'

Hailey nodded. 'We all fell apart when that happened.

Mom and Dad totally went to pieces. For a while I practically ran the store. If I hadn't it would probably have shut down.' She shrugged, then let loose with another of those small laughs. 'And, look, I'm still here.'

'You never made it to Chicago, did you?'

A slow shake of the head. 'No.'

'What happened to the boyfriend?'

'He was there for me when I needed him most, but in the end the sadness got too much for him and we broke up. I don't blame him, though. I couldn't have been easy to deal with. And it wasn't like I could just up and leave my mom and dad. Families have to stick together, right?'

Family. The word momentarily threw Winter. He'd been on his own for so long he could barely remember what it meant to be part of a family. After his dad was caught, his mother had become a totally different person. He'd tried to keep things as normal as he could, and some days he actually managed to pull it off. Those were the days when he didn't come home from school to find her passed out on the sofa, the days when she didn't make him sit opposite the extra place that had been set for his father at the dinner table.

This was the heart-breaking reality of the ripple effect. The spotlight always fell on the primary victims, but what about the secondary victims? The partners, parents and loved ones? They'd survived the blast, but there was never any guarantee they were going to survive the aftermath. If ever he needed a reminder of that all he had to do was look at Hailey Reed.

18

Mendoza walked over to one of the shelves, her feet tapping gently against the wooden floorboards. She picked up a bag of potato chips, studied the label for a second, then put it back on the wrong shelf.

'Is it true that Lester and Melanie had known each other since kindergarten?' she asked.

Hailey smiled like she actually meant it. 'It's true. It was like they were made for each other.'

'What was she like?'

'Mel was basically the nicest person you'd ever want to meet.'

Mendoza raised an eyebrow.

'I'm serious. Ask anyone around here and they'll tell you the exact same thing. And I know what you're thinking, you're thinking I'm just saying this because she's dead. I'm not.' A couple of tears slid slowly down Hailey's cheeks. She wiped them away with the backs of her hands, then rubbed her eyes and swallowed hard. 'She would have made a great mom.'

'She would have,' Winter agreed. 'It was Melanie who painted the mural in the nursery, right?'

'You've been in the house?'

He nodded.

'They should bulldoze that house into the ground. I

haven't been there in years. I can't bear to even look at the place. My father tried to sell it, but after what happened, nobody wanted to live there. I mean, who would? When it became clear that it wasn't going to sell he had it boarded up. He didn't even bother to clear the place out, just left it how it was after the murders. I take it all their stuff was still there.'

'It was.'

Hailey shook her head. For a moment it looked as though she might start crying again. 'Mel loved that house. So did my brother. They should be living there now, bringing up their kids. It's just not fair.'

'I was impressed with the mural. Melanie clearly had talent.'

'Yeah, she did. She loved to paint.'

'I get the sense that her and Lester were old for their years. I mean, twenty-one's young to be starting a family.'

Hailey almost smiled, but the sadness won out. 'We used to joke that Lester was born middle-aged. Was it a surprise that he wanted to marry his high school sweetheart? No. Was it a surprise that he wanted to have kids and stay in Hartwood? Again the answer's no. Most people want to get out of this place as soon as they can.'

'So he wasn't a party animal then?'

This time she did smile. 'You could say that.'

'Do Melanie's parents still live in Hartwood?'

The smile faltered and the sadness returned. She shook her head. 'The last I heard her mom had moved back to Kansas City. That's where she was originally from.'

'Divorce or death?' Winter asked softly.

'Her father was hit hard. He died three years ago. They

said it was a heart attack, but I think it was a broken heart. After Mel died he just kind of faded away.'

'Did Lester and Melanie have many friends?'

'Plenty. Everyone loved them.'

'Everyone except Nelson Price,' Mendoza put in. 'So how well did your brother know Nelson?'

Hailey crossed her arms. 'Nobody really knew Nelson. Come to that, nobody really knew any of the Prices.'

'Nelson was the same age as your brother?'

A nod. 'They went to school together. He was in the same grade as Lester and Melanie.'

'Did your brother or Melanie ever mention him? For example, did they ever argue or fight, anything like that?'

Hailey shook her head. 'I went through all of this with the police at the time. No arguments, no fights. Nelson didn't register on my brother's radar, not even a little bit. Mel was kind to everyone, but even she barely spoke to Nelson.'

'But she did speak to him.'

'Maybe once or twice, if that. Mel was the sort of person who'd find a bird with a broken wing and want to nurse it better. She'd always try to find the good in a person.'

'What was Nelson like?' Winter asked.

Hailey hesitated, searching for the right words. 'He just kind of drifted through high school like a ghost. If you weren't looking straight at him you wouldn't have known he was there.' She hesitated again, her face screwed up into a frown, then shook her head. 'I'm sorry, I'm not making much sense.'

'Can you think of any reason why Nelson would want to kill Lester and Melanie?' Winter asked. 'Anything at all? And take a second before answering.'

Another hesitation, another shake of the head. 'I'm sorry. I couldn't think of anything back then, and I can't think of anything now. As far as I know Lester and Mel had nothing to do with Nelson. The attack was completely random.'

'What about Amelia Price? Is there anything you can tell me about her?'

'Only that she was a ghost too. As far as I know she still lives out on the edge of town, but I haven't seen her for years.'

'Do many people manage to escape from Hartwood?'

Hailey almost laughed at that. 'It's occasionally been known to happen.'

Winter held his hand up. 'The woman I'm looking for is this tall. She's thin, and she was a little bit older than Melanie and Lester, which means she'll be in her late twenties now.'

Hailey was shaking her head. 'Sorry, I can't think of anyone. Is there anything else you can tell me about her?'

'She's confident and arrogant, someone who wouldn't take kindly to being told what to do.'

Another shake of the head. 'Sorry.'

The bell above the door tinkled and they turned towards the sound. A middle-aged man with salt-and-pepper hair was standing in the doorway, watching them suspiciously. He was wearing denim jeans and heavy work boots, and his red plaid shirt was mostly hidden by his waterproof coat.

'Everything okay, Hailey?' he asked as he walked up to the counter.

'Everything's fine, Carl.'

'Are you sure? You look like you've been crying.'

'I'm fine. I promise. These folks are from the New York Police Department. They were just asking me some questions.'

'Uh-huh.' Carl stared at Winter and Mendoza. 'You're a long way from New York.'

Winter smiled. 'Three hundred miles, give or take.'

'Is that supposed to be funny?'

'Are you always so suspicious of the police? You know, you'd think it would be the other way round. Maybe we should be suspicious of you. After all, you look like a man with plenty to hide.'

Carl went to say something to Winter and Hailey put her hand up to stop him.

'It's okay,' she told him.

'You sure?'

'I'm sure.'

A beat of silence. 'I'll have a pack of my smokes, please.'

The words were aimed at Hailey, but Carl's eyes didn't leave Winter's. He paid for his cigarettes, pushed the pack into his jacket pocket, then turned and headed for the door. The bell tinkled, a blast of cold rushed in, then the door banged shut again.

'Sorry about that,' said Hailey. 'Carl can be a little overprotective sometimes. People around here tend to look out for one another. Most times that's a good thing.'

'But not always,' Winter finished for her.

'Sometimes it can get a bit much,' she agreed.

Winter walked over to the shelves and picked up four Snickers bars for himself. On the way back to the till, he lifted up the bag of chips that Mendoza had moved earlier and put it back on the correct shelf. He found his wallet and laid down a twenty-dollar bill.

'Don't worry about the change.'

Hailey reached for the money and put it in the till.

'Do you have to travel out of town to get your supplies?'

She frowned. 'What?'

'When you're low on stock do you get deliveries, or do you have to drive somewhere to pick stuff up?'

'We get deliveries from Rochester on Tuesday and Friday mornings.'

'So Lester never travelled when he worked here?'

She laughed. 'Lester never travelled anywhere.'

'There was no way that Lester could have met someone outside of the town then?'

'Like a woman, you mean? No! No way! He wouldn't do that. He loved Mel.'

Winter nodded. 'And sometimes people do things they shouldn't, even when they love someone.'

'You're wrong. Way off the mark. They were in love. Ask anyone. The year before they died had been hard on both of them. Mel had two miscarriages, so she was in a bad way, and Lester didn't know what to do. But they sorted it out, and they were so happy. And then they died.' Tears filled her eyes but she ignored them. 'I didn't know it until afterwards but Mel was pregnant. She'd never made it to the second trimester with either of the other pregnancies.' The tears turned into a sob. 'That baby was all they ever wanted.'

'What about Melanie? Did she ever go out of town on her own?'

'What! You think that Mel was having an affair now! Weren't you listening? They loved each other and they were having a baby together.' She took a deep breath and pulled herself together. 'I think I'd like you to leave now.'

Winter didn't move. Hailey's face was a mix of emotions, part anger and a lot of sadness. The tears that had been threatening since they got here were now flowing freely.

'Please,' she whispered. 'Just go.'

19

Winter sat on the kerb outside the store staring past a parked car, not really seeing anything. Mendoza was still inside, no doubt doing her best to calm Hailey down. Five minutes and counting. He hadn't wanted to push so hard, but they were questions that needed to be asked. Sometimes the break came from asking the questions that nobody wanted to ask. Not often, but it did occasionally happen. Given how popular and loved Lester and Melanie had been, he doubted those questions had been asked at the time of the murders.

In the distance, the street hung to the right before disappearing altogether. He could see their BMW parked outside the station house. Winter could imagine what Birch and Peterson were up to. Birch would be sat there on his fat ass, while Peterson kept him fuelled up on coffee and doughnuts. Winter took out his cell and dialled the police department's number. Peterson answered after a couple of rings and he asked to speak to Birch.

The line clicked and a computerised version of *Eine Kleine Nachtmusik* drifted through the static. He hated hearing Mozart being brutalised like this. It was like all the life had been sucked out of it. Another click, then Birch said, 'What is it now?'

'I was just wondering if you'd found that file yet.'

'We're still looking.'

'That's good to hear. As soon as it turns up, I want to see it.'

'And as soon as it turns up I'll be sure to give you a call.'

Yeah, right, thought Winter as he hung up.

When Mendoza finally came out of the store, he was still sitting on the kerb staring along the street, his ass going numb from the cold concrete. He heard footsteps coming up behind him, heard them stop. He glanced over his shoulder, hand on his forehead, squinting to block out the sun. Mendoza was glaring down at him.

'Let's get going,' he said. 'Places to be, people to see.'

He jumped to his feet, brushed off his jeans, and started back towards the station house. Before he'd got six yards, Mendoza dragged him to a stop and spun him around. He moved her hand off his shoulder.

'You're upset because Hailey's upset. I get that. You don't like seeing her cry. I get that, too. But someone has to ask tough questions.'

'This has nothing to do with Hailey, and everything to do with the fact that you've dragged me all the way up here into the middle of nowhere to look into a murder that was solved years ago. That's why I'm pissed.'

'Liar.'

'Excuse me.'

'You're not the hard ass that you'd like everyone to believe, Mendoza. If you were you wouldn't have spent the last seven minutes and forty-three seconds in there talking to Hailey.'

'You'd just assassinated the memory of her brother and sister-in-law. Someone had to pick up the pieces.'

Winter raised an eyebrow. 'And for the record, I wasn't

114

trying to hurt Hailey, I was trying to help her. The best way to do that is to uncover the truth. The Reed murders aren't as straightforward as everyone is making out.'

'No, they are straightforward. The truth is that Nelson snapped and killed the Reeds. Hailey believes that. Hell, the whole town believes that, and right now so do I. So everything you did back there was for nothing. Admit it.'

'No, it wasn't. If we're going back to first principles with this, then we need to examine motive. How many murders have you dealt with that turned out to be crimes of passion? Plenty, right? They look complicated to start with, and there are all sorts of theories flying around, but when you get down to it the reason behind the murder was that someone was screwing someone they shouldn't have been. Bottom line: I did what needed to be done. Those questions needed to be asked.'

'But did you learn anything new?'

'Okay, do you want to know the fundamental difference between us? The difference is that taking down the bad guy is your endgame.'

'And it's not yours? Don't give me that crap, Winter. I saw your face when we took down Ryan McCarthy. It was like all your birthdays and Christmases had been rolled into one.'

'But that's not my endgame. My endgame is to *stop* these assholes.'

Mendoza's eyes narrowed and she shook her head. 'Sorry, I don't see the difference.'

'The difference is that I couldn't care less about the bad guy, or woman as is the case with Omar's murder. No, all I care about is that they're off the streets. If Ted Bundy hadn't been stopped how many more women would he have killed?'

'So you do this for the all the victims-who-might-have-been? Is that it?'

'Look, we can't be certain that Nelson Price killed the Reeds. Not a hundred per cent, at any rate. Yes, the evidence points that way, but the only people who really know what happened are all dead. Lester, Melanie and Nelson. What we do know, however, is that there's a very dangerous and unpredictable killer out there and she needs to be stopped. If I need to upset a few people to do that, then I'll do that again in a heartbeat. Hurt feelings I can deal with, but another dead body would *really* piss me off.'

Ten minutes later they drove over the kissing bridge, heading out of town, a charged silence filling the BMW. Winter was guessing that they weren't the first two people to cross this bridge when kissing was the last thing on their minds. They passed the sign that marked the town boundary and a couple of seconds later the sky disappeared behind the tree canopies.

'The mom's suicide doesn't sit right,' he said finally.

Mendoza glanced over from the passenger seat. 'People commit suicide every day, Winter.'

'They do, but the kids make this situation different. If Eugene Price was beating his wife, chances were he wasn't a candidate for Father of the Year. You heard Granville Clarke, everyone suspected that the kids were being abused but nobody could prove anything. The maternal bond is one of the strongest bonds there is. Knowing what Eugene was like, things must have gone beyond unbearable for her to leave the kids on their own with him.'

'Maybe that's exactly what happened. Things went beyond unbearable.'

'I don't think so.'

Winter was thinking about his mother again. Things had gone beyond unbearable for her, yet she'd hung on in there. He had often wondered why she hadn't killed herself, and the only reason he could come up with was that she hadn't wanted to leave him on his own. After he started college, he had expected to get a phone call informing him that she'd taken a handful of pills or slashed her wrists in the bath, but the call never came.

He only saw her once at the end. She'd been in the hospital, her body failing and her mind going. In her confusion she kept calling him by his father's name, and that had made a hard situation impossible. He'd lasted less than five minutes before he left. He'd gone back to work at Quantico, arranged for her to be moved to a better hospital, made sure that everything was done that could be done to make her last days more comfortable, and waited for the call. In the end, it hadn't been pills or a razor blade that killed her, it was the booze.

'What do you think happened to the mom then?' Mendoza asked.

The road hung a sudden right and sunshine poured through the windshield, blinding him. He shielded his eyes and turned towards her.

'I think that she was murdered. I think that Eugene Price took her out to the barn, put a rope around her neck and hung her. And I think he made the kids watch.' He paused a moment. 'What I can't work out, though, is how any of this links to a New York diner at two in the morning, and a psychopath who likes making grand statements.'

20

The Monroe County Medical Examiner's office was based in Brighton, a town buried in the southern suburbs of Rochester. Next door, the Lego-brick buildings of the Monroe Correctional Facility rose up out of the ground. The prison looked like it had been built by an unimaginative kid.

They parked up and Winter got out. He stretched, lit a cigarette, zipped up his jacket, then stretched again, popping his bones and overextending his joints. Mendoza walked around the front of the car to join him. She repositioned her sunglasses, then brushed down her suit. Winter had only ever seen her look immaculate. First thing in the morning or the middle of the night, it made no difference. It really was a gift.

They walked across the parking lot to the squat red-brick building that housed the ME's office. It looked like it had been built by the same unimaginative kid who'd built the prison. Winter took a final pull on his cigarette, put it out in the ashtray next to the entrance, then ducked inside behind Mendoza before the door slid shut.

The inside of the building was as bland as the outside. Beige was the dominant colour, and there was plenty of concrete and laminated wood. A large cheese plant provided the only real colour. The woman behind the reception desk looked up from her computer and showed a smile that contained plenty of teeth.

'Detective Mendoza?'

Mendoza smiled. 'That's right. We're here to see Dr Griffin.'

The receptionist looked momentarily perplexed.

'Anything the matter? Dr Griffin is here, isn't she?'

'Yes, she's here. It's just that your voice sounded different on the phone.'

Winter answered the accusations in Mendoza's eyes with a shrug. The receptionist came around to the front of the desk and motioned for them to follow.

'You know it's illegal to impersonate a police officer,' Mendoza hissed as they headed deeper into the building.

'So, arrest me,' Winter whispered back.

They turned into another corridor and stopped at a door three-quarters of the way along. The brushed-steel plaque read DR ROSALEA GRIFFIN CHIEF MEDICAL EXAMINER. The receptionist knocked once, a light gentle tap.

'Enter.'

The receptionist pushed open the door and stood aside to let them past. Dr Griffin walked over to greet them. She was a good-looking woman in her mid-fifties. Her grey hair had been cut recently, the style short and easy to manage. Her short fingernails were manicured, and, although her suit wasn't designer, it was made-to-measure. Either that or she'd got a lucky fit. Given that she was at least six and a half feet tall, it would have been one hell of a lucky find. She had a patch over her left eye, the outline picked out in diamante. Red, white and blue. Very patriotic.

'Childhood accident,' she offered by way of explanation in a slow Southern drawl. Winter waited for more, but there wasn't any.

'Would you like a coffee?' she asked.

'Black with two, please,' said Winter.

'White and no sugar for me,' said Mendoza.

'Make that three coffees please, Angela.'

Angela ducked out of the doorway, pulling the door closed behind her. Griffin sat down and waved them into the chairs in front of the desk. Aside from the telephone, laptop and a single manila folder, the surface of the desk was empty. Winter unzipped his jacket and sat down. There was plenty of laminated wood here too. The floor, the desk, the bookcase. Certificates proclaiming Griffin's competence were hung in matching pine frames behind the desk.

'If you don't mind me asking, why is the New York Police Department interested in a murder case that was closed six years ago?' Griffin aimed the question at Mendoza.

'The case impacts on our current one, but that's all I can tell you.'

There was a single gentle knock on the door and Angela entered carrying a tray. She found some mats and put the mugs down before slipping back out of the room.

'Okay, let's start over,' Griffin suggested after the door had closed. She tapped her finger on the manila folder, drawing everyone's attention to it. 'Seems to me we've got a straight trade here. I have something you want. You have something I want.'

'Why are you so interested?' asked Mendoza.

Griffin laughed like the answer was so obvious she couldn't

believe anyone would bother asking. 'Because I'm nosy, and because I love mysteries. I get a mystery, I just have to solve it.'

Winter smiled. He could relate. An unsolved puzzle drove him nuts. He looked Griffin straight in her good eye, then glanced down at the folder. It was unlikely the folder contained all the answers they were looking for, but it might contain some of them and that meant it was a no-brainer.

He began to talk.

21

'Interesting,' Griffin said when Winter finished talking. She drummed her fingers on the file again, drawing his attention back to it. 'However, if you think you're going to find proof in here that your mystery woman is guilty, or any clue as to who she might be, you're going to be disappointed.'

'You seem pretty sure of that.'

'The statistics are on my side. Your mystery woman, was she right-handed?'

Winter's mind flashed back to the diner. He could see the blonde standing there. Her left arm was curled around the cook, the knife was in her right. He had a pretty good idea where Griffin was going with this. Roughly nine out of ten people were right-handed, and the doctor had said the statistics were on her side. 'The person who killed the Reeds was left-handed?'

Griffin nodded. 'And I'm guessing your mystery woman isn't.'

'No she's not.'

'There's absolutely no doubt in my mind that the Reeds' killer was left-handed.'

'And Nelson Price was left-handed?'

Griffin nodded. 'Yes, he was. Could your mystery woman be ambidextrous?'

'Possible, but it's a statistical improbability.'

'You've already concluded that she didn't do it, haven't you?'

'Going on the available evidence, it looks like Nelson Price did it.'

'That wasn't what I asked.' Griffin narrowed her good eye and fixed it on Winter. He became aware that Mendoza was staring, too. It felt like they were ganging up on him. Strike that, they *were* ganging up on him.

'What?'

'Spit it out,' Mendoza said. 'Whatever crazy idea is swirling around in that massive over-sized brain of yours, I want to hear it.'

Winter reached for his coffee and blew across the top to cool it down. He took a sip then put the mug back down. 'How do you prove a negative?'

'With difficulty,' said Griffin.

'Exactly. But, if you think about it, that's what's happening here. We're trying to prove that our mystery woman *didn't* kill the Reeds.'

Mendoza looked momentarily puzzled. 'Haven't we already done that? I mean, all the evidence is pointing to Nelson Price being the killer. It seems straightforward enough to me.'

'And that's the point. Proving that Nelson did it is not the same as proving that our mystery woman didn't do it.'

'Okay,' Mendoza continued, drawing each syllable out. She shook her head. 'Sorry, I'm not following you. *Really* not following. If Nelson did it, he did it. End of story.'

Griffin propped her elbows on the desk and leant forward. 'What your friend here is alluding to is that this is a logical fallacy.'

'A what?'

'How about this?' said Winter. 'If I tell you that some men are doctors and that some doctors are tall, then you would be happy to conclude that some men are tall, right?'

'That makes sense.'

'Except it doesn't make sense. Okay, how about this? If some doctors are men and some doctors are women, then it follows that some men are women.'

'That's crazy.'

'Invisible pink unicorns.'

'Excuse me.'

'Invisible pink unicorns have immense spiritual power. What other creatures have the ability to be both invisible and pink at the same time?' Mendoza gave him the look, and he added, 'The existence of invisible pink unicorns is an argument that is often used to refute a negative proof. How can you prove it isn't pink if you can't see it? Or to put it another way: just because Nelson Price is guilty, it doesn't necessarily follow that our mystery woman is innocent. Two people can commit a murder, right?'

'So why the hell didn't you just say that, instead of making me sit through all that crap about pink unicorns and transgender medics?'

Winter looked over at Griffin. 'Was there any evidence pointing to a second person being involved?'

Griffin shook her head slowly. 'Not that I remember. But I'm really not the best person to ask. I just deal with the corpses. If memory serves, the investigation was headed up by Jeremiah Lowe.'

'That doesn't really help since he's dead.'

Griffin surprised him by laughing. 'No, he's not.'

'Are you sure about that?' Mendoza asked.

'I'm positive. He retired a couple of years ago but I still see him occasionally. The last time was at a police function back in the summer.' She laughed again. 'Speaking in a professional capacity, I can assure you that he was very much alive. What made you think he was dead?'

'That's what we were told when we contacted the sheriff's department last night. I can't say that I'm surprised the mistake got made, though. When I pull a graveyard shift, I sometimes have trouble working out if I'm alive or dead.'

'She needs her beauty sleep otherwise she gets cranky,' Winter put in.

Mendoza flashed him a dirty look.

'See,' he added. 'Cranky as hell. And you must have had at least three hours' sleep, which, I might add, was three hours more than I had.'

'Well, I'm glad I could help to straighten things out,' Griffin said. 'If you talk to Angela, I'm sure she'll be able to track down Jeremiah's number.'

'That would be great.'

Griffin pushed the file across the desk. 'Here, you can keep this. I got Angela to make you a copy. I don't know how much help it's going to be, though. Any more questions?'

Winter and Mendoza shook their heads.

'In that case I'm going to have to bid you a good day.' She glanced at her watch. 'Damn, I'd better get moving otherwise I'll be late for my meeting. No rest for the wicked, eh?'

22

Jeremiah Lowe lived in Webster, a small town situated up in the north-east corner of Monroe County. It was close enough to Rochester to commute, but far enough away to breathe fresh air. His house was in Dunning Avenue, a wide street lined with trees and whitewashed clapboard houses. A scattering of leaves lay across the sidewalks. The area was middle class, respectable, a nothing-much-happening kind of place.

Mendoza parked the BMW outside one of the smaller properties a quarter of the way along the street. Three bedrooms, Winter guessed. Big enough to raise a family, but just that little bit too big when the kids finally left home. The lawn had been mown within the last few days and the weed-free flower beds had been set straight in anticipation of the coming winter. The leaves had been raked that morning and lay in a neat heap near the garage. A Stars and Stripes flag flapped loosely in the breeze.

Mendoza killed the engine, then reached into the back for the Reed's autopsy reports and started reading. Winter had been through them already. Twice. Like Dr Griffin had said there wasn't anything in there that could help them prove anything. Then again, there was nothing in there that disproved the blonde's innocence, either.

Logical fallacies.

There were two people-shaped diagrams on the page

Mendoza was reading. Two dots and a line had been used to create a face on one of them so you could tell which diagram was the front, and which was the back. Griffin had marked Melanie Reed's injuries on it in her neat handwriting.

Winter got out and leant against the car. Lake Ontario was only a couple of miles away. Beyond the lake lay Canada. Toronto was to the north-west, roughly eighty or so miles away as the crow flies. He lit a cigarette and waited for Mendoza to finish with the file. He'd got down to the final drag before he heard the driver's door open. He crushed the cigarette out and picked up the butt. There wasn't anywhere obvious to dispose of it, so he opened the car door and dropped it in the side pocket. Mendoza gave him a dirty look.

Winter smiled. 'I'll get rid of it later when I find a trash can.'

'See that you do.'

'So, what do you make of the report?'

'Nelson Price did it, and he was working alone.'

'Yes, Nelson Price did it, but it doesn't necessarily follow that he was working on his own. Remember our pink unicorn. So what do you think happened?'

'What happened was that Nelson killed Lester Reed first, and the reason he did that was because there was one of him and two of them. He needed to take Lester out, and he needed to do it fast because he was bigger and stronger and posed more of a threat. So he slit Lester's throat, dropped him to the ground, then went after Melanie. That's what happened.'

'I agree with you up to a point.'

Mendoza raised a disbelieving, quizzical eyebrow. 'Up to a point?'

'The injuries the Reeds sustained tallies with your interpretation of events. Lester Reed's carotid artery was sliced, as was his windpipe. That was the cause of death. The contusions on his skull were caused by his head hitting the floor. There were no defensive injuries because at this point in the proceedings Lester would have been pleading for Melanie's life. He was more concerned about what was happening to his wife than to him.'

'Up to a point,' Mendoza repeated.

'The injury that killed Lester happened quickly and took him by surprise. And that's the second reason there weren't any defensive wounds. Everything happened too quickly. There wasn't time for him to process what was happening. His brain never had a chance to catch up. Which is understandable. A knife-wielding maniac comes crashing uninvited into your home, there's going to be a certain amount of disbelief, a certain amount of denial.'

'Up to a point,' Mendoza said for the third time, eyebrows arching upwards. 'I've got to tell you, Winter, there are no real surprises in what you've said so far.'

'Melanie, on the other hand, did have defensive wounds,' he went on. 'She'd seen what had just happened to Lester and was fighting for her life. The life of her unborn baby, too. Let's not forget that. Judging by the extent of her injuries, she put up one hell of a fight. Nelson's blood was up, too. He'd been in control when he killed Lester, but with Melanie any attempt at keeping control was long gone. This attack took place in a complete frenzy. Nelson kept stabbing until she stopped moving. Griffin reckoned that she'd died from a stab wound to the heart. That's academic, though. She would have died from her other injuries anyway.'

'Again, no real surprises. Nelson killed the Reeds and he was working alone. End of story.'

'Invisible pink unicorns.'

'No, Winter. No goddam unicorns. What? You think that your mystery woman was just standing by watching while Nelson went on a complete rampage?'

'That's exactly what I think.'

'Well you're wrong. What's more I'm going to prove you're wrong.'

'Okay, if you're so sure that you're right, how about we have a little wager? I want to drive back to New York.'

Mendoza pressed a finger to her lip. It was curled like a question mark. Her head was going from side to side. 'No way. I do the driving.'

'You've got real control issues. Has anyone ever told you that?'

'This has nothing to do with control issues. I don't gamble.'

'Everyone gambles, Mendoza, every day of their lives. When you get out of bed it's like rolling a dice. You don't know what's going to happen. Are you going to walk out the door and get hit by a truck, or are your lottery numbers going to come up.'

'You're not driving.'

'Help me out here, Mendoza. Two seconds ago you were convinced I was wrong. What's changed?'

'Nothing's changed. You are wrong.'

'In which case you've got nothing to worry about.'

Mendoza just stared. Winter held the thumb and forefinger of his right hand up in an L-shape and pressed it against his forehead. The sign of the loser. More staring. More silence. Mendoza thrust her hand out and they shook to seal the deal.

'I'm telling you now. No way are you driving us back to New York.'

'Well you'd better hope you're right then.'

23

The front door swung open before they reached it and Jeremiah Lowe greeted them with a warm bone-crushing handshake, a slap on the shoulder, and a 'get your asses out of the cold and get on in here'. At first glance he looked to be in his late sixties, but Winter was betting he was much younger. Whereas Rosalea Griffin was weathering the years just fine, Lowe hadn't fared so well. He had a deep-lined worn-out face, and there were large dark pouches beneath his tired eyes.

He was doing his best to hide behind a wave of exaggerated gestures and cheery words, but not quite managing. When he moved, he had a slight stoop, as though the weight of the world had been pressing down on him too heavily, and for too long. Winter had seen this before in ex-cops, particularly murder detectives. It was as though every corpse they'd ever seen had stayed with them, like unwanted ghosts.

Winter had learned early on in his career to compartmentalise. For the most part, when he closed a case he was able to walk away. Occasionally, however, there would be one that stayed with him. More often than not it would involve kids. Trying to understand how someone could intentionally hurt another human being was tough enough. Understanding how they could hurt a kid was ninety-nine point nine per cent impossible.

The front door opened on a large open-plan space that was

part kitchen, part diner, part living room. Each section was defined by a single eye-catching object. A large cooking range in the kitchen, a ten-seat table in the dining area, and a sixty-inch TV in the living room. The second they stepped inside, the smell of Lake Ontario was replaced by the smell of hot coffee and reheated pizza. Lowe offered coffee and Mendoza declined. Winter didn't. Today was the sort of day where you couldn't have too much caffeine.

They sat down at the table, Lowe at the head, Mendoza and Winter to the right of him. There were framed photographs dotted all around the room. They were on every wall, and any flat surface where there was space. Winter saw evidence of a wife, two sons, two daughters, and an indeterminate number of grandchildren.

Lowe saw where he was looking. 'What can I say? Noreen's big on family.' The glow in his voice made it obvious that she wasn't the only one. 'So you want to know about the Reed murders over in Hartwood?'

'That's right, sir,' said Mendoza.

Mendoza gave Lowe a quick rundown of what they'd learned so far. Because they were both cops, she talked in bullet points. Being able to skirt around the bullshit and get straight to the point made life a whole lot easier. After Mendoza had finished, Lowe sat there shaking his head, his frown emphasised by the deep lines carved into his face.

'There's no way this woman was involved. Nelson Price did it and he was acting alone.'

'That's what we've been told,' said Winter.

'But you don't believe it. That much is clear. Look, I was with the Monroe County Sheriff's Department for thirty years. During that time I worked more murder investigations than I care to remember, and I'm telling you now that this one was about as straightforward as I ever saw. I'm sorry but you're barking up the wrong tree.'

Winter said nothing, injecting a little inquisitor's silence into the proceedings. Lowe lasted almost ten whole seconds.

'We had a witness who saw Nelson Price go into the Reed house, and he saw him come out again. The Reeds were alive when he went in and dead when he came out, which is pretty damning in my book. His prints were all over the murder weapon, and they were all over the house. Nelson Price did it. No two ways about it.'

Winter could feel Mendoza's eyes drilling into the back of his head. He could sense all those told-you-so's hanging in the air between them. 'I take it you've heard of a cognitive interview? I'd like to try one on you, if that's okay.'

Lowe glanced suspiciously at Mendoza, then looked back at Winter. 'You're not a cop, are you?'

'No, sir. But I was with the FBI's Behavioral Analysis Unit for over a decade.'

'That figures.' Lowe did nothing to hide his hostility. There was little love lost between the FBI and the local cops. Until the locals needed the FBI's help, of course, then it was a different story. Those old resentments ran long and deep, and, it would seem, all the way into retirement.

'This won't take long. And it would really help us out.'

Lowe's face softened into something approaching a smile. He snorted out a small laugh. 'What the hell? Knock yourself out.'

24

Jeremiah Lowe sat at the head of the long dining table, eyes closed, palms flat on the wood. His wrinkles and worry lines had smoothed out, shaving a decade off his age. Winter gave it almost a full minute. He watched Lowe's chest rising and falling, watched his breathing slow down into a rhythm that was moving away from awake and closer to sleeping. When he finally spoke, he kept his voice quiet and gentle.

'You're in your car and you're pulling up in front of the Reeds' house. You park as close to the house as you can, kill the engine, get out. For a moment I just want you to stand there, taking it all in. Make a note of what you can see, what you can hear.'

Lowe was nodding to himself, his head moving forward and back by just a fraction of an inch. Winter waited for him to go still before continuing.

'What time of day is it?'

'Somewhere around noon. I can't remember the exact time, but what I do remember was that I had to have lunch on the run.'

'What's the weather like?'

'It was raining, but it was that slushy rain you sometimes get before snow. There had been blizzard warnings all over the news, but it hadn't hit at that point. Later that night we had one of the worst snowstorms I can remember. That really hampered things.' Lowe shook his head. 'Listen to me. That's got to be the understatement of the century. It's a good job the investigation was so straightforward. At least we had that working in our favour.'

'So, you walk up to the house, and you're moving quickly because you want out of the cold. Can you feel the rain biting into the exposed parts of your face?'

Lowe nodded.

'What cán you see?'

'Yellow crime tape. And people. Lots of people. Neighbours, cops, journalists. The Christmas wreath on the door has bright red berries. It's early January and the decorations haven't come down yet.'

His voice was as relaxed as Winter's, which was a good sign. He'd also slipped from the past tense to the present. Another good sign. Lowe was right there in the memory, reliving it. Winter was surprised that Lowe was remembering so much. Six years was a long time. By the same token, he wasn't completely surprised. You could forget what you'd had for dinner the day before, but you could remember every single detail of a crime scene from a decade ago.

'Is there any sign of forced entry?'

Lowe shook his head. 'No.'

'Okay, I want you to go inside now. Go along the hall and into the living room. What can you see? What can you hear? What can you smell?'

'Lester's body is lying near the dining table. Melanie's is by the fireplace. It smells like a death house. You know, like a slaughterhouse.'

'Is there anything about the scene that catches your eye?'

Winter was working hard to keep his tone gentle so he didn't shake Lowe out of the memory. It wasn't easy. Now they were getting to the good stuff, the temptation was to hurry.

'The dining table is laid out like it's a special occasion. There are wine glasses, candles. A tablecloth. It's set for four, one place on each side.'

'Tell me about the candles. Are they lit?'

Lowe shook his head. 'No, they've gone out.'

'What colour are they?'

His brow wrinkled then relaxed again. 'They're red. At least I'm pretty sure they were. I can't remember for sure. It was too long ago.'

Winter sensed Lowe slipping out of the memory. 'Okay, I want you to take a couple of deep breaths and imagine that the candle is lit. See how the flame flickers and dances.' He watched Lowe's chest, waiting for his breathing to slow down again. Mendoza leant forward, her hands, forearms and elbows resting flat on the table. Winter tuned her out. 'I want you to go over to where Lester's lying and tell me what you see.'

'He's on his stomach, arms out like he's trying to drag himself across the floor, and he's bled out. Most of the blood is pooled around his body but there's a trail that leads to the other side of the dining table. It's all smeared from where he's dragged himself through it.'

'Now tell me about Melanie.'

'She's lying curled up in a ball with her hands clamped over her belly. I've no idea how many times she's been stabbed, but it's a lot.'

It was forty-seven times, according to Rosalea Griffin's

autopsy report. And that was more than a lot. The poor kid had never stood a chance.

'What's she wearing?'

Lowe shook his head. 'Sorry, I can't remember.'

'That's okay. Now don't say anything for a second. I want you to look at the fireplace. Maybe there's a fire going. Maybe it's gone out.'

'It's gone out.'

'In that case I want you to imagine that it's lit. Nod when you've done that.' Winter counted off four seconds before he got the nod. 'Good. Now lose yourself in the flames. Watch the way they swirl, see the different colours, hear the crackle and pop of the wood. Feel the heat and smell the wood smoke.' Winter gave him a second to process this. 'Now look back at Melanie and tell me what she's wearing.'

'Sweatpants and a baggy T-shirt.'

'What about Lester? What was he wearing?'

'Jeans. I'm pretty sure he had a T-shirt on but it might have been a shirt.'

'Thanks. You can open your eyes.'

Lowe opened his eyes, blinking and squinting away the daylight. He rubbed his hands over them, once, twice, then reached for his coffee.

'So how do you think this whole thing played out?' Mendoza asked him.

Lowe fell into a thoughtful silence. He was staring over her shoulder, his eyes fixed on a framed wedding photograph on the mantel. Lowe and his wife from way back. They were roughly the same age as the Reeds at the time of the murder.

'You want to know what I think? I think Nelson Price

knocked on their door, and I think Lester Reed opened it, inviting a whole world of hurt into their lives. And I also think, without a shadow of a doubt, that Nelson Price was working alone. I'm sorry, I know that's not what you want to hear, but that's the way it was.'

25

It was hitting five by the time they passed the HARTWOOD sign and rattled across the picture-postcard bridge again. Winter found the note that Granville Clarke had given him and read out the directions to the Price place. A short while later they were bumping down a narrow rutted dirt track that was surrounded by dense woodland on both sides. Conditions were so bad Mendoza was forced to slow to ten miles an hour.

'Why were you so interested in what the Reeds were wearing?' she asked.

'Just crossing those T's and dotting those I's. I was ninety-nine per cent certain that they hadn't been celebrating, but that turned a "definitely maybe" into a definite "no". You go to the trouble of laying the table for a special occasion, you're going to go the trouble of changing out of your sweats.'

'Which proves beyond a doubt that Nelson Price laid the table after he killed them.'

'Except that doesn't work.'

'It doesn't?'

'You saw the autopsy report, and you heard what Jeremiah Lowe said. Nelson was feral when he killed Melanie. There was no way he did what he did to Melanie then got himself together enough to go and lay that table.'

'I see where you're going with this, Winter, but it's not

going to work. This doesn't prove that your mystery woman was involved. It's not even good enough to be classed as circumstantial.'

Winter waved a hand through the air. 'Look around you, Mendoza. Not a courtroom. I don't need to prove anyone's guilt here, I just need to work out what happened.'

'You're not driving back to New York.'

'I'm picturing myself behind the wheel right now. I've got my foot down and we're burning those miles up.' He smiled. 'A bet's a bet. It's time to pay up.'

'Not until we've got hard evidence. And I'm talking evidence of the irrefutable kind, evidence that you *can* take all the way to court.'

Thirty seconds later they drove into a wide clearing. Mendoza pulled to a stop and ratcheted the handbrake. She killed the engine. Up ahead was a dilapidated two-storey farmhouse. Once, long ago, it had been white. Now it was a mix of rancid shades. Yellows, greys, blacks and browns. In places the paint had peeled away entirely to expose the bare wood beneath. The windows were even filthier than the diner windows. All the lights were off and the place appeared to be deserted.

Off to the left was a barn that was as neglected as the house. It loomed out of the ground, dark and depressing. It was the only barn Winter could see, so presumably this was where Nelson Price and his mother had hung themselves.

Winter got out of the BMW and stared up at the darkening sky. There were no stars yet, no moon either, but they'd be along soon enough. A sky this clear, this far from any large cities, you were looking at the perfect canvas for the full show.

He walked around to Mendoza's side of the car. The detective was staring up at the house. Since they'd got there, they'd seen no signs of life. This far off the beaten track, if Amelia had been home, he would have expected her to come out and see who was on her land. At the very least, a light or two should have gone on.

No lights. No sounds. No Amelia.

There was no sign of a vehicle either. You couldn't live way out here in the woods without transport. It was just too impractical. Granville Clarke had said Amelia worked as a nurse over in Rochester, so that's where she probably was right now, no doubt pulling a night shift.

'Here's a question,' said Mendoza. 'Why the hell would anyone in their right mind choose to live in a place like this? I mean, you heard what Clarke said. The whole town guessed both the kids were being abused, and had been for years. So why would Amelia Price stay?'

Winter didn't say anything for a moment. He knew better than anyone that the past clung to you, keeping you stuck and treading water. A memory of his mother filled his head, this one from when they were still living in California. His father had been arrested a couple of weeks earlier so it was just the two of them. He'd woken in the night to the sound of crying and found her sobbing in the living room. Even though she knew exactly what her husband was, she'd still grieved for him. The mourning period ended when she put the house on the market. Looking back now, he saw that her heart had never really left that house.

'Well there's money, for starters. Looking at this house, it's a safe bet that the Prices weren't rolling in it. Where would she go with no money? Also, it's her home and, no matter what hell you've been through, that's where your heart stays trapped.'

'That's one way of looking at it, I guess. Okay, here's another question: how come she hasn't strung a noose up in the barn? I mean, this place goes beyond depressing. If I had to live here, I'd kill myself.'

Winter looked up at the house, then glanced over at the barn. 'You've got a point there.'

'I'm thinking nobody's at home.'

'And I'm thinking you might be right. Maybe she's working a late shift.'

'Hold that thought.'

Mendoza took out her cell phone and made a quick call. It took Winter two seconds to work out that she was talking to Hitchin, and another two seconds to work out that they hadn't yet found what hospital Amelia was working at. The rest of the conversation was taken up with Mendoza filling Hitchin in on what they'd been up to in Hartwood, and Hitchin giving an update on the New York end of the investigation.

'Did you get all that?' she asked as she hung up and put her phone away.

'I got what I needed to. Have you got a pen?'

'Try the glove box.'

Winter clicked it open and rummaged around until he found one. He tore Granville's note in half and scribbled down a short message asking Amelia to call his cell.

'Nice writing,' Mendoza remarked. They both looked down at his scrawl. 'You realise that even if she could read that, she's going to take one look and pitch it in the trash.'

'We'll see.'

'What's that supposed to mean?'

'It means we'll see.'

'Yes, I heard you, but you're doing that thing where you pretend to be all mysterious. You're thinking that Amelia's our mystery woman, aren't you?'

'And you're not.'

'Well, I wasn't until thirty seconds ago. After all, you did a pretty good job of convincing me that it wasn't her back in Clarke's office. So is Amelia our woman or not?'

Winter shrugged. 'For now how about we class her as a person of interest?'

'In which case we need to talk to her sooner rather than later.'

'Agreed. The problem is that she's not at home and we still don't know which hospital she works at.' He held up the note. 'This is all we've got at the moment. If Amelia is our mystery woman then I'm figuring that she won't be able to resist getting in touch. If it's not her then she'll probably pitch it in the trash.'

He folded the note in half, wrote 'Amelia' on the front, then made his way up the porch steps. The old wood creaked underfoot, and the air smelled of decay. A couple of rust-streaked metal chairs sat abandoned near the door. Over his shoulder, he caught sight of high branches backlit by the sun. Before the rot had set in, before the nightmares, this would have been a good place to come with a whisky and a cigarette to watch the day wind down.

On the off chance that Amelia was in and hadn't heard

them arrive, he knocked on the door. No footsteps, no signs of life. Winter knelt down and pushed the note through the narrow gap at the bottom of the door. Then he straightened up, creaked back down the stairs and walked over to the car. He climbed in, pulling the door shut behind him.

'So what now?' Mendoza asked.

'Since it doesn't look as if we have any reason to head back to New York any time soon, I vote that we go and find somewhere to stay.'

26

Myrtle House was a mom-and-pop guesthouse situated opposite the cemetery way up at the north end of Main Street. It looked Victorian, but there was no way it was that old. For a start, the location was all wrong. If this house had been built in the 1800s, it wouldn't have been built here. Land had been cheaper and more plentiful back then. This site wouldn't even have been a fourth or a fifth choice, because there would have been plenty of sites with a better view. You only built opposite a cemetery when your options were severely limited.

Mendoza parked out front and they climbed from the car. Sunset was still half an hour away and the sky was lit up like a Van Gogh, purples, pinks, blues and greys all swirling together. The guesthouse was painted light grey, and the small front yard was tidy and well-maintained. There were rooms on the first and second floors, dormers protruding from the attic rooms. A VACANCIES plaque hung beneath an illuminated sign that had Myrtle House printed in neat gold letters.

Mendoza popped the trunk and Winter grabbed his suitcase and heaved it out. It was a top-of-the-range black Samsonite that had seen plenty of action. After escaping from the Seventh Precinct's interview room, they'd detoured via his hotel to pick it up. His whole life was in that case, everything he needed to get through the day, which wasn't much. Clean clothes, clean underwear, his laptop, a carton of cigarettes and a bottle of single malt whisky. Mendoza's bag was much smaller, and presumably contained everything she needed to survive a couple of nights out here in the middle of nowhere. Winter made an 'after-you' gesture, and they climbed the steps to the main entrance. He followed her inside, the wheels of his suitcase trundling over the hard wooden floor.

The guy behind the desk welcomed them with a beaming smile and a cheery 'good evening'. He was well into his sixties, smartly dressed in a white button-down cotton shirt and chinos. Judging by the wide smile he was glad of the extra business.

'Can I help you?'

'Two rooms, please. If you've got anything that resembles a suite I'll take that. If not I'll take the best room you've got.'

The guy behind the desk looked him up and down. Winter could almost read his thoughts. He was probably thinking about the extra dollars a suite would bring, but then doubting that anyone who looked as scruffy as he did would pay extra for anything.

'What my colleague is trying to say', added Mendoza, 'is that we'd like your two best rooms.'

'Certainly, ma'am. The Presidential Suite is currently unoccupied, and I've got a very nice room on the first floor that I think would meet with your approval.'

'We'll take them.'

They went through the paperwork and Mendoza paid with her card. Then the guy showed them to their rooms, filling the silence with small talk and empty observations. Winter's suite was in the converted attic at the top of the house, two floors above Mendoza's room. He dragged his suitcase inside and abandoned it in the middle of the floor. The décor was no real surprise. Dark wood and sepia-tinted framed photographs, and plenty of lacy Victoriana frills and decorations. The window looked out over the cemetery.

To call the room a suite pushed the definition. At best, it was a large room. Still, it had an en-suite bathroom, and it seemed clean enough, and it made the tatty suite the NYPD had booked for him seem like a palace. There was no way in hell a president had ever stayed here, though, or ever would. Winter had been named after Thomas Jefferson, president number three, and he reckoned that was as close as they were ever going to get to hosting a president.

He had just started arranging the room when there was a gentle knock on the door. 'Give me a second,' he called out. He put his laptop bag down on the bed then opened the door. Mendoza was standing there. She had a pained expression on her face and was biting her lip.

'What's wrong? Has something happened?'

'Everything's fine.' Mendoza was looking at her hands, her feet, anywhere so she wouldn't have to meet his gaze.

'You're starting to freak me out. Whatever's on your mind, just say it.'

'I was out of order,' she blurted out.

'When?'

'Earlier, at the Reeds' house. I shouldn't have said all that stuff about you being like your father.'

Winter waved the apology away. 'Is that all. I thought something serious had happened.'

'I was out of order,' she said again.

'No you weren't. You had something you wanted to say and you said it. I'd much rather that than you feeling like you can't say what's on your mind. That's not going to help us. Anyway, one of the advantages of having a serial killer for a father is that I don't take offence easily.'

'How about I buy you dinner? That could be my way of saying sorry.'

'I appreciate the invite, but I can't. I've got a date.'

Mendoza frowned. She opened her mouth to speak then closed it again.

'Yeah, I know, who'd ask me on a date?'

'Since when? Who?'

'Ah, that would be telling.'

'So, are you going to tell me who the lucky girl is?'

'Who says it's a girl?'

Mendoza opened her mouth, but nothing came out.

'You know, you remind me a little of someone I used to work with. She liked the world to think she was a hard ass, too, but deep down she was a pussycat.'

'I am not a pussycat.'

'Yeah, I believe you.'

'Okay, if you won't let me buy you dinner, how about I buy you breakfast instead?'

Winter considered this a second. 'I tell you what, if it's going to help you to feel better, how about you tell me the real reason you were going to Vegas?'

'I already told you, I like the shows.'

'And I believe that as much now as I did then.'

'Why do you want to know?'

'Because everyone knows about Mendoza the cop, but nobody knows a damn thing about your personal life.'

'That's because it's personal.'

'Look, anything you tell me stays with me. I promise I won't breathe a word to your colleagues. And anyway, when this is over, I'm out of here. Chances are you'll never see me again.'

'That's what I thought last time.'

Winter said nothing and Mendoza let out a long sigh.

'Okay, okay. I split up with my boyfriend a couple of months ago. He got fed up with coming second to work, and I can't say I blame him. He was always going on about taking a vacation and I always had an excuse for why it wasn't a good time. He was the one who wanted to go to Vegas.'

'So, what? You figured it was a case of better late than never?'

'Something like that. And, yes, before you say anything else, I know how crazy that sounds. All I can say in my defence is that it made perfect sense to me when I made the booking.'

'You say he was your boyfriend, but this wasn't some casual thing, was it? How long had you guys been together?'

'Twelve years.'

'Twelve years. That's not a fling, that's a marriage.'

'And that's a whole other issue.'

'Okay, here's a question. If you had the opportunity to do it all over again, would you change anything?'

'I'd like to say yes, but that would be a lie.' Mendoza shook her head and gave a small laugh. 'The one thing they don't tell you when you sign up is that this isn't just a job, it's a way of life.' She paused and caught his eye. 'I don't have to tell you that, though, do I?'

She turned and walked off along the corridor. Winter watched her until she disappeared around the corner, then went back into his room and gently closed the door.

27

Winter attached the speakers to his laptop and navigated to his Mozart file. He selected Piano Concerto No. 24 in C minor and hit play. It was six-thirty, so he had half an hour to shower and change before he went out.

This concerto had been written towards the end of Mozart's life and was widely considered to be a masterpiece. Influential, too. Beethoven's Piano Concerto No. 3 in C minor was inspired by this. It was also something of an oddity in that it was one of only two minor-key concertos that Mozart wrote, and one of only three where the first movement was in 3/4 time. Technical details aside, Winter loved it for the drama of the opening movement. And the playful variations on the main theme near the start of the third movement always made him smile.

Over the years he'd collected recordings of every piece that Mozart had written. For some of the more popular pieces he had three or four versions. His aim was to own the defining performances of each work. It was a never-ending task. Mozart was more popular now than he'd ever been, so new recordings were appearing all the time.

Eyes closed, he stood in the middle of the room conducting an imaginary orchestra. It was springtime in Vienna, and he was in the original Burgtheater, and the orchestra was on fire. He silenced the strings, leaving space for the woodwind to do their thing, and then the clarinet floated in with a hint of the main melody.

Heaven.

Winter opened his eyes and sat down on the bed to check his emails. For once there weren't any requests for his help, which made a welcome change. Most days there would be at least one request. Two or three weren't unusual.

There was an email from the lead investigator in the Paris case wondering why he hadn't appeared at Charles de Gaulle airport. He was pissed off, but there was nothing Winter could do about that. Right now his priority was finding the blonde. And anyway, time was on their side there. That killer was on a two-week cycle and the last body had been found a couple of days ago. Winter typed out a quick reply to say that he'd been unavoidably detained in New York and would get there as soon as he could. He hit send, reckoning that would buy him a few days.

Next he poured a whisky, then hung out the window to smoke a cigarette. Full dark had fallen and there was an ominous low moon hanging in the sky. Winter looked up at the stars and wondered how many of them were already dead. The idea that he could be looking at stars that had died millions of years ago had always amazed and fascinated him.

For a while he smoked and sipped and thought things through, the cold night air blowing into his face, the silence broken by the occasional vehicle and a dog barking off in the distance. It had been a long day. He was looking forward to climbing into bed and shutting his eyes. Best-case scenario, he might manage eight hours of unconsciousness and wake up feeling like a new man. Unfortunately, four or five hours of disturbed sleep was probably more likely.

Even though he was trying not to, his thoughts kept straying back to the mystery woman. She was a puzzle, and when he got his head into a puzzle he just couldn't let go. It was just the way he was wired. He had one of those brains that never quite stopped. The best he could hope for was to get it ticking over in a lower gear for a while. And figuring the puzzle out didn't help. Not really. There were always going to be new puzzles to solve.

Winter shut his eyes and imagined himself back into the diner again. He could smell the grease in the air. He could hear Elvis, and the clatter of the dying heater. And he could see the blonde reflected in the window. She walked down the aisle between the counter and the tables and came over to where he was sitting. They spoke for a bit, then the cook appeared with his breakfast and she grabbed hold of him and stabbed him in the eye. Winter rewound the memory and played it again with everything slowed down to half speed. He heard those soft padding footsteps, watched her come closer. He went over every word that had passed between them, looking for hidden meanings and subtext, trying to crack the code.

Nothing.

He trawled through the memory again, this time at quarter speed, looking for anything he might have missed. He felt he was on the verge of a breakthrough, but wasn't sure what that breakthrough might look like. Then again, that might just be wishful thinking.

The diner door in his head banged shut, the woman

walked off into the night, and Winter was left none the wiser. Tonight he'd get a halfway decent sleep, and tomorrow he'd hopefully wake up with a clearer head and a less jaded perspective. Sleep usually did wonders for getting his head straight.

He grabbed some clothes from his suitcase and laid them on the bed. Clean underwear, a fresh pair of Levis, and a T-shirt that had a photograph of a psychedelically stoned Lennon taken during his Sergeant Pepper days. The clothes were laid out head to toe, like the person wearing them had suddenly vanished. All except the socks, which were in a neat ball on the pillow. He never bothered unpacking because he never stayed anywhere longer than two weeks. What was the point in putting your clothes in drawers and hanging them up in closets if you were going to be moving on in a couple of days?

He hit the shower, blasting it as cold as he could stand for as long as he could stand in order to blow away the worst of his fatigue. By the time he'd towelled himself dry he was feeling almost human. Not all the way there, but close enough to pass a casual inspection. He dressed quickly, smiling to himself as those playful variations from the third movement filled the room.

The world he inhabited was one where the human imagination had been set on 'destroy'. From time to time he needed a reminder that it was also a place filled with light, a place where incredible and wondrous things could be created. That was where Mozart and Lennon and Hendrix and all those other amazing musicians came into their own. To hear the world as they heard it, even just for a moment, gave him reason to hope.

He whistled along to the music as he got dressed, improvising countermelodies and harmonies, and just having fun. Even in his darkest moments there had always been music. The movement reached its conclusion and a blissful silence settled across the room. Winter took a moment to appreciate this, then shut down his computer and headed out to meet his date.

28

Willow Avenue ran parallel to Main Street and was filled with large houses that looked like they'd been built back when the town was founded. It was a short ten-minute walk from Myrtle House, a one-cigarette walk. Winter took out the note Granville Clarke had given him and unfolded it. An invitation to dinner was tagged on the bottom, the wording old-fashioned and kind of endearing.

Winter checked he'd got the right house then climbed the steps to the porch and gave the old iron bell pull a sharp tug. Deep inside the house, a lonely bell sounded. Footsteps in the hall, then the door rattled open. Clarke stood there, the dull light softening the sharp angles of his face. He was dressed in tweed trousers and a plain white shirt that had the top button undone. He waved Winter inside and shut the door.

'Hope you like takeout Chinese,' he said.

'Always. Do you want me to go pick it up.'

'Not necessary. I've got an arrangement with Mr Li. He knows where I live. At least, his son does. I slip the kid a couple of bucks and he brings the food straight to my door. I've never been much of a cook. That was Jocelyn's department.'

Winter held up the half-full bottle of Springbank that the NYPD had got for him. 'I wasn't sure what meds you were on, but I brought this along in case you fancied a drink.'

Clarke smiled. 'Let me go grab a couple of glasses. Ice?'

'Not for me.'

'Good man. People who put ice in a single malt ought to be shot.'

Winter laughed and followed Clarke through to the kitchen. The inside of the house looked as old as the interior of Myrtle House, with one major difference: this wasn't fake. Maybe the grandfather had bought it, and it had been passed down through the generations, like the *Gazette*. Clarke got some glasses down from a cupboard, placed them on the antique oak dining table and Winter poured out two decent-sized measures. He handed one of the drinks to Clarke. They clanked glasses and said 'Cheers'. Sips and smacked lips followed.

'This is good.'

'It's not bad,' Winter replied.

'So what do you want to eat?'

'I'll leave that one to you since you're obviously the expert.'

'I guess you could say that. I'm thinking about buying shares in the place. Of course, the only problem with that is that I won't be around to see them mature.'

Clarke chuckled gently then pushed his wire-rimmed spectacles back into place. He picked up the phone, dialled a number from memory, and ordered the food. No name, no address. No need. Winter glanced over at the stove and wondered if it had been used since Jocelyn passed away. Breakfast at the diner was a regular thing, so was Chinese takeout from Mr Li. With those meals bookending the day, you'd only need a quick sandwich at lunchtime to keep you going. Winter tried to work to a similar dietary plan. A large breakfast, a large dinner, and regular snacks in-between to keep his blood sugar level on an even keel.

They walked through to the living room, their footsteps loud on the bare wooden floors. The room had a lived-in feel. One wall was made up entirely of wall-to-floor bookcases that were crammed to overflowing. There were a real mix of titles. Classics at the upper end of the scale, trash at the lower. This library wasn't here for show, this was the library of someone who loved to read.

Clarke saw where he was looking and said, 'Most of those were Jocelyn's. She was the reader.' He let loose with another soft chuckle and added, 'My contribution are all those airport thrillers. Jocelyn used to give me such a hard time about those. Said I was turning my brain to mush.'

Clarke fell into a long silence, and Winter had a pretty good idea what he would have said next if he'd been able to get the words out. He would have told him that he'd give anything to be with Jocelyn for just one more day, even if she was nagging him half to death. Winter walked over to the chessboard that was set up on the coffee table. Like the board back in Clarke's office, this one was frozen mid-game too. Winter took a closer look and saw that it was the same game.

'You used to play with Jocelyn?'

'All the time.'

'And this was the last game you played together?'

A nod.

'White or black?'

'Black.'

'She was kicking your ass all the way into the middle of next week, you realise that, don't you? Checkmate in five.'

Another chuckle. 'Yeah, I know. She always won.'

Winter nodded down at the board. 'Fancy a game. And don't worry I can put the pieces back where they are.'

Clarke gave him the look.

'I'm good at remembering things.'

'How good? Photographic-memory good?'

Winter grimaced. 'I've never been a fan of labels.'

For a moment, Clarke looked like he was about to snap into journalist mode. Instead, he started moving the pieces back to the start position. 'Loser pays for dinner?'

'Sounds good to me.'

Clarke held out a couple of pawns in his closed fists and Winter tapped the left one. Black. The old guy sat down and moved his pawn to e4. Winter countered by moving his pawn to e5. As opening moves went, it was pretty uninspiring.

They were a couple of dozen moves in to the game when the doorbell rang. The Li boy with their food presumably. Clarke excused himself and Winter killed time studying the board. As things stood it was pretty much a tie, which was what he was aiming for. If he wanted to, he could get checkmate in nine. That said, if he didn't move his bishop, then Clarke could push forward and get checkmate in six.

The game eventually ended in a draw and Winter reached for his wallet. Their empty plates were pushed to the side of the coffee table, chopsticks lying neatly on top. The smell of Chinese food hung in the air.

'Put your money away,' Clarke told him.

'We had a bet, remember? Winner pays for dinner. Since it was a draw, I say we split it.'

Clarke narrowed his eyes. 'You threw the game. That was a

nice touch, by the way. Playing for a stalemate. Now, if I'd actually won, then I would have been *really* suspicious.' Winter said nothing and Clarke added, 'You're way smarter than the average bear, right?'

There was no point denying it, so he kept his mouth shut. He wasn't the only person in the room who was smarter than the average bear. Clarke might be on the last lap, his body failing, but there was nothing wrong with his mind. He began moving the pieces back to the start position.

'Here's what we're going to do. We're going to play again, and this time you're *not* going to pull your punches.'

'You sure? I'm warning you now, it won't be pretty.'

Clarke laughed softly. 'I'll get over it.'

Winter played white this time, and showed no mercy. As soon as Clarke moved, he responded. Attack, attack, attack. The game was over in minutes. Clarke sighed out a 'Phew-wee' and sunk back in his seat, clutching his whisky glass to his chest. He was grinning, though, a wide ear-to-ear beamer.

'That was mighty impressive, young man. Where the hell did you learn to play like that?'

'Books and computers.'

'You could have been a pro.'

'I don't have the discipline.'

'So, what are we talking about here? Have you got one of those freakishly high IQs?'

Winter answered with a shrug.

'How high?' asked Clarke.

'Let's just say that I'm way above average but a mile behind Da Vinci, and leave it at that.'

'You know what Da Vinci's IQ was? How the hell does that one work? I didn't think the IQ test was around in his day.'

'It wasn't. The figure attributed to him is just some expert's best guestimate.'

'Yet you still know what it is. So what does that say about you?'

'I don't know. What does it say?'

'It says that you're an overachiever.' Clarke paused for a moment and studied Winter closely. 'Also, you're bright, that much is obvious. And you like people to know that, but pretend you don't. You've got a high degree of empathy, too. I'm sure if I asked you what you're doing here this evening you could give me a dozen justifications, and they'd all be bullshit. And it really doesn't matter anyway. The truth is that today has been one of the best days I've had in a long, long time. You've no idea how much I appreciate this.' He lifted his glass and chuckled softly. 'And this.'

Winter gave him the look. 'I don't believe it. You're trying to profile me. *Me!*'

Clarke chuckled again, but didn't deny it. Winter reached for the whisky bottle and topped up their glasses. He glanced over, trying to figure the old guy out. He might have been able to beat him at chess, but he'd think twice before taking him on at poker.

'Okay. How do you fancy playing cop?'

'Well, I've got to say that it sounds way better than being annihilated at chess.'

Over the next ten minutes Winter outlined everything that had happened. Clarke had promised he wouldn't breathe a word, and Winter believed him. You didn't survive this long as a small-town journalist without knowing how, and when, to keep a secret. And it was good to have his thoughts out there in the open. All the same there were still far too many questions and nowhere near enough answers.

Never enough answers.

After he finished, Clarke didn't say anything for a long time. He just sat there and nursed his drink. Little thoughtful sips. He placed his glass back on the table.

'You feel guilty about the cook's death?'

'Not guilty as such, but I need to catch this woman. Let's face it, if I hadn't been there, he'd still be alive. Incidentally, his name was Omar.'

'So what can you tell me about Omar?'

'Not much. He'd been living in the US for almost a decade and was married with a couple of kids. And he was a really good cook.'

Clarke smiled and they fell into another long silence. Winter picked up his glass, swirled the whisky around and took a sip. Clarke was staring off into space, miles away. Patience wasn't Winter's strong suit but he was happy to wait this one out. He was enjoying the old guy's company, enjoying the whisky. It was good to get off the merry-go-round for a short while.

'Way back when, I did a front-page lead about a boundary dispute,' Clarke said eventually. 'On one side you had the town committee. They owned the disputed land. At any rate, they *claimed* to own it. I can't remember the name of the person involved because we're talking decades rather than years, so, for argument's sake, let's call him Mr X. With me so far?'

Winter nodded for him to go on.

'Anyway, Mr X was adamant about where his boundary lay, and was very vocal on the subject. As far as he was concerned the committee was made up of scum-sucking bottom feeders. And that was one of the more polite phrases he used. So I write the story, get a few quotes from the mayor to balance out Mr X's argument, and as far as I'm concerned, that's the end of things.'

'Except that wasn't the end of things.'

'No it wasn't. The mayor accused me of being biased, and he probably had a point. So the next week I write the story again, this time from the committee's point of view. The thing is, all I did was rewrite the first couple of paragraphs of the original story and rework a few of the other paragraphs.'

Clarke stopped talking and repositioned his spectacles, pushing them back into place with his fingertips. Winter sat patiently waiting. Yet again the only time that had any real meaning was time as defined by Granville Clarke.

'For all intents and purposes the two stories were identical,' Clarke continued. 'To this day the thing that gets me is that nobody noticed. *Nobody*. Not even my father, and he edited both of them. Don't you find that incredible?'

'Yes and no. If I'm honest, nothing much surprises me any more.'

'So cynical for someone so young. The point is, you can take a whole bunch of facts and use them to tell a dozen different stories. Now, it seems to me that what you've done here is take the facts as presented by your mystery woman and weave your own narrative from it. I can see why you've done that, but I think it's a mistake. The story you manage to divine from the facts is irrelevant. What you should be asking yourself is what story is your mystery woman trying to tell you? That's all that matters here. The story she wants to tell.'

29

Winter walked up to the tall iron cemetery gates and peered through the bars. Hundreds of gravestones stretched out into the distance, following the gentle downward slope of the land. At the far edge of his vision the gravestones and darkness merged together, making it difficult to tell them apart.

The gate was padlocked shut, but that was no real deterrent. If anyone wanted to get in all they had to do was climb over. Winter was betting that plenty of kids had done that over the years. This was the perfect place to come and share a bottle, or a few stolen teenage kisses. He rattled the chain a couple of times. It was pulled tight and, at first glance, it seemed secure enough.

He checked both ways along the street to make sure he was alone. There were a few lights on in the upstairs rooms of the nearby houses, but aside from that this stretch of Main was deserted. Winter reached into the inside pocket of his jacket and found the leather wrap that contained his lock picks. He took one last look to make sure no one was watching, then inserted the torsion wrench into the big brass padlock and pushed it all the way to the back of the lock, away from the pins. Next he inserted the feeler pick and used it to put pressure on the pins. Ten seconds later there was a click and the padlock sprung open.

Winter put his picks away and loosened the chain,

carefully so he didn't make too much noise. He opened the gate just wide enough to slip through, then pulled it closed behind him. Within a dozen yards the darkness had claimed him, the night turning him into a shadow. He followed the access road a bit further then stepped on to the grass and wound his way between the headstones.

Clarke had mentioned that Lester and Melanie were buried here and he spent the next half an hour trying to find their graves before giving up. The problem was that the cemetery was just too big. Locating theirs in the dark would require a whole load of luck, and the whole concept of luck was something that made him uneasy. He'd been looking out for Nelson Price's grave, too, but wasn't expecting to find it. Cremation was more likely there, the symbolism of the flames too strong a lure for a small town like Hartwood.

Winter stopped at the next grave, flicked his beat-up Zippo to life, and read the inscription in the dancing light.

VICTORIA BURGESS
24th SEPTEMBER 1911–30th MARCH 1944
LOVING WIFE AND MOTHER
CALLED HOME TOO SOON

Winter did the math. Victoria had been thirty-three when she'd died, which was definitely too soon. He wondered how many kids she'd had. However many there had been, they would probably have been young when she died. And how had she died? Long and slow like the way Granville Clarke was dying, or quickly like Jocelyn Clarke?

What story is your mystery woman trying to tell you?

The memory of Clarke's words drifted through his mind. Winter had to concede that the old guy had a point. The problem was that he was just too close to this one. Usually when he walked into a crime scene, he was able to view it from at least one step removed. That hadn't happened here because he'd been part of the scene. Yes, he'd approached the investigation in his usual logical, methodical manner, and, yes, he'd listened to what the victims had to say and followed the trail step by step. But that was where the similarities ended. Instead of looking down from the high ground, he was looking up from the low ground, and the perspective was all wrong.

Question: if he walked into this scene cold, what would he see?

To begin with he'd see an incredibly well-executed murder. It was unlikely that this was the blonde's first. Nobody showed that level of proficiency first time out. If it had been, she would have hesitated. She would have pulled that punch. Stabbing someone wasn't as simple as the movies made out. How hard did you have to thrust? What angle did you go in at? Where did you need to be standing? And that was before you got on to all the added complications, like the fact that she'd been punching through the bone at the back of the eye socket. Also, her choice of weapon made life difficult. Stabbing someone in the eye with a food knife wasn't easy.

Another thing that would have jumped out at him was the fact that this wasn't a robbery. Nothing had been stolen from the till. And nothing had been taken from Omar. The reason Omar had been killed was because she'd wanted to get Winter's attention. The problem with this motive was that it spawned a whole load of new questions. Like why did she want to get his attention?

Earlier he'd told Mendoza that he had never seen the woman before, and he still believed that. If he had met her before he would have remembered her face. Another possibility was that she was connected with someone he'd put in prison, just like Mendoza had suggested. One of the main reasons he tried to stay under the radar was to avoid reprisals. He never gave interviews and did his best to avoid having his photograph taken. The last time he Googled his name all he'd found were some newspaper articles where he'd gotten a short mention. In addition, there were a couple of features on his father and some press releases that dated back to his FBI days, but that was it. There had only been two photographs.

That said, despite the precautions he took, it wouldn't be the first time an irate relative or lover had sought him out. He'd spent eleven years with the FBI, and since quitting he'd worked more cases than he cared to remember. Add it all up, and you were looking at plenty of potential grudges and a whole lot of motivation. Even if Mendoza was right, it didn't really help. Without knowing specifically who he'd pissed off, there was no way of using this to work back to the woman.

Winter rummaged in his pockets for his cigarettes. He lit one then stared up at the sky, smoking and thinking. He loved these big skies, the ones that stretched on for ever where you could imagine that you were looking at the whole universe. Occasionally it was good to get a reminder of how insignificant you really were. Without those perspective shifts it was too easy to get lost in your own dramas and crises. A seventy-year lifespan wasn't even a blink of the eye when measured against the 13.7 billion years that the universe had existed. It was less significant than a single heartbeat. No matter how important you thought you were, the truth was that you weren't. In the grand scheme, your actions accounted for nothing.

Rather than depressing him, he found the idea appealing. He now understood what Clarke was getting at when he said that his cancer was liberating. Basically, if nothing you did mattered a damn, then you might as well go and do whatever the hell you wanted.

He walked back through the cemetery, glancing at the graves he passed on the off chance he stumbled across Lester's or Melanie's. He reached the gates and let himself out, then headed across the street to Myrtle House. For once, insomnia wasn't an issue. Within minutes of letting himself into his room he was unconscious, his sleep dreamless.

30

'Wakey, wakey.'

A soft voice tickled Winter's ear, cutting through the fog in his brain. His first thought was that it was Isabella. But that couldn't be right. He'd left Izzy behind seven hotels ago. She was the reason that he'd stayed in Rome a week longer than he'd needed to. She'd been a distraction of the best kind, a welcome change in focus, albeit a brief one. It wasn't Izzy, though. The accent was all wrong, the pitch of her voice, the cadence.

These thoughts took a millisecond to process and were immediately replaced by a more worrying one. *What the hell?* Winter's eyes snapped open and the first thing he saw was the beam of a flashlight. Then he saw the shadow of a woman standing beside his bed, the unmistakeable silhouette of a gun in her hand.

'Don't move or speak.'

Winter kept completely still. It wasn't easy. The adrenaline was pumping and his breath was coming in fast shallow gasps. He concentrated on his breathing, willing it to slow. Although this latest development was surprising, it wasn't completely unexpected. She'd said that they'd meet up again, but he hadn't expected her to be this brazen. Then again, she did like dramatic gestures. The woman took a pair of handcuffs from her bag and tossed them on to the bed. They landed with a rattle and a clink.

'Attach one end to the headboard and the other to your wrist.'

Winter complied. The click of the bracelet was loud in the silent early morning stillness.

'Tighter.'

He clicked the cuffs two notches tighter and the cold steel dug into his wrist. She turned on the bedside lamp and the narrow beam of the flashlight was replaced by a weak jaundiced light that struggled to fill the room. She was wearing the same baggy leather jacket that she'd had on in the diner, the same sneakers. He glanced over at the nightstand. His cell phone was next to his watch, within touching distance. It was almost three-thirty. She saw where he was looking and slid the phone to the edge of the cabinet.

She positioned a chair next to the bed then sat down, crossed her legs and leant forward. She was close enough for him to catch all her fragrances. Deodorant, soap, shampoo, laundry detergent. A delicate mix of flowers and fruit. Close enough to reach out and touch her white skin. Close enough to see the slight ridges at the edge of her irises, and know for definite that she was wearing lenses again. Close enough to see she was wearing a wig. Close enough to see how painfully thin she was.

'What are you thinking?'

'I'm thinking you should put the gun away. You're not going to use it.'

'You sound pretty sure of that?'

'I am. Whatever game you're playing, I'm a part of it. If you kill me, that's going to spoil your fun.'

She aimed the gun, her finger curling around the trigger.

Her left hand was supporting the right, which implied a degree of competence. That said, it was a moot point. Even if she had been holding the gun side on and pointed downwards like a street punk, there was no way she could miss at this range. Her face and eyes were empty, and Winter wondered if he'd overplayed his hand.

'You're not going to shoot me,' he repeated.

'Bang, bang,' she whispered. She gave a quiet playful laugh, then lowered the gun and laid it across her lap. 'So what conclusions have you drawn with regards to the murders?'

'Nelson Price did it. His prints were all over the murder weapon and there are witnesses who place him at the scene of the crime.'

'But?'

'But you know this already, because you were there. You're Amelia Price, aren't you? You're Nelson's sister.'

For almost a whole minute she just sat there. While she studied him, he studied her. Now that his eyes had adjusted to the light, he could see her better. Her eyebrows were darker than the wig, her teeth slightly crooked. She wanted him to believe that she was relaxed, that she was taking all this in her stride, but he could see the tension in her face and shoulders.

'You'd like me to be impressed,' she said eventually. 'After all, that's the way things work in your world. You come strolling in, solve the crime, and everyone cheers. I've got to tell you, though, I'm really not impressed.'

'I'm right, though.'

'Yes, you're right.'

'You set the table after the Reeds were murdered, didn't you?'

A nod. 'Yes, I got to play mother.'

'Why?'

'Does there have to be a reason?'

'In my experience, yes there does.'

'So what's the reason?'

Winter fell silent while he thought this over. 'The Reeds were already dead so laying the table had no direct bearing on the actual murder. Nor did it help you when you escaped. You could argue that it gave the cops something to think about, and anything that muddies the water could be advantageous, but I don't think so. That would require the local cops to be operating with a degree of subtlety that I just don't see.'

Amelia nodded for him to go on.

'Therefore the act was a symbolic one. There were four places set at the table, and that was symbolic as well. Why four places? Why not three? Or five? Or six?' Winter thought this through for a second longer, then shook his head. 'Wrong question. The correct question is who were those places laid for?'

Amelia just stared, her face blank.

'Dinner time was a big deal in your family, wasn't it? Your father wanted everything set out in a certain way, and he wanted everyone playing their parts. I'm guessing that you only got to speak when you were spoken to, right?' When it became clear that she wasn't going to answer, he added, 'Did he make you wear your best clothes? Did he make you sit just so?'

'You're wrong.'

'That's the thing, we both know that I'm not.'

Amelia picked up the gun and aimed at his head. 'You're wrong.'

'Okay, I'm wrong.'

He glanced at the gun, then shifted his focus so he was looking at Amelia. She took a couple of deep breaths and the moment passed. She was still pointing the gun at him, but he sensed that he was out of danger for now. He needed to keep her talking, needed to stretch things out. The longer she talked, the more he could learn. A dozen questions jumped into his head, two dozen. What he needed was one where she had the opportunity to show how clever she was.

'Tell me about the file.'

'What file?'

'You stole the Hartwood PD's file on the Reed murders. Why?'

'Why do you think? After all, you're the ace detective. The go-to guy who's got all the answers.'

'You stole it because you didn't want me to get hold of it. And the reason for that was that you didn't want to make things too easy for me.'

'Not everything's about you, Jefferson. Try again.'

Winter shook his head. 'I don't know then.'

'And I'm betting it kills you to admit that.'

'Why did you kill Omar Harrak?'

She frowned. 'Are you talking about the cook?'

Winter nodded.

'I killed him because I needed to make sure that you were taking me seriously.' She paused. 'He was my first, you know.'

It was Winter's turn to frown. 'No he wasn't. It takes time and practice to get that proficient.'

'And you're sure about that?'

Winter studied her carefully, but saw no evidence that she

was being disingenuous. For a split second he was back in the diner again, reliving Omar's murder. Amelia's attention had been fixed fully on him. It was almost as though Omar was an afterthought.

'You're a psychopath, there's no doubt about that,' he said. 'But killing doesn't really do it for you. It's all about control, isn't it? That's what gets you off. So how long did it take to persuade Nelson to murder Lester and Melanie?'

Amelia tapped her fingertips against her lips. Winter watched them move. One, two, one, two, his heart thumping in time with the beat. She stood up abruptly, placed the gun on the nightstand, then unzipped her jacket and lifted her top. Her pale stomach was covered with cigarette burns. There were dozens of them, ugly patches of scar tissue erupting through the smoothness. She ran her fingers across them, the tips reading the shapes.

'There are sixty-three burns in total, and I remember every single one.'

'And I guess this is how you justify things to yourself. How you sleep at night. You were abused, therefore that gives you a licence to destroy. Do you have any idea how many times I've heard that particular story? Do you have any idea how tedious it is?'

Amelia tugged the top down and pulled it straight. 'You think you're so clever, but you're not. Not really. When you get right down to it you don't know anything.'

'I know enough to guess that the person who did that to you was your first.'

'And I've already told you: the cook was my first.' She paused a moment. 'You talk about firsts like they're important. They're not. Does it matter if the cook was my first, or my second, or even my tenth?'

'His name was Omar.'

'So what? If he's got a name that somehow makes him more real?'

'He was real.'

She smiled but didn't say anything.

'Okay,' he went on, 'if he was your first like you claim, I want to know how you were able to kill him so efficiently.'

The smile widened to show the tips of her teeth. 'Cat skulls aren't as thick as a human's, but I was able to get a good idea of what was involved.'

Winter was studying her carefully again. As far as he could tell, she wasn't lying. 'Thank you for sharing.'

'You're welcome.' The smile slid away and her face turned serious. 'Where's your passport?'

'Excuse me.'

'Your passport. Where is it?'

'It's in my suitcase.'

Winter watched her walk over to the stand. She popped the catches on the Samsonite case and lifted the lid, rummaged around until she found the passport. She held it up for him to see, then very deliberately dropped it into the pocket of her leather jacket.

'Why me?'

'And you call me a narcissist.' She smiled. 'You know, not everything's about you, Jefferson.'

Winter shook his head. 'No way is this random. You've targeted me. Why?'

'Maybe you'll have that one worked out by the time we

next meet. Then again, maybe you won't. I guess this is where we find out if you're as smart as you think you are.' Her smile turned into a laugh. 'As much as I'm enjoying this little chat, I really should get going.'

'Before you do, I've got one more question. Back in the diner you said that I was a work in progress. What did you mean by that?'

For a moment Amelia looked as though she was going to ignore the question. 'We're more alike than you think.'

Winter shook his head. 'I'm nothing like you.'

'Yes you are. You've been shaped by your experiences, the same as I've been shaped by mine. The difference is that I wear some of my scars on the outside.'

'Don't think for a second that you know me. You don't.'

'Don't I? When you shut your eyes I'm betting that you dream of blood. Isn't that right? Your dreams are decorated with arterial spray patterns, and your head is filled with thoughts of what it's like to play God. There's nothing more thrilling than being the breath between life and death. I know that, and you know it, too.'

'You're wrong.'

'That's the thing, I'm not.'

Before Winter could say anything else, Amelia leant forward until they were almost touching. He could smell her scent again, and he could see the tell-tale signs of her disguise. He could see the tight angles made by her bones. She was so thin she might blow away. She paused for a moment then started moving her head gently from side to side, her eyes scanning every inch of his face like she was trying to memorise it.

'You don't scare me,' he whispered.

'Yes I do.'

Amelia stood and picked up his cell phone from the night-stand. She looked at it for a second, then tossed it across the room. It tumbled through the air and come sliding to a stop next to the dresser.

'Lie down on your front with both hands above your head.'

Winter shuffled down the bed and a couple of seconds later heard the click of a handcuff bracelet being unlocked. He tilted his head and saw her winding the chain around the headboard. She grabbed his uncuffed wrist and fastened the bracelet to it. Then she took out a large handkerchief and motioned for him to raise his head so she could gag him. The handkerchief was dry and abrasive against his lips. She checked everything was tight then turned to go. Before leaving she turned off the bed-side lamp and turned her flashlight back on. The door opened, then closed, and he was alone again.

So what now? The handcuffs meant that he couldn't move from the bed and the gag meant that he couldn't shout for help. Not that it made much difference if he was gagged or not. Even if he could call out, Mendoza wouldn't hear him. There were two fire doors, two staircases and another floor between them. No matter how loud he shouted, it wouldn't be loud enough.

He looked around for something he could use to pick the handcuffs, but there was nothing he could reach. His lock picks were in his jacket pocket in the closet, and, even if he could get hold of his watch, the prong on the buckle wouldn't be long enough. As far as he could see there was only one op-tion open to him.

Winter shut his eyes and willed himself to sleep.

31

The banging on the door sounded like cannon shots. Three loud thumps followed by a pause, then three more, the noise working to create an unpleasant syncopation with the blood pounding in his head. *Boom boom boom. Boom boom boom.* This was a serious cop knock, one designed to scare the life out of you and get the adrenaline pumping and get you running to answer the door. Winter's eyes snapped open and for a moment he didn't have a clue where he was. Then he noticed the pins and needles in his arms and everything came flooding back. He tried to move his arms and the handcuffs rattled against the headboard.

'Time to get up,' Mendoza yelled through the door. 'I've heard back from Hitchin. Amelia Price doesn't work in a hospital.'

He tried to shout for her to come in but the words were blocked by the gag.

'Winter, is everything okay in there?'

He tried to shout again but all that came out was a muted mumble.

'Is everything okay?' she repeated.

This time he didn't even bother trying to speak because there was no point. Five more seconds passed then the door swung open and Mendoza came in. It took a couple of seconds for her brain to catch up with her eyes. Winter saw the exact moment that realisation dawned. Her eyes widened, as did her grin. She looked at the handcuffs, looked at the gag, looked at him lying there in his boxer shorts and John Lennon T-shirt.

'Your date get a little out of hand, Winter? You know I never would have had you pegged for this sort of thing. Then again, I'm standing here seeing it with my own two eyes and I'm asking myself if I'm really that surprised. The answer is no, by the way.'

She walked over to the bed and took the gag out of his mouth.

'This isn't what it looks like.'

'So you're not cuffed to the bed, and you don't look like hell.'

'Just get my lock picks from my jacket pocket, please. It's hanging up in the closet.'

Mendoza went over to the closet and searched through the pockets until she found the leather wrap. She walked back over to the bed, flicked it open and extracted a pick. Winter motioned for her to give it to him and she shook her head.

'What?' she said. 'You think you're the only person around here who can pick a lock? Okay, let's see those hands.'

Winter didn't bother arguing. He held up his hands and Mendoza went to work. Fifteen seconds of fiddling and the left cuff released. Another ten seconds and she had the right one open as well. He stood up and rubbed his arms to get the circulation going. Mendoza was looking him up and down like he was some sort of previously undiscovered life form.

'Are you just going to stand there in your underwear or are you going to put some clothes on?'

Winter grabbed a clean pair of boxers and a T-shirt from his suitcase, then stood looking at Mendoza until she got the message and turned around. He swapped his dirty clothes for clean, dressing quickly. The T-shirt was one of his favourites. Mozart was wearing a large pair of headphones and there was a large spliff burning between his fingers. It was irreverent and tasteless, and he reckoned that the composer would have loved it. He pulled on his jeans and rubbed a hand through his hair to get rid of the worst of the tangles.

'It's safe to look now.'

Mendoza turned to face him. 'So are you going to tell me what the hell is going on here?'

'Amelia Price is our mystery woman. She cuffed me to the bed.'

For a moment Mendoza just stood there staring. 'You're sure it was Amelia Price?'

'I'm sure. She even admitted it.'

'And this is the point where I'm going to remind you that this woman is a psychopath, and that psychopaths have been known to lie from time to time.'

'Granted, but she wasn't lying about this.'

Mendoza considered this, then shook her head. 'Just because this woman says she's Amelia Price it doesn't mean that that's who she is.'

'Okay, but why would she lie? What would she have to gain?'

'Like I said, she's a psychopath. Who knows what the hell's going on inside her head.'

'Would it help if I told you that my inner psychopath agrees with me on this one?'

He cracked a small smile, then locked eyes with her, daring her to argue some more. The small nod she gave indicated that although she wasn't convinced, she was prepared to go along with him for now.

'There's more. She also admitted that she was with her brother at the Reeds' house on the night they were murdered.'

Mendoza laughed. 'Yeah, nice try.'

'I'm serious.'

'You remember what I said about psychopaths being known to lie? So, how did she outsmart you a second time?'

Winter didn't like the way she was staring, nor did he like the emphasis that she'd placed on those last three words. *A second time.* Like he needed a reminder. But it was a good question, even if he didn't have an answer to it just yet.

'I always knew that she was going to come back. What I didn't consider was that she'd risk coming to my room in the middle of the night.'

'Is that another way of saying that you screwed up?'

'I didn't screw up, I just slightly misjudged the situation.'

Mendoza stood there thinking for a moment. 'Okay, we need to contact the Monroe Sheriff's Department and get them to issue a BOLO alert for Amelia. They'll also need to send someone out to secure the Price place.'

'Agreed, but who do we have them looking for? A shy dark-haired little church mouse, or a platinum-blonde green-eyed psychopath?'

'And who's to say she's not using a different disguise?' Mendoza added with a sigh. 'Shit. She's got us running around in circles and looking like fools. You realise that, don't you? Did she say what she wanted? I mean, why target you?'

'I asked her that, but she threw the question right back at me.'

'You must have a theory, though.'

Winter shook his head slowly. 'Other than the fact that she likes playing control games, I've got no idea why she's doing this. As for why she's singled me out, your guess is as good as mine.'

Mendoza pulled out her cell phone and called the sheriff's department. While she did this, Winter went over to the dresser and picked up his. There was one missed call and a message. He connected to the messaging service and put the phone to his ear. The electronic voice was followed by Granville Clarke's.

'Thanks for last night. I had a great time. I couldn't sleep so I've come over to the office to dig out my old notebook from the time of the murders. Maybe there's something in there that can help you out. Maybe not. Anyway you can catch me at the diner for breakfast.'

The line went dead and Winter put his cell away. He took out one of the Snickers bars he'd bought yesterday and started eating it. He'd taken two bites before he realised that Mendoza was watching him.

'What? I'm hungry, and it doesn't look like we're going to be getting away from here any time soon.' He took another bite. 'By the way, Clarke left a message. He wants us to take a look at one of his old notebooks.'

'Could be useful, I guess. Okay, I spoke to the sheriff's department and they're going to issue that BOLO immediately. They've got some sort of a crisis going on so they can't send anyone to the Price's house just yet. Some guy held up a minimart and now he's holed up in his apartment in Rochester with a gun, a bag of money, and his four-year-old daughter. The police have got the place surrounded. Because of the kid, they're reluctant to go in with all guns blazing. They promised to send someone as soon as they could.'

'It doesn't matter. Amelia won't go back there.'

'Of course she won't. But there could be evidence there. If that's the case it needs to be preserved. It also means that we need to get over there as soon as possible.' She leant against a wall and waited for Winter to meet her eye. 'But first I need you to tell me exactly what happened here last night.'

So Winter went through the whole thing. Recounting it like this, the whole incident had the surreal feel of a dream. Put aside the handcuffs lying on the bed and the ache in his arms, and it was like none of it had ever happened.

'You could have shouted for me,' Mendoza said when he'd finished. 'If you'd done that maybe she'd be in custody by now. But no, you had to go it alone.'

'What was the point? You would never have heard me.'

'But one of the other guests might have.'

'What other guests? Have you seen anyone else?'

'Now you mention it, no I haven't.'

'And even if there were other guests, what do you think would have happened? Amelia wants to play games with me, not hurt me. If Omar's murder is anything to go by, that's a courtesy she's not extending to everyone.'

'The fact that she took your passport is encouraging. She obviously doesn't want you to leave the country.'

'Which means that she's planning to make good on her promise to see me again.'

'My thoughts exactly.'

Mendoza took out her cell phone again and started hitting buttons.

'Who are you calling?'

'Hitchin. If Amelia Price is a viable suspect then he needs to know.'

'Mendoza, Amelia isn't a viable suspect, she did it.'

'And you're still working on the assumption that the woman who was in your room last night was Amelia Price, an assumption based on the fact that she told you that's who she is.'

'Which brings us back to the question of why she'd lie.'

Mendoza shrugged dismissively. 'Who the hell knows why she does anything? Maybe she's just screwing with you.'

'And why would she do that? She's highly organised, and she's a control freak. There's a reason behind everything she does.'

Mendoza waggled her cell phone at him. 'Well, we'll find out if she's lying soon enough. She's got a vehicle, which presumably means that she's got a licence, which means that there will be a picture of her in New York State's Department of Motor Vehicles database.'

'Before you do that, you said earlier that she wasn't a nurse?'

'Yeah, that's right. There's no record of her ever working in any of Rochester's hospitals.'

'What about hospitals outside of Rochester?'

'Nothing in a thirty-mile radius.'

'Nursing homes? Hospices? Veterinary surgeries?'

'I'm sure that whoever looked into it was thorough. Amelia Price is not a nurse.'

While Mendoza made her call, Winter walked over to the door, opened it, and examined the lock on both sides. It was a deadbolt, sturdy and secure. The lock hadn't been forced. Either Amelia had picked it or she'd had a key. He became aware of Mendoza at his shoulder.

'There's no way to tell if it's been picked,' she said.

'No there's not.' Winter straightened up. 'Okay, question one: how did she get in my room? And question two: how did she get into the guesthouse?'

'Let's go find out, shall we?'

32

Mendoza dinged the bell on the reception desk and stepped back. The man who appeared from the back room was the same sixty-something man who'd checked them in last night. Once again, he was wearing chinos and a white button-down shirt. The clothes were freshly pressed and clean on. Winter could smell the laundry detergent.

'Good morning. I trust you slept well. How can I help?'

'What's your name?' asked Winter.

'Jerry. Jerry Barnes.'

'Are you the owner?'

'I am. Well, the co-owner. I run this place with my wife.' He looked suspiciously at Winter.

Mendoza showed her badge and Barnes's face turned white. 'It's okay,' she added quickly. 'You haven't done anything wrong.'

His eyes followed the badge all the way back to Mendoza's pocket. 'Obviously I'll help in any way I can.'

'Someone broke into my room last night. We're trying to work out how they got in. Do you have any cameras?'

'No we don't, sorry. There's no need. There's very little crime in Hartwood.' Concern suddenly filled his face. 'Someone broke into your room? Did they take anything?'

'No they didn't.'

'Are you okay?'

'I'm fine.'

'Did you see them?'

Mendoza and Winter shared a look. This was a tangent they didn't need. 'Mr Barnes,' she said, 'we're trying to ascertain how this person got into my colleague's room. I take it you've got spare keys for all the rooms.'

He nodded. 'We do.'

'Can you show us where you keep them?'

'Certainly.'

He waved them around the counter and led them through to the small back room that he used as an office. It was no bigger than a broom closet. It might well have been a broom closet once upon a time. The desk was the same length as the wall it was pushed up against. There was an outdated monitor on top and a tower hidden away beneath.

On the wall to the right there was a varnished wooden board containing the room keys. Most of the hooks held two keys. The only exceptions were the hooks assigned to the Presidential Suite and Mendoza's room. Winter crouched down to examine the door lock. It was another deadbolt, as sturdy and substantial as the one on his room. In most situations it would be an effective deterrent. There was one definite exception, though.

'Do you ever lock this door?' he asked.

Barnes shook his head. 'No. We've never felt the need to.'

'Well that explains how she got into my room. She sneaked in here and stole the key.'

'I am so sorry,' Barnes said to him. 'If I'd thought something like this might happen, of course I would have kept it locked.'

Mendoza pushed her way past them and took a closer look at the hook containing the spare key for the Presidential Suite.

'Have you got any envelopes?' she asked Barnes. 'Some latex gloves would be good too.'

'Let me go and see what I can find.'

Winter watched him go, then turned back to Mendoza. 'I don't hold out much hope of you getting a decent print off that key. How many people do you think have handled it?'

'Even so, we still need to check it out. Who knows, maybe we'll get lucky.'

'There's no such thing as luck.'

Barnes returned with a bright yellow pair of kitchen gloves and a white self-sealing envelope, and handed them to Mendoza. 'I'm sorry, this was all I could find.'

'This'll do fine. Thanks.'

Mendoza pulled on the rubber gloves and removed a bag from the box. She lifted the key carefully from the board and dropped it into the envelope. Then she sealed the flap and put the envelope into her pocket. She peeled the gloves off and gave them back to Barnes.

'What time do you lock the guesthouse at?' Winter asked.

'Usually around midnight.'

'And if anyone comes back later than that, then they ring the bell and you let them in? Like you did for me last night?'

Barnes nodded. 'That's right. The system works pretty well. There's not much to do in Hartwood in the evenings so most of our guests are back well before midnight.'

'Did you notice anyone acting strangely around the guest-house yesterday?' Mendoza asked.

He shook his head. 'No. Sorry.'

'What about your wife? Maybe she saw something.'

Another slow shake of his head. 'She's in Seattle for a couple of days. Her sister hasn't been well.'

'So you're running this place on your own at the moment?'

'Pretty much. Nicole comes in most days to clean the rooms, but aside from that it's just me.'

'Does Nicole have a key for the front door?'

'Yes she does.'

'Could you call her and see if she's still got it?'

'Certainly.'

The call lasted a little over a minute, just long enough for Barnes to explain what he wanted, and for Nicole to go and check her bag, or wherever it was she kept her keys.

'She's got her key.'

'Who else has one?' Winter asked.

'I've got one, obviously. My wife has one on her key ring. And Nicole. That's it.'

'Do you leave any downstairs windows open?'

'Not at this time of the year.'

'Can we take a look around?'

'Of course.'

It took ten minutes to do a circuit of the first floor to check the windows. They were all locked and secured, and, as far as Winter could tell, they hadn't been tampered with. He checked the front door as well, but, again, there were no obvious signs that it had been tampered with. He tapped out a quick frustrated drum roll on the reception desk.

'So how the hell did she get in?'

'Beats me,' said Mendoza.

'It's a pity that we were the only guests staying here last night. Extra eyes wouldn't do us any harm right now.'

'But you weren't the only guests,' Barnes said. 'What makes you think that?'

'The keys on the board. You give one key to the guest and keep the other for emergencies, right? At the moment there are two keys for all the rooms except ours.'

'That's correct. But there was someone in room five. She's already checked out, so her key has gone back on the board. She was catching an early flight from Rochester.'

Winter and Mendoza exchanged a look. 'Can you describe her for us please?'

'She was roughly your height with blue eyes. Her hair was short and black. I don't know what the correct term for the style is, but I think I've heard my wife call it a pixie cut.'

Winter nodded. This was the confirmation he'd been looking for that Amelia was using disguises. 'Was there anything about her that struck you as strange?'

Barnes thought this over for a second, his face creased in concentration. 'Now you mention it, there were a couple of things. She was a lot younger than our usual guests, mid-twenties, maybe a little older. And I guess I thought it was a bit strange that she was travelling on her own.'

'What was she wearing?'

'She was dressed casually. Jeans, a denim jacket. It looked like she had a white T-shirt on underneath.'

'Was she wearing the same clothes both times you saw her?'

'It was the same jeans, that I'm sure of. They were

decorated with blue sequins. Same jacket, too. She had a white T-shirt on but I don't know if it was the same one.'

'It's her,' Winter told Mendoza.

'Let's not get too excited. We could be looking at a whole string of coincidences here.'

'There's no such thing.' He turned to Barnes. 'Who did she sign in as?'

Barnes reached under the counter for the register and started flicking through the pages. 'Here we go. Wren J Firestone.'

'That sounds like a false name,' said Mendoza. 'Women don't normally use a middle initial.'

'It's definitely a false name,' Winter agreed. 'It's almost an anagram of my name. She couldn't work out what to do with the extra F.' He paused for a second. 'Rowen J Stiffener, would have worked better. That uses all the letters. Or Owen Stiffener Jr. Obviously the junior gets condensed to a J and an R. Of course the problem with that one is that Owen is a male name.'

Mendoza gave him the look then turned to Barnes. 'When did Ms Firestone check out?'

'Early this morning, around seven.'

'And when did she check in?'

'Yesterday evening around nine.'

'Did you notice if she had a suitcase?' Winter asked.

'She had a small case with her.'

'Did you carry it upstairs for her?'

'No.'

'But you offered.'

'Of course.'

'How did she know we were staying here?' Mendoza asked. Before Winter could respond, she added, 'Because she saw the BMW parked outside.' She turned back to Barnes. 'Okay, we're going to need to see her room. And if you have any more gloves and envelopes, that would be really useful.'

33

They stopped at a door halfway along the second-floor corridor and Barnes used the emergency key to unlock it. He pushed the door open, then stood aside. Winter went in first and walked over to the bed. It was neatly made up, the pillows plumped, the comforter pulled straight and square. The yellow rubber gloves that Mendoza had made him wear were making his hands sweat and itch.

'Has Nicole been in today?'

Barnes shook his head. 'No. I'm not expecting her until lunchtime.'

Winter pulled back the comforter and checked the sheet. It was tight and smooth, not so much as a single crease. 'This bed hasn't been slept in. Now, that's unusual, right? Why would someone pay for a room then not sleep in the bed?'

'Yeah, that's unusual,' Mendoza agreed. She turned to Barnes and gave him a quick smile. 'Thanks for your help. We can take this from here.'

Barnes paused, then reluctantly left the room, the door clicking shut behind him. A chair had been positioned next to the window. Winter walked over and sat down on it. He was almost the same height as Amelia, so what he was seeing would tally with what she would have seen. From this angle, he could see the cemetery curving gently down into the distance, and he could see Main running from north to south.

The chair was far enough from the window to make it difficult for anyone passing by to see him. The only way that would happen was if someone was looking directly at the window, and even then it wouldn't be easy.

Mendoza had put her rubber gloves back on and was going through the closet. Winter tuned her out, shut his eyes, and started running scenarios in his head. He could imagine Amelia sitting here in the dark, watching the street. She would have seen him walking back from Granville Clarke's house. She would have seen him pick the padlock on the cemetery gate and disappear into the graveyard shadows. And she would have seen him reappear and walk across the street. She would have heard Barnes letting him into the guesthouse. Then she would have waited until she was sure he would be asleep before breaking into his room.

'What are you thinking?' Mendoza asked.

'I'm thinking that she has the patience of a saint. After breaking into my room she wasn't in any hurry to escape. Instead, she waited until morning then calmly checked out.'

'Isn't that risky?'

'Yes, but whichever way she'd chosen to play this there would have been a risk involved. If she'd sneaked away in the middle of the night, either you or Barnes might have heard her leave and gone to investigate. That would have looked suspicious. Alternatively, she stays until morning and leaves first thing, but what if I'd woken up and managed to raise the alarm before she could get away?'

'Or I might have found you earlier than I did. It still seems like a massive risk to me. And for what?'

'But that's one of the things that defines her, Mendoza.

She's a risk taker. Look at Omar's murder. She killed him in cold blood then calmly walked off into the night. There were massive risks involved, but she did it anyway, and the reason she did it is because beating the odds gets her blood pumping. She gets a buzz from it. That said, the risks she takes are calculated ones. They might seem extreme to you and me, but she's weighed the situation up carefully before acting. And so far, so good. We haven't caught her yet.'

'*Yet.*'

Winter nodded. 'Right now she's riding her luck. The problem with that is there's no such thing as luck. That's how we're going to catch her. She's gotten away with it so far and that's going to make her overconfident. Eventually she's going to fall down, and when that happens we'll be there to catch her.'

'Let's hope you're right.'

Winter nodded towards the closet. 'Anything?'

'Not a damn thing. It's like she was never here.'

'Her suitcase would have contained all the things she needed for her visit to my room last night. The handcuffs, her disguise. There would also have been some sort of padding to stop any rattles, a large bath towel, something like that. She didn't need anything else. If Barnes had carried the case upstairs he would have noticed that it was too light.'

Winter stood up and glanced around the room. It looked like a thousand other rooms he'd stayed in. Tidy enough, but completely lacking any sort of personality. The Gideon Bible suddenly registered as an anomaly. Most rooms he'd stayed in had one, but they were usually hidden away in the top drawer of the nightstand. This one was sitting on top of the dresser.

He went over, picked it up and flicked through the pages. Something fell out and landed on the carpet. He crouched down to get a closer look. It was a ripped-out page that had been folded into eighths.

'I've got something here,' he called out.

Mendoza came over and knelt beside him. She picked it up with her gloved hand and unfolded it carefully. Wrapped inside was a clump of hair that had been torn out at the roots. The hair was grey and long. She put the hair into an envelope sealed it, then flattened out the page and placed it on the dresser. Three verses from Exodus 21 had been circled in red.

But if there is serious injury, you are to take life for life, eye for eye, tooth for tooth, hand for hand, foot for foot, burn for burn, wound for wound, bruise for bruise.

'Revenge, Old Testament style,' Winter suggested.

'That's what I'm thinking.' Mendoza gestured towards the envelope. 'You think they're still alive?'

'I'm guessing that they were alive when that clump of hair was ripped out, but further than that I can't say.' Winter fell silent for a moment, pieces of the puzzle tumbling around in his head. 'Who does the hair belong to? That's got to be the first question.'

'Judging by the length and the colour, an older woman.'

'Except when you factor in question two that answer just looks plain wrong.'

Mendoza raised an eyebrow. 'Question two?'

'Who does she want to get revenge on?'

'Whoever gave her the cigarette burns you mentioned, would be my guess.'

'And that would be her father. Eugene Price.' Winter fell

silent, thinking things through. 'They're wrong,' he said softly.

'Who's wrong?'

'Everyone. Nelson Price didn't kill his father. If anyone killed him, it was Amelia.'

Mendoza was nodding. 'And that "if" brings us back to one of our earlier questions: is Eugene alive or dead?'

'One thing's for sure: if the length of those hairs is anything to go by, he didn't die the night the Reeds were murdered.'

'Jesus,' Mendoza whispered. 'For his sake it might be for the best if he is dead. If he's still alive, then Amelia has had six years to make him pay for what he did to her. That one doesn't bear thinking about.'

34

The first thing Winter did when they got outside was light a cigarette. He'd missed his morning hit of caffeine but at least he could get some nicotine into his system. Mendoza was on her cell trying to arrange for someone from the Monroe County Sheriff's Department to pick up the evidence that she'd collected. Winter could only hear one side of the conversation, but that was enough for him to conclude that this was turning into a logistical nightmare. She hung up and swore at the phone.

'Problem?'

'They're still tied up with this emergency they've got going on, so they can't send anyone over to Hartwood to pick up the envelopes. And we need to get over to the Price place, so we don't have time to detour via Rochester. They said they might send someone to meet us there. Then again, they might not. It depends on how things pan out.'

'You're stressing about nothing, Mendoza. If you're not careful you're going to get wrinkles.'

'This isn't nothing, Winter. We need to know if that hair came from Eugene Price.'

'It came from him.'

'You *suspect* it came from him, which is a completely different thing. Also we might be able to use the room key to get a positive ID on Amelia.'

'It was Amelia. No doubt about it.'

'No Winter, you *suspect* it was her. Again, that's a completely different thing.'

She tapped her phone against her chin, then started thumbing the screen.

'Who are you calling now.'

'Hitchin. I want to know what Amelia is driving these days.'

'Good idea. While you're at it, see if there are any cars registered to Nelson, Eugene or Linda Price.'

'Like I haven't already thought of that.'

'Just crossing those T's.' He took a drag on his cigarette. 'Tell you what, you make your call and I'll drive. We want to get to the Price place as soon as possible, right?'

Mendoza made an I-don't-think-so face and shook her head slowly. 'Not going to happen. A couple of minutes won't make any real difference.'

While Mendoza made her call, Winter took out his phone and tried to get hold of Birch. Peterson answered.

'Hartwood PD. How can I help?'

'I need to talk to Chief Birch. Tell him it's Jefferson Winter.'

'He's not here yet.'

'Still at breakfast?'

Peterson didn't respond.

'Maybe you can help. We need someone to go over to the Price house and secure it for us. It's a crime scene.'

'I don't know if I can do that.'

'Sure you can. Just jump into the PD's beaten up old Crown Victoria and head on out there.'

'I'll need to run this by Chief Birch.'

'Do what you need to do, but make sure you get there sooner rather than later. No one goes in or out of that house until we get there. Understand? If you do happen to see Amelia Price be careful. She's armed and dangerous.'

Winter hung up then stubbed out his cigarette and got into the BMW. Mendoza was behind the wheel, the engine running.

'We need to swing by the diner so I can tell Clarke that we'll meet him later,' Winter told her.

'That's what cell phones were invented for.'

'I also need coffee.'

'No, what we need to do is to get over to the Price place.'

Winter grinned. 'A couple of minutes won't make any real difference.'

The journey to the diner took them past the *Gazette*'s office and the police department's station house. It was another glorious fall day. Mendoza found a parking space and told him to be quick. Winter got out and jogged over to the diner.

He opened the door, then stood in the doorway searching for Clarke. He started at the window seat and worked his way counterclockwise around the room. Like yesterday, everyone turned and stared at him. By the time he'd finished his sweep of the room, everyone had gone back to their own business again.

No sign of Clarke.

He headed across to the counter. Violet broke off from what she was doing and came over. Today she offered him a real smile, which probably had everything to do with the tip he'd left yesterday.

'I need a coffee to go,' he said. 'Also, I'm supposed to be meeting Granville Clarke here. Has he been in yet?'

Violet shook her head and started pouring. 'Not yet. Sorry, hon.'

'What time does he usually get here?'

'Normally he's an early bird. It's not unusual for him to be waiting at the door when we open up. That said, he can turn up any time through until about ten. The actual time depends on how well he's slept the night before.'

Winter pulled out his cell phone and the note that Clarke had given him yesterday. He punched in the *Gazette*'s number. A dozen rings then it went through to the answer machine. The message was delivered by a woman, the accent local, and Winter would have bet everything he owned that he was listening to the ghost-voice of Clarke's dead wife. He hung up without leaving a message, then punched in Clarke's home number. Eight rings before the answering machine kicked in. The voice was the same, the message similar: there was nobody around to take the call, please leave a message after the tone. He hung up.

'He's not picking up.'

Violet frowned at Winter and shrugged. 'Granville's getting on in years. Maybe he didn't hear it.'

'Maybe.'

Violet gave him a worried look. 'Is everything okay, hon?'

'I hope so. If you see him could you please ask him to call Jefferson Winter.'

'Sure, and when you get hold of him, tell him to call me.'

Winter sugared his coffee, paid for it, then hurried back

to the BMW. He opened the passenger door, leant across the seat and put the cardboard cup into the holder.

'What's up?' Mendoza asked him.

'Clarke hasn't been seen today. I need to head over to the *Gazette* office and see if he's there.'

'No, we need to head on out to the Price place.'

'It'll only take a minute.'

'No, Winter. No more minutes.'

'Come on Mendoza, you're a cop. If Amelia's clever enough to break into my room in the middle of the night, she's clever enough to work out who we've been talking to. You saw what she did to Omar, and he was a damn sight younger and fitter than Clarke.'

Mendoza shook her head then sighed. 'Okay, go, but be quick.'

Winter slammed the car door shut and jogged along Main to the *Gazette* office. A light was burning on the second floor and the door was unlocked. Not a good sign. If the lights were on and the door unlocked then Clarke was here, and if that was the case then why the hell hadn't he answered the phone? He tried to open the door but it was stiff and wouldn't budge. He banged the sweet spot at the top and tried again. This time it screeched open.

He went inside and turned the lights on. The reception area looked as abandoned as he remembered. The whole place was eerily silent. All Winter could hear was his breathing. The soft drag of each inhalation, the gentle rasp of every exhalation. He could sense his diaphragm pulling down to create a vacuum in his lungs, and he could imagine the air molecules rushing in to fill the void. A sense of unease crowded around him. The feeling was similar to the one he got when he walked into a murder house. The prickling in his scalp, the heavy, acidic swirl in his stomach.

He climbed the stairs to the second floor and stopped outside the door to Clarke's office. This was the most obvious place for him to keep his notebooks. Winter was convinced that he was going to open the door and find Clarke lying dead on the floor. He took a deep breath and opened the door. There was no sign of Clarke. He stepped inside, glanced around. The blinds were up and the sun was pouring in. The peace lily sat still and silent, glowing in a patch of perfect light.

He left the office and went back downstairs. Instead of going into the reception area, he followed the narrow corridor that led to the records room. He turned a corner and saw a faint glow sneaking from under a door. He reached for the handle, hesitated for a second, then pushed the door open and went inside.

The back wall was lined with bookshelves that held the leather-bound back issues of the *Gazette*. The older editions were on the bottom shelves. Tall and tatty and timeworn. And thin, because the newspaper had been a broadsheet back then. It had become a tabloid some time during the nineties and, from that point on, the books were fatter and squatter. In the middle of the room was a large table with one of the newer tabloid-sized ledgers sitting open on it.

And lying on the floor beside the table was the lifeless body of Granville Clarke.

35

Winter crouched down and pressed his fingers against Clarke's neck, searching for a pulse. Nothing. His skin was cold, his face bloodless. Those rheumy blue eyes that had been so alive and full of stories were staring blankly at the ceiling. Winter straightened up and stepped back into the doorway so he could get a different perspective. The scene was peaceful. There were no signs of a struggle. Clarke was lying sprawled out in a way that was natural rather than posed. One second he'd been upright, the next he was down on the ground, dead. Whatever happened, it had happened quickly.

Winter knelt beside the body and lifted the arms one at a time, testing for rigor mortis. There was some stiffness. At a rough guess he'd been dead for six hours. Full rigor mortis occurred after twelve hours and things hadn't progressed that far yet. It was nine-thirty now, so he'd died sometime around three-thirty this morning. Which was around the time he'd been speaking to Amelia. On the slim chance that he was wrong about this being natural causes, that gave her a potential alibi.

He took out his cell phone and checked the call log. The missed call from Clarke had come in at ten after three. His last conversation had been with a machine and that didn't seem right. Even though logic dictated that death was the end of everything, Winter wondered if he might be wrong about that. Maybe there was a hereafter, and maybe Clarke was there now, reunited with Jocelyn. Maybe, but Winter wasn't convinced. When Jim Morrison sang that this is the end, he'd been bang on the money. There were few happy-ever-afters in this world, so what was the chance of getting a happy hereafter?

The sound of Mendoza yelling pulled him from his thoughts. Judging by the choice of words, and the timbre of her voice, she was standing at the bottom of the stairs shouting up to the second floor.

'What the hell are you doing up there, Winter! Your minute's up. We need to get going.'

'I'm in the records room,' he called back.

Footsteps in the corridor. Cursing and questions. The footsteps stopped in the doorway. So did the cursing and the questions.

'It's natural causes, in case you're wondering,' he told her. 'My guess is a heart attack or a stroke.'

Mendoza was looking around the room, taking it all in. 'You sure about that? There's no way it could have been Amelia?'

Winter shook his head. 'Griffin will need to confirm the time of death, but if my estimate's right then Amelia was with me when this happened. That aside, the sense of drama's missing. Look what she did to Omar. That wasn't just a murder, it was a statement. What statement is being made here?'

Mendoza took another look around the room, then nodded down at the body. 'We still need to call this in.'

'We do.'

'You really liked the old guy, didn't you?'

'Yes I did.'

Clarke's notepad was lying on the table next to one of the ledgers. Winter picked it up and flicked through it. The pad contained page after page of shorthand, but without Clarke it was no use to them. Given enough time Winter reckoned he might have been able to decipher the symbols. Maybe. The problem was that Clarke had been a journalist for most of his life. Over the decades he would have developed his own form of code, and the chances were those symbols wouldn't have made sense to anyone except him.

'Looks like Greek to me,' Mendoza said at his shoulder. 'Does it mean anything to you?'

'Unfortunately no.'

He put the notepad back on the table and looked down at the ledger. It was open to the front page of the edition that had come out the week after the Reed murders. He scanned the lead story. There were two main differences between this story and the one that had appeared the previous week. First, it was more detailed. There was less speculation and more fact. The prose had been calmed down, too, and was less inflammatory. The second difference was that Nelson Price had been mentioned in connection with the crime.

'Anything interesting?' Mendoza asked.

'Only that it's like I thought, the Reed murders happened right on the paper's deadline. It might have even happened close enough to the deadline for Clarke to stop the presses. A story this big in a place this small, it would merit that. If he was that close to the deadline, it would explain why there was no mention of Nelson Price in the original story.

Everything would have been chaos when the crime occurred and Clarke would have been battling to discern fact from fiction. Chances were that he knew Nelson did it but didn't have enough time to get confirmation.'

Winter turned the page and felt the air catch in his lungs. Amelia Price was staring back at him from an old black-and-white high school photo. This was her in her natural form. No wigs, no contact lenses, no disguises. Her hair was a light colour that brought to mind Clarke saying that she had mousy brown hair. As for her eyes, it was impossible to tell. Maybe they were blue like her father's, but they could just as easily be brown or green.

'What?' said Mendoza.

Winter tapped the picture. 'You wanted irrefutable proof that Amelia Price is our mystery woman? There's your proof.'

36

It was after ten by the time Peterson arrived to process Granville Clarke's death. Birch was nowhere to be seen. According to the deputy, Birch had insisted on heading over to the Price house to secure the scene, which led Winter to wonder why. Perhaps Birch saw himself stopping Amelia single handed. If that was the case then he was going to be seriously disappointed. Amelia wouldn't be going anywhere near her old home today. Then again, that was probably a blessing. If Birch tried to arrest her he'd probably end up as dead as Omar.

Mendoza tapped Winter on the shoulder. 'We need to get going.'

Winter took one last look at Clarke then headed for the door. Leaving him in Peterson's hands felt like a betrayal, but Mendoza was right. Fifteen minutes later they arrived at the Price's house. Mendoza parked in the same spot as yesterday and reached over to open the glove box. She removed the yellow rubber gloves she'd got from Jerry Barnes and held a pair out to Winter.

'Do I have to? They make my hands sweat.'

'The alternative is that you stay here in the car and I go in alone.'

Winter gave her a pleading look and she shook her head.

'Okay, give me the damn gloves.'

She handed them over and he put them on and they got out of the car. Their doors closed one after the other in quick succession. *Bang bang.* There was no sign of Birch. No sign of the Hartwood PD's battered old police cruiser.

'So much for Birch securing the scene,' said Mendoza. 'Do you think he stopped off somewhere for doughnuts?'

'That would be my guess.'

Winter stood next to the car, waiting for something to happen, but nothing did. No lights came on, and Amelia didn't come screaming out on to the porch waving a gun at them. The house looked as still and deserted as it had done when they were here last. Mendoza took her cell phone out and called the sheriff's department again. Winter was able to hear enough to get the gist of the conversation. The standoff was over and the kid was okay. Unfortunately, the father was, too. Mendoza hung up with a promise that they were going to get someone over to the Price place as soon as possible.

'Did you get all that?' she asked as she put her cell away.

'It sounded like you were getting palmed off.'

'Yeah, that's my take. You can't blame them, though. I'm sure they've got better things to do than look into a six-year-old murder case that they've already signed off on.' She added a brisk 'Shall we?' then walked off towards the house without waiting for a reply.

Winter caught up with her at the bottom of the porch steps and they climbed them one at a time again. This time he went first. Mendoza caught up with him at the door and knocked hard. She stepped back and waited. No response. The house was so quiet Winter was beginning to wonder when it had last been inhabited. A year ago? Six years?

Mendoza stepped forward and thumped the door again. *Bang bang bang.* She hit it even harder this time, hard enough for the vibrations to rattle through the brittle porch floor and into their feet. He stepped back and they waited some more.

Still nothing.

'Looks like no one's in again,' Mendoza said.

'Looks that way.'

Winter removed his right glove and stuffed it into his jacket pocket, then took out the leather wrap containing his lock picks and held it up for Mendoza to see. She nodded for him to go ahead and he went to work. The lock was old and stiff and in need of oil, and it took a bit of persuasion, but he got there in the end. He put the picks away, pulled the glove back on, then opened the door and motioned for her to go in. Mendoza didn't move.

'When we arrived we found the door open,' she told him. 'Amelia Price was supposed to be in, but she wasn't answering. Naturally, we were concerned about her safety so we went inside to make sure she was all right. How does that sound?'

'It sounds like you're a natural born storyteller.'

'I'm serious, Winter. I'm a cop. I can't just break into someone's home.'

'Technically, I'm the one who's broken in so you're off the hook.'

She gave him a look that said she wasn't convinced, then followed him through the door. The inside of the house was as tired and old as the wood stretching around the outside of the building. It smelled stale, like all the air had been used up long ago. The carpets were threadbare, the wall coverings jaded. There were dark rectangular marks on the walls where pictures had once hung.

Four doors led off the hall and a flight of stairs disappeared up into the gloom. The first door they tried opened into the dining room. Winter went in first. Behind him, Mendoza let out a whispered elongated 'Shit'. Winter knew exactly where she was coming from.

The first thing that caught his eye was the table. Like the table at the Reed's house, it was big enough for four. For some reason, though, it had been laid for two. The white tablecloth had turned grey with age, as had the napkins. The place mats had faded from red to pink. There were wine glasses and water tumblers, and silverware for three courses. Starter, main, dessert. A three-arm candelabra sat in the mid-point between the two place settings. There was melted wax around the bases of the red candles. All three had blackened wicks. Everything was covered with a layer of dust and cobwebs. Six years' worth, at a guess.

The second thing that caught his eye was the portable record player on the credenza. It was covered in red vinyl and looked like it dated back to the sixties. Winter walked over to get a better look. The LP on the turntable was old. Strauss performed by the Vienna Philharmonic Orchestra. He picked it up, blew the dust away, put it back down. Then he turned the record player on and placed the needle at the start of the disk. The gloves made this tricky but he got there in the end. There was a series of crackles then the unmistakeable sound of the *Blue Danube* filled the room.

Mendoza appeared at his shoulder. 'That thing looks ancient. I'm surprised it still works.'

'I'm not.' He lifted the needle up and turned the record player off.

Mendoza nodded towards the table. 'Why are there only two places set? Why not four?'

'A better question is who are those places set for?'

'Mom and dad?'

'I don't think so. The mom would have been long dead before this table was laid. I'm thinking it's for Amelia and her father.'

'This would have been before Nelson died. So where did he eat?'

Winter shrugged.

'What are you thinking?'

'I'm thinking that we've got one very screwed-up family here. An abusive father, a mother who hung herself in the barn, a son who brutally murdered two innocent people, and a daughter who stood by watching while it happened.'

'And turned into a killer herself. Let's not forget that.'

Winter nodded. 'Okay, let's back up a second. One day, the Prices ups sticks and move to Hartwood. Why? What does this place offer?'

'Anonymity.'

'Exactly. According to both Clarke and Hailey Reed, the Prices kept to themselves. Nobody really knew them. Remember what Hailey said about Nelson and Amelia. She described them as ghosts. So where did they come from? And why did they move? In this case the why is easier than the where. If they changed their names, which is a distinct possibility, then that's going to make it harder to work out where they came from.'

Winter paused for a second then added, 'The reason they moved here is because life became uncomfortable for Eugene Price. Maybe the kids were turning up to school with bruises and questions were being asked. Maybe the mother walked into one door too many.'

'So they move here,' continued Mendoza, 'a smallholding in the middle of nowhere, and Eugene wises up and makes sure the bruises don't show. The abuse gets worse because that's the way it works.'

'And the mother is the first casualty,' Winter added. 'Maybe Eugene murdered her or maybe it was suicide. Whichever way it played out the end result was the same. And who becomes the substitute mother and wife? Amelia does. She more or less told me as much last night. We were talking about why she'd set the table after the Reed murders and she said that she got to "play mother". At the time I thought she was making a joke, but I think she was being literal. She didn't just play mother, there were times when she *became* her mother.'

Winter fell quiet again, thinking this over, rearranging the pieces in his head. He glanced over at the table and saw the ghostly figures of Amelia and her father sitting down to eat. Amelia was dressed in clothes that were a couple of sizes too big and a couple of decades too old for her, clothes that had once belonged to her mother. She was awkwardly filling the space in their lives that had been created when her mother died. Strauss was playing gently in the background, creating an illusion of civility that was light years from the truth.

'After the mother hung herself, that's when Amelia's nightmare really began. However bad it had been for her mother, it would have been infinitely worse for Amelia since she would have been dealing with the fallout from her mother's death. Eugene Price needed someone to blame, and that someone was Amelia. Every time he looked at her he would have been reminded of what happened. He would have been filled with guilt, hate and self-loathing, and Amelia would have borne the brunt.'

'And she was just a kid.' Mendoza was shaking her head. 'You know something, Winter? I could almost feel sorry for her.'

37

Winter lifted the tablecloth with a gloved finger and checked under the dinner table. Nothing but floorboards and dust. He let the tablecloth drop back into place and straightened up. Mendoza was walking around the room, looking but not touching.

'Amelia was obviously mentally stronger than her mother,' she said. 'So instead of killing herself, she killed her father. But she didn't do it straightaway. If the length of the hairs we found back in the guesthouse are anything to go by, then she kept him alive for years before she did it.' She stopped walking and turned to face Winter. 'Assuming, of course, that he's dead. So what do you reckon: alive or dead? I'm thinking dead.'

Winter nodded. 'I think so too. Omar's murder proves that. For years she flies under the radar, then suddenly changes her MO and actually goes out of her way to get noticed. A change like that, there's got to be a trigger. The death of her father would do it.'

'You're frowning. What's the problem?'

'The problem is that the chronology doesn't work. Amelia claimed that Omar was the first person she'd killed. Before you say anything, I don't think she was lying. Nor am I over-analysing the situation.'

Mendoza gave him a cynical look.

'She wasn't lying, Mendoza.'

'You're words are saying one thing and you're body language is saying something different.'

Winter sighed. 'Okay, before I talked to her last night I'd come to the conclusion that she must have killed before.'

'And maybe you were right about that.'

'Except I'm trained to tell when someone is lying to me, and she wasn't lying.'

'And that lie detector of yours is one hundred per cent accurate? I don't think so. We know she likes to play games, Winter. That's all that's going on here. She's trying to mess with your head. What's more, it's working. Anyway, what does it matter if she's killed one person or two? The fact is she's a murderer. That's all I need to know.'

'It matters.'

'If you say so. Okay, moving on. The one thing we can be certain of is that she kept him alive for a very long time. In which case the question we should really be asking ourselves is where she kept him locked up. The cellar would be my first choice.'

'Mine, too.'

They left the dining room and tried the next door along. This one led to the living room. Like the dining room, it looked as though nobody had been in there for years. The next door they tried opened on to the kitchen. It was clean and tidy. Plates, bowls, pans and flatware neatly put away in cupboards and drawers. The tiled floor was scrubbed to a high sheen, as were the work surfaces. All the appliances were clean, too, the metal gleaming.

'This I wasn't expecting,' said Mendoza.

Winter opened the refrigerator and peered inside. No junk, just healthy options. Fruit, yogurt, salad vegetables, fresh juice. One shelf was taken up with low-fat microwave meals, the packets piled neatly on top of one another. He opened the milk and sniffed it, then checked the vegetables in the bottom drawer. Everything was relatively fresh, bought within the last week or so.

'She cooks here,' Winter called over his shoulder. He picked up a tomato, ate it in two bites, then picked up another.

'What the hell are you doing?'

'I missed breakfast, remember. All I've had today is a candy bar.'

'And you're kind of missing the point. As usual.'

Winter smiled and took a bite out of the tomato, leaving Mendoza shaking her head. He finished eating then carried on searching the kitchen. The second drawer he looked in contained tablecloths. The difference between these and the one in the dining room was that these were clean and dust-free, smaller too. The next drawer contained candles and place mats.

'Weird,' Mendoza said at his shoulder.

'Not really. I think that Amelia is still playing mother. At least she was until her father died.'

'Maybe she still is.'

Mendoza's comment sparked an image of Amelia sitting down at a table neatly set for two, something healthy on her plate. He could hear an orchestra playing, and he could see her lifting her glass in a toast to the empty chair opposite. Alone but alive.

218

'These tablecloths are smaller. They'd be more appropriate for a two-set table.'

'You think that they were still eating their meals together after she imprisoned him.'

'It's possible.'

'Weird,' Mendoza said again.

The door at the far side of the kitchen led down into the cellar. Mendoza and Winter peered into the darkness, neither one in a hurry to cross the threshold. Winter leant forward and sniffed the air. 'I don't think Eugene's down there.'

'I'm not smelling anything either.' A pause. 'Unless he's down there, and he's still alive.'

Winter turned on the light and leant through the doorway again. 'Anyone there?' he called out.

No response.

'Satisfied?' he asked.

'Not really.'

Winter led the way, Mendoza trailing two steps behind. The stairs creaked under their weight, but held up okay. The cellar was colder than the kitchen by at least ten degrees. At the bottom he zipped his jacket to the chin and drew his hands back into his sleeves.

The shelves lining two of the walls held enough jars and tins to keep a family fed for a year. And the shelves on the third wall held a variety of items that didn't seem to have anywhere else to go. Mousetraps, a flashlight, empty glass jam jars, a tower of metal dog bowls and a couple of boxes of batteries.

The small freezer was square topped rather than rectangular, presumably because it would have been impossible to get a full-size model through the cellar door. The freezer was filled with TV dinners. Winter lifted two of them out. Macaroni cheese and spaghetti bolognaise. He put them back again.

'Well there's your proof that she kept her father alive. No way would she eat crap like this. If she did she'd be twice the size she is.'

'So where was he kept?'

'Good question.'

Winter spun through a full three hundred and sixty degrees. The cellar was large but it wasn't as big as the footprint of the house. He walked over to the nearest wall and tapped it with his knuckle. It seemed solid enough. He followed the wall, moving counterclockwise, tapping at random intervals.

'What the hell are you doing, Winter?'

'Rooms within rooms. Serial killers love them.'

It took a couple of minutes to do a full circuit of the room. All the walls were solid. He stopped by the freezer. 'Okay, let's take a look upstairs.'

They headed back up to the kitchen. At the top of the stairs Mendoza turned off the light, closed the door, then they retraced their steps to the hall and climbed the stairs. The first door they tried opened on to a bathroom that was as clean and tidy as the kitchen. The porcelain and fixtures sparkled, the floor tiles were scrubbed. There was plenty of evidence that a woman lived here, and no evidence of a man. No shaving stuff, no cologne, and lots of female-friendly labels on the bottles. The toothbrush was pink. Like Clarke had told them, she lived here alone.

The next two doors led to Amelia's and Nelson's bedrooms. These appeared to have been abandoned long ago as well. They were coated with an accumulation of dust that was best measured in years rather than months. Cobwebs dangled in the high places, dancing in the gentle currents blowing through the doorway.

The rooms were devoid of personality, which, in a weird kind of way, created its own personality. There was nothing to indicate that they'd once been inhabited by a couple of teenagers. No posters, no TV, no games consoles. No CDs, no DVDs, no books. There were no diaries or personal touches of any kind, either. The walls had been painted an off-white that had faded to an unpleasant yellow that reminded Winter of curdled cream.

Thin, scrappy floral drapes hung on the windows in both rooms. The hems were uneven, the hooks were spaced unevenly, and the material looked like it had been given away rather than bought. The bed linen in both rooms was identical: plain cheap white cotton that had faded to grey. There was little life or colour left in the rugs. They were so worn that the brown woven jute backing was showing through.

The only way to tell the rooms apart was by looking in the closets and drawers. The clothes were hand-me-down thrift-store rejects. Cheap and functional, rather than fashionable. Even six years ago these clothes would have been well out of date.

'I can't be sure about this,' said Mendoza, 'but I think Amelia's room was abandoned long before Nelson's. If I'm right about that then there's a good chance she stopped using it when her mother committed suicide.'

'You're thinking that this is another example of her playing mother, aren't you?'

'That's not how I'd put it, but yeah, I'm thinking along those lines.'

Winter nodded. 'You could be right.'

'Unfortunately. It's like I said earlier, I could almost feel sorry for Amelia.'

They left Nelson's room and walked along the corridor to the door at the far end. It was the last room left to search, so by a process of elimination it had to be the master bedroom. Based on what they'd seen so far, Winter was expecting this room to be as clean and tidy as the kitchen and bathroom. This house was an exercise in compartmentalisation. Six years ago, Amelia had closed the doors on the rooms she no longer needed. When those doors had closed, it was as though she was drawing a line in the sand. That was then and this is now.

Winter opened the door.

38

The main bedroom was twenty feet by fifteen feet, and larger than both Amelia's and Nelson's put together. Sharp October sunlight spilled through the windows, cutting bright angles on the wooden floorboards and the bed. There were no drapes, just an empty pole fixed to the wall above the window. The room was nothing like Winter had expected, but at the same time there were no real surprises. He'd expected a functional space, much like the bathroom and the kitchen, and this space definitely ticked that box. Where it differed was the way in which it was functional.

Mendoza stepped into the room, but Winter held back. He needed a moment to get his head around what he was seeing. He'd witnessed his share of the bizarre over the years, and this was definitely bizarre.

The focal point was the wall of tall mirrors. They were attached to the room's longest wall, stretching from one end to the other, twenty feet of glass. The two large spotlights set up in the corners opposite the mirror wouldn't have looked out of place on a fashion shoot or a film set. They were positioned so they shone down on the middle of the room.

A small bookcase sat next to the head of the single bed and a freestanding clothes rail had been positioned near the foot. The placement of the bookcase was odd. Rather than being pushed flat against the wall, it was side-on to the bed so it jutted out into the room. There was no dresser, no closet, none of the things you'd expect to find in a bedroom. Seven naked plastic mannequins stood like sentries in a careful semicircle around the bed. Bald heads, closed mouth, blank staring eyes.

Mendoza walked up to one of the mannequins and started examining it, her eyes moving from its head to its toes. She turned to Winter, a baffled expression on her face. 'How do you even begin to make sense of this?'

'Let's start with the bed.'

She gestured towards the mannequin. 'But these are more interesting.'

'And I'm betting that as a little girl you always ate your meat before your vegetables.'

Mendoza flashed him a brief smile.

'You define a bedroom with the bed,' he went on. 'A big double bed for mom and dad, singles for the kids, and bunks for the twins. Now, a room this big and this bright, surrounded with all of this wood, it makes sense to have a big king-sized bed. Something substantial built from pine or oak. Something that makes a statement and works the space.' He gestured towards the single bed. 'You're not going to have something like that.'

'Amelia slept alone so she didn't need the space. There's no mystery here. You're making a big deal out of nothing.'

'No I'm not. The big deal is that she doesn't view this as a bedroom. You do, because it's on the second floor, and it's in a room next to the other two bedrooms, and it has a bed in it. Ergo, a bedroom.'

'Okay, so what does she view it as?'

Winter circled the room twice, then walked up to the mirrored wall and put his gloved hand on the glass. He tilted his head to the left and looked along the surface of the mirror, tilted it to the right. The mirror was perfectly flat, the joins as good as you were going to get. There wasn't a single smudge, which meant that it had been cleaned recently. And it was probably cleaned regularly, too.

'This was installed professionally, and I'm betting it cost ten times as much as the bed.'

Mendoza came over and stood next to him. She studied her reflection for a moment, then straightened the sunglasses on top of her head and tightened her ponytail.

'*This* defines the room,' he said. 'So, if Amelia doesn't view this as a bedroom what does she view it as? Or let me put it another way. Where have you seen a mirror like this before? The wood floor? Good lighting?'

Mendoza turned in a tight circle, studying the room. 'A dance studio?' Winter nodded and she added, 'Why?'

'Dancing is movement elevated to an art form. She's practising moving.'

'But why would she do that?'

Winter looked at the mannequins, then looked back at the mirror. Mannequins, mirror, mannequins, mirror. He shut his eyes and imagined Amelia was in here. Perhaps she was wearing the platinum-blonde wig, or maybe the black pixie wig she'd worn when she checked in to Myrtle House. The one thing he was certain of was that she wouldn't have her own hair showing. He imagined her parading up and down in front of the mirrors, and asked himself why she'd do that. What was she trying to achieve? The reason wasn't vanity.

She wasn't parading for gratification, she was parading for a purpose. But what was that purpose?

Because the room was so sparse, it held little in the way of clues. This was Amelia's sanctuary, the place she felt safe, yet there was no real sense of her personality here. The spartan feel of the room reminded Winter of the bedrooms further along the hall. It also reminded him of a monk's cell. This was somewhere you came to reflect and think and get away from the distractions of the world. It was a place where the ego had been stripped completely away and left at the door.

But when the ego was erased, what did that leave?

Winter glanced over at the nearest mannequin and had a partial answer. Strip away the ego and you were left with a blank canvas. Like a mannequin. And what did you do with mannequins? You dressed them up and created snapshot personalities for them, and you posed them in shop windows in order to tell a story.

'So what story are you trying to tell me?' he whispered, echoing the question Clarke had asked last night. He looked over at the mannequins, a quick glance for each one, and the question in his mind changed subtly, singular becoming plural. 'What *stories* are you trying to tell?'

He did another slow circuit of the room and stopped at the clothes rail. Empty hangers were interspersed amongst the ones that held clothes. They jagged out at odd angles, like someone had left in a hurry grabbing the first thing that came to hand. He ran a gloved hand across the clothes, rattling the hangers and making the fabric shift and shiver.

There was a pale pink dress, a black leather skirt, low-cut tops, T-shirts, a couple of pairs of jeans. Female clothes.

Feminine clothes. A rack beneath the rail held footwear: sandals, pumps, a pair of suede ankle boots. He couldn't see the Converse sneakers she'd had on at the diner, but there was plenty of empty space on the bottom of the rack, so maybe that's what she was currently wearing. The wire basket next to the shoe rack contained underwear that was practical rather than sexy. No lace, just cotton. Winter picked up a bra and read the label. He frowned. What was written there didn't make sense. He picked up another one, read the label, frowned again.

'This can't be right. No way was Amelia a 34C. She was flat chested.'

Mendoza took the bra from him and checked the label. She glanced down into the basket. 'They're all the same size,' she confirmed. 'So what? She strapped her breasts down?'

Winter closed his eyes and pictured Amelia in the diner. Then he pictured her in his bedroom last night. He opened his eyes and glanced over at the clothes rail and another piece of the puzzle dropped into place.

'I assumed she was flat chested because she's so thin, but I was wrong. That's the reason she was wearing a leather jacket that was a couple of sizes too big. She was disguising her real shape.' He nodded towards the clothes rail. 'She clearly likes to dress in feminine clothes, yet both times I've seen her she was dressed more like a man. And on both occasions she was wearing the exact same clothes. Same sneakers, same leather jacket, same jeans.'

'And that's significant?'

Winter smiled for the first time since entering the house. 'Damn right. She's wearing fancy dress.'

Mendoza moved next to him and pushed aside the clothes on the rail with a gloved finger. 'What? Like Halloween?'

'Exactly like Halloween. If you want to dress up as Dracula you go to a fancy-dress shop and they'll give you a black cape with a red silk lining, a fancy waistcoat, and a set of pointy plastic teeth. You put those on, you become Dracula for the night. So Amelia puts on a wig and inserts her coloured contact lenses and puts on her jeans and sneakers and that baggy leather jacket, and she becomes a completely different person. I bet that if you looked under the jacket, you'd find that she was wearing the same jumper and top on both nights, because that's how she designed the disguise.'

Mendoza nodded slowly then walked over to the nearest mannequin. 'Okay, moving on to these. There must be a reason why they're arranged like this. They were the last thing she saw before she went to sleep, and the first thing she saw when she woke up. That means they're important to her. The way they're positioned around the bed, it's almost like they're guarding her while she's asleep. Although, how that might work, I've got no idea. Any normal person trying to sleep here would end up having nightmares.'

Winter walked over to the bed and sat down, looking for a different perspective. Finding it. He shook his head. 'They're not guarding her. If they were, their eyes would all be aimed towards the pillow. Three of them aren't even looking at the bed.' He did a slow sweep from left to right, taking in the mannequins one at a time, and saw something that made him smile. 'Come over here a second. I want you to take another look at the mannequins and tell me what connects them.'

Mendoza sat down next to him, her gaze falling on each

mannequin in turn. Winter could tell by her expression that she just wasn't getting it. And then she did.

'The body shapes are identical,' she said. '34C right?'

Winter stood up and pointed a yellow glove finger at the nearest mannequin. '*This* is what Amelia looks like.'

'That still doesn't explain why they're arranged like this.'

Winter did a slow circuit of the room. As he walked, he tried to imagine himself into Amelia's shoes. He could see her in the baggy leather jacket, jeans and sneakers, posing in front of the mirror, examining the way she moved, the way she carried herself, the way she gestured, imagining that she had become another person.

'The outfit she wore at the diner doesn't belong on the clothes rail,' he said finally. 'It's too precious for that. Too *special*. She puts it on display where she can see it. That's why the mannequins are positioned this way. They're not watching her. She's watching them. She dresses them up in her special clothes then lies in bed admiring them.'

'And the reason she has seven mannequins is because the outfit you saw her in last night isn't her only disguise. She actually has seven of them.'

'Something else we need to bear in mind here is that these are more than just disguises, Mendoza, they're personalities for her to inhabit. It's like a little girl playing dressing-up, but taken to its ultimate conclusion. She's not just trying to look the part, she wants to *own* that part. To be that person.'

'Like a method actor?'

'Yeah, just like a method actor.'

Winter crouched down in front of the empty bookcase. There were a number of odd things about the picture being

229

presented here, but this was perhaps the most incongruous. In its own way, it was even odder than the mannequins. At least with those, he could see a reason for them being here. This bookcase he couldn't see any reason for whatsoever.

He leaned in closer to get a better look. It was three feet high and made from pine. Solid wood rather than laminate. This wasn't a cheap flat-pack piece of furniture, it had been handmade. Someone had spent time building this. They'd cut the wood, sanded it and assembled it. And they'd taken pride in how the end result turned out. He ran a finger over the shelves. No dust. The small dark rectangular patch on the top was roughly six inches by four inches. Over the years the sun had faded the wood, but it hadn't touched this part. Clearly something had been covering it, but what?

'What's this bookcase all about?' Winter asked. 'Because it sure as hell wasn't used for keeping books on.'

'Maybe there was nothing on it.'

'No way. Everything in this room is here for a reason. If it wasn't being used, it wouldn't be here.'

Winter took a step back and studied the bookcase for a moment. Then he moved to the bed and lay down. From this angle the top shelf was at eye level. The bookcase was close enough to reach out and touch. Whatever this was for, it was important enough for Amelia to want to keep it close. And, like the mannequins, it was important enough for it to be the last thing she saw before she went to sleep. Mendoza came over to join him. She batted his feet away to make a space and sat down at the end of the bed. She studied the bookcase for a moment, eyes moving from top to bottom.

'This looks old. It also looks more like the sort of thing

you'd find in a kids' room.' She pointed to the dark patch of wood on the top of the bookcase. 'What do you think caused this?'

'No idea, but whatever it was, it was important enough to have pride of place.'

Winter stood up, went back over to the rail and ran a gloved hand over the clothes. The house was cool but his hands were sweating inside the rubber. He glanced around the room, his eyes moving from the mirror to the mannequins, then back to the free-standing clothes rail.

'So who exactly are we looking for here?' Mendoza asked him. 'We've come across two versions of her so far. The blonde, and the black-haired woman who checked in to the guesthouse. But what about the other five? Because that's the problem here, isn't it? We're hunting a chameleon.' She paused. 'You know something? It's a shame that your inner psychopath can't just tell us where she is. That would make life a whole lot easier.'

Winter laughed. 'It would.'

'Well, if he does come up with anything, I want to know about it.'

'I'm hearing you.'

Winter got up and walked over to the window. He looked out at the back yard, and his inner psychopath started shouting.

39

'Mendoza!'

Winter stood staring out the window, not daring to move in case what he was seeing suddenly disappeared. He heard Mendoza's shoes clomping over the wood, then she was standing beside him.

'Do you see it?'

He didn't turn around. He didn't *want* to turn around in case it somehow changed things. Not until he had confirmation that she was seeing this, too.

'See what?'

'The path that's been trodden through the backyard?'

'Of course I see it.'

He jogged from the room and ran down the stairs, his feet thudding on the bare floorboards. Mendoza was yelling after him, demanding answers, but Winter ignored her and kept running. He sprinted along the hallway, pushed through the front door and took the porch steps sideways. He stopped and looked around for the best way to get to the back yard.

Mendoza caught up with him and started to ask something, but he ignored her again and sprinted around the left side of the house to the yard. From down here, it looked even more of a jungle. He didn't even want to guess when it had last been tended to. It was longer than six years, though. He could just about make out the ruined wire and wood of something that might once have been a chicken coop, and a fenced area that might once have been used for growing vegetables. The grass was waist high, and the path that cut a line through it went on for about thirty feet before disappearing into the trees. Mendoza came to a halt beside him, their arms momentarily touching. Winter looked at the path, his eyes tracing the route all the way to the treeline.

'The only reason you make a path, or a road, or an interstate, is because you need to get from A to B. And this path is well trodden, which means that Amelia used it regularly, maybe even every day, so the question I'm asking myself is, why?'

Mendoza moved past him and stood there looking for a moment, her eyes following the same route as his.

'There's no evidence of a dog,' he added. 'So she doesn't come out here to exercise it.'

'What about the bowls in the cellar?'

'Yes, but where were the tins of dog food, the dog basket, the lead and the chew toys? There might have been a dog here once upon a time, but there isn't one here now.'

'Maybe she goes running then? You said she was thin.'

'Maybe, but I don't think so. Judging by the food in her refrigerator her weight is controlled by diet, not exercise.'

'So where does it lead to? If we can work that out, then maybe we'll be able to work out why she needs to use it so regularly?'

'That's what I'm thinking.'

Winter broke into a run again, the grass stems brushing against his jeans. Mendoza was close behind, her stride matching his. They reached the treeline and the day disappeared behind the tangle of high branches. The path snaked from left to right, navigating a course defined by the trees. A couple of hundred yards further on, they came to a small clearing. At first glance, it appeared to be empty. Winter looked around, his eyes tracing a quick counterclockwise circuit around the trees, but he couldn't see where the path started up again.

'Looks like we've found Point B.'

'But there's nothing here.'

'There's something here. We just haven't found it yet.'

Winter stepped into the clearing, back into the October sunlight. He stopped for a second to let his eyes adjust, then carried on walking, looking high, looking low, searching. The path suddenly stopped a part of the way into the clearing. He glanced down. Smiled. The scattering of leaves at his feet were too ordered to have been blown here.

'Strike that earlier comment. *This* is Point B.'

He crouched down and brushed the leaves away. The ground underneath appeared to be covered in moss. He ran a hand over it. Not moss. It had an artificial felt-like texture. Winter banged down hard with the flat of his hand. A hollow wooden echo rang back. Once he'd brushed the rest of the leaves away it was easy to see the outline of the trapdoor. The hinges were on the left side, and on the right was a gap just big enough for a small hand to get beneath.

He squeezed his fingers into the gap. It was a tight fit, and he could feel the dirt scratching at his skin. He kept pushing until he managed to get a good hold, then heaved the trapdoor open. It went up and over and smacked against the ground, revealing a set of concrete steps leading down into the dark.

'We need to call this in,' said Mendoza.

'And who do we call? Birch? Who knows where he's got to. And Peterson would be no help at all. As for the sheriff's department, I wouldn't hold my breath.'

'Now we've got something solid, that should get them moving.'

'Tell you what. You make your call and I'll go see what's down there.'

Winter moved to the top of the steps and Mendoza laid a firm hand on his shoulder.

'Wait. What if this is some sort of a trap?'

'It's not a trap. Amelia doesn't want to hurt me. I'm too important to whatever game she's playing.'

Mendoza sighed, then tried again. 'She's a psychopath. You can't know what she's thinking.'

'Newsflash, Mendoza: I can.' Winter shrugged her arm away and placed his foot on the first step. He turned to face her and softened his tone. 'It's probably best if you stay up here. If it turns out that this is a trap, then I'm going to need you to come and save my ass.'

'Don't count on it. There's no way I'm going down there without proper backup.'

40

Winter walked down into darkness, the temperature slowly dropping the deeper he went. Up above he could hear Mendoza talking on her cell. Halfway down he removed his rubber gloves and stuffed them into his jacket pocket. Then he took out his Zippo and lit it. The flame danced yellow and red and orange, creating patterns on the whitewashed cinderblock walls. He sniffed the air. It smelled damp and earthy, but underpinning that was the faint smell of decay. By the time he reached the bottom that was all he could smell.

He held his lighter up higher and stepped forward into an empty space that was about five yards wide and four yards long. The floor was rough-cast concrete and the ceiling was concrete, too. Like the stairwell, the walls down here were made from whitewashed cinderblock, There were empty shelves fixed to one wall and an empty gun rack pushed up against another. An old-fashioned gas hurricane lamp hung from a nearby hook. He lit the lamp and put his Zippo away. Then he pulled his rubber gloves back on, lifted the lamp down from the wall and stepped back into the stairwell.

'It's not a trap,' he called up. 'It's an old bomb shelter.'

There was no answer. Maybe Mendoza had heard, maybe she was still on the phone. He moved away from the stairs, the lamp held high. The smell of decay was stronger than ever, but there was no sign of the source. He walked into the middle of the room and the light from the lamp crawled up the end wall. This wall wasn't made from cinderblock. It glittered darkly in the dim light.

He stepped closer and saw that it was made entirely from jars of different shapes and sizes that had been stacked carefully on top of each other. All were filled with some sort of translucent yellow liquid, the colour differing subtly from jar to jar. The overall effect was to create a kind of mosaic. In its own weird way it was really quite beautiful. He bent forward to get a closer look, moved the lamp right up against the jars. Flames played inside the liquid. He tapped one of the jars with his fingernail and a dull *tink* sound whispered through the room.

Winter reached up to the top of the wall and carefully removed a jar. He could see a second jar behind it. As far as he could tell the jars had been arranged to create a wall that was two deep. He took a closer look at the jar in his hand. There was no label but judging by the size and shape he figured it had contained some sort of cook-in sauce. He removed the lid and the unmistakeable smell of ammonia wafted out. Urine.

He stepped back so he could see the whole wall. There had to be hundreds of jars, thousands even, and they were all full. Suddenly it felt much colder in here. He pulled up the zipper on his jacket but it did nothing to alleviate the chill crawling down his spine. He waved the lamp in front of the jars, making the contents shine and glisten and darken. Organised serial criminals loved to make statements because it made the game more exciting. They loved to pose puzzles then watch to see if the cops could solve them. Winter had seen plenty of those puzzles. He'd been presented with plenty of those statements, too. However, if that's what was going on here, this was one of the grander, and stranger, statements he'd come across.

This wall represented hours of painstaking, methodical work. It would have taken time, effort and patience to construct. One jar at a time, one row at a time, the wall slowly climbing higher. Winter leant in close enough for his nose to touch glass and peered through the gaps. Because the jars differed in shape and size all he saw were the ones on the second row.

He knelt down and tried looking lower. Again, all he saw was liquid and glass shining back. He tried a little to the left. Same thing. A little more to the left, and this time he found what he was looking for, a place where the gaps between the two rows lined up. He moved the lamp around to make sure that his eyes weren't playing tricks.

There was a void beyond the wall of jars.

41

'You're sure this isn't a trap?' Mendoza yelled out from the stairwell.

'I'm sure.'

Footsteps on the stairs, footsteps crossing the room. He tore his gaze away from the jars and turned around. Mendoza was standing there holding her cell phone in one gloved hand and her service revolver in the other.

'So where's your backup?'

'The sheriff's department are on their way.'

'But they're not here yet.'

'I couldn't hear you and I got worried, okay? And before you read too much into that. I'm a cop and technically you're a member of the public, therefore it's my duty to protect you.' She nodded towards the wall of jars. 'What the hell is this? And why can I smell a dead body when I can't see one?'

Winter lifted the hurricane lamp up, making the jars sparkle.

'Some sort of coloured water?' she suggested.

'Not exactly. It's urine.'

She stepped back so she could see the wall better. Her eyes scanned from left to right, starting at the top and working downwards. Winter could almost read her thoughts. She'd be counting the jars and calculating how long it would take to fill them all. She pushed her cell into her pocket, but kept the gun out.

'This is really messed up, Winter.'

'It gets worse. The wall is two jars deep.'

'Jesus. So where's the body?'

Winter nodded towards the jars. 'My guess is it's behind here.' She gave him a puzzled look. 'Rooms within rooms,' he reminded her.

She stepped up to the wall and gently tapped one of the jars on the top row, making it wobble. 'I don't think it would take much to bring this whole thing down.'

'Well we'd better be careful then.'

Mendoza caught his meaning and shook her head. 'We need to wait for the sheriff's department before we go back there.'

'Because a sheriff's department out here in the middle of nowhere is going to be better qualified to deal with this than we are. Come on, Mendoza, you know how territorial cops can be. When the sheriff's department gets here we're going to be left sitting on the sideline. Now by my reckoning it'll take about half an hour to get here from Rochester, so we need to hurry. Assuming, of course, that they are actually on their way.'

Mendoza stood there weighing up the pros and cons, her mouth shut tight. She seemed to come to some sort of decision because in the next second she had her gloves off, her cell phone out and she was ushering him out of the way. She started taking photographs from different angles, the small flash cutting through the gloom.

'You get to leave when this is all done,' she told him. 'But I have to deal with the aftermath. There's no way I'm letting you screw up a conviction by moving all of these, not without having some sort of photographic evidence of what we found.'

'Fine, but please be quick.'

Mendoza took one last picture. The cell phone disappeared into her pocket and the rubber gloves went back on. They started in the right-hand corner and quickly got into a rhythm. Winter was able to reach higher, so he lifted the jars down and passed them to Mendoza, who put them in a neat pile against the nearest wall. They stopped a couple of times and tried to look through, but couldn't see anything. Once they'd cleared a two-foot-wide corner from the first layer, they started on the second. Winter stripped the second layer back to eye level then held up the hurricane lamp. Mendoza squeezed in next to him and stood on tiptoes so she could peer over the top. He couldn't see anything at first, but then his eyes started to adjust and he was able to make out vague shapes.

'I think we've just found Eugene Price,' he said.

'At least we now know where the smell is coming from.'

Winter put the lamp down on the floor and reached for another two jars. They worked their way down until the jars were low enough to step over. Mendoza went through first, sideways so she didn't nudge any jars and send them crashing to the floor. Winter passed the lamp through, then followed.

Eugene Price was lying naked on a small single mattress. A thick grey beard covered the lower half of his face, long white hair covered the rest. His skin had blistered and the body had begun to bloat. He was chained to the wall by his left wrist. Judging by the scarring on his other limbs, Amelia had rotated the limb she had used. When his wrist got too raw she would have moved on to a different arm or leg, eventually working her way back to the left wrist.

'Going on the smell, and the state of the body, I'd say he's only been dead for about three days,' Mendoza said.

'Maybe a little longer. It's cold down here. That would slow the rate of decomposition.' Winter became aware of Mendoza watching him and turned to look at her. 'What?'

'Maybe you were right about this being the trigger for Omar's murder. Maybe this is the reason for changing her MO.'

'The timings work, but why New York? And why target me?'

'New York's one of the biggest cities in the world. It's much easier to kill someone there and get away with it.'

'Agreed. But why me? Because that's the question we keep coming back to here.'

Mendoza shrugged and Winter turned his attention back to Eugene. When his heart stopped pumping, gravity had taken over and caused his blood to pool in the parts of his body lowest to the ground, making the skin look bruised. As you looked higher the purples and blacks turned to yellow and grey. The untidy scars that covered his body were more noticeable on the top part where the background was lighter.

'What do you think Amelia used to make these?' Mendoza asked.

'She didn't do this, Eugene did. Can you see how the scarring gets less as you get to the parts that are harder to reach?'

'In which case these weren't done with a knife or a razor blade. If he'd had access to something like that he would have killed himself.' She leant in for a closer look, then suddenly straightened up, a look of horror on her face. 'Jesus, he did them with his fingernails, didn't he?'

'Griffin would need to confirm that, but yeah that's my guess.'

Winter held the lamp up high and moved closer. Eugene's hair and beard was thick and dirty and matted together in clumps, making it impossible to see his face. Griffin would be able to get a match to the hair left in the Bible. He used a gloved finger to move the hair from Eugene's face. Mendoza inhaled sharply and exhaled a breathy 'Holy shit.'

Winter shined the lamp closer. The scarring here was different from the scarring on the rest of his body. It was hard and dark. Melted. The empty eye sockets made him think of black holes. 'Amelia did this. She burned his eyes out with a cigarette.'

Mendoza just stood there staring. 'So what does your inner psychopath have to say about this?'

Winter ignored her and lifted the lamp higher. The small table that had been positioned near the back wall was like a miniature version of the one in the house. White tablecloth, a red place mat, silver flatware. The main difference was that it had been set for one. Because everything was scaled down, there was a single candle in a silver holder instead of a candelabra.

And instead of a record player there was a small portable CD player. Winter hit play and the unmistakeable sound of Strauss's *Blue Danube* filled the air. He looked back at the mattress, saw the scuffmarks on the concrete floor near the top end.

'I know what the dog bowls in the cellar were for.'

Mendoza's head was tick-tocking between the mattress and the table. 'Amelia ate at the table, while Eugene ate from a dog bowl on the floor.'

'Exactly. She heated up one of those TV dinners, scraped it into a dog bowl, then prepared a nice healthy salad for herself. Then she came out here, turned on the CD player and they ate together.'

Empty jars had been piled up in one corner beside a black bucket. Next to the bucket was a urine-stained plastic funnel, and next to that was a cardboard box filled with medical supplies. There were bandages and tubes of antiseptic to dress Eugene's wounds, and packets of over-the-counter painkillers. Winter picked up a small orange medicine tub and looked at the label. A prescription for Vicodin made out to Amelia Price.

He put the pills back in the box and walked over to the mattress. The manacle and chain was attached to a metal plate that had been fixed to the wall. The metal was tarnished and speckled with rust. It looked years old. He knelt down and lifted up the manacled arm. It moved easily, which was to be expected. The effects of rigor mortis were temporary and usually started to wear off after twenty-four hours. The fingers were curled into the palm, the skin felt waxy. He put the arm back down carefully, then stood up and lifted the lamp to eye level. More white cinderblock, but unlike the blank walls on the other side of the glass jars, these ones were decorated with crude childlike paintings. Long sweeping diagrammatic brushstrokes in black and red.

'I should go back up top and update Hitchin,' said Mendoza.

'Yes you should.'

'And you should come with me.'

Winter shook his head and met Mendoza's eye. They stood frozen like that for the best part of ten seconds. It was Mendoza who broke the silence.

'Okay, stay here, but please try not to touch anything.'

42

The sound of Mendoza's footsteps faded into silence, leaving Winter alone with the shadows. He placed the hurricane lamp down beside the body and, for a time, just stood there. This scene was the latest episode in a whole chain of events. The flow of those events had started back at the house and pushed him gradually towards this place. It was almost as though Amelia had taken hold of his hand and led him here.

Except that wasn't quite right, because that chain hadn't started back in the house, it had started when he stepped into a New York diner and watched Amelia stab Omar. It was like a movie. You started at the opening scene, then worked through, moving from frame to frame and scene to scene until you reached the end credits. Except that still wasn't right, he realised. This film would have started with Eugene dying. That was the trigger event.

He reached into his jacket pocket for a Snickers, ripped it open and took a bite. While he ate, he walked over to one of the walls and studied the paintings. The one that caught his eye was easy to interpret. It showed two stick figures positioned side by side. Both had nooses around their necks, and crosses for eyes. The figure on the left was wearing a triangular skirt and was larger than the one on the right. Mother and son.

He stepped back and another picture jumped out at him.

This one had been drawn beside the mattress. Once again, it was easy to interpret. A little girl holding a knife as big as a pirate's sword was standing over a cowering man. Father and daughter. Revenge, Old Testament style.

The position was interesting. Every time the light came on it would have been one of the first things that Eugene Price saw from his mattress. The positioning reminded Winter of the mannequins back in Amelia's room. He started at the mattress and traced a circuit around the room, moving from picture to picture. Some he could interpret, but most he couldn't because there wasn't any context to work with. The stories those pictures told was just too personal. He was able to form an impression of the overall story, though. A tale that began in suffering and ended in redemption.

A small picture of Amelia and her father caught his attention. It was near floor level, hidden away in one corner. Winter crouched down beside it and passed the lamp back and forth, making the picture come to life.

This drawing was more detailed than the others. Instead of sticks, there were fully formed limbs and bodies, and instead of dots for eyes and a line for a mouth there were carefully realised facial features. Amelia was cowering against the headboard of a bed, while Eugene Price loomed over her. There was more detail in the background too. Enough for Winter to be fairly certain that this was the bed from Amelia's childhood room.

There was a small bookcase next to the bed, a ballerina music box sitting on top. Amelia had drawn a couple of crochets and quavers, giving the impression that there was music coming out of it. The music box was clearly a cherished possession from childhood, precious enough for her to have kept it all these years.

The subtext of this picture was as easy to interpret as the one of Nelson and his mother with the nooses around their necks. But how long had the abuse been going on for? Had it started after her mother's suicide, or had it been going on longer? Winter was leaning towards the latter. Amelia was screwed up. No doubt about that. She might even be one of the most screwed-up individuals he'd ever encountered, which was saying something. If she'd had a loving childhood, would she have still ended up a killer, or would her life have taken a different route?

Winter had been battling with the question of nature versus nurture since he was eleven and the FBI had taken his father away. The answer wasn't black or white, it was mired in grey. That was the only conclusion he could allow himself. *We're the same.* The statement contained more truth than he was happy to admit to. There was a reason he was so good at what he did, and that reason had little to do with the training he'd received at Quantico. A part of him understood the monsters he hunted. And that part had been with him for as long as he could remember.

When he was a kid his father had taken him on hunting trips to the forests of Oregon, the same forests that he'd taken his victims to. The difference was that when Winter wasn't around his father had hunted young women instead of deer.

He could clearly remember the first time he killed a deer. He could feel the cool damp bark of the tree that he'd used to support himself. He could smell the soft, moist stench of the forest crowding around him. Electricity was flowing through his veins and his heart was pounding. During their previous trip his father had wanted him to take the shot and he'd purposefully missed. At the last second he had shifted his aim and the deer had run off. His father hadn't said anything, but he'd known. The silent disapproval had somehow been worse than if he'd raged at him. This time it would be different.

So he'd lined up the sight on the deer's body mass, and he'd willed his breathing and heart to settle. The world had shrunk until the deer was the only thing that existed. He'd breathed out one final exhalation, and, as he did so, gently squeezed the trigger. Before the bullet left the barrel he knew the shot was true. In the time it took to finish the exhalation the deer lay dead on the ground.

As natural as breathing.

His father might have taught him the art of killing, but the ability to take a life had come from that part of him that lived to dance with the dark. That said, the crucial difference between them was that he had never killed a person in cold blood. But what would have happened if he'd had a different childhood? If he'd suffered the abuse that Amelia had, what might he have become?

He finished the Snickers, put the empty wrapper into his pocket, then took another look at the wall of jars. Six years was a long time. Working on a year being 365.25 days, you were looking at 2,191.5 days. The average male produced between two and four pints of urine a day, so in six years that added up to anything between 4400 and 8800 pints. The actual amount would be dependent on fluid intake, which worked in Amelia's favour. If she needed more urine all she had to do was make him drink more. He took a closer look at the jars. They were all different sizes, but at a rough guess each one held about a pint.

Assuming Amelia had taken six thousand pints over six years, that would equate to around six thousand jars. Winter didn't think there were that many in the wall, but it couldn't be far off. That meant she'd started collecting the jars near the start of Eugene's incarceration. Every day he would have seen the wall getting higher and that would have been torture in itself. Eventually it would have got to the point where there was just a narrow walkway for Amelia to come and go, but still she collected the jars. She would have piled them up near the gap and Eugene must have known what they were for. As a form of punishment, this was as cruel and unusual as anything Winter had ever seen.

Satisfied that he'd answered the question of *how* she had done this, he moved on to the question of *why*. That one was tougher. Maybe she'd done it for some sort of symbolic reason, or perhaps she'd done it because she thought it looked nice. Serial killers did all sorts of strange things that made sense to them, but would baffle a rational mind. Often the motivation for the behaviour only became clear after they were caught. Winter had a feeling that this was one of those occasions.

He walked back to the corner where Amelia had drawn the picture of herself with her father, sat down on the cold floor and traced her lines with the tip of his gloved figure. He started with the bed, before moving on to Amelia, and finishing with Eugene. He took a closer look at the picture of Amelia and saw that the black marks he'd taken for dirt were actually tears.

Because there was no stave, the musical notes she'd painted made no sense. Even if there had been he doubted it would help. This was figurative rather than literal. Even so, he was interested to know what tune the music box had played.

He leant back against the cold wall and extinguished the lamp. The room disappeared into pitch darkness. Winter waited for his breathing to steady and his heart to slow, just like he had done when he had shot his first deer. When it had, he closed his eyes and thought back to the hours following the Reed murders.

43

'What happened to the light?' Mendoza shouted from the stairs.

'I needed to think,' Winter called back.

He fumbled the Zippo from his pocket and relit the lamp. Footsteps echoed in from the entrance room and a second later Mendoza walked through the gap in the wall of jars. She looked at the body, then cast a quick eye across the room, before finally looking at Winter.

'How long have you been sat down here in the dark for?' she asked as she climbed through the gap.

Winter shrugged. 'A while, I guess.'

'Communing with your inner psychopath again?'

'Something like that.'

'The sheriff's department had another emergency, hence the reason they're not here yet. I didn't even bother asking what, since I'm sceptical there was one. After I told them about Eugene Price it was a totally different story. They've promised to get someone here as soon as possible. What's more, this time I actually believe them. I also managed to get hold of Dr Griffin. When I told her what we'd found she sounded unhealthily interested.'

'There's no such thing.'

'So says the guy who's happy to sit in the dark alongside a corpse with no eyes.'

They started at each for a moment.

'I don't think Amelia blinded her father,' Winter said.

'So who did? We've seen nothing to indicate that she has a partner.'

'No, she's definitely working alone. Eugene blinded himself.'

Mendoza frowned.

'Okay, put yourself in Eugene's position. For six years Amelia tortured him. She kept him chained up in the dark, just like he'd done to her and Nelson, and she made him eat from a dog bowl. When the lights were on, he'd watch her painting pictures on the wall. When the lights went off he would still see those pictures because the images were seared into his memory. Amelia would have noticed the scars appearing on his body. Maybe she started off by suggesting that he scratch his eyes out, and this progressed to her suggesting he burned them out. Six years is a long time, but under these conditions it would seem like an eternity. Eugene would have plenty of time to think things through. He would have been eaten up by the guilt.'

'So he blinded himself out of remorse,' Mendoza finished for him. She shook her head. 'I don't think so.'

'He wouldn't have had to look at the paintings any more.'

'You're just speculating here. You don't have any proof that that's what happened.'

'The eyelids were scarred, but there were no marks on the outer edge of the sockets or the upper cheeks. If someone is trying to take your eye out with a cigarette you're going to struggle.'

'But to burn out your own eyes, Winter.'

'A desperate unhinged person is going to do desperate un-hinged things. You don't need me to tell you that.'

'But his eyes.'

'Okay, think of the worst thing you've ever seen, then tell me I'm wrong.'

Mendoza fell silent for a second. 'Jesus,' she whispered to herself.

'There's more. I think Eugene died of natural causes.'

She laughed at that. 'Winter, there is nothing natural about this situation. Nothing whatsoever.'

'Okay, Amelia is ultimately responsible for killing him. No argument there. But how did he die? He wasn't shot, bludgeoned or stabbed. Yes, he might have been poisoned, and we'll have to wait for the tox screen before we can rule that one out, but I doubt he was. So that leaves natural causes. Because of all the painkillers, my money's on cancer. Towards the end things would have got bad, that's why she got the Vicodin. The over-the-counter pills would have stopped working.'

'And that's significant?'

'Mendoza, everything that happened here was significant. Put yourself in Amelia's shoes. You hate your father more than you hate any other person on the planet, so you lock him away down here and torture him for six years. You tell yourself it's all about revenge, you even go to the trouble of looking up Bible passages to justify your actions, but that's not the real reason.'

'So what's the real reason?'

'Love.'

'Excuse me.'

'Yes, you're a killer, and yes you hate him, but there's a tiny part of you that loves him. That's why you can't take that final step.'

Mendoza walked over to Eugene and looked down at him. Her attention was fixed on the two empty spaces where his eyes had been. She shook her head. 'I don't know, Winter.'

'You had a pretty normal childhood, right? You loved your mom and dad, yet I bet there were times you hated them. Love and hate are not absolutes. They're like yin and yang. Each one contains a little of the other.'

'I'm still not seeing it.'

Winter hesitated, debating whether or not he should go that extra step. 'I hated my father for what he did to me and my mom. I probably hated him as much as Amelia hated her father. But despite everything, there was a part of me that still loved him.'

Mendoza looked at him long and hard. 'Okay, I can see how that might work.'

Winter came over to join her. 'Eugene would have known he was dying. It's like Clarke said, that's going to give you a whole new perspective.'

'And that's when the guilt finally got the better of him. That's the point when he realised that everything he'd done to his family was wrong.'

'He spent more than two thousand days down here. That's a long time. And every day he had to look at those paintings, and fill the jars, and watch the wall getting bigger. When he realised he was dying something flipped inside his head.' Winter paused. 'But it wasn't all about the torture for Amelia. In her own weird way she was looking out for him.

Think about it, he's not malnourished, so she clearly wasn't starving him. You saw all those TV dinners in the freezer, all the food tins in the cellar. Those were for Eugene. The fact that he managed to fill all those thousands of jars is proof that she wasn't denying him water.'

'Which would explain the medicine. It's another example of her looking out for him. She didn't want him to die.'

Winter nodded. 'But there's more to it than that. For the past six years her life here has been defined by her father. Caring for him is a full-time occupation. Amelia had come to need her father as much as he needed her. With him gone, she's been cut adrift. Her father has cast a shadow over the whole of her life. His death has forced her into a position where she needs to completely re-evaluate everything.'

'So how does the thing with the eyes fit into this? Amelia would have had to provide the cigarettes. Doesn't that count as torture?'

'Yes and no. If you view it is an act of atonement then the answer is no. It wouldn't have been enough for Amelia if they'd just kissed and made up. She needed some sort of symbolic act, and that's what happened.'

'So he blinded himself?'

Winter shrugged. 'It's only a theory.'

'It all sounds crazy.'

Winter nodded. 'No arguments there.'

Mendoza looked down at Eugene's bloated body, then stepped back and looked around the room. 'Do you know what this place reminds me of? It's like an Egyptian tomb. You've got the hieroglyphs all over the walls. And you've got the jars, although, these contain bodily fluids rather than his organs. And everything's sealed up like a tomb. What do you think?'

'I think you might be on to something there.'

'And your inner psychopath? What does he say?'

Winter turned to face her and waited until she met his gaze. 'He says that when Eugene Price died he was sorry for what he did. Very sorry. He also says that right now Amelia Price is a very, very angry young woman.'

44

Birch and Peterson were first to arrive. They bounced into the clearing in the Hartwood PD's battered old Crown Victoria and came skidding to a stop beside the BMW. Peterson got out first and slammed his door. The pathetic look of boyish enthusiasm on his face reminded Winter of an over eager puppy. Birch wasn't so quick. He eased himself out from behind the wheel and stood there breathing hard for a moment or two, his face flushed, his piggy-like eyes so narrow they were almost shut.

'Would someone mind telling me what in the name of sweet Jesus is going on around here? First Granville Clarke, and now this.'

'Where have you been?' asked Winter.

'That's none of your business.'

'It is our business. You were supposed to secure this house.'

'I do not work for you Mr Winter.' Birch's eyes turned even more piggy like. His expression was more smirk than smile. 'You aren't even a police detective, nor are you with the FBI any longer. You have no authority over me whatsoever.'

Winter went to reply, but Mendoza touched his arm.

'Chief Birch, we need you to identify the body of Eugene Price.' She was aiming for placatory, but her Brooklyn accent made it sound like a threat.

'It can't be him. Eugene Price has been dead for six years. All you'd have left is bones.'

'That's the thing, he hasn't been dead for six years.'

'What the hell are you talking about?'

'Eugene died sometime during the last week, and so far as we can tell he died of natural causes.'

'That's impossible. Eugene Price died six years ago. He was murdered by his son.'

'And the body was never found.'

Birch's blood pressure was creeping up, the skin on his face and over-sized neck turning pink. 'It's not Eugene.'

'Maybe you should reserve judgement until you've had a chance to look for yourself.'

'I'll look, but I'm telling you now, you're wrong.'

Mendoza gave Birch directions to the bomb shelter and watched him waddle off towards the side of the house. Peterson was hurrying along behind him, looking more like a puppy than ever. Winter walked over to the porch and sat on the bottom step. He took out his cigarettes and lit one. He reckoned Griffin should be here in fifteen minutes or so, probably fewer if she found it as 'unhealthily interesting' as Mendoza had made out.

He was contemplating a second cigarette when he heard the distant sound of a car moving through the trees. Thirty seconds later a black SUV with County Medical Examiner markings on the hood and doors drove out from between the trees and parked beside their BMW. Griffin got out of the passenger side and stood for a moment gazing over at the dilapidated farmhouse. Winter didn't recognise the man who'd climbed out of the driver seat. He was in his early forties. Short black hair that was greying at the sides and a pair of John Lennon spectacles. The guy started pulling bags from the rear seat of the SUV.

Griffin came over, a smile on her face. Today's eyepatch had a five-pointed star picked out in white diamante. Her laden-down assistant came over to join them and she introduced him as Barney. He was almost as tall as Griffin, well over six feet. Handshakes and 'Hellos', then it was down to business. Mendoza got the ball rolling by signing over the evidence she'd collected to Barney. The hotel key, the Bible page, the clump of hair. He put everything into one of his bags for safekeeping, then it was Griffin's turn.

'So, you've found Eugene Price,' she said, her voice as slow and lazy as ever.

Mendoza nodded.

'How bad?'

'That's a matter of perspective. If you're talking about the condition of the body, then it's not bad at all. In fact for someone who's supposed to have been dead for six years, the body is in surprisingly good condition. But that's because he hasn't been dead for six years. If we're talking about injuries to Eugene Price, then I guess you could say it's pretty bad. We think he burned his eyes out with a cigarette.'

Griffin just stared at her for a moment. 'Do you have any idea how many questions I've got going around in my head right now?'

'My guess would be a hell of a lot more than Chief Birch but a damn sight less than me.'

'Birch is here already?'

'I'm afraid so.'

Griffin groaned.

'Not a fan, then?'

'The official line is that Chief Birch is an upstanding citizen and a shining example of everything that a good law enforcement officer should be. The unofficial line is that the man's an idiot.'

Mendoza laughed. 'That's pretty much the same conclusion we've come to.'

'You know, the original investigation would have gone so much smoother if he'd been on vacation that week. He viewed the whole thing as though Jeremiah Lowe and the sheriff's department had some sort of vendetta against him. It was completely counterproductive.'

'Clearly there was no vendetta,' Winter said. 'We met Lowe. The impression I got was that he's competent and professional. He knows his stuff.'

'Of course there wasn't, and yes he does. Birch is just a little man who desperately wants to believe that he's a bigger fish than he actually is.'

'Not so little,' Winter added. He pointed to the side of the house. 'The crime scene is that way.'

'Lead on.'

They arrived at the clearing just as Birch was hauling himself from the ground. Peterson was already at the top, offering his hand to help his boss. Birch batted the hand away and climbed the last couple of steps. He stopped at the top to catch his breath, wiped his brow with a handkerchief, then dipped his head towards the medical examiner.

'Dr Griffin.'

'Chief Birch.'

He shook his head slowly, profoundly. 'That's a hell of a thing down there. A hell of a thing.' He turned to Winter. 'Okay, Mr Bigshot Profiler. How about you tell us what we're looking at here?'

Winter met Birch's eye. 'You know, I can't help wondering how you didn't find Eugene six years ago. How did that happen? I mean, he's right there under your nose, and he's been here all this time.'

Birch huffed and puffed like the answer was on the tip of his tongue. In the end he didn't say a word, he just turned and stomped out of the clearing, Peterson trailing a few steps behind.

Mendoza lifted her sunglasses and stared at Winter. 'What happened to playing nice with the other children?'

Winter looked back along the path, back the way they'd just come. In his mind, he was retracing his steps all the way to Hartwood. He saw the BMW pulling away from the house and driving along the pitted dirt track that cut through the trees. He saw them turn on to the winding two-lane road that led into town.

'Jeremiah Lowe would have been thorough. He would have turned this place upside down. So why wasn't Eugene found during the initial investigation?'

Nobody answered. Winter went over the interview with Lowe in his head. The detective had said that there had been a snowstorm, and that it was one of the worst he'd ever seen. He retraced the route from Hartwood to the Price house, the roads blocked with snow, the bumpy track leading to the house as good as impassable. The ground would have been covered by snow, the path to the clearing hidden beneath a blanket of white. And they were looking for Nelson at this point, not Eugene.

He turned to Griffin. 'Lowe said that the investigation was hampered by a snowstorm. Do you remember how long the snow stayed on the ground?'

'At least a week, maybe longer.'

'And did the storm block the roads in and out of Hartwood?'

Griffin nodded.

'As for this place, I'm guessing that you couldn't even get in here with a snow plough. Does that sound about right?'

'I managed to escape after four days, but that was still four days too long.' She laughed. 'That's not something I'm hoping to repeat any time soon.'

All of this fitted his theory. After four days stranded in Hartwood, Lowe and his people would have been itching to get back to Rochester, leaving Birch to clean up. Would Birch have bothered coming back here to search the woods? Not a chance. That would have been way too much like hard work. Which meant that this place would have only got a perfunctory onceover right at the start of the investigation. After all, the main crime scene was at the Reeds' house. That's where everyone would have congregated.

'What's on your mind?' Griffin asked him.

'I'm just wondering how long Amelia had been hanging around waiting for the perfect storm to hit.'

45

'Alive or dead, hiding someone isn't easy,' Winter continued. 'With a dead body you've got all that hassle of dragging them out into the middle of nowhere, in the middle of the night, and digging a shallow grave, and you've got to do all that without anyone seeing you. And if they're alive, well, that's even tougher. You then need to keep your victim fed and watered, and you need a hiding place, somewhere well out the way so no one can find them.'

He looked over towards the trees, saw the sun playing on the leaves. No one else spoke. They just stood in a ragged circle, the light wind and bird calls breaking the silence. He glanced down at the open trapdoor.

'Okay, so what if you're trying to hide a live body and you've got cops crawling all over your house? That's going to be even tougher, right? And you'd better believe that they're going to be crawling all over the place, because your brother has just committed one of the worst murders that this town has ever seen. So if you're Amelia Price what are you going to do?'

'You're going to muddy the waters as much as you can,' said Griffin.

'Exactly. Most people would like you to believe they're happy to go that extra mile, but that's bullshit. The truth is that most people are looking for an easy life. They're searching for the path of least resistance.' Winter turned his attention back to the hole and for a split second it was six years ago. Scenarios span through his mind, possibilities and hypotheses and almost-certainties. 'Amelia's timing was perfect. She waited until she knew the storm was going to hit then went to the Reeds' house with Nelson. Then she stood and watched while he murdered them.'

'Woah,' said Griffin. 'Back up there a minute, cowboy. There's no evidence Amelia was in the house while the Reeds were murdered.'

'That's because nobody was looking for that evidence. In this case everyone was happy to accept that there was only one gunman up on the grassy knoll. Of course, the fundamental problem with evidence is that it's open to interpretation. One set of facts can lead to more than one story.'

Griffin studied him, sunlight bouncing off the diamante stars on her eyepatch. 'At this point I'll just have to take your word that she was there.'

'But how did she get her father into the cellar? asked Barney, breaking into the conversation. 'The cops would have searched this place. They would have seen a line of footprints leading through the backyard, and they would have gone to investigate, and they would have found this place. Except that obviously didn't happen.'

'Amelia must have hidden her father somewhere else,' Griffin suggested.

'Why?' asked Winter. 'There's a perfectly good hiding place right here, so why go to the trouble of finding somewhere else? She just wouldn't. Remember, she would have been looking for the path of least resistance.'

'And she couldn't have brushed over the footprints,' Mendoza cut in. 'That would have left a trail that was just as obvious.'

'Exactly. So how did she do it?' Winter pulled out another cigarette and played with it while he spoke. 'I think Eugene was right here all along, under the ground and out of the way. He was here on the night the Reeds were murdered. He was still here when the snow cleared enough for the cops to be able to get out here, and he was still here long after they'd gone.'

Mendoza shook her head. 'Except that doesn't work. We're back to the fact that they would have seen the footprints leading out to the woods.' She went to say something else and stopped at the last moment. 'Shit. Amelia brought him here before the snow hit, and she didn't come back until she was certain as she could be that the cops weren't coming back.'

Winter nodded. 'That's the way I see it.'

'How long did she leave him for?'

'It took four days for the snow to clear enough for people to escape from Hartwood, so at least that long. But she would have wanted to give it a few days longer to allow for the police turning up unexpectedly. You're looking at a minimum of a week, but probably longer.'

'What about food and water?' asked Griffin.

'Amelia would have left water, bottles of the stuff. Crates of it. As for food, there were shelves full of cans back in the cellar. I'm sure she could have worked something out. And even if she didn't, it wouldn't be that big a deal. The way I see it, it comes down to the rule of threes. In an extreme situation you can't survive for more than three minutes without air, three hours without shelter, three days without water, and three weeks without food. Eugene was okay for air and shelter, so as long as he had water, he'd be good for three weeks without food.'

'You think she left him there for three weeks?' Griffin asked.

'If she'd needed to, then yes, that's exactly what she would have done.'

'What if he'd died?'

'We know that she's clever, and careful. She also has patience and can plan. She would have been confident that that wasn't going to happen.'

'But she couldn't have been a hundred per cent certain.'

'And that was the gamble. She needed to stop her father. At that point, that was the most important thing to her. If he had died, then I guess she would have waited until the ground thawed, and then she would have gone deep into the woods and buried him, and then she would have probably packed up and quietly left town. With her father dead, there would be nothing to keep her here.'

Griffin stared down into the hole, down into the dark. 'I've seen some things, but this has got to be the coldest thing I've ever come across. It's the length of time she held him for that I find incredible. Six years. How can someone do something like this?'

'That's the wrong question.'

'So what's the right question?'

'There are two actually. Where is she? And why involve me at all?'

46

Winter watched Griffin and Barney disappear into the ground. He took out his Zippo, clicked the lid open, flicked up a flame. For a moment he just stood there watching the fire dance, then he clicked the lid shut. *Click, flick, click.*

'You're doing that thing with your lighter again,' Mendoza told him. 'The thing you do when you've got something on your mind.'

'I was just thinking about the question I asked Griffin. Why involve me?'

'Yeah, that one again. Still no thoughts?'

Winter frowned. 'Not really.'

'Maybe that's because you're too close to see things clearly. Okay, here's an idea. She's read on the internet that you're the best there is when it comes to hunting serial criminals and she wanted to prove you wrong.'

'I guess, that's one possibility.'

'Okay, I'm sensing you're not convinced, so try this on for size: could you be looking for reasons that don't really exist? Overcomplicating for the sake of overcomplicating? You know, chasing shadows?'

Winter gave a wry laugh. 'Mendoza, I spend most of my life chasing shadows. It's what I do.'

'Even so, my question stands. You know, more often than not the simple explanation *is* the correct one.'

'And what if this is one of those occasions where the complicated explanation is the correct one?'

'So what does that look like?'

Winter sighed. 'I don't know.'

'In which case, we go with the simple explanation. She wants to go toe-to-toe with the monster catcher.'

Winter kicked at the earth and said nothing.

'You're still not convinced, are you? You know what this is like? It's like the Ryan McCarthy case all over again. Even when we had that asshole in custody you were still tugging at the threads. It's like you go out of your way to make life difficult for yourself.'

'That's not it. I just don't trust things when they look too neat. Reducing this down to some sort of competition smacks of convenience.' He switched to the voice of a WWE announcer. 'And fighting on the side of evil we have Amelia Price. And marshalling the forces of good we have Jefferson Winter.' He switched back to his real voice. 'Nothing's that clear cut. Nobody's a hundred per cent good, and nobody's a hundred per cent bad. It's like yin and yang again.'

'Your father has a lot to answer for.'

'And what the hell has my father got to do with this?'

Mendoza met his eye. 'He's the reason you're so damn suspicious of everything. You thought he was one thing and he turned out to be something else entirely. Even now, all these years later, you still haven't forgiven yourself for calling that one wrong, have you?'

Winter didn't respond for a while. Mendoza was right about one thing. He had gotten too close to this case. He was too emotionally involved. Amelia had made sure of that by killing Omar.

'My relationship with my father was a sham from start to finish. You think you know someone, but you don't really. Nobody does.'

'Is that your way of saying that I'm right.'

'No, it's my way of saying it's complicated.'

'No, Winter it's actually quite simple. You hate being wrong and I'm guessing you've been that way since birth. What's more, the fact you were wrong about your father kills you. That's what this double guessing is all about. Admit it.'

Winter kept his mouth shut.

'Newsflash: sometimes you actually get things right. Like you did with Ryan McCarthy. But sometimes you won't know all the answers. It's called being human. I know you like to think you're better than us mere mortals, but the truth is that you're flesh and blood, too. If I cut you, you will bleed.'

They drifted into a long, deep silence. The only distractions were the chirping of the birds and the gentle shushing of the wind blowing through the branches. Winter wanted to know what Amelia was up to right now. He wanted to know where she was. *Who* she was.

One thing was for sure, she wouldn't be using last night's disguise. Right now she'd be trying to merge into the background. That meant dull hair and dull eyes and boring conservative clothing that no one would look twice at. But not too boring. Go too far in that direction and people might take notice.

As for where she was, that one was tougher to call. At a rough estimate, six to eight hours had passed since she broke into his room back at the guesthouse. If she'd run, she'd be using the interstates to get as far away from Hartwood as quickly as possible, and she'd be careful to stick to the state speed limit of fifty-five miles an hour because she wouldn't want to get pulled over.

In eight hours she could easily have covered more than four hundred miles. By now she could be in Pittsburgh or Philadelphia or two-thirds of the way to Chicago, which was as good as saying that she could be anywhere. And the bad news was that with every passing minute that area was getting bigger. Then again, maybe she was still in Monroe County. Not that that helped. Not really. Monroe County might be out in the middle of nowhere but there were still plenty of places to hide.

Wherever she was, and whatever she was doing, she'd be planning her next move. He was sure of that. Yes, she might decide to disappear completely, but he didn't think so. Not quite yet. She was clearly intending for their paths to cross again, and he figured that would happen sooner rather than later. The longer she waited, the more time there was for him to regroup. As for where their next encounter might happen, he didn't know. What he needed was to engineer a scenario where they crossed on his terms. Right now, she was calling the shots and he was playing catch up. So how could he turn the tables? It was something to think about.

He zipped up his sheepskin jacket then sat down cross-legged on the grass and got settled in for the long haul. They were heading into the lull. Every investigation suffered from this phenomenon. Everything you could think of had been done, the bases were all covered, and there was nothing left to do except wait and see how things played out. Only then could you plan your next move.

Winter hated the lull. He hated waiting, hated having to be patient. It had been that way since for ever. Even as a kid he had always been doing something to keep his mind occupied. When his brain was idling, that's when the problems began. His thoughts would chase themselves down dead ends and get stuck there. He'd start to obsess over things that he had no control over.

For instance, what if someone had worked out earlier what his father was? How many young women's lives would have been saved? And these were young women who would maybe have gone on to get married and have kids. Sometimes when he closed his eyes he saw golden threads running out from their hearts, spreading out into the future, splitting and separating and multiplying. Then, in the next heartbeat, they'd burst into flames and it would be like they'd never existed.

Of course, when he asked that 'What if', the real question was what if he'd worked it out? Ultimately, the question was pointless. It didn't matter how he answered, nothing changed. Those fifteen women were dead, his mother was dead, and his father had been tried and executed, and there wasn't a damn thing he could do about any of that.

Then there was the question of how early was early enough. If he'd realised at victim number eleven or victim eight or victim four, would that have changed how he felt? The answer was no. Even one victim was one too many, which rendered the question invalid. His father had started killing before he was born. Winter was only eleven when he was caught. He'd just been a kid. What could he have done to change things? Yet here he was, all these years later, still trying to make amends.

He understood the futility of this way of thinking, but couldn't have stopped himself even if he'd wanted to. He'd made an uneasy peace with himself years ago. This was what he was. This was *who* he was. There was nothing he could do to affect the past, but he could do something about the future. Every time he took down a killer he was saving lives, and that had to mean something.

The sound of footsteps on the stone stairs broke into his thoughts. A couple of seconds later Rosalea Griffin appeared, rising out of the ground. She was wearing latex gloves and her good eye was twinkling.

'Was it natural causes?' he asked her.

'You're stretching the definition to breaking point, but yes I'm pretty sure it was natural causes. Obviously, that's just my best guess at the moment. I'll be able to give you a definitive answer after I've examined the body.'

Winter motioned towards her hand. 'What's that?'

Griffin held up a crumpled seven-by-five photograph. 'I thought you might want to take a look. I found this wedged between Eugene Price and the mattress.'

The ME was talking, but Winter couldn't hear a word she was saying. Mendoza was talking, too, but he couldn't hear what she was saying, either.

The photograph had been taken in front of the Alice in Wonderland statue in New York's Central Park. Amelia had her arms around a man who was an inch or two taller than she was. The man was smiling like he'd won the lottery and his head was turned towards Amelia as though he'd just kissed her. She was smiling, too. It was a smile that lit up her whole face, a smile that made her look just like a normal person.

Anyone looking at this photograph would conclude that these were two people who were very much in love. It would be easy to build a whole story based on that assumption. Maybe they'd met at college, or maybe they'd bumped into each other in a bar, or perhaps they had met online. They'd hit it off straightaway, and quickly discovered they had loads in common. They thought the same way about things. They finished each other's sentences. They even owned the same DVD box sets.

The future was as easy to divine as the past. Marriage, kids, and their Golden Years spent living down in Florida because the heat was better for your arthritis, and watching the sun set was more pleasant than watching the rain. Two people this much in love, you just knew you were looking at one of those couples who would end up dying within days of each other.

They'd probably saved for a while before booking their vacation to New York, and while they were saving planned exactly what they were going to do when they got there. They'd have wanted to do all the tourist things. A trip to the top of the Empire State, a visit to the Statue of Liberty. Shopping expeditions and meals out and a Broadway show. And, of course, the obligatory stroll around Central Park.

It was easy to imagine things playing out this way. Except that wasn't what had happened. There had been no Broadway shows or meals or shopping trips, and there had been no slow-burn evenings where they'd shared a bottle of wine and dreamt about what they were going to get up to when they finally hit the Big Apple. And there would be no kids, or twilight years spent wishing away the sunsets in Miami or Fort Lauderdale.

'What the hell?'

Mendoza's voice pulled Winter's attention away from the photograph. She was standing at his shoulder, shaking her head from side to side and biting her lip. There were frown lines on her forehead and tiny crow's feet at the edges of her eyes.

'This makes no sense, Winter. No sense whatsoever. Why would Amelia Price be hanging out with Ryan McCarthy?'

47

'Who's Ryan McCarthy?' Griffin asked.

'Ryan McCarthy's the reason I came to New York,' Winter answered. 'He preyed on young gay men who were visiting the city on business. He'd hook up with them then go back to their hotel rooms. Instead of a nightcap, he raped and dismembered them.'

'If he was doing this in a hotel room then he probably wasn't using power tools. Even battery operated ones. Too noisy.'

'The markings were consistent with hand tools,' he confirmed.

'How small were the pieces?'

'Small.'

'Yikes, that's going to take time. How did you catch him?'

'We worked out that the victims used the same websites to arrange dates while they were in the city, then we created an online avatar that ticked all of McCarthy's boxes and went fishing.'

'And once you got a bite, I'm guessing you got dressed up in your tightest pair of jeans and went out there to reel him in.'

Mendoza laughed. 'That was never going to happen. Winter doesn't like getting his hands dirty.'

Winter frowned at her. 'For the record I have no problem getting my hands dirty.'

'Yeah right. Anyway, we sent Greg Behringer out to meet him. He's one of my colleagues in Homicide, and the closest match we could find to McCarthy's victim profile. He was white, the right age group, and with a bit of work we managed to get it so he looked the part. And it worked. Before the clock struck twelve, McCarthy was in custody.'

For a moment the three of them just stood in silence, everyone lost in their thoughts. A plane was cutting through the blue sky, heading towards Canada, a long white contrail flowing in its wake.

'I guess it's time to discuss the white elephant that's just walked into the clearing,' Winter said. 'Where does Amelia Price fit into all of this?' He turned to Griffin. 'Can I see the photo again, please?'

'Sure, but before you ask there's no way you're getting to touch it.'

Griffin held the photograph up by the edges to make as much of the picture visible as possible, and Winter and Mendoza leant in closer to get a better look. All he saw was the obvious lovers' story he'd seen earlier, which, in light of everything else he knew about Amelia and McCarthy, was clearly a fabrication.

The more he looked, the more questions the picture provoked, but the one question he kept returning to was how had Ryan McCarthy's and Amelia's orbits collided? What circumstances had conspired to bring them together? Right now the only solutions he could come up with involved fate or coincidence, which was as good as having no solutions at all.

The idea that they just happened to be in the same place

at the same time was too big a coincidence. Sure, people met every day, and some of them would go on to spend the rest of their lives together. But Amelia and McCarthy weren't your everyday people, they were psychopaths, which meant there was little to no chance of them bumping into each other in the street. The odds of that ever happening were just too long. Compounding this was the fact that serial killers didn't tend to advertise themselves, which lengthened those odds even further. So how did they meet?

Winter found his cell phone and took a quick snapshot of the photograph. He studied it again, but no matter how hard he looked, no matter what angle he came from, there were still too many questions and nowhere near enough answers. The crunching of twigs interrupted his thoughts. The sound was coming from the path leading to the house.

Mendoza and Griffin had also heard the noise and were staring towards the path. As the footsteps got louder and closer, voices floated into the clearing on the wind, dislocated fragments of sentences that made little sense. A moment later Birch appeared from between the trees, along with a dozen men from the Monroe Sheriff's Department.

The guy at the front talking to Birch was obviously the sheriff. His hat was cleaner, his buttons shinier. This was someone who didn't get out of the office much, and when he did it wasn't to go traipsing through the woods. The body language was interesting. Birch was overcompensating, trying hard to get taken seriously, while the sheriff wasn't trying at all.

Griffin walked over to meet them, and Winter sidled up next to Mendoza. He leant towards her ear. 'Unless you want to spend the rest of the day sitting in an interview room, we need to get out of here,' he whispered. 'You know how this one plays out. We found Eugene and everyone will want to know how. There are much better things we can be doing with our time.'

'Like getting our asses back to New York so we can talk to Ryan McCarthy,' Mendoza added in a low whisper.

'Exactly.'

'So, what's the plan?'

'I'm going to make like I need to use the bathroom. Give it a minute or two then make your excuses. Everybody's going to be more concerned about what's happening underground to worry about us at this point. But they will at some point, and before that happens I want to be long gone. We'll meet at the car.'

48

Winter was standing by the driver door of the BMW when Mendoza appeared a couple of minutes later. She came striding around the side of the house, saw him, and her body language switched from slightly amused to out-and-out pissed. She stalked over and stopped in front of him. Winter held his hand out.

'No chance,' she said.

'A bet's a bet, Mendoza. Amelia was there when her brother killed the Reeds.'

'I've only got your word for that.'

'No, you've got Amelia's word. She told me she was there.'

'Was I sitting there in the room while she confessed? No. Do you have a motive for lying? Yes you do. And have you proved in the past that you're prepared to lie and cheat to get what you want? Absolutely.'

'We're wasting time here. It's going to take at least five hours to get back to New York. Maybe longer if the traffic is heavy.'

'You're the one who's wasting time, not me.'

When he didn't move, she sighed then pulled out the key, zapped the doors and slapped it into his hand. 'Don't say a word.'

Winter got in the car and altered the seat position. Then he adjusted the rear-view mirror, fixed his seatbelt and got himself comfortable. Mendoza climbed in the passenger side and buckled up.

'This isn't over, Winter. Not by a long shot.'

'You done?'

'For now.'

Winter hit the gas pedal and drove out of the clearing. For the next couple of minutes, he kept his mouth shut and concentrated on avoiding the ruts and potholes. The hardest thing was taking it slow. He hated driving slowly. The second they reached the highway, he put his foot down.

'Are you just going to sit there sulking all the way back to New York.'

'I'm not sulking, I'm pissed. There's a difference.'

'Okay, here's a question: how does Amelia know Ryan McCarthy? And don't answer straightaway. I want you to think about it.'

Mendoza gave it the best part of mile then sighed. 'I don't know. Maybe they attended the same meeting of Psychos Anonymous.'

'If only it was that simple. The problem is that the numbers don't add up. The population of America is over the three hundred million mark, and conservative estimates put the number of active serial killers in the region of a hundred. That means one in every three million people in this country is a serial killer. In other words, those church halls are going to be lonely old places.'

'I was joking. You know what a joke is, right?' Winter glanced over and she waved him away. 'Eyes back on the road. I'd like to get there in one piece. And anyway, why are you suddenly so happy? This has made everything so much more complicated.'

'What's not to be happy about? We finally have a decent lead. Incidentally, I caught that it was a joke. Believe it or not I was joking, too.' He glanced over again. 'They met on the internet. Using the internet would fit with what we know already about Ryan McCarthy. After all, he used the net for stalking his victims. Did you see a computer at the Price house?'

Mendoza shook her head.

'Which means Amelia has a laptop. Which means she has it with her. You keep going on about evidence, Mendoza. My guess is there will be plenty of evidence on her hard drive.'

'But why would they be searching for each other in the first place?'

Winter went quiet for a mile or two, thinking hard. 'Having someone to share the fantasies with makes the game more exciting. They can talk about what they're going to do and work themselves up into a frenzy. And when they're done, there's the added bonus that they have someone to re-live the memories with.'

'Okay.'

'Also, in any intimate relationship a power dynamic comes into play. One person is subservient, the other dominant. In a healthy relationship the power play won't be too extreme. However, when you're dealing with the fractured personality of a psychopath everything becomes more exaggerated. There are plenty of psychopaths out there who suffered horrific abuse as kids. That's going to leave scars on the psyche, and those scars are going to get carried through to adulthood.'

'And all of that's going to get played out in their crimes. Yeah, I get that. The pain that was inflicted on to them gets projected on to their victims.'

'But that's only part of it. When two killers get together, that's when things get really interesting. One plays out the abuse sadistically, the other masochistically, and that can lead to some pretty extreme behaviour.'

'So in this case, Amelia is the dom and McCarthy is the sub,' she replied.

'At this point, that's consistent with what we know about McCarthy. Everyone we spoke to said the same thing, his neighbours, his boss, everyone. He kept himself to himself and didn't make waves. But the rage was there. It was squashed all the way down and looking for a way out.'

'And the common ground that brought them together was that they were both abused by their fathers.'

Winter went quiet for another half mile. 'It's an unfortunate truth that plenty of people have been screwed up by their fathers. Agreed?'

'Agreed.'

'Which means you'll have chat rooms dedicated to the subject. Places where people go to vent.'

'And that's where McCarthy found Amelia. He went trawling around those sites looking for a kindred spirit. So when do you think the killing started? Before or after he met her?'

'Good question.' Winter glanced over and Mendoza gestured for him to get his eyes back on the road again. 'The MO was pretty much the same from the first murder to the last. Any variation could be put down to McCarthy gaining confidence and looking for ways to improve his methods, which is entirely consistent with the route most serial killers follow. What I'm not seeing is any evidence that he hooked up with Amelia after he got started. If that had happened we would have seen a definite change in MO as a result of her influence. Or to put it another way, the fantasy becomes a joint effort rather than a solo project. Therefore Amelia was there from the start.'

Winter stared at the highway on the other side of the windshield, the miles falling away behind them, his thoughts chasing themselves around and around inside his head.

'What are you thinking?' Mendoza asked.

'It's nothing.'

She looked over at him. 'And that's what you said just before you worked out how to catch McCarthy. So with all due respect, even if it is nothing I want to hear it.'

Winter blew out a sigh. 'Okay, because we haven't seen any evidence to the contrary, we've assumed that McCarthy's kills were based on his fantasies. But what if we're wrong about that? What if they were actually based on Amelia's fantasies? He had the urges, but what if he didn't have the imagination to channel them?'

Mendoza nodded. 'It's possible. So where does that lead us?'

Winter sighed again. 'Maybe somewhere, maybe nowhere. It's just an idea.'

They fell into another long silence. The road rumbled away beneath the BMW's tyres, while the breathtaking scenery of upstate New York paraded past on the other side of the glass. Questions, questions, questions, thought Winter, always too many damn questions and not enough answers.

Never enough answers.

Winter kept his foot down all the way back to New York and only got pulled over once, just outside Cortland. The bored highway patrolman had his pen out ready to write them up, but had a change of heart after Mendoza flashed her badge. A couple of minutes later they were back on the road, heading south again, the needle on the speedometer hitting a hundred. The only other stop they made was at a gas station near Binghamton so they could grab something to eat.

When they reached the city, Mendoza directed them to Queens. She took them down shortcuts and side streets with the skill and confidence of a cab driver, the buildings rising higher and higher on both sides. New York was a tall city, a busy city. There was noise and bustle everywhere. The closer they got to Rikers, the more depressing the landscape got. Even the junkies and the homeless didn't want to live out here. They smelled the East River before they saw it.

'You know that this isn't an actual river, don't you, Mendoza? It's a tidal strait.'

'I don't care, Winter.'

'How can you say that? Education is the cornerstone of civilisation. Anyway, a strait is a navigable waterway that separates two larger bodies of water, like the Straits of Gibraltar, which links the Atlantic to the Mediterranean. The East River connects Upper New York Bay to Long Island Sound. On one side you've got Long Island and on the other you have Manhattan and the Bronx.'

Mendoza yawned dramatically. 'Are you quite finished?'

'Yeah, I'm done.'

'Okay, when we see McCarthy, I want you to take the lead. He'll be expecting me to, since that's how I played it last time we spoke, but I'm not going to do that. He's smooth. If we're going to get anything out of him, we need to shake him up a little. Can you do that?'

'I reckon so.'

They drove over the three-lane bridge that joined Queens to Rikers, bleak concrete structures looming large and foreboding in the windshield. A mist had rolled in off the water, cloaking everything in grey and silver. Off to their left was the Bronx, and beyond that, the ghostly shape of the George Washington Bridge rose out of the fog. The prison complex was a washed-out mess of concrete and steel. There seemed to be no real cohesion in the architecture. Tall spotlights surrounded the perimeter, along with plenty of open flat space. Anyone attempting to break out would be seen before they'd managed to get a couple of yards.

Winter thought that there was something cruel about having a prison so close to a city. Every time the inmates went outside they'd see skyscrapers reaching up into the sky and it would be a stark reminder of everything they'd lost. And maybe that was the point. Maybe when the decision was made to build here that was one of the things that had been considered.

They left the bridge behind and drove on to Hazen Street, the main thoroughfare that cut through the middle of the island. Rikers was a small city in its own right. The place was massive, a maze of roads and buildings. It was made up of ten prisons that housed in excess of twelve thousand prisoners. A staff of more than ten thousand people looked after them, and the annual budget ran close to a billion dollars.

Mendoza knew her way around well enough to direct them to the building where Ryan McCarthy was being held. They'd called ahead, but even though they were expected, it still took half an hour to process them. That was another thing with prisons. Time was long and moved slowly. In the outside world it slowed and accelerated depending on how much fun you were having. Trapped behind the tall walls and the razor wire, the second hand seemed to be going backwards.

The guy who escorted them to the interview room was a foot taller than Winter. He was white and bald, with a neck as thick as his thigh. No jokes, no laughter, and definitely no small talk. He opened the door and stood aside. Mendoza went in first, Winter following. The door slammed shut behind them with a bang that echoed around the room.

49

Ryan McCarthy was sitting in handcuffs on the far side of the table, watching them. The steel cuff around his ankle was attached to a steel hoop on the floor and his bright orange prison uniform was two sizes too big. He'd aged since they last saw him. It had only been two days, but it could have been years. There were lines around his eyes that hadn't been there before. His skin had already taken on the grey pallor that came from eating crappy food and spending most of the day under artificial lights.

Even so, there was no doubting that he was a handsome guy. Blue eyes, a disarming smile, dimples in his cheeks and chin. His fair hair still held the shape from when it was last cut, but it wouldn't last much longer.

Mendoza sat down in the left-hand seat and Winter took the one on the right. For almost a whole minute nobody spoke. Winter had played this game before, more times than he cared to remember. The FBI's Behavioral Analysis Unit regularly interviewed convicted serial criminals in a bid to find out what made them tick. The programme had one of those immediately forgettable bureaucratic titles that managed to say everything and nothing. It was known informally as the 'Interview an Asshole' programme.

During his eleven years with the BAU, Winter had carried out as many interviews as he'd been allowed to. Unless it was a high-profile criminal, his colleagues hadn't wanted to know. It was one of those assignments where you bitched and shook your head and went on and on about your workload. Not Winter. You could only learn so much from reading about what a killer had done. Sitting opposite one while they laid it all out in graphic detail, well that was another matter.

It was Winter who finally broke the silence. 'Good to see you again, Ryan. So how's life treating you?'

'How do you think it's treating me? I'm locked in a cell for twenty-three hours a day.' McCarthy's voice was quiet and gentle and a little too high-pitched to ever be described as macho. Winter figured this was how he'd disarmed his victims. He didn't look like a threat, and he didn't sound like much of one either.

'That's for your own protection.'

McCarthy's eyes narrowed. 'What do you want?'

'I want you to tell us how you know Amelia Price? Then I want you to tell us everything you know about her.'

'Who's Amelia Price?' asked McCarthy.

Winter gave him a hard stare. 'Come on, Ryan, let's not play this game. We know that you know her.'

'No games. I've no idea who you're talking about.'

'Sure you don't.'

'It's the truth. I don't know anyone by that name.'

Winter was watching carefully. Words lied, body language didn't. McCarthy seemed to be telling the truth, but that was impossible. They knew that he knew her. They even had the photograph to prove it. Mendoza gave him a puzzled look from the next seat. She was clearly thinking along the same lines as he was. Winter pulled out his cell phone and found the photograph he'd taken back at the Price place. He slid the phone over the table and McCarthy glanced down at it.

'You'll have to excuse the quality,' Winter told him. 'It's a photo of a photo, so inevitably you're going to lose something, and it would obviously be better if we had a bigger screen. However, you can see enough of what's going on for our purposes.' He stood up and leant over the table and started pointing things out. 'Now that's the Alice in Wonderland statue in Central Park, no question about that. And that's you, no question about that, either. And that's Amelia Price cuddling up to you, which is where the confusion seems to be creeping in.'

'I don't know who Amelia Price is.'

Winter snatched the phone up and placed it neatly on the table, making sure it was parallel with the edge. He looked McCarthy in the eye. 'Now that is a lie Ryan. Please don't lie to me.'

'It's the truth. Obviously that's me in the photograph. I'm not denying that. And I remember the picture being taken because it was all a bit strange. I was walking through the park and this tourist stopped me and asked if she could have my photograph taken with her. It would have been rude to say no.'

'No it wouldn't have been rude, it would have been the New York thing to do. The New York thing would have been to keep walking and not say a word. Also, you're a serial killer, and no self-respecting serial killer would let some random stranger take a picture of them.' Winter did a fast *rat-a-tat-tat* drum roll on the table, making McCarthy jump. 'Lastly, and this is the clincher, you're not a Hollywood A-lister. I mean, you're a good-looking guy and everything, but seriously, who's going to want to have their photograph taken with you?'

McCarthy locked eyes and said nothing, trying for the hard stare, and failing by a mile.

'Computers rule the world,' Winter continued. 'For all intents and purposes our whole lives have been reduced to a series of ones and zeroes. Like in here, for example. Your name's in the computer system. There's a whole file devoted to you. It contains everything that anyone might want to know from your date of birth to your blood type. Now somewhere in there you'll find a little tick box, and next to that box are the words *Protective Custody*. At the moment there's a tick in that box.'

McCarthy smiled, but he was looking worried. He started tapping the table, realised what he was doing and stopped.

'Here's what's going to happen Ryan. There's going to be an administrative screw up and that tick is going to disappear.' Winter brought his fingers up to his lips and blew them apart with a *phh*. 'And like that it's gone.'

'You can't do that.'

'I can and I will. But you're focusing on the wrong thing here. Now I know for a fact that you've imagined what life would be like if you were in the general population. The thing is you're looking from the perspective of a jail cell where you're locked down for twenty-three hours of the day, and you're thinking about how you managed to dodge a bullet there. Now here's another way of looking at it. Imagine what it would be like if you were sharing a cell with one of those tattooed sweethearts from the Aryan Brotherhood. That would give things a different spin. I mean, how terrifying would that be? Just the other morning I was in a similar situation, contemplating a similar fate, and I've got to say it scared the shit out of me.'

McCarthy looked across the table, his gaze flitting between Winter and Mendoza. 'Let me see that photo again.'

Winter activated the cell phone and slid it across the table. McCarthy picked it up and studied the photograph. Before passing it back, he touched Amelia's face through the screen, the tip of his finger gliding gently across the glass. His expression was ambiguous. He looked as if he was holding back a smile, but it could just as easily have been the start of a scowl or a frown.

'Okay, I know who she is,' he said eventually. 'However, if I help you, I'm going to need something in exchange.'

Winter reached for his cell phone and put it back in his pocket. 'The only thing we've got to offer is peace of mind. Let's face it, sleeping with one eye open can't be much fun. It's really going to screw with your biorhythms.'

'Not good enough.'

Winter leant forward. 'We haven't come here to negotiate. That's not what this is about.'

'Isn't it?' McCarthy stared at him and said nothing.

'Okay, I'm done.' Winter jumped to his feet, startling McCarthy. 'We're clearly wasting our time here. If you don't want to help, then that's your prerogative.'

Mendoza scraped her chair back and stood up too. They turned and began walking to the door. Winter counted off the seconds in his head. He got to four before McCarthy cracked.

'Okay, okay. The name Amelia Price means nothing to me. As far as I'm concerned the woman in the photograph is Maddie Phillips.'

Winter studied him for a moment then sat down. He waited for Mendoza to get comfortable before speaking. 'So where did you meet Maddie?'

'On the internet.'

'And your father abused you, right?'

The smile dropped from McCarthy's face. 'What's that got to do with this? Are you trying to get inside my head, is that it?'

'Maddie's father abused her, too. But you know that already, don't you?'

No response.

'Don't you?' Winter repeated.

McCarthy shrugged, then nodded.

'I'm guessing you met in a chat room for victims of childhood abuse. Trust is always an issue, which means it probably took some time before you guys got down to the really interesting stuff. So how long ago did you meet Maddie online?'

Another shrug. 'A while ago, I guess.'

'You guess?'

'Eighteen months.'

'In the early days there would have been plenty of hypothetical conversations about what you'd both like to do to your fathers, and somewhere along the line those hypothetical conversations turned into more detailed discussions about what you'd *really* like to do. And further down the line still those conversations turned into actual plans. Your first murder took place back in April, so you had eleven months of dancing before you got down to business.'

McCarthy licked his lips.

'So who was leading the dance? I'm thinking Maddie. But that's not the real question, is it? The real question is, who did you think was leading it? She had you believing that you were calling the shots, didn't she? She made you believe that you were the big man.'

McCarthy grinned and waited for Winter to meet his eye. 'You think you're so damn clever, don't you?'

50

The interview room fell silent. Winter could hear breathing, and air being pushed through the vents, but they were the only sounds. On the other side of the walls thousands of prisoners were going about their day-to-day business, and thousands of guards were keeping an eye on them, but it was like they didn't exist. There was a tickle of panic in his stomach. The idea that he'd missed something significant was running around inside his head.

'Don't play games,' said Mendoza from the next seat.

McCarthy ignored her. He was staring across the table at Winter, his eyes cold and unforgiving. The grin had disappeared and for the first time since they got here, Winter could believe that he was looking at someone who was capable of hacking someone to pieces just for the fun of it.

He'd seen this sort of transformation before. Highly organised serial killers were masters at hiding in plain sight. They created personas to disappear behind, friendly non-threatening ah-shucks disguises that were designed to disarm. And the thing was, it worked. John Wayne Gacy used to dress as a clown for fundraisers, parades and parties. None of his friends or neighbours had any idea that he'd murdered more than thirty people. And Winter knew how charming his own father could be. He'd seen this side of his personality whenever they were out in public. Albert Winter had always been quick with a smile and a joke. If you'd got into a tight spot he would have been more than happy to help you out.

And if you were a young woman who fitted his victim profile he'd have been more than happy to take you into a forest under a killer's moon and hunt you down with a high-power rifle.

That was the thing with these disguises. Scratch hard enough at that veneer and the killer's true nature would eventually surface. Like now. On the other side of the table, McCarthy smiled again.

'Okay, here's how I see things. I've got something you want, you've got something I want. I need assurances that I'm not going to be moved out of protective custody. And I need access to any books I want from the library. No waiting list. No vetting.'

'Why do you care?' asked Mendoza. 'If I was in your shoes, being moved into the general population and ending up stabbed would be a blessing. As for the books? Why would you want to read about a life you're never going to see again?'

He shook his head. 'But you're not me. You see, I'm a hopeful kind of guy. My glass is always half full.'

'Even in here. I don't think so.'

'You've got a deal,' Winter told him. Mendoza glared at him, no doubt wondering what the hell he was up to now. He ignored the dirty look and added, 'You tell us what we want to know and you get to read all the airport thrillers and romances you want. That works for me.'

'How can I trust you?'

'That strikes me as incredibly cynical, particularly coming from someone who claims their glass is half full.'

McCarthy said nothing.

'Okay, how about this? The idea of you rotting away in a cell for the next fifty years appeals to me more than the idea of you getting shanked in a shower.'

'You're serious, aren't you?'

'As a heart attack.'

McCarthy looked at him over the table, sussing him out, weighing up his options. 'You think I'm sick in the head, well, I'm telling you this for nothing, I've got nothing on Maddie. That girl is a whole new brand of crazy.'

'All well and good, Ryan, but we need specifics.'

'Earlier you were talking about how Maddie and me were dancing together in that chat room. You wanted to know who was leading the dance, right?'

Winter nodded for him to go on.

'You were right. It was Maddie. She initiated our first conversation, and pretty much led things from there.'

Mendoza laughed. 'Of course he's going to say that. He's angling for a reduction in his sentence on the grounds of diminished responsibility.' She leant across the table and waited for McCarthy to meet her gaze. 'It's not going to work. You're going down for the rest of your miserable life.'

'Is that what's going on here?' Winter asked. 'Are you really trying to pull the diminished responsibility card? Are you trying to play me, Ryan?'

McCarthy shrugged. 'I am not trying to play you. Why would I do that?'

Winter leant forward, edging towards McCarthy's personal space. He heard Mendoza shift in the seat beside him. 'Okay, I'm listening.'

'It was Maddie who suggested we meet. I didn't want to at first, but she can be very persuasive. So we met up in a bar and hit it off straightaway. She really got me. Got me in a way nobody ever had before?'

'No she didn't.'

McCarthy went to fold his arms and the handcuffs rattled tight. The spark of rage that flashed in his eyes was there and gone in seconds. He leant forward, moving towards Winter, and put his hands back on the table. 'So you say.'

'Let me guess how it went down. You both loved the same movies, the same music, the same TV shows. Right?'

McCarthy stared across the table, eyes narrowed. His small pink tongue snaked out and moistened his lips.

'She was mirroring you, Ryan. You'd tell her that you loved *The Sopranos*, and she'd come back telling you that was her favourite series too. So she takes that on board and a little while later she tells you that one of her favourite movies was *The Godfather*, just slides it into the conversation real casual. No bite there, so she tells you that she loved *Goodfellas* too, and you're all, *Oh my god that's my favourite movie in the whole universe.* Now chances are she hated the film, but that doesn't matter. All that matters is that you loved it, and you think that she loves it. So what's your favourite movie?'

'It's not *Goodfellas*, if that's what you're thinking.'

'No it's not. It's either *The Usual Suspects* or *The Shawshank Redemption*.' Winter was watching McCarthy closely. '*The Shawshank Redemption* it is then. But that's only just moved up to the number-one spot, hasn't it? For obvious reasons.'

McCarthy scowled. His lips were pressed hard together,

turning them into two narrow strips. 'What me and Maddie had was special. I don't care what you say.'

Winter shook his head. 'You were in love with her, weren't you?'

McCarthy said nothing.

'Oh this is priceless. She really got you good, didn't she?'

McCarthy's cheeks turned red and he went to stand up.

'Sit down,' said Mendoza.

They were all staring at each other. Winter counted off thirty-three seconds before McCarthy sat back down. Mendoza let him settle, then said, 'Help me out here, Ryan. I thought you were gay.' When McCarthy didn't respond she turned to Winter. 'So what? He's bi?'

Winter aimed his answer at McCarthy. 'This isn't about sexuality, it's about power. Isn't it, Ryan? When those men were begging for their lives I bet it felt so good, didn't it? I bet you felt like a god. But what you had with Amelia, that was love, wasn't it?' Winter shook his head. 'Except it wasn't. You believed that she loved you, and she let you believe that. Because she was the one who held all the power, right? It's like you said, she was leading the dance. You might want to believe that it was the other way around, but it wasn't. And do you want to know something else? She's still leading it. Think about it. While you're stuck in here, she's out there living it up. I doubt she even thinks about you these days. That's how much she loved you, Ryan. You know, when you get right down to it, she has as much respect for you as you had for your victims.'

'We're done here,' McCarthy said.

'Yeah, you're right. We're done.' Winter did another quick *rat-a-tat-tat* on the table top, then got up and headed for the door. He banged on it hard and a couple of seconds later there was a heavy clunk as the lock released. The door swung open and the same guard as earlier was standing there filling the doorway. Mendoza went out first, but Winter didn't follow straightaway.

'One last thing, Ryan. Where did you and Maddie stay when you were hanging out together?'

'My place.'

'No you didn't. You suggested it, but she didn't take you up on the idea. No offense, but she's much cleverer than you. And she's a planner. She wouldn't have wanted there to be anything to connect her to your life. So there's no way she would have gone to your place where your neighbours would have seen her. Secondly, it would have put her at a psychological disadvantage. Your place, your rules. No way would she have gone for that. So try again, but this time imagine how uncomfortable I could make things if you lie.'

For a moment he was convinced that McCarthy wasn't going to respond. He looked broken. Winter had a sudden flash of what his relationship with Amelia had been like. In his own way he'd loved her but she would have kept him at arm's length. She would have given him enough attention to keep him interested, but not too much because she wouldn't have wanted him getting too comfortable. She was in charge. She held the power. That was one of the big problems with love. There was no guarantee that it would be reciprocated to the level you needed. McCarthy had learned that the hard way.

'We stayed at a hotel,' McCarthy said softly.

'The same one each time?'

A nod. 'The Hyperion. It's on the Upper East Side.'

51

They stepped out into the early evening sun and just stood there for a moment breathing in freedom. Winter lit a cigarette and took a drag. His exhale was part sigh, part smoke. He hated prisons. The way the walls pushed in on him made him feel claustrophobic. His father had been in prison for two decades, most of that on Death Row. Every day the same, your world defined by the walls and the bars. Hour after hour, day after day, year after year, and the only thing you have to look forward to at the end of it all is your execution. Ryan McCarthy said his glass was half full, but Winter didn't believe that. How could it be in a place like that?

He took another drag and looked out over the water at the ghost city rising from the mist and thought about the interview with McCarthy. Then he thought about the photograph. Amelia had left it on Eugene's body for them to find, which meant that she wanted them to head straight to Riker's to question McCarthy. And she knew McCarthy well enough to know how he'd react and that he would eventually cave in and give them the name of the hotel.

'We need to go to the Hyperion,' he told Mendoza.

'Why? Amelia's not going to be there.'

'Agreed, but I'm betting she's going to be somewhere close by, watching. She's laid her trail of breadcrumbs and this is where she wants us to go next.' Winter took a final drag and crushed the cigarette out under his boot heel. 'Amelia is a textbook psychopath. She's sitting right up there at the top of the psychologists' charts. Now, the one part where her score is off those charts is the section that deals with the Machiavellian traits. Look at how she operates. With McCarthy she pulled the strings then stood back and watched. I'm betting she did the same thing with Nelson. She wasn't hiding in the shadows on the night the Reeds were murdered, she was out there front and centre, cheering her brother on. That's what she does. She jerks the strings and makes those puppets dance.'

'She's making us dance too. You realise that, don't you?'

'She's trying.'

'She's doing more than that, Winter. Think back to that first time you saw her in the diner. She knew who you were, she chose the venue. Basically, she was running the show, even back then. She left the newspaper behind knowing you'd go charging up to Hartwood, and she left the photograph of her and Ryan because she knew we'd come here. Which brings us back to our earlier question: why you?'

Winter stared out over the city, looking for answers in the tall towers, concrete and steel. He smiled to himself as another piece of the puzzle finally dropped into place. 'It's all about revenge, and that's one of the oldest stories there is. I helped catch Ryan McCarthy and she wants payback.'

'Yeah, that makes sense. She'd invested in him and he was doing what she needed, and then he got caught. No Ryan McCarthy, no more games. So she went looking for a new game.'

Winter nodded. 'She's *mightily* pissed off, but open

warfare isn't her style. We've seen that. So she took a long, deep breath and pushed the anger down, and kept doing that until she was thinking clearly again. Then she worked out what she could do to redress everything she perceives as being wrong in her world. McCarthy is history and there's nothing she can do about that, but she can affect the future. That's where I come in.'

He stopped talking and looked out over the water at the misty city again. Noises filtered in from all directions. The industrialised clang and bang of the jail behind him, the distant clatter of the city in front, the screeching of some high-wheeling birds. Everything seemed dull, like the fog was acting as a muffler. The sharpest, most defined sound was the sound of Mendoza breathing less than a yard away. A light breeze was blowing in from the water, bringing an unpleasant smell that was difficult to categorise.

'Clarity,' he said finally. 'That's important to her. She doesn't act unless she sees the board clearly. So when the anger and disappointment finally fade, what does she see?'

'She sees that everything has gone to hell, so she starts looking around for someone to blame.'

'Exactly. She knows that the cops are responsible for spoiling her fun, but she can't go up against the whole of the NYPD. She needs the target to be more specific. So she does a bit more digging and my name comes up in connection with the investigation. Now she has someone she can target.'

Mendoza went quiet while she considered this. 'It's all about control,' she said. 'Or to be more precise, it's all about the loss of control and doing whatever she needs to do to get that back. So here's a question: how do we take control of the board?'

It was Winter's turn to fall quiet. 'Her overconfidence is her biggest weakness. That's how we're going to catch her. We're going to follow the breadcrumbs, but we keep our eyes wide open. At some point she's going to make a mistake. When she does we need to be ready.'

They walked back to the parking lot where they'd left the car. Mendoza went around to the driver's side and stood there expectantly with her hand held out. 'Key, please.'

'But I'm a much better driver than you are.'

'The deal was that you drove back to New York. We're in New York, so hand over the keys, or I will shoot you.'

'A threat is only effective if the person being threatened thinks it might be carried out.'

Mendoza unbuttoned her jacket, took out her gun and aimed at his head. 'Give me the key.'

Winter craned his head around so he could see the side of the gun. 'The safety's still on.'

'Don't push it. Just give me the damn key, Winter.'

52

The Hyperion was a six-storey building with dirty stonework and a sense that its glory days were long gone. The owners no doubt wanted their customers to believe it was on the Upper East Side, but that was stretching things. Winter reckoned it was closer to East Harlem. Parking was a nightmare and they'd ended up abandoning the BMW four blocks away and walking. They still had a couple of blocks to go when his cell phone started ringing. He looked at the number flashing up on the screen, but didn't answer. It was a number he was unfamiliar with.

'Aren't you going to answer that?' Mendoza asked.

Winter ignored the question. 'Whatever happens over the next couple of minutes, I want you to look straight ahead and keep walking. Nod if you understand.'

Mendoza's eyes narrowed, but she did what he asked and carried on walking. 'I want to know what's going on, Winter?'

'And I'll tell you. Just not now, okay?'

For a second it looked as though she was going to argue. Instead, she nodded once and kept on walking. Winter was charting a route that took them right down the middle of the sidewalk. Anyone dumb enough to play chicken got bumped out the way. He barely noticed the collisions, or the abuse. He was concentrating on the cell phone, counting the rings. His cell died halfway through the fourteenth ring. Three seconds, four seconds, five. The phone started ringing again and he smiled to himself.

'What's going on?' Mendoza asked again.

Winter ignored her and kept walking. The phone was still ringing in his hand, insistent and annoying. Nine rings, ten rings. They were a block and a half away from the Hyperion. Directly opposite was another hotel. Architecturally, it looked different, but in every way that mattered it was identical. Same location, same clientele, same three-star rating. Twelve rings, thirteen. The cell cut off halfway through the fifteenth ring. Winter held the phone up. 'It's Amelia.'

Mendoza stopped in the middle of the sidewalk. 'Why the hell didn't you answer it?'

'Keep moving,' he replied without breaking stride.

She took a large step and came back in line with him. 'I need to know what the hell's going on, and I need to know now. If I'm going to be any help here, you need to let me in.'

'We're taking control of the board. Amelia is in the hotel opposite the Hyperion. She has to be. My cell started ringing the second we came into view. It's the obvious place to watch from.'

Before he could finish, Mendoza was already sprinting along the sidewalk, arms and legs pumping. Winter's cell phone rang again. He counted the rings off, waiting for the thirteenth, then stopped walking and connected the call.

'Hi Amelia. How's it going?'

There was a slight pause. 'Hello, Jefferson. How did you know it was me?'

He'd hoped that ignoring her calls would wind her up, but

she sounded as calm as ever. He glanced across the road, eyes searching the hotel's windows, wondering which one she was behind.

'I didn't recognise the number so I assumed it was a junk call. A telemarketer might have phoned back a second time in quick succession but not a third. So I asked myself two questions. Who might want to speak to me so urgently, and whose number didn't I have? Yours was the name I was left with.'

'How clever of you.'

'Not really. This isn't exactly rocket science.'

'Modesty doesn't suit you.'

'Clever is developing a cure for cancer, or picking up the ball from Einstein and finally coming up with a Unified Theory of Everything. Using deductive reasoning to work out who might be calling your cell phone is not clever. That's just a parlour trick. So what do you want Amelia? Or should that be Maddie?'

'You've been to see Ryan, then? How is he?'

Her voice had changed. It sounded as though she was talking while she was walking, the rhythm of her feet dictating the beat of her words. Winter listened harder, trying to hear her footsteps. Nothing. Perhaps they'd been muffled by carpet. In which case she was still inside the hotel. A door opened and the rhythm changed again. It sounded like she was descending a flight of stairs. Mendoza needed to hurry or Amelia was going to get away.

'I think he's probably been better. Prison life isn't agreeing with him. You really enjoy pulling those strings and making people dance, don't you?'

'You have no idea.'

'Enlighten me.'

'I'd love to, but it would take too long. I want to meet up, Jefferson.'

'Why?'

'Since when does there have to be a reason?'

'Of course there has to be a reason. It isn't like we're friends getting together for lunch and a chat. You're a killer and my job is to catch you.'

'I'm sensing that you're still upset about the cook's death. What was his name again? Oscar?'

'Omar. His name was Omar.'

'Poor Omar. But then, if I hadn't killed him, we wouldn't be here now. So you see, his death was necessary.'

'Why do you want to meet, Amelia?'

'That would be telling.'

Before Winter could say anything else, the high-pitched sound of a fire alarm ripped through the earpiece. He jerked the cell phone away from his ear. An old trick, but a good one. He put the phone back to his ear. The ambient noise had changed. Clanging metal and bright echoes. A kitchen. Not good. While Mendoza was working her way towards Amelia's room, Amelia was down on the first floor, escaping out the back way.

He looked along the sidewalk towards the hotel entrance. Nobody had come out yet, but it wouldn't be long. And while everything was in chaos she'd just slip away. Judging by the sounds coming through the earpiece she was still in the kitchen. But she wouldn't be there much longer.

'You've gone very quiet,' she said. 'I can almost hear those cogs turning inside your head.'

'You want to meet? Fine let's meet.'

'I want you to come alone.'

'Of course you do.'

'I'm serious. This one's a deal-breaker. If I get even a hint that you're not alone then I disappear.'

'You're going to have to give me some time. A couple of hours at least. I need to give Mendoza the slip.'

'No you don't. You could give her the slip right now. Just walk away while everything's going crazy, and don't look back. New York's a great place to lose yourself in.'

'You know I can't do that, Amelia. As long as you're in that hotel I've got to come after you.'

'But what's the point? I'll be gone long before you get here. I know that, you know that, so why bother?'

'I've still got to try.'

Amelia let out a world-weary sigh. Winter could almost see her shaking her head on the other end of the line. 'What is it with you men? You're all so stupid.'

'Two hours,' he said.

'I'll give you half an hour.'

Winter noticed a new change in the background noise. She was outside. Which meant they'd lost her. 'I'll be there in an hour.'

'Be where?'

'If you think about it, I'm sure you'll work it out.'

He killed the call and broke into a run, his thumbs working his cell phone. He found Mendoza's number, typed *shes gon out thru kichn*, then hit send.

53

Winter scanned the abandoned kitchen, taking everything in. The discarded pots and pans, the pile of half chopped vegetables, the open back door. He crouched down and picked up a large knife that had fallen on the floor. The blade was shiny and sharp. He laid the knife on one of the work surfaces. A door banged open behind him and Mendoza came rushing in.

'Shit, Winter! We lost her.'

'It's not all bad news.'

'She's still out there. That doesn't sound like good news to me.'

'She's taking more risks than ever, which means there's more chance of her making a mistake. That's the best news I've heard in a while.'

Winter went over to the back door. It was wider than an average door to make it easier for deliveries. You opened it by pushing the bar across the middle. Beyond the doorway was a narrow alley. The tall buildings on either side kept everything in shadow, and the dumpsters stunk of garbage. Once Amelia had reached this point she was home and dry. A quick jog along this alley and in no time she would have been swallowed up by the city.

'How did you find out which room she was in?' he asked.

'She used the Wren J Firestone alias again. Her room was up on the fifth floor.'

Without another word, Winter ran out of the kitchen and retraced his way back through to reception. There was a queue for the elevators so he headed for the stairs, taking them two at a time. By the time he reached the fourth floor he was out of breath. He stood there for a second, his hand on the rail, breathing hard, then got going again. Mendoza had caught up with him by the third floor and sailed passed him without breaking stride. Her face was a little flushed but she looked as though she could easily manage another four flights.

'You really should think about quitting the cigarettes,' she told him.

'Really not the time for a lecture. So which way to Amelia's room?'

'This way.'

Mendoza banged through the heavy door that led to the corridors. Winter took one more deep breath then followed. It occurred to him that their journey from the kitchen to the fifth floor was the exact same journey he'd heard Amelia taking, but in reverse. Mendoza turned left and walked quickly along the narrow corridor, glancing at the room numbers. Room 516 was two-thirds of the way along the corridor. The door was ajar, wedged open with a bath towel. Winter looked at the towel, looked at Mendoza.

'I figured we might want to take a look at the room,' she said. 'This way saves all the hassle of finding someone to unlock the door.'

The room was decorated for a business traveller from the lower rungs of the ladder, or a tourist on a budget. It was comfortable and functional with a funky modern vibe. Lots of white interspersed with bright splashes of colour. The throw on the bed was bright purple and the surrealist prints on the wall veered heavily towards primary colours. There was a suitcase on the stand in the corner. It had a hard shell and was small enough to be taken on to a flight as carry-on luggage. Mendoza walked over and popped the catches.

'I wouldn't bother. It's empty.'

She ignored him and lifted the lid, peered inside. She checked the pockets, ran her hands over the lining. 'You're right. It's empty.'

'It's probably the same suitcase she used back at Myrtle House.'

'And I'm thinking she brought it here for the same reason. Someone checking into a hotel without luggage is going to stand out, right? And it's empty because she knew that there was a good chance she might have to clear out in a hurry. Carrying this with her would have slowed her down.'

A chair was positioned in front of the window, just like there had been back at the guesthouse. The biggest difference was that this chair was pushed up close to the window. Clearly Amelia wasn't as worried about being seen here. New York was much busier than Hartwood so it was easier to blend into the background, and being on the fifth floor made it difficult for anyone looking up from the street to see into the room.

It was a different story for the person sitting in this chair, though. They'd have a great view. Winter sat down and peered through the gap in the drapes. The window was open and a fresh breeze was blowing in, cold against his skin. The rowdy noise of the street rose up from below, fragmented jigsaw-puzzle pieces of sound. Car engines and horns and a stereo playing too loud. Laughter and shouting.

Straight ahead on the other side of the street was the Hyperion. Five stories up and twenty yards away it looked just as shabby as it had done from street level. Shabbier, perhaps, since there weren't so many distractions up here. Winter leant on the window sill and peered left, peered right. The view on the near side of the street was restricted to a block in either direction. He could see way into the distance on the other side of the street.

Mendoza pulled one of the drapes aside. 'She would have seen us coming from a mile away.'

'Yes she would. Any idea what disguise she was using?'

'The guy at the desk said she was dressed like a business woman. Dark hair, brown eyes, somewhere around five-eight or five-nine, and that was about as much as he could tell me. It didn't help matters that it was a very quick conversation. After all, I was in a hurry to find her.' She paused, frowned. 'Chances are she changed her disguise as soon as she got outside. She probably hit the streets as a blue-eyed blonde.'

'Probably. Not that it really matters what disguise she's using.'

'Of course it matters. What are you talking about?'

Winter grinned. 'I've arranged to meet her.'

Mendoza stared at him. 'And you've only just thought to mention this. Is there anything else you're not telling me?'

Winter was staring out of the window again. He could picture Amelia in his mind's eye. She didn't look anything like a businesswoman, though. The version his imagination conjured up had platinum-blonde hair, bright green eyes and a baggy leather jacket. He saw her walking out of the hotel kitchen, saw her reach the end of the alley. She glanced over her shoulder like she had done two nights ago back at the diner in New York, and then she was gone. He turned around and looked at Mendoza.

'Yeah, there is one thing. I think I know how to catch her.'

Winter sat down on the edge of the bed and spent the next couple of minutes outlining his idea. The whole time Mendoza just stood silently in front of him, the frown on her face slowly morphing into a scowl.

'No way, Winter,' she said when he'd finished. 'It's too risky.'

'Okay, if you've got a better plan, let's hear it.'

'You're not doing this without backup. It's crazy.'

'Still waiting to hear your plan.'

'Winter, Amelia is a psychopath.'

'No argument there. She probably scores higher than me on the Hare psychopathy checklist and that's saying something.'

'This isn't funny. She stabbed that cook with a cutlery knife.'

'I know. I was there.'

Mendoza closed her eyes. She had her fingers pressed against her forehead like she had a migraine coming on. She opened her eyes, lowered her hands, then took a deep breath. 'I don't know who's crazier, you or her.'

'I'm going to be fine, Mendoza. She's not going to lay a finger on me.'

'And you're sure about that?'

'I am. If she wanted to hurt me she would have done so already.'

'She cuffed you to a bed.'

'But she didn't hurt me.'

'But she could have.'

Winter jumped up from the bed and Mendoza took a step back in surprise.

'Look, Amelia isn't going to hurt me, and the reason I know that is because she craves an audience, and right now I'm that audience. Her brother, her father, Ryan McCarthy. She wasn't just toying with them, she needed them to validate herself.'

'And as a result of getting mixed up with her, two of them are dead and one is looking at spending the rest of his life in prison.'

'I'm going to be fine,' he said again.

'I don't like this, Winter.'

'You don't have to like it, you've just got to help me out here.'

Mendoza's head started moving slowly from side to side. He doubted she was aware of what she was doing.

'Are you going to help me or not?'

A sigh. 'Yeah, I'll help you.'

'Thanks.'

'I wouldn't go thanking me just yet. Let's see how this plays out first.'

'It's going to be fine. *I'm* going to be fine.'

Mendoza smiled at him. 'To be honest, I'm more concerned that you catch her.'

54

Winter pulled up the collar of his sheepskin jacket and lit a cigarette. Darkness had fallen over an hour ago, and the temperature was slowly dropping. He clicked the Zippo closed, then clicked it open again and flicked up a new flame. *Click, click, flick.* The smell of lighter fluid drifted up towards his nose. Central Park was busy. It was a perfect fall evening and people were making the most of it. December was just around the corner. Snow, sub-zero temperatures and everybody praying for spring.

The Alice in Wonderland statue was hidden away in its own secret grove. Trees crowded around in a circle, stealing away the city and giving the impression that you'd actually tumbled down the rabbit hole. Hugging the curve of the trees were benches for the parents to rest on, and laid out inside that was a circle of paving slabs that had been worn smooth by millions of little feet. The main path led down to a lake but there was a smaller path off to the side that wound away between the trees.

The kids clambering all over the statue were probably here on vacation. No doubt they'd been allowed to stay up late because all the usual routines had been put on hold. Winter stood watching them for a moment, a dusty old memory surfacing. He was three and a half and he was sat up on his bed with his back against the headboard, a copy of *Alice's*

Adventures in Wonderland lying open on his lap. This book was one that he kept coming back to. He could recite whole sections from heart. The caterpillar had always been his favourite character. He was rude and chain-smoked. What wasn't to like?

His mother was sat beside him, listening and smiling, her body warm through the thin material of his pyjamas, the smell of her soap and perfume comforting. Looking back, what got to him most was how relatively normal the scene was. *Relatively* normal. Most three-year-olds weren't reading books this advanced, but that was just a detail. The point was that back then he'd had no idea that 'normal' was just an illusion, that real life was as screwed up as anything that Lewis Carroll could dream up.

He took a drag on his cigarette and scanned the area around the statue to make sure he wasn't being watched. Mendoza had promised, but she was a cop, and you could never completely trust a cop. He finished his sweep. Nobody had set off any alarm bells.

There were three benches to the left of the Mad Hatter. It was a good position since it gave an unobstructed view of both entrances. The old woman on the middle bench was staring off into the distance. Her expression was tinged with sadness, but there was an air of acceptance there too, a sense that this was the way things were and there was nothing she could do, so why fight it. Whatever memory she was lost in, she'd made peace with it long ago.

Winter stared a little longer than he should have, just in case it was Amelia. He knew she was good with disguises, and the best disguises were the ones that enabled you to merge completely into your chosen environment. Dressing up as an old woman would definitely fall into this category. Nobody ever paid much attention to the elderly.

He looked away then glanced back. If it was Amelia then it was one hell of a disguise. To start with you'd need a Hollywood make-up artist and hours of work to come up with a prosthetic mask that good. Amelia was driven and resourceful, but he doubted even she could pull off something like that.

He sat down on the empty bench to the left of the woman, arms outstretched along the top of it. For a while he just sat there smoking and thinking, and did his best to appear as though he didn't have a care in the world. Butterflies were buzzing in his stomach and his nerve endings were jangling. There was just too much information coming in from his senses.

He checked his watch. Still a couple of minutes to go. He did another sweep, checking faces. Checking the way people moved. Undercover cops moved in a certain way, even the best. Unless you were deep undercover there was always going to be the occasional giveaway, no matter how good you were. Even then, it was hard to stay consistently in character. No cops. No Amelia.

Winter counted off the seconds in his head. At T minus sixty seconds he took a final pull on his cigarette, crushed it under his heel and dropped it into the nearest trash can. He checked his watch, counted down the last ten seconds. Still no sign of Amelia. Patience, he told himself. It wasn't easy. He hated inactivity. He took out the last Snickers he'd bought back in Hartwood and ate it quickly.

The old woman was still on the next bench. He glanced over again, just in case he'd called this one wrong. He hadn't. The woman had to be well into her seventies. She was still staring off into the distance as though the rest of the universe had ceased to exist. A laughing family came up the main path. Mom, dad, two boys. Scandinavian accents and good genes. Tall, strong, blonde. The kids were young. Five, six, seven, somewhere around there. They broke away from their parents and sprinted towards the statue, racing each other, laughing and squealing.

Winter contemplated having another cigarette. He needed something to do with his hands, something to do with his mind. The wait was killing him. If there had been another way of doing this then he would have done it, but he'd needed to arrive first to assure Amelia that he wasn't being followed. And she needed to arrive late to show him that she was calling the shots. Because he had chosen the venue for their meeting she would be looking to redress the balance of power.

He checked the time again. He figured that she'd want to be nine minutes late. The figure wasn't entirely random. If she just wanted to show who was in charge then she'd aim to be fifteen minutes late, maybe twenty. She'd want him to sweat. But it wasn't just about that. She was as anxious to see him as he was to see her, so she'd be aiming to be ten minutes late, but she'd be in that little bit too much of a hurry.

A Japanese family came up the path. Mom, dad and a little girl. Because the girl was on her own she wasn't anywhere near as hyperactive as the two Scandinavian boys. She wandered timidly over to the statue and her father started snapping photographs.

Winter kept glancing at his watch, counting off the minutes. Six, seven, eight. He took another quick look around. No undercover cops. No Amelia. He reached nine minutes and realised he'd called it wrong.

Patience.

As it got closer to the twenty-minute mark, he began wondering if she'd gone to the wrong place. Except that didn't work. If she'd done that then she would have called by now to find out where he was. So where the hell was she? It crossed his mind that she might have left the city. It was possible, but he wasn't convinced. Whatever game she was playing, it wasn't quite over yet.

A kid on Rollerblades came skating into the clearing and did a fast circuit of the statue. He was about eighteen or nineteen with acne scars on his cheeks and piercings in his ears, nose and upper lip. Despite the temperature he was wearing baggy shorts that came down past his knees and a black T-shirt with a stoned yellow smiley face on the front. No coat or jacket.

The kid skidded to a stop near the old lady and pulled out his cell phone. He thumbed the screen and put the phone up to his ear. The call connected and he said 'Hi'. A pause, then, 'Tell me where the money is.' Winter's first thought was that he was probably a low-level dealer chasing up a debt, but the explanation didn't ring true. Another pause then, 'Yeah, he's here but I'm not putting him on until you tell me where my money is.'

Winter didn't need to hear any more. He covered the distance between them in less than two seconds, barrelling into the kid and knocking him to the ground. The kid might have been pushing six foot but he couldn't have weighed more than a hundred and twenty pounds. For once Winter had the weight advantage. He pinned the kid down, knees on his arms, weight on his chest. The kid was squirming around and trying to break free, but Winter was just about managing to hold him. He plucked the cell phone from the kid's hand and put it up to his ear.

'Hi, Amelia.'

55

'You sound like you've got your hands full there, Jefferson.'

'Yeah, give me a second.'

Winter pressed the phone against his chest and looked down at the kid. His face was red and he looked worried. People were starting to stare, and a few of the braver ones were moving in closer.

'FBI! Please stay back!'

It had been a while since he'd played this particular card, but he was able to deliver the warning with enough authority to make it sound convincing. People were still staring, and some didn't look convinced, but he'd planted enough doubt to keep them at arm's length. He turned his attention back to the kid. 'How much did she offer you?'

The kid just stared.

'Fifty bucks? A hundred?'

The kid's eyes narrowed. 'It was actually two hundred.'

Sure it was, thought Winter. 'And she was going to tell you where you'd find the money after you delivered the phone, right?'

'Yeah, that's right.'

'But you don't trust her to pay up, hence the reason you were stalling.'

'Man, you can't trust anyone these days.'

Winter stared at the kid until he had his full attention.

'Okay, listen carefully. She was never going to pay up. You need to understand that. It was never going to happen. On the other hand, I will pay up. That's a promise. So here's the deal. I'm going to get off you and you're going to sit on that bench over there until I've finished my call, and then we're going to have a little chat. Do that and I'll give you two hundred bucks. However, if you try to run I will use every resource at my disposal to hunt you down, and when I catch you, I will make sure you go to prison.'

The kid considered this for all of two seconds. 'You don't have to worry, man. I'm not going anywhere.'

Winter stood and pressed the cell phone to the side of his head. He stepped back to let the kid up and watched him skate over to the nearest bench and sit down.

'Are you still there?'

'I'm still here.'

Winter heard the smile shining through in her voice. 'I thought you wanted to meet.'

'I do, but on my terms not yours. I'm figuring that Central Park is crawling with cops by now. Does that sound about right?'

'You told me to come alone, and that's exactly what I've done.'

Amelia laughed. 'I'm sure you'll understand why I'm not going to take your word for that. The kid on the skates, he's still with you, yes?'

'He is.'

'Put him on.'

Winter walked over to the bench and held out the cell phone. The kid stared at it for a second, then reluctantly reached out. He listened, said a couple of 'uh-huhs', then looked up.

'She says that you need to give me your cell phone. And she says if you don't hand it over in the next five seconds then she's going to hang up and disappear. By the way, she's started counting, and she's already on four.'

Winter pulled his cell out and tossed it into the kid's lap.

'Okay, got it.' The kid told Amelia. He listened some more, said a couple of 'Yeahs', then glanced an apology up at Winter and started dismantling the cell phone. 'She says you need to give me your lighter.'

Winter took out his Zippo and handed it over. He had a pretty good idea what was coming next. Sure enough, the kid removed the SIM card from the cell and, holding it carefully by one corner, started to burn it, the flame turning green from the melting plastic. Next, he dropped the phone and battery on to the ground and crushed them under his skate.

'Okay, done it,' he told Amelia. He listened some more then held the Zippo and cell phone out for Winter to take. 'She wants to talk to you.'

Winter took the phone and pressed it against his ear. The Zippo went back into the pocket of his sheepskin jacket. 'So how does this work then?'

'You're going to catch a southbound train from the 77th Street station and get off at Grand Central. Call me when you get up to the concourse. If you get there in time I'll answer. If not, then I'm out of here. It goes without saying that you come alone.'

'You need to tell me how long I've got.'

'No I don't. Either you'll get there in time or you won't. My advice would be to get moving.'

The line went dead and Winter pushed the cell into his jacket pocket. He pulled out his billfold and stuffed two hundred-dollar bills into the kid's hand.

'What did she look like, and where did you meet her?'

'The south end of the park,' the kid replied quickly. 'She had brown shoulder-length hair. Well kind of brown. Maybe it was more blonde. You know a brown-blonde sort of colour. She was wearing thick black spectacles that were on a string like you sometimes see on a teacher or a librarian.' He nodded to himself. 'Yeah, that's what she reminded me of, a librarian.'

'Thanks.'

The kid started to say something else, but Winter was already jogging down the path that led away from the statue. He upped his pace a little, his lungs complaining. He still couldn't see any cops. Mendoza had promised she wouldn't get in his way, but she had her own agenda and one thing he'd learned long ago was that you could never fully trust anyone with an agenda.

By the time he reached the subway station his lungs felt as though they were about to explode, his heart too. He caught his reflection while he was buying a ticket. His face was red and there were beads of sweat on his forehead. The Mozart T-shirt was sticking to his chest.

He made his way down the stairs and reached the south-bound platform just as a train was pulling out. He watched the red tail-lights disappear into the tunnel. This was one of the city's busiest lines. Another train would be along soon enough. The only positive was that the platform was now empty. If Amelia was following him it would make her easier to spot. Since she knew where he was headed, it was unlikely she was, but he wasn't taking anything for granted. There was no way she was going to get the drop on him again.

He walked to the midpoint of the platform and leant against a pillar. From here he had an unobstructed view of any new arrivals. He checked out every person who appeared, but no one stood out. Was she still dressed like a librarian or had she changed disguise again? He thought she'd probably have switched to a new one by now. That's what he would have done.

He took a couple of deep breaths and felt his heart begin to settle. No doubt Amelia was hoping he would underestimate how much time he actually had, and that would make him hurry. The quicker he was doing things, the less he was thinking. The less he was thinking, the more chance there was of him doing something dumb. The flaw in her thinking was that she was as anxious to see him as he was to see her, which meant that the threat was almost certainly an empty one. As long as he didn't waste too much time getting to Grand Central Station then he should be okay.

Winter glanced over at the woman who'd just walked on to the platform, then quickly looked away. Those couple of short seconds were all it took to confirm that this wasn't Amelia. She was the right height, and the right sort of age, but she was too fat. Bulking yourself up so you appeared bigger was fairly straightforward, but this was too extreme.

The train arrived and he got on. He hovered in the doorway until it pulled away, glancing up and down the platform, watching for anyone attempting to beat the doors.

The warning sounded and he took one last look along the platform. No one was trying to squeeze in at the last second. The doors started to close and he stepped back into the subway car.

It was only four stops to Grand Central. Five minutes, ten max. Winter found an empty seat and sat down, then did a quick sweep of the car, checking out the other travellers. Nobody raised any suspicions. There were a couple of dozen people in total. All ages, all races, but definitely no Amelia. He took a moment to straighten his clothes, then rubbed a hand through his hair to tidy it up. When they did eventually meet, he wanted to look as unflustered as possible.

Mendoza would no doubt be wondering where the hell he was, and why he hadn't called. That was part of the deal. As soon as he'd made contact with Amelia he was supposed to call her. Unfortunately, he couldn't see a way to do that. His cell had been destroyed, and although he had the one that the skater kid had given him, it didn't really help. At the moment he was underground and had no signal.

He glanced around the subway car, wondering if he could get one of the other passengers to pass on a message. It was a long shot. Chances were they'd either think he was crazy, or they'd just blank him. He did another quick sweep. The priest at the far end seemed like his best bet. Winter got up and walked over.

'Excuse me.'

The priest didn't seem to hear. He was staring out the window, lost in thought. The rattle and whine of the train didn't help.

Winter tried again. Louder. 'Excuse me.'

The priest turned to face him. He was the same height as Amelia, and for a split second Winter thought it was her. He shook the thought away. The priest was in his fifties, tidy and serene. There was a small wooden crucifix around his neck and a small multi-coloured cloth bag hanging from his shoulder.

'Can I help you?' he asked. His voice was clear, every word enunciated. His accent had been South American once upon a time. Brazilian, maybe.

'I need you to pass a message on to a colleague, please. She's a detective with the NYPD. I need you to tell her that I'm okay, and that I'll contact her as soon as I can.'

The priest frowned, then glanced along the subway car. 'Is this a joke?'

'I know how strange this sounds but I promise you this isn't a joke. If I could do it myself then I would. The problem is that I'm working undercover. It would be too risky.' It wasn't quite the truth, but it was close enough. Winter just didn't have the time or energy to get into long drawn-out explanations. 'Please help me out here,' he added.

The priest took a breath, then nodded. 'What exactly do you want me to do?'

'I take it you have a cell phone?'

'I do.'

'What about paper and a pen?'

The priest rummaged around in his bag until he found a small notepad and a biro. 'Here we go.'

Winter dictated his message and watched him write it down. It was short and to the point. He was okay, but the venue for the meet had changed. The message needed to go to Lieutenant Carson Jones at the NYPD's headquarters. Jones would make sure that it got through to Mendoza. The train pulled into the 51st Street station and the priest stood up to leave.

'Thank you for doing this,' Winter told him. 'I appreciate it.'

The next stop was Grand Central.

56

The doors opened and Winter got out. Two seconds earlier the platform had been empty. Now it was a crush of bodies, everyone anxious to get wherever they were going. He pushed his way through the crowd and pressed himself up against the wall to wait for things to ease off. If he was being pulled along by a sea of bodies it would make it much harder to spot Amelia. The train pulled away from the platform, quickly picking up speed. The last car rattled and sparked into the dark, leaving a large silence in its wake.

Winter gave it another thirty seconds then followed the signs and the crowds to the upper level. There were plenty of people heading the same way, but at least he could move without constantly bumping elbows and arms.

The main concourse reminded him of a cathedral. Solid stone, large windows and a massive vaulted ceiling. He walked slowly into the middle. With every step, he checked faces. Left, right, in front, behind. There were too many to track. Grand Central was one of the world's largest stations. Tens of millions of passengers used it each year, tens of thousands every day. Winter could feel his senses overloading. There was just too much information to process.

He stopped walking. Straight ahead were the three massive windows that the photographers loved. He turned a slow three hundred and sixty degrees, looking for Amelia, and saw too many possibilities. *The brunette in the jeans and leather jacket. The blonde winding through the crowds. A redhead in a business suit.* They were all the right height and the right body-shape and the right sort of age, but none of them were Amelia.

He found the cell phone. There was only one number in the call log. He hit the button to connect the call and pressed the phone hard up against his ear, to try to block out as much of the station noise as possible. The call connected and his heart beat a little faster. It rang a second time, a third. By the fifth ring she still hadn't picked up.

He let it ring out. Just because she said something, it didn't mean it was true. Like Mendoza kept saying, she was a psychopath and psychopaths were known to lie. It was all about control. By telling him that she might or might not answer his call, she was trying to put him on the back foot. She wanted him doubting himself. She wanted him to keep dialling her number until she deigned to pick up.

Winter pushed the cell phone back into his pocket. If she wanted to play control games, then that was fine with him. To kill time he turned in slow circles, checking out faces. He wouldn't put it past her to try and sneak up and tap him on the shoulder.

One minute passed, two. No calls, no taps on the shoulder. Five minutes came and went, six. The cell phone started to buzz in his pocket and he pulled it out. He didn't answer it straightaway. Instead, he turned through another three hundred and sixty degrees, eyes searching the crowds. He saw plenty of people with phones pressed up to ears, plenty of people texting, plenty of people with their eyes fixed to phone screens. No Amelia, though.

He connected the call. 'I'm here.'

'I know. And you came alone.'

Which meant that she was here now, watching. Or maybe she'd watched him until she was satisfied he wasn't being followed then gone to another part of the station to make her call. He pressed the phone harder against the side of his head, listening for anything that might give some idea where she was, but there was just too much ambient noise. He turned through another full circle. No Amelia.

'You said you wanted to meet here. So where are you?'

'No, I told you I wanted you to come here. You really need to pay attention to those details.'

Winter sighed into the mouthpiece. 'Enough with the games, Amelia.'

'Or what? You're just going to walk away?'

'What do you want me to do?'

'I want you to head on over to Brooklyn. Take the 4 train to Fulton Street, then switch to the 2 train and get off at High Street. I'll text through details of where I want you to go after that. Now, in case you're tempted to call in backup, I've paid someone to follow you.'

'No you haven't. It's one thing to get that kid on skates to deliver a cell phone, it's something else entirely to get someone to follow me. They'd need to know about surveillance, which they won't. Not unless they're ex-cops or PIs, and I can't see you hiring someone like that. As for someone who wasn't trained, well I'd spot them in two seconds flat.'

'You didn't see me when I followed you to the diner.'

'I wasn't looking. Big difference.'
'See you soon, Jefferson.'
A click and the line went dead.

57

Winter held the cell phone as high as he could and hurried up the subway steps, searching for a signal. An electronic beep sounded halfway up and he checked the screen. *Brooklyn bridge park, pier one. Call me when you get there.* He broke into a run, taking the remaining steps two at a time. At the top, he stopped and used his phone to get directions. Five minutes later he was jogging towards the park entrance.

Winter took a moment to straighten his clothes and run a hand through his hair. Appearances were important. The last thing he wanted was for Amelia to arrive fresh and breezy, and find him looking as though he'd just run a marathon.

He counted slowly to three, psyching himself up, then walked into the park. Within a couple of strides he was struck by the same sensations he sometimes got when he walked into a murder scene. That familiar tightening in his stomach, the way his heart felt uncomfortably big for his chest. The rational part of his mind knew these were physiological responses to the excess of adrenaline flooding his system, but the irrational part was searching for ghosts.

Winter glanced around quickly, looking for Amelia. There was no sign of her. Up ahead the Manhattan skyline twinkled and glittered in the dark, and off to his right was the bridge. He had the impression that the park hadn't been here long. The trees dotted around the large grass lawns looked young, as though they still had plenty of growing to do, and there was a sense that this whole stretch of the East River was slowly coming back to life.

He did another scan of the park, more slowly this time. There were a couple of women who were the right sort of height and age, but neither one was Amelia. He took out the cell phone and made the call. It was answered on the third ring.

'I'm here.'

'I know. You just strolled right past me.'

Winter fought the urge to glance over his shoulder. 'No I didn't.'

'And you're sure about that?'

'If you'd been planning on being here when I arrived, then you wouldn't have needed me to call.'

'I'll meet you down by the waterfront.' There was a smile in her voice. 'Five minutes.'

The line went dead and Winter put the cell phone away. He walked down towards the river and found a bench, then sat and looked out over the water and waited. It was closer to six minutes before she finally appeared. Winter recognised her straightaway because she was dressed in the same clothes she'd worn at the diner two nights ago. She stopped fifty yards away from the bench and had a quick look around. The impression she gave was that she was taking a moment to appreciate the view, but she was actually checking one last time to make sure he'd come alone. Satisfied, she walked over to the bench and smiled down at him.

'Hi Jefferson, it's so good to see you again.'

Winter studied her for a moment, his eyes taking in

everything. He was wrong. This wasn't the same outfit she'd worn when they first met. It was close, but there were differences. The wig was the same platinum-blonde colour, a colour that was almost white. Same battered Levis, same scuffed Converse sneakers. The first difference was that she had a laptop bag slung over her shoulder. Secondly, she'd swapped the baggy leather jacket for a suede one that was lined with sheepskin.

'Hi Amelia. So who are you pretending to be today?'

58

Amelia's smile widened to show the tips of her teeth. Her fake green eyes met his. 'Do you like my new jacket? I found it in a thrift store. Then again, I'm guessing that's where you buy most of your clothes.'

'You haven't quite got the hair right. It should be white.'

'Artistic licence. I didn't want to stand out too much.' She fluffed the wig with her hands. 'This was as close to white as I felt comfortable going. So what do you think? Just like looking in a mirror, right?'

Winter said nothing. He looked at her and wondered what the hell she was up to. Why go to all this trouble?

'Okay,' she said eventually, 'I want you to stand, and I want you to do it slowly. Then we're going to hug like we've really missed each other.'

Winter got up and stepped into Amelia's open arms. He felt her hands moving efficiently across his body as she patted him down. A couple of people glanced over, but all they saw were two lovers meeting up, or perhaps a couple of close friends, nothing more suspicious than that. Amelia stepped back and held her hand out.

'The cell phone please.'

Winter gave her the phone. He watched as she worked the screen with her thumb, watched as it disappeared into her laptop bag. She sat down on the bench and patted the space next to her. He sat down. Amelia moved the laptop bag to her side and rested one hand protectively on top of it. Winter found his cigarette pack and tapped one out.

'Didn't you see the signs at the entrance?' she asked him. 'No smoking.'

He pushed the cigarette back into the pack but kept the lighter out. *Click, click, flick* with the flame. He did this a second time, a third time. He felt her watching him.

'What's the story with the Zippo?'

'Who says there's a story?'

'There's a story.'

He clicked the lighter closed and looked at it for a moment. The brass was pitted and scratched. The combination of the park lights and the moon made the metal appear yellow. He pushed the Zippo back into his pocket.

'It belonged to my partner in the FBI. When she quit smoking, she gave it to me. Like I said, there's no story. Not really.'

She leant towards him, eyes locked on his and kept going until the tip of her nose touched his cheek. Slowly she moved her head upwards, her nose dragging across his stubbly skin. Winter sat dead still, staring straight ahead. She reached the top of his cheek, paused a moment, then settled back into her own space, a hint of perfume trailing in her wake.

'You're lying. I can smell lies, you know.'

'There's no story, Amelia. She quit smoking and gave me the lighter. That's all.'

'This partner meant something to you. You wouldn't have kept it if she didn't. That's a story in itself right there. So where did she get it from?'

Winter hesitated. 'Her father. He gave it to her when he quit smoking.'

'See, it's not just a lighter, it's an heirloom. You two were as close as family. Close enough for her to want to give you an heirloom. So what happened? Did she die of lung cancer?' When Winter didn't respond, Amelia put her hands up. It was a gesture that could have been contrite or apologetic, but was neither. 'You don't want to talk about it, don't talk. I get it. Personal is personal.'

'Why did you want to meet?'

'I wanted to see your reaction. It was dark the first two times we met, and I didn't quite have the jacket right. This one's much better, don't you think?'

'Okay, you've seen my reaction. Can I go now?'

'What's the hurry? It's a beautiful evening. I thought we might chat for a while.'

'You want to chat, fine. Tell me about your father.'

Amelia smiled. 'How about you tell me about your father first?'

Winter smiled back. Move and countermove, just like a chess game. In another world, another life, it would have been so easy to be disarmed by her.

'My father was one of America's most notorious serial killers. Over a twelve-year period he murdered fifteen young women. He kidnapped them then took them out into the forest in the dead of night and hunted them down with a high-powered rifle. He was highly intelligent, but obviously not intelligent enough, because he got caught. He spent twenty years on Death Row and then he was executed. Okay, your turn.'

Amelia shook her head. 'You're going to have to do better than that. You haven't told me anything I couldn't find out online. I want something that I can't read on a computer screen.'

Winter took out the Zippo and lit it. A thousand and one random images were flooding through his mind, pictures from the years before the arrest. Good times, fun times. Happier times. He narrowed the list down to six, then picked the memory that shone the brightest. He clicked the lighter closed and put it away.

'He made the best banana pancakes you've ever tasted.'

'Banana pancakes!' Amelia shook her head. 'Is that the best you can do? Your father was one of the world's most notorious serial killers and you give me pancakes.'

'Up until I was eleven my dad was my dad. He could be distant at times, controlling at others. Sometimes I hated him, sometimes I loved him. Like I say, he was my dad, the guy who made the best banana pancakes in the world.'

She considered this for a moment, then nodded to herself. 'You didn't have a clue what he was, did you?'

'No I didn't. I should have, though.'

'And this is where I'm supposed to tell you that you were just a kid? I mean, how could you have known? That's what everyone else says, right?' Her face brightened. 'Yes, you should have known, Jefferson. You should have seen him for what he really was. But what then? Would you have turned him in? The guy who made the best banana pancakes in the world? Not a chance.'

'Okay, your turn.'

Amelia didn't say anything straightaway. She broke eye

contact and watched a middle-aged guy walk by, trailing a golden retriever on a lead.

'My father loved music,' she said eventually.

Winter waited for more, but there wasn't anything. 'A lot of people love music. I love music. With all due respect, you're not exactly giving me banana pancakes here.'

Her eyes moved away from the guy with the dog and back to Winter. She smiled one of the most disturbing smiles he'd ever seen. 'His favourite composer was Strauss. He had one LP that he would play continuously while we ate dinner. Over and over and over. As soon as it finished, he'd get up and put the needle back to the start again.'

'I saw the CD player and the table in the bomb shelter. I'm guessing you carried on the tradition, right? You ate at the table, your father ate out of the dog bowl, and Strauss played gently in the background.'

'Wrong again, Jefferson. Well, mostly wrong. Dinner time was quiet time.'

'So what was the CD player for?'

'That was so he didn't get lonely in the dark.'

The statement didn't make sense to start with, and then it did. 'The stockpile of batteries in the cellar was for the CD player, wasn't it. Day and night, you made him listen to that same CD. Over and over and over.'

'I told him that I'd turn it off if he burned his eye out. It took a while to convince him, but eventually he believed me. It took longer to convince him the second time.' She paused. 'When I was little I wanted to be a dancer. When my father found out, do you know what he did? He made me dance for him every night after dinner, and he'd just sit there laughing at me. I hate Strauss almost as much as I hate him.' Another pause. 'Okay, your turn. When we were in the diner, you wanted to kill that cook, didn't you?'

For a split second the world shrunk down until all it contained was the bench that the two of them were sitting on.

'You're way off the mark,' he said evenly.

'Liar. I saw the way your pupils dilated. I saw your breathing speed up. You were imagining what it would be like to stick that knife into his eye.' She smiled brightly. 'Go on, admit it.'

'You're wrong.'

Amelia leant in close, closer. Her nose touched his cheek and she sniffed. She let out a long breath that warmed his skin, then settled back into her own space again.

'You're wrong,' he repeated.

'We could kill someone right now, you know.' Her left hand moved in a loose arc that seemed to take in the whole park and everyone in it. 'Pick a sheep, any sheep.'

'I'm not playing this game.'

'Come on, Jefferson, loosen up a little. Okay, how about that guy over there wearing the red NYC ball cap? So tacky, and the way he's staring up at the bridge, he's got to be a tourist. He deserves to die just for that, don't you think?' She dropped her voice to a confidential whisper. 'What about that old guy over there near the next bench? He must be at least a hundred. If we kill him, we'd be doing him a favour. He's probably riddled with cancer.'

Winter said nothing.

'I could make you choose, you know.' She patted her laptop bag. 'I've got a gun in here. Either choose one or I'll shoot both. I'd happily waste two bullets to put those little sheep out of their misery.'

Winter sighed and shook his head. 'Amelia, you're not going to shoot anyone, so let's drop it. How far do you think you're going to get before you get taken down? Sure, you might make it out of the park, but I can't see you getting much further than that. A gun goes off around here and someone's going to call the cops. This isn't exactly the Bronx.'

'The question isn't how far I'm going to get, it's how many people will I kill before that happens?'

'Both questions are irrelevant. Yes, you're a psychopath, but you're not a killer. At least you're not one who likes getting their hands dirty. It's much more fun to get other people to do the killing for you, right? That's what happened with Nelson and Ryan McCarthy, wasn't it. You wound them up then stood back and watched. Control and manipulation, that's what you get off on.'

'I killed Omar.'

'But why did you kill him? That's the crucial question here. Why? You didn't do it because you wanted to see him suffer, or you wanted to hear him scream, or you needed to right some perceived wrong. You did it to get my attention. Basically, he was collateral damage. If you could have got my attention another way, you would have, but you knew that would work. What's more, you were right. It was probably the only thing that could have stopped me catching my flight to Paris.'

'But that's not the only reason? People always hide from their true selves. They keep their secret desires locked down

343

inside their heads. Nelson did that. Ryan, too. I just helped them to reach their full potential.'

'Maybe so, but that doesn't explain why you killed Omar.'

'What secret desire do you keep locked away, Jefferson? Or, let's put it another way, what do you fantasise about? I couldn't find any online interviews with you, but I managed to find some that had been done with the people you'd worked for. The common theme was the way you got into the heads of your prey. So the question I'm asking myself right now is: how do I help you to reach your full potential?'

'I know where you're going with this, and you're way off the mark.'

'I don't think so. It starts with the fantasies and progresses from there. One day you're daydreaming, the next your hands are covered in blood. And it's not as though you've never killed. Sure, you can try telling yourself that it was in the line of duty, that the kills were righteous, but we both know the truth. Killing someone is easy. The trick is getting away with it. With all your training, you know all the tricks, don't you? So would you like to know what it felt like to kill Omar?'

'No, Amelia, I wouldn't'.

She stared at him for a second, then her face broke into a wide smile. 'Liar.'

Winter took out the Zippo and lit it. He snapped the lid shut and put the lighter away. She was trying to rattle him. What's more, she'd almost succeeded. He forced himself to put his personal feelings aside, forced himself to inject some ice into his thoughts, forced himself to look at what she was actually saying without taking it personally. Amelia said that she was helping Nelson, but that was bullshit. The only person that she was looking out for was herself.

'What did Melanie do to you?'

The smile slid away. 'Melanie didn't do anything to me.'

'Then why did you want her dead? Was it because she was the popular girl at High School, and you were the girl everyone despised?'

Amelia laughed. 'Do you really think that I care about other people's opinions?'

'Okay, not that.' Winter glanced over the water at Manhattan then looked back at Amelia. 'How about this then? Nelson got a crush on Melanie and you couldn't handle that. When you latch on to someone, you need to be the only person in their universe. You did that with Nelson, and Ryan McCarthy, and your father. And you're trying to do it with me.'

'You don't know what you're talking about.'

'Yes I do. What's more, it's working. Right now, you're right at the centre of my universe. You're pretty much all that I've thought about for the last two days. But what happens when the object of your obsession starts to stray? How does that make you feel? Angry, I bet. Absolutely furious. I'm figuring that you filled Nelson's head with poison. You took his love for Melanie and turned that into hate, then convinced him to kill her. You're lucky Nelson didn't turn on you.'

'Nelson would never have hurt me.'

'And you're sure about that?'

Amelia said nothing.

'You lost control of him, didn't you? But that's the thing

with fantasies. When they become real it's never quite how you imagine. So why didn't you stop Nelson killing himself? My guess is that it's because you didn't trust him not to implicate you. He was too unstable for you to trust with a secret that big.'

A sly look came over Amelia's face. It was an expression that Winter had seen during those FBI prison interviews. He was circling close to the truth. She wanted him to know, but she was going to make him work for it.

'Where are you going with this?' she asked gently.

'You told him to kill himself. That was your idea. It's the ultimate control game. Manipulating people into killing is one thing, manipulating them into killing themselves takes it to a whole new level.'

Amelia smiled again.

Winter took out the Zippo again. *Click, flick, click. Click, flick, click.* 'Earlier you were talking about sheep. What does that make you? A wolf.' He watched her closely. 'Not a wolf then, how about a tiger?' He studied her again. 'Close but not quite. Okay, how about a lioness? That's what this is really all about, right? You're trying to nurture your inner lioness.'

'Don't mock me.'

'And what am I supposed to do? Take you seriously? No, that would legitimise you, and that's not going to happen. You think that what you do makes you special, but it doesn't. Take it from me, you're not the first psychopath with delusions of grandeur, and you won't be the last. Do you want to know the truth? You're a nobody, Amelia. Just another nothing in a long line of nothings.'

Her face contorted with anger, all pretence gone. One

second she was doing a poor imitation of him, in the next he glimpsed the monster she was. The transformation was both terrifying and fascinating. Winter was waiting for her to say something. Waiting for the explosion. It never happened. She took a deep breath and by the time she'd finished her exhalation the mask had gone back up.

'Sticks and stones, Jefferson. Sticks and stones. Okay, we're done here.'

Winter was watching her closely, waiting for the right moment. Timing was everything. Amelia went to stand and he stood up, too. They bumped arms and the laptop bag fell to the ground. Winter bent down and scooped it up. He held it out and waited for her to take it. Their eyes locked.

'What are you up to, Jefferson?'

'It was an accident.'

'No it wasn't.' She snatched the bag back and started going through the pockets. Her hand went into the small side pocket and a grin lit up her face. She removed her hand slowly. Clasped between her thumb and forefinger was Winter's Zippo. She held it up. 'Lost something?'

Amelia sat down again and dismantled the lighter. She examined each part then laid it neat on the bench. The tracking device was hidden in the wad of cotton wool used to soak up the lighter fluid. She held it up for him to see. 'You're so predictable.'

Winter looked at the pile of parts on the bench, then looked at Amelia. She dropped the tracking device on the ground, crushed it underneath her sneaker, then stood up and walked away without looking back. Fifty yards on the path curved gently to the right. After another ten yards she'd disappeared from sight. Winter reassembled the light, then walked over to an old guy who was stood looking out over the river and asked if he could borrow his cell phone. The guy looked at him like he'd gone crazy. So did the next two people he asked. The fourth person actually believed him when he told her he was an undercover cop. She dug a cell phone from her bag and handed it over. Winter punched in 911 and asked to get put through to Mendoza.

59

The stoned Asian guy working the graveyard shift looked like he'd been teleported in from the sixties. His Grateful Dead T-shirt was faded and old, and his long grey ponytail was wound into a plait. He watched bug-eyed as the police filed through the door. At the same time he was trying hard to avoid looking directly at anyone. Up until ten seconds ago the world had been a mellow place, now it was a living nightmare. Winter felt kind of sorry for him.

Given that this motel was two-star at best, the reception area didn't look anywhere near as shabby as he would have expected. The computer monitor on the counter was reasonably up to date, the cheap furniture matched, and the plants dotted strategically around the room were both real and alive. The plastic holder next to the monitor contained business cards. The Paradise Motel was printed in bamboo letters above a nasty graphic of a palm tree. Beneath that was a Bellefonte number. The town was in Philadelphia, just off I-80. They'd done the four-hour drive from New York in a little over three hours and fifteen minutes, the BMW's big engine working hard.

Mendoza laid a tablet down on the desk and pointed at the screen. 'See that flashing red dot? Which room?'

The guy just stood there with his mouth hanging open, his gaze following three points of a triangle. Mendoza, Winter, the tablet, before moving back to Mendoza and starting all over again. The other six cops who'd come in with them no longer seemed to be registering on his radar.

'It's okay,' Winter told him. 'This isn't a bust. What's your name?'

'Marty.'

'Okay, Marty, how about we start with you killing the sound on the TV set.'

Marty turned and looked blankly at the TV on the corner of the desk. A DVD of *Pulp Fiction* was playing. Samuel L. Jackson was on the screen, intense, righteous and cooler than cool. Marty broke out of his trance and leant over to hit the off button. Winter tapped the desk to bring his attention back to the tablet.

'What room is this?'

Marty slid the tablet closer and peered at the screen. 'If I'm reading this right, then it's either 107 or 117. I'm not sure which since they're on top of one another. Give me a second and I might be able to tell you.' He reached for the mouse and the computer monitor flared to life. A couple of clicks, then he nodded to himself. 'Yeah, it's 107. There's no one in 117.'

'What name did they use?' asked Mendoza.

'Wren Firestone. Middle initial J.'

She exchanged a glance with Winter. 'Is Ms Firestone on her own?'

Marty nodded. 'So far as I can tell.'

Mendoza turned to the cop standing immediately behind her. 'I want to know what's happening in room 107. And be discrete, okay? I don't want her spooked.'

When the cop reappeared a couple of minutes later he

was carrying a laptop. He placed it on the counter and lifted the lid. At first glance the heat signatures looked psychedelic. Amelia was represented by colours from the upper end of the spectrum. Red, orange, yellow, white. The rest of the screen was filled in with cooler colours. Black, blue and purple.

'This is in real time, right?' Mendoza asked.

'Yes ma'am,' the cop replied. 'As far as we can tell she's sleeping like a baby.'

Winter leant in for a closer look. He could make out Amelia's chest moving. It looked as though she was in the deepest part of her sleep cycle, which would make things a bit easier. The jagged splash of white near her head puzzled him to start with, then he got it.

'She's left a night light on, hasn't she?'

The cop answered with a nod.

Mendoza turned away from the laptop and addressed the cops standing directly behind her. 'We use the battering ram, then take her down as quickly as possible. I want it so she doesn't know what's hit her. Does everyone understand?'

Nods all around

'Okay, let's do this.'

The six cops turned for the door in unison, tugging at their Kevlar vests, reaching for guns. Pumped and primed and ready for action.

'Wait up,' Winter called out.

Everyone froze then turned to face him.

'This isn't going to work. If we force her into a corner she's going to choose suicide by cop. Are we all agreed that the aim here is to bring her in alive?'

Winter focused on Mendoza. This was her show. She was calling the shots.

'So what do *you* suggest?' she asked evenly.

'I go in alone, and persuade her to come out quietly.'

'With all due respect, that doesn't sound like much of a plan.'

'I can do this, Mendoza. This isn't the first takedown I've been involved with. A little faith, please.'

'What makes you so sure that she'd pick suicide over prison.'

'Because of what her father did to her when she was a child. All that time spent chained up in the dark, there's no way she'd choose to go to prison. She'd rather die first.'

The lies were delivered smoothly, so smoothly that Winter almost believed them himself. The truth was that Amelia would do anything to stay alive. She'd survived being abused by her father for all those years, she wasn't just going to give up now. Suicide by cop was not on the agenda.

Mendoza stared at him a second longer. 'You need to wear a vest. You're not going in there without one.'

'Sure. I'll need a gun as well.'

She unclipped the gun from her shoulder holster and handed it to him butt first. Then she motioned for one of the cops hovering near the doorway to come forward, the one who was closest to Winter's size. She told him to take off his vest. Told him that he was to stay put in reception and keep his head down since she didn't want to be on the wrong end of a lawsuit.

Winter put the Kevlar vest on and made sure the Velcro straps were done up tight. It was heavy and bulky and restricted his breathing. He thumped his chest once, and felt the reassuring thud echo through his chest.

'You sure you want to do this?' Mendoza asked. 'You don't have to, you know.'

'What's this? You're actually worried about me?' Winter smiled. 'See, you do like me really.'

60

Winter made his way slowly around the edge of the deserted parking lot, hugging the side of the motel building and merging with the shadows being cast by the motel lights and the fat full moon. The vest was digging into him and the gun felt heavy in his hand, but there was something reassuring about that.

Room 107 was easy to find. It was the only first-floor room with a light on. The car parked out front was a small nondescript Ford. It was impossible to tell the exact colour because it was dark, but it was towards the lighter end of the spectrum. There were hundreds of thousands of cars like this one on the road. It was the sort of vehicle you wouldn't look at twice, a good choice for a killer on the run.

There was no way to see inside the room. The drapes were pulled tight together and the edges had been stretched past the window frame so you couldn't see around them. They glowed dimly from the light being thrown off by the bedside lamp. He crept past the window and stopped outside the door. Mendoza's voice was whispering through the earpiece, telling him that Amelia was still asleep. Even so, he pressed his ear to the thin wood and listened. No noise from the other side.

He pushed the key into the lock. Slowly, carefully. In the quiet still of the night, the sound of metal scratching against metal was as loud as a klaxon. He slid the key out of the lock and dropped it back into his pocket. The door opened easily. No creaks, no squeaks.

Winter stepped inside and stopped dead. The room appeared to be full of headless two-dimensional people. He took a closer look and realised that he was seeing her disguises. Amelia had screwed hooks into the door frames, run clotheslines across the room, and hung her outfits up. There was a hanger for the top half of the outfit, and tied to this was a second hangar for the bottom part. The sheepskin jacket and jeans were hanging near the bed.

He didn't recognise Amelia at first. She was wrapped up in the quilt, breathing slow and easy, little muffled snores tickling the silence. This was the first time he'd seen her without a wig. Her shaved head made her look like an androgynous automaton, more machine than human. Winter tiptoed deeper into the room, Mendoza's service pistol leading the way. He kept the gun trained on her, aiming at her body since it offered a larger target. Her Glock was on the nightstand, next to a music box. The laptop bag was wedged between the bed and the stand. He picked up the gun, then leant down towards her ear.

'Wakey wakey,' he whispered softly.

He took a couple of quick steps backwards, his gun still aimed at her centre mass. Amelia came awake in an instant, making the transition from fully asleep to fully alert in the space of a single heartbeat. Her hand slapped down into the empty space where her gun had been. She glanced at the nightstand, then looked at Winter. He held up the Glock so she could see, gave it a little wiggle.

'Looking for this?'

Amelia didn't reply. She'd thrown off the quilt and was sitting on the pillows. She was wearing a shapeless baggy white T-shirt and plain white panties. Winter pushed the Glock into the waistband of his jeans then unhooked a pair of handcuffs from one of the belt loops. He tossed them on to the bed and they landed with a muted jangle. Amelia glanced at them, then looked back at him.

'I don't think so.'

Winter reaffirmed his grip on Mendoza's gun and made a big show of aiming it. 'Attach one cuff to your wrist and the other to the bed. Do it now.'

'Or what? You're going to shoot me.'

'Last chance.'

Amelia shook her head slowly, a wide smile playing on her lips. 'Looks like we've reached a stalemate.'

'No, we haven't.'

Winter shifted his aim slightly to the left and pulled the trigger. The gun boomed and the bedside lamp exploded in a shower of ceramic. The darkness that followed was sudden and absolute. The muzzle flash had destroyed his night vision making everything look even darker than it actually was.

There was a brief moment of stillness before hell broke loose. All Winter could hear were voices. They cut through the dark and broke into the silence. Mendoza was shouting in his earpiece, demanding to know what the hell was going on, and Amelia was screaming from the bed. She sounded like a wounded animal, her terror evident in every strangled sob. Winter touched his throat mike.

'I'm fine, Mendoza.'

'I heard gunfire. What the hell just happened?'

'Later, okay?'

'We're coming in.'

'No you're not. Just give me five minutes. I've got this under control.'

Winter walked over to the door and hit the light switch. Amelia had pulled herself into a tight foetal ball at the head of the bed, knees tucked into her chin. Tears were streaming down her face. She'd stopped screaming the second the light came on, but she was still sobbing.

'The cuffs,' he prompted.

Amelia shook her head and he hit the light switch again. More darkness, more screaming. He left it longer this time, let time stretch to a minute and beyond. Her screams intensified with every passing second. This was no longer the sound of a wounded animal, this was the sound of madness. He let things run past the point where he thought he couldn't take any more then hit the lights. Amelia was cowering at the end of the bed. With her bald head and wide terrified eyes, she looked like a crazy person.

'Next time the lights stay off. Do you understand?'

Amelia nodded, then reluctantly reached for the handcuffs. She fastened one end to the bed, the other to her right wrist. She was still breathing fast, but she was coming back down. The fear in her eyes was fading fast, replaced with something more calculating. Her eyes were a dull everyday blue, and Winter was almost certain that this was her natural colour.

He walked slowly over to the nightstand, her eyes following every step. The music box was the sort of thing that you'd find in a little girl's bedroom. A place to hide treasures. It was pink and rectangular and, even before he opened it, he knew there would be a plastic ballerina turning endless pirouettes, while a piece of music played on an endless loop. He lifted the lid and sure enough, the ballerina started to dance. It only took four notes for him to place the tune. 'Twinkle Twinkle Little Star'.

Inside the music box was his passport. He recognised it from the scratches and creases on the cover. He lifted it out, Amelia watching his every move. Underneath was a second passport, and beneath that was another, and another. He lifted them out. There were seven in total.

He laid the passports on the nightstand, then picked up the one that had been on the bottom of the pile. Linda Price, Amelia's mother. Next was Melanie Reed's. He didn't recognise the names on the next four, but the picture in the last one rang a bell. The photograph showed a young woman with a black pixie haircut. According to the passport her name was Caroline Mathers.

Winter took out his cell and typed *Caroline Mathers homicide*. He looked at what he'd typed, changed homicide to suicide, then hit search. Top of the list was a link to a story printed in the *Atwood Herald*. Caroline Mathers had hung herself. She was only twenty-two. A second search placed the town of Atwood in Illinois.

Seven passports. Seven mannequins. He looked at the clothes hanging around the room. Seven outfits.

'These aren't just disguises. These were real people.' He walked over to the scarlet dress. It looked old-fashioned, whereas the other outfits appeared to be more up to date. It

was the sort of thing an older woman might wear. 'This belonged to your mother, right?'

Amelia said nothing.

'Your father made you and your brother watch when she
hung herself, didn't he? The three of you just stood there
watching her dance and twitch at the end of a rope. Did
Daddy make her do it? Is that how it worked? Did he march
everyone out to the barn and taunt her until she finally put
the rope around her neck?'

Still nothing from Amelia. It might not have gone down
exactly like this, but he could tell from her expression that he
was in the right ballpark.

'After your mother's death, you took her place. You'd put
on this dress and take her seat at the dinner table, and after
dinner you'd dance for your father. That was the start. That
was the point the behaviour was established. Next you became Melanie Reed. And after that you became someone
else. And somewhere down the line you became Caroline
Mathers. And now you're trying to be me.'

Still nothing.

'So who are you, Amelia? I mean, who are you really?
Because my feeling is that you don't know any more. You've
spent so long pretending to be other people that you've lost
sight of who you actually are.'

'I want to know how you found me?'

'There's a tracking device stuck to the back of the sheepskin jacket you were wearing in the park. It's a tiny adhesive
thing that I borrowed from the FBI. You'd have to look hard
to find it. I planted it on you when you patted me down. I
put the lighter in your bag because you were expecting me

to do something. After all, I'm so predictable. If you hadn't caught me planting the lighter you would have kept looking. I couldn't run the risk of you finding the real tracking device.'

They fell into silence. Winter walked around the room, looking at the outfits. He could feel Amelia watching him again. He stopped at the scarlet dress and ran his hand over the fabric.

'You know something? I almost feel sorry for you, Amelia.'

'And I could say the same thing to you.'

He touched the throat mike and told Mendoza that the coast was clear. Thirty seconds later he heard footsteps outside the room. Mendoza appeared in the doorway, gun drawn, a couple of cops covering her back. She looked Winter up and down like she needed to convince herself that he was still in one piece. She glanced over at Amelia then turned back to Winter.

'So your mystery woman exists, after all.'

'Admit it, Mendoza, this beats the hell out of Vegas.'

'Maybe.'

'Look at the two of you,' Amelia whispered. 'You think you've got this whole thing all sewn up, don't you?'

'Yeah,' said Mendoza, 'You can see why we might make a mistake like that, what with you being cuffed to the bed and everything.'

Amelia shook her head and met Winter's eye. 'What I did with Ryan marked a change in my MO, right? But that's okay, because that's the way it works. When fantasy becomes reality you're always chasing the original high. So you adapt and change in an attempt to find that high. But what if Ryan wasn't a change of plan? What if there are more Ryans out there? If I were in your shoes, the question I'd be asking right now is what exactly has Amelia been up to for the last six years.'

Winter felt his heart jump uncomfortably. She was right. He had assumed that McCarthy marked a mutation in her MO. The behaviour was still based on control, the difference was that the risk factor had increased. But what if he was wrong about that? What if there were a dozen Ryan McCarthys out there? Two dozen?

'I don't believe you.'

'Whether you believe or not is irrelevant.'

He studied her face for any indication that she might be lying. Any tic or tell. He couldn't see anything, nothing at all. Not a damn thing. 'How many?'

'That would be telling.' She smiled. 'You know, I don't know which I prefer. Watching someone put a noose around their neck, or watching someone take a life. One coin. Two sides.'

'Get her out of here,' Mendoza shouted.

Two of the cops stepped forward and walked over to the bed. Amelia ignored them. All her attention was focused on Winter. He met her gaze, refusing to back down. One of the cops unlocked the cuff from the bed, while the other grabbed her arm and dragged her upright. He pulled her arms behind her back, clicked the bracelet closed on her wrists, then marched her unceremoniously from the room. She flashed Winter one last smile from the doorway, and then she was gone.

Mendoza walked across to the bed and sat down on the edge.

'She's full of shit, you know that don't you? No way does she have an army of Ryans all prepped and ready to go.'

'I think she was telling the truth.'

'Bullshit.'

Winter said nothing.

'Is this you or your inner psychopath talking here?'

'What do you think?'

Mendoza studied him for a second, then shook her head and swore to herself. 'So, what now?'

Winter walked over to the bed and knelt down beside the nightstand. He pulled the laptop bag out, then straightened up and handed it to Mendoza. 'Well, this is the obvious place to start looking. There's got to be something on there. You're going to have to go careful, though. She might have it set up to wipe the hard drive.' He considered what he'd just said. 'Actually, I'd say that's a definite.'

'How many Ryans do you think we're talking about?'

Winter shrugged. 'Maybe one, possibly two.'

'Is that all?'

'You saw what McCarthy did. Even one is one too many.'

'That's not what I meant. The way she was talking, there's more than two out there. Maybe a lot more.'

'She was toying with us. Again. Creating another Ryan McCarthy is not going to be quick, or easy. Creating two would be harder still. As for a dozen of them, I just don't see it, not in six years.'

'I hope you're right about that.'

'So do I.'

Winter walked over to the door and stepped out into the chilly early morning air. A couple of the other rooms were now lit up, the occupants peering around doors and drapes to see what was happening. The sound of a car engine starting broke the silence. He looked over and saw a cop car backing out of a parking slot. The shadow figure on the rear seat turned its head towards him. He had no trouble filling in the blanks with the face she'd shown him back at the diner. Platinum-blonde hair that was so light it was almost white, bright green eyes, and a playful I-know-something-you-don't smile. A mirror image of himself, but not quite. The car slowed when it reached the motel entrance but didn't stop. It swung hard to the right, and a couple of seconds later the taillights disappeared from sight.

Epilogue

The small tent that had been erected over the coffin was unnecessary. After three days of solid rain, the clouds had finally dispersed and it was another beautiful fall day. Winter glanced up at the wide swath of blue stretching above his head and reckoned that Granville Clarke would have approved.

At a rough estimate there had to be at least a couple of hundred mourners here, all dressed in black, faces grim, eyes fixed on the coffin. He wasn't sure what Clarke would have made of all of this, though. No doubt he would have been dismissive of everyone making such a fuss, but deep down he would probably have been pleased.

He was watching from the shade of a sugar maple a couple of hundred yards from the grave site. He was far enough away to be able to see what was going on, but too far away to hear what the preacher was saying. He didn't feel as though he was missing much. These things tended to pretty much follow the same bleak script. The grave was halfway down the hill. Over his shoulder, he could see the big old cemetery gates. Main Steet was quiet, presumably because everyone who was anyone in Hartwood was here.

He'd flown in from Paris so he could attend Omar Harrak's funeral service yesterday. The Paris investigation was still ongoing, but they'd hit a lull and he reckoned he could afford a couple of days off without it causing any real problems. Winter wasn't in the habit of turning up uninvited at funerals. He wasn't in the habit of attending funerals, period. The last one he'd been to was his mother's, and that had been so depressing he'd vowed never to go to another. And now this. Two funerals in two days.

Omar's funeral had been a very different affair. Clarke had been old and sick. He'd been the first to admit that he was on borrowed time. Omar, on the other hand, wasn't. His death was a complete bolt from the blue, and the faces of the mourners had reflected this. Winter had snuck in at the start of the funeral prayer, and snuck away again before the mourners began to file out. No one had known he was there. He had paid particular attention to Omar's wife and children. What he saw in their faces confirmed that Omar had been a good husband and father. Their grief was real, raw and heartfelt.

*

The laptop had been a bust. All the police had found on it was a folder that contained information on him. Amelia had scoured the internet and managed to put together a sketchy biography based on the information she'd collected. She'd also got hold of two photographs. In both of them he'd been wearing his leather jacket instead of the sheepskin one. He was sure there was another laptop somewhere that could be used to connect her to her other victims. A laptop that could help them find all those other Ryans she claimed were out there. But where? She'd managed to successfully hide her father for six years, how hard would it be to hide a laptop?

Caroline Mathers' parents had confirmed that one of Amelia's disguises was made up of clothes that had belonged to their daughter. Three of the other outfits had been connected via the passports to young women who had also hung themselves. All four women had a history of depression, and all of them frequented internet chat rooms dealing with the illness. There was no evidence to suggest that Amelia had witnessed their suicides, but Winter was betting she had. She wouldn't have missed an opportunity like that.

Amelia had recently been moved to the maximum security unit at New York's Bellevue Hospital to undergo a psychiatric evaluation. As far as Winter was concerned, the question wasn't whether she was insane, it was whether she wanted people to believe that. For her, it would just be an opportunity to assume a new personality. He wasn't surprised that she'd been moved to Bellevue. If anything, the only surprise was that it hadn't happened sooner. Doctors and nurses were always going to be easier to handle than prison guards.

*

Even though he couldn't hear what was happening at the grave, he got the sense that things were winding up. Sure enough, a short while later the coffin was lowered into the ground. A couple of mourners stepped forward to drop dirt on to the coffin. Violet was one of them. Winter didn't recognise her at first because the context was wrong. He was used to seeing her in the diner. He waited until the last mourners left before heading over. The headstone had Jocelyn Clarke's birth and death dates chiselled into the marble. There was space underneath for her husband's name and dates to be added.

Winter took the two chess pieces from his pocket and turned them over in his hand. They'd been hand carved, the old wood smooth to the touch. While the mourners were gathering at the chapel for the memorial service, he had broken into Clarke's house. The chessboard in the living room was frozen mid-game, just like it had been on the night they'd eaten Chinese and drunk whisky together. He had played the game through to its logical conclusion then pocketed the black king and the white queen.

He held his hand over the grave, the chess pieces lying flat on his palm, then slowly tilted his hand and watched them fall. They hit the coffin lid with two sharp cracks, one after the other.

Winter took one last look at the coffin then turned and made his way back up the hill. He'd gotten halfway to the gate when his cell phone buzzed in his pocket. There was one new email. It was from Amelia. At first he thought his eyes were playing tricks, but they weren't. He hesitated a second, his thumb hovering over the screen, then opened it and read through it quickly, speeding over the words. It was short and to the point, the tone casual, the subtext anything but.

Feel free to visit any time you want. It would be good to catch up.

Amelia

Winter read through the email a second time, wondering

how the hell she'd managed to send this. It had to be her lawyer. She must have requested a meeting, and when it was just the two of them, she gave him the message and the email address. The rest of the time she would have had people watching over her. Cops, prison guards, medical personnel. Given time, Winter didn't doubt that she could manipulate one of them to do something like this. But it was too soon. The lawyer was the only way she could have gotten this email to him, because that was the only variable she could currently control. Lawyer/client privilege could be a real bitch.

She was screwing with him. Again. She wanted to show that, even though she was locked up, she could still reach out and mess with his head. So, how did you disempower a psychopath who liked to play games? Simple. You didn't play along.

Winter glanced at the email one last time, then hit delete.

Acknowledgements

I couldn't do this without the support of my family. Karen, Niamh, Finn . . . I love you guys.

I'm fortunate to be represented by the best agent in the business. Camilla Wray, please step forward and take a much deserved bow.

Katherine Armstrong has done yet another fantastic editing job.

Thanks also to Hannah Griffiths, Miles Paynton, Kate O'Hearn, KC O'Hearn and Nick Tubby; and to Clare, Mary, Sheila, Emma and Rosanna at the Darley Anderson Agency.

Finally, a huge thank you to everyone who has taken the time to read the books. Your continued support means the world to me.

ff

Broken Dolls

It takes a genius to catch a psychopath

Jefferson Winter is no ordinary investigator.

The son of one of America's most notorious serial killers,
Winter has spent his life trying to distance himself from his
father's legacy. Once a rising star at the FBI, he is now a
freelance consultant, jetting around the globe helping local
law enforcement agencies with difficult cases. He hasn't got
Da Vinci's IQ, but he's pretty close.

When he accepts a particularly disturbing case in London,
Winter arrives to find a city in the grip of a cold snap, with a
psychopath on the loose who likes abducting and lobotom-
ising young women. Winter must use all his preternatural
brain power in order to work out who is behind the attacks,
before another young woman becomes a victim.
As Winter knows all too well, however, not everyone who's
broken can be fixed.

'Strikingly well-researched and written with a real
swagger, it leaves you desperate for more.'
Daily Mail

ff

Watch Me

Everybody's got something to hide . . .

Ex-FBI profiler Jefferson Winter has taken a new case in sunny Louisiana, where the only thing more intense than the heat is a killer on the loose in the small town of Eagle Creek.

Sam Galloway, a prominent lawyer from one of Eagle Creek's most respected families, has been murdered. All the sheriff's department has to go on, however, is a film of Galloway that shows him being burned alive.

Enter Jefferson Winter, whose expertise is serial criminals. But in a town where secrets are rife and history has a way of repeating itself, can Winter solve the case before someone else dies?

'Toe-clenching, nail-biting, peep-from-behind-your-fingers suspense.' **S. J. Bolton**

'Jefferson Winter is a welcome new genius, and I can't wait to meet him again.' **Neil White**

ff

Presumed Guilty

The first in a special eBook only series. The Jefferson Winter Chronicles, featuring Jefferson Winter from *Broken Dolls*, and introducing his mentor, Yoko Tanaka. Together they make an unforgettable team.

Special Agent Yoko Tanaka is one of the best profilers in the FBI. She's observant, smart and professional, but doesn't really play well with others. She's been called in to consult on the case of 'Valentino', a killer who steals his victims' hearts. Literally.

With five women already dead, time is running out for the police to catch the killer before he strikes again. Within twenty-four hours of Yoko's arrival they have a suspect in custody: a precocious nineteen-year-old kid called Jefferson Winter whose IQ is off the charts. He's also a textbook psychopath and the son of one of America's most notorious serial killers. Not only does he confess to the murders, he knows details of the crimes that only the killer could know. It's an open and shut case, or is it?

'A brilliant, conflicted profiler.' **Stephen Fry**

ff

Hush Little Baby

<small>(A JEFFERSON WINTER NOVELLA)</small>

Don't say a word . . .

FBI profiler Yoko Tanaka is in Tampa, Florida helping the local P. D. with their 'Sandman' case. Three mothers and their daughters have been found murdered in their homes. The mothers have been brutally stabbed while the little girls' have been smothered in their beds and posed to look like they're sleeping.

Defying FBI protocol, Yoko makes a detour to Sarasota to entice Jefferson Winter to join the case. Winter has now graduated from college and is playing piano in a tourist bar. At first he's reluctant to get involved but that's the thing with Winter, what he says and what he means are usually two different things. All Yoko knows is that he's the only person who can help her before the Sandman claims another two victims . . . but what Winter doesn't know is that Yoko might also be able to help him.

'Leaves you desperate for more.' *Daily Mail*